Praise for the novels of Sheila Roberts

"No one writes emotionally satisfying, warmhearted tales of small-town life quite like Roberts."
—*Booklist* on *Starting Over on Blackberry Lane*
(starred review)

"An irresistible story... Lighthearted and full of colorful, quirky characters and surf-side warmth, this latest foray into Roberts's picturesque coastal world is sheer delight."
—*Library Journal* on *The Summer Retreat*

"Roberts once again works her easy, breezy brand of romance magic in the latest sun-dappled, ocean-splashed, and superbly satisfying addition to the endlessly charming Moonlight Harbor series."
—*Booklist* on *The Summer Retreat*

"Roberts kicks off her new Moonlight Harbor series with this delightful story of family, friendship and new beginnings. The vividly-drawn coastal Washington setting comes alive."
—*RT Book Reviews*
on *Welcome to Moonlight Harbor*

"*Welcome to Moonlight Harbor* will be sure to capture your attention as well as your heart."
—*HarlequinJunkie.com*

SHEILA ROBERTS

beachside beginnings

mira

mira™

Recycling programs
for this product may
not exist in your area.

ISBN-13: 978-0-7783-6089-6

Beachside Beginnings

This edition published by arrangement with Harlequin Books S.A.

For questions and comments about the quality of this book,
please contact us at CustomerService@Harlequin.com.

Mira
22 Adelaide St. West, 40th Floor
Toronto, Ontario M5H 4E3, Canada
www.Harlequin.com

Printed in U.S.A.

For Charlene, who has helped so many women.

beachside
beginnings

One

"He kicked Harry," Moira Wellman told her boss, Michael Rozzi, owner of Chez Michael's Salon.

The memory of her boyfriend booting her poor little cat across the room pulled tears of rage from her. When Lang yelled at her or hit her, she knew she'd somehow brought it on herself. But Harry Pawter had done nothing to deserve such treatment other than try to slip back into the apartment after Lang had put him out.

Her cat had yowled and she'd cried and Lang had told her to shut up or she'd be out with the cat. That had been the night before and now she was out with the cat. For good.

After Lang had fallen asleep, she'd brought Harry back in. The poor little guy had yowled in pain when she picked him up. She'd cuddled him while she sat on the couch, steaming. And thinking. And then steaming even hotter. And then worrying about what would happen if she got up the nerve to do what she wanted to do.

Before Lang woke up, she'd put Harry in his cat carrier and stowed him in the back of her fifteen-year-old Honda, cracking the window so he'd have fresh air. Then she'd set out the last maple bar from the donut box (Lang always got the maple bars), showered and dressed and mentally readied herself for…whatever. Who knew what that would be? Usually, after a bad night he woke up ready to pretend nothing was wrong. But sometimes, if she looked at him wrong, said something wrong, he'd go off again like a firecracker.

Right on time at seven o'clock, he came out of the bedroom in his boxers, all smiles. "You're up early."

I couldn't sleep. No, that implied he'd upset her and if she implied he'd upset her, then she also would have been implying he'd done something wrong.

She'd opted for "Ready for a new day." That sounded positive.

He'd nodded and moved on to the kitchen. She already had the Keurig ready to go with his favorite coffee. She'd gone into the bathroom and begun putting on her makeup. *Just another day in paradise.*

He'd joined her there with his coffee and maple bar, setting the coffee on the bathroom counter and watching her, like a prison guard would watch a prisoner. "Where's the cat?"

"Outside."

He'd nodded his approval and that had been that. She'd breathed easier.

Until right before he went out the door. He'd studied her, eyes squinting as if he was trying to read her mind. "Are you okay?"

"I'm fine."

He'd half frowned, but all he said before he went out the door was, "I'll call you later."

She didn't want him to call her at all.

After Lang left for work, she'd brought Harry back inside and fed him, then let him rest on the bed while she loaded his food, litter box and toys in the car. Next came her clothes, purse and makeup, and the fifty bucks she'd hidden in a boot. She wished she could take the cute set of dishes that she'd found at Goodwill, but the idea of spending the extra time to pack them gave her the whim-whams. She'd start again somewhere with new dishes.

Now Harry was in his carrier once more, this time on the passenger seat, and she was sitting behind the wheel. They were still in the parking lot in front of the apartment. She had her cell phone in one hand and was gripping the steering wheel with the other. The key was in the ignition but she was finding it hard to reach over and turn it. If it wasn't for the fact that her hands were shaking, she'd have thought she was paralyzed.

"How could he do a thing like that?" she whispered.

"Haven't I been telling you for the last three years? The guy's scum," said Michael.

"He does have a temper," Moira admitted. But was he really that bad? If he wasn't, why was she sitting here in her car, ready to bolt?

Michael let out a disgusted snort. "Girl, you are the queen of understatement."

Okay, Lang had issues. But didn't everybody?

"That goon has slapped you around, broken your arm and made you feel like the bottom of the shit pile. And now this. Come on, Moira, it's a cosmic message. Are you getting it?"

Yes, she was, although if Lang hadn't done what he'd done to Harry, she'd never have dreamed of leaving. In spite of the problems they'd had, she'd still loved him.

And feared him.

No, no, not fear. It was more like she'd treated him with care. Lang was a man who had to be finessed, the same way she would finesse a haircut. You had to do things just so or it got ugly. She could take the ugly. Wasn't that what love was all about? You accepted the person, faults and all. But to hurt a defenseless animal? Uh-uh. That was a deal breaker. She couldn't stay.

Of course, he would come to the salon on his lunch hour to make sure they were good, maybe even bring her one of those chocolate roses you saw in all the drugstores in February because he knew how much she adored them— so romantic—and he'd assure her that all was well, they were fine and they belonged together.

It was how they rolled. No matter where they were or how hard they fought, she always wound up back home with him. He'd tell her that he'd never meant to hurt her. He loved her. She just made him so mad. Why did she always have to push his buttons? She'd ask herself the same thing, tell him she was sorry and then it would be as if nothing ever happened, him putting an arm around her as they sat on the couch, watching TV. Except she'd have a purpling memento on her cheek or a sprained wrist.

One time it was a broken jaw. But what had she expected? That time she'd mouthed off to him, called him the scum Michael said he was. She'd told the emergency-room doctor that she'd tripped and fallen on her face. She never told people what really happened when Lang accidentally hurt her. People asked too many questions. And their relationship was, well, complicated. So no matter how concerned a doctor would look, no matter what questions he'd ask, she always stuck to her story. Anyway, how did you explain that you were as much at fault as your boyfriend?

She knew whose fault last night was, though, and it wasn't hers. And she wasn't staying.

Something Lang had said back in January crouched at the back of her mind, like Death slipping into the back row of a church at a funeral. They'd gone out on New Year's Eve and had rung in the New Year with beer and a major fight. He'd accused her of flirting with another guy. She'd insisted she hadn't been and it had all slid into ugliness from there. The next morning, she'd been covering her black eye with makeup and, once more, they'd had that conversation about who'd really been the problem.

"You make me crazy, Moira, but I love you," he'd said. "I couldn't live without you."

So romantic.

"If you ever left me, I swear to God I'd kill you."

So…romantic? She'd tried to lighten the moment. "Aw, you wouldn't even miss me. You'd just sit around drinking beer and playing *Call to Arms* with your online buddies and blowing each other up."

His eyes had turned to slits and his jaw to granite. "What's that supposed to mean? Are you saying I ignore you?"

Wrong move. She'd backpedaled quickly. "No. It was a joke. Jeez."

"Well, I didn't think it was funny."

What would he think if he came home from the office today and found her gone? A chill crept up her spine. Her heart rate picked up and she felt suddenly sick.

She shot a look over her shoulder, half expecting Lang to come driving back in his fancy car. "What am I going to do?" she whispered into her phone.

"You're going to get out of here," Michael said.

"I need to take Harry to the vet."

"Take him to the vet in another town."

"Another town?"

Michael might as well have said another universe. She was moving out, but she hadn't thought of moving that far out. She'd always lived in Seattle, grown up in the city— the fringe ends and not the best neighborhoods, but still, it was what she knew. The farthest she'd ever gotten outside the city limits had been a day trip to Wild Waves in nearby Federal Way with some friends.

She'd first gone to the amusement park when she was a reckless teenager, partying and shoplifting mascara from Walmart and snitching money out of her mom's purse. It was the closest she'd probably ever get to Disneyland.

Her mom sure hadn't taken her anyplace. No Disneyland, no zoo, no trips to see Grandma, who'd disowned her mother the day she moved in with Moira's father. (Not too hard to figure out why. According to her mom, her dad, who'd left when she was one, had been a mean drunk.) She'd never seen her dad since, hadn't seen her mom in the last year and a half, either. Lang had come between them.

Even though her life in the city wasn't all that great at the moment, it was at least familiar. Where should she go? What was she going to do?

"Come by the salon," Michael commanded.

"He'll find me there." If he did, she'd lose either her resolve or a tooth.

"Where are you now?" Michael asked.

"In the parking lot at the apartment."

"He'll find you there, too, and you'll be all alone. Get over here right now."

She bit her lip and nodded. Like Michael could see her nod? If Lang had been with her in the car, he'd have said, "You're such a dumb shit."

Maybe she was, but maybe she didn't have to stay dumb. She ended the call, took a deep breath and told her racing heart to chill. Then she started the car and screeched out of the parking lot like the devil himself was after her.

Michael had been watching for her when she walked up to the salon, bringing Harry along in his pet carrier. He unlocked the glass door of Chez Michael's and let her in, then shut it behind them.

Even standing behind a locked door with someone right next to her it was hard to feel calm. Where was Lang right now? Was he at work? He'd called her cell phone twice since she left the apartment but she hadn't answered. He knew. He knew he'd finally pushed things too far when he went after Harry.

Michael's first client would be arriving any moment and then he wouldn't have time for her or her problems. She wished she could turn herself invisible. Or travel in time back to…when? When had her life ever been really good?

"You need a plan," Michael told her.

A plan. Yes, a plan. She had no plans. She had no idea what she was going to do beyond making sure her cat was okay.

Their receptionist, Rebecca, came in and hung her coat on the coat-tree. "Hi, Moira," she said. "What's with the cat?"

Michael answered for her. "It's bring-your-cat-to-work day." With a jerk of his head, he motioned Moira back into the stockroom, where they kept their supplies—towels, colors, shampoo and other products along with mannequin heads, color swatches and the lighting equipment for when they did photo shoots for Instagram. Once they were in, he reached into his back pocket and pulled out his wallet. "You can't stay here. You gotta get out of Dodge."

She looked on in horror as he took out three one-hundred-dollar bills and shoved them at her. "Take this."

"I can't," she protested.

"Yeah, you can. You need something to tide you over. I'll send you your last paycheck once you're settled."

She could feel tears prickling the back of her eyes. "Aww, Michael." How could she take his money? He had a wife and two young kids and a third one on the way.

"Go on," he urged. "If you won't take this for yourself, take it for Harry. Vets are expensive. And if that doesn't cover it, have the vet send the bill for the rest to me. In fact, send the whole damn bill. You'll need this to tide you over until you get settled."

The tears escaped and started down her cheeks. "Shit," she muttered as he grabbed her hand and pressed the money into it.

"Yeah, that's what you've been in for the last three years. Now you're getting out of it." He took his cell phone and began texting. "I know this woman, Benito's aunt. She's got a salon and she could use someone like you who's good with color and can do makeovers."

Her phone pinged, signaling a text from him.

"That's the name of her salon and the town it's in," he said as Moira read the information on her phone screen. "Her name's Pearl Edwards. I'll let her know you're coming."

Moonlight Harbor. It sure sounded pretty. But, "Where's that?"

"The end of the world."

The end of the world?

Michael's cell rang. He frowned and turned the screen for her to see.

The incoming call was from Lang. Seeing it sent adrenaline racing through her and she backed away.

Michael took the call. "Lang. I was just gonna call you

and ask if you knew where Moira is. I've been trying to reach her and she's not answering her phone. She's got a color scheduled for nine thirty. Yeah, yeah. I'll tell her. If you find her, tell her to get in here or she's fired. I have plenty of other girls who'd like to work at Chez Michael's if she doesn't want to," he added, sounding like the big meanie he wasn't.

Moira was shaking by the time he ended the call. "Thank you," she whispered. Michael was the best. He and his wife had been good friends to her ever since she'd come to work for him. More like family, really. Well, as much like family as Lang would let her have.

Michael reached out an arm and pulled her to him for a hug. "Things are gonna work out for you. Hang in there."

There wasn't much else she could do.

"Okay, now," he said brusquely, releasing her. "Get your stuff and get going. Close your checking account and trade your phone in on a new one first chance you get. Don't go back to your place and don't stop until you hit the Washington coast."

"The Washington coast?" she echoed. That was hours away.

"Trust me. You'll love it there. Now, get out of here."

She nodded, gave him one final hug and then gathered the tools of her trade, took Harry and hurried out of the salon, barely saying goodbye to Rebecca, who was setting out a box of Valentine candy for their clients.

Valentine's Day. How ironic that Moira was leaving Lang on Valentine's Day. Ironic. Paradoxical, even. *Paradoxical*. She loved that word.

Lang hated it when she worked fancy words into her vocabulary. "Who the hell do you think you are all of a sudden, a college graduate?" he'd taunt.

College? Yeah, right. She only been able to manage beauty school because she'd gotten a scholarship in high school.

But she had a library card and she wasn't afraid to use it. Her favorite books were biographies. She liked reading about successful people and how they'd gotten where they were. Someday, she was going to get…somewhere.

"I'm a lifelong learner," she'd insist. She loved that term. She'd learned it from one of her favorite clients, a middle-aged woman who loved trying the latest cut or color fashion. "You don't have to be in school to learn," she liked to remind Moira.

Sadly, the most important lesson Moira hadn't learned was how to make things work with her man. And now she was leaving him.

And she wasn't sorry.

Two

"I look like a chia plant with legs," wailed Jo Murphy as she whipped off the scarf she'd tied over her head.

Pearl Edwards, owner of Waves Salon, blinked. She'd seen some home perm disasters in her time, but Jo's took "hair disaster" to a whole new level. Her brown hair—the color was also a do-it-yourself job—was a frizzy, fried mess.

Looking at it, all Pearl could manage was, "Oh, Jo."

"I know, I know," Jo said miserably. "I shouldn't have tried to give myself a perm."

By the age of fifty-five, she should have known better. Jo could well afford to come in and have a professional help her get the look she wanted, but Jo was cheap. She pinched pennies until they bled copper.

"But you can fix this, right?" Jo pleaded.

"I can use a bond builder."

Jo's lips pursed in thought. "How much is that?"

"Do you care?"

"I am on a budget."

It was all Pearl could do not to roll her eyes. "The other option is to cut it all off. How do you feel about a pixie?"

"My hair grows so slowly," Jo bemoaned. As if Pearl didn't know. As if she didn't know everything about all her clients and their hair.

"Then you should be more careful what you do with it. Honestly, Jo. All this talk about budgets is baloney. You can afford to come in and have me give you a perm."

Jo scowled. "How would you know what I can afford?"

"How many years have you been coming to me?" Pearl retorted.

Nine years, and over those years Pearl had heard about every thrift-store bargain Jo found and every garage sale treasure she'd bargained for. Jo knew the days and hours for the specials of every restaurant in town. She clipped coupons, and cut napkins in half to save money. She also drove a Lexus, owned a house twice as big as Pearl's and she and her husband took a cruise to some exotic locale every year. She could probably afford to buy Pearl's hair salon.

She never tipped.

"Okay, okay," Jo said, a little testy. "Just cut it. And put on some conditioner."

"All right," Pearl said, and led her to the shampoo bowl to get the fix-up started.

As Pearl worked, Jo brought her up to speed on all the local gossip. Had she heard that Kiki Strom's daughter had a boyfriend now and it was serious? Maybe this marriage would work. The third time was the charm. Oh, and Natalie Bell's youngest boy, Joey, was caught trying to shoplift candy at Cindy Redmond's candy shop.

"Already a juvenile delinquent at thirteen," Jo said. "But hardly surprising. With her and her husband so busy running their hot dog stand and the hamburger joint, they can't have time to watch those boys."

Their oldest son, Jeff, was graduating from high school and was college bound. He worked summers as a lifeguard at the community pool. Their other son James was a high school baseball star and wanted to play for the Mariners someday. Joey was a bit of a mischief, but he'd be fine. If people didn't start branding him as a bad kid.

"Lots of kids get into trouble," Pearl said. "That doesn't mean they can't straighten out." She had to believe that.

· "I suppose," Jo said. Of course, her two daughters were perfect, married to lawyers and producing gorgeous grandchildren. But Pearl had watched them grow up. They were both selfish pills.

She finished shampooing Jo and then put on conditioner, covered her hair with a plastic cap and set her in a chair to stew. Of course, what she really needed was that bond builder but there was no point wasting breath arguing.

Pearl then turned her attention to her next client, Gloria Collins, who, as usual, was frustrated with her daughter.

"Honestly, Pearl, there are times I could wring her neck," Gloria finished after fifteen minutes of sputtering. "Wouldn't you think that by thirty-five she'd start to get her act together?"

"It takes some people longer than others to figure things out," Pearl said as she started texturing Gloria's hair. What she didn't say was, *At least you still have a daughter*.

All her friends had come alongside her and given her much-needed emotional support when her daughter died from an aneurysm and then again when her granddaughter went off the rails. But that had been five years ago and people tended to forget. They got used to your loss.

Gloria frowned at her reflection. "She needs to start figuring soon. That's all I can say."

It wasn't all she could say. Gloria went on. And on. But that was the nature of hair salons. Regular clients became like family and hair sessions either turned into shrink sessions or gossip fests. And by the time Gloria was done sputtering, Jo would have a lot more to gossip about.

"There you go," Pearl said at last. "You're good for another six weeks." She held up a hand mirror and turned Gloria's chair so she could see the back of her head in the big mirror. Thick gray hair—lucky woman!—cut short like she preferred it. *Thick* not only described Gloria's hair. It pretty much described the rest of her, too. Pearl envied Gloria's thick hair, but she was glad she didn't have to worry about dieting.

Like Gloria, Pearl's body shape fell in line with her hair, both a little on the thin side. She was happy with her figure—not every woman finishing up her sixties could say that. Her hair was another matter, though. It was an unremarkable ash blond with a heavy invasion of gray. She kept it pulled back in a ponytail. She wasn't exactly a walking advertisement for her salon but considering the fact that she'd had pretty much the same clientele for years, what was the point?

"Fabulous as always," Gloria declared when Pearl had finished with her. "You have a gift."

Sometimes Pearl thought it would be nice to expand that gift beyond the styles she'd been doing since the seventies and eighties. Her women were aging and if she didn't reel in some young blood, she'd be out of business in a few more years.

Or retired. She could retire.

But she wasn't exactly swimming in money. Her husband's life insurance hadn't gone far. Anyway, what would she do with herself? It was only her now. No one to travel with. Glen had died two years before she lost her daughter. She detested gardening. (Weeding—ugh!) And, much as she enjoyed reading, she couldn't picture herself glued to her armchair all day doing nothing but that. Hair was what she did and working was the only thing that kept her sane.

She thanked Gloria, took her charge card and gave her the Valentine's Day discount she'd advertised in *The Beach Times*.

And Gloria added a healthy tip to the bill. "Love my hair. Now I'm all ready to go to dinner at the Eagles Club," she said. "Of course, if I hadn't made the reservation, Willie and I would have been sitting at home, eating in front of the TV. And you know who would have cooked dinner. I warned him before he left for the gym that he'd better pick up flowers on his way home. Otherwise it will be no Valentine's Day fun for him later."

Gloria and Willie having Valentine's Day fun. There was an image Pearl didn't need burned into her brain. "I'm sure he won't fail you," she said.

"What are you going to do for Valentine's Day?" Gloria wanted to know.

"I'll probably dig out one of my movie classics like *Charade* or *You've Got Mail* and enjoy that." Kids, husbands, flowers—so many things women took for granted. But, "I might pick up some flowers for myself after work today." After all, why not?

"Good luck with that. By then everything will be picked over." Gloria studied her. "You are still so pretty. You really should try one of those online dating sites. Get out and have some fun."

Valentine's Day fun. Sigh. When it came to sex, things down there had closed for business years ago. "And who's going to come all the way to Moonlight Harbor to have fun with me? Tyrella Lamb's been trying the internet dating thing and so far she hasn't found anyone worth keeping."

"You never know unless you try. That's all I'm saying."

"She's right, Pearl," put in Jo.

"I'll think about it," Pearl said, even though she knew she wouldn't.

"Good. Meanwhile, you treat yourself. You know, in some ways you're better off not having a husband. At least you can get exactly what you want for Valentine's Day. And Christmas."

Well, there you had it.

Pearl was still trying to decide what to say to that when Chastity Morgan burst through the door. Chastity was young, in her twenties and married to one of the checkers at Beachside Grocery, and she worked part-time for Pearl doing manicures and pedicures.

"Oh, my gosh!" Chastity cried. "I'm going to have a heart attack."

Chastity was always on the verge of a heart attack about something.

"What happened?" asked Gloria, taking the bait.

"I almost hit a deer!"

"That's it?" Jo sounded disappointed.

"What do you mean, that's it?" Chastity demanded, outraged.

"I mean, with as many deer as we've got wandering around down here, we all come close to hitting one sooner or later."

"Well, I haven't. It jumped right out in front of me when I was coming down Butter Clam. What would I have done if I hit it?"

"Had dinner taken care of for the rest of the year," Gloria said. Unlike Pearl, Gloria was into gardening and the deer were not her friends.

Chastity made a face. "That's heartless."

"No, that's the food chain," Gloria said. "See you later, Pearl. Don't forget to buy yourself some flowers," she added, as she pulled open the door.

"She has no heart," Chastity muttered. Then, "Why does she want you to buy yourself flowers?"

"Valentine's Day. She doesn't want me to lose out."

Chastity knit her brows. "I should have brought you something."

"Valentine's Day isn't for bosses. It's for sweethearts."

"And friends. And good bosses. It's all about love, right?"

Pearl smiled. "Yes, it is." So maybe she'd show herself some love and get those flowers. And some chocolate, too. "Are you and Cole doing anything special tonight?"

"Not much. He's bringing home pizza and we're gonna stream a movie."

A simple evening, two happy people cuddled up on a couch, enjoying being together. Pearl remembered cuddling on the couch with her husband, watching movies. At least she still had Pumpkin to cuddle with. They could watch a movie together. Maybe something with a cat in it for Pumpkin. *Bell, Book and Candle*, perhaps.

Chastity got ready for her first client and Pearl poured herself a cup of coffee from the pot in the back room, then came back out and sat down in her chair to enjoy a quick break. She'd barely turned on her cell phone when it signaled a text from Michael Rozzi.

Sending someone to you. She's great and she needs a job.

Pearl had her regulars but she wasn't exactly swamped with clients. She couldn't afford to bring in another stylist, no matter how great she was.

Boyfriend smacked her around for the last time. She needs a new start.

Oh, dear. Pearl didn't like to turn away someone in trouble.

She's on her way down.

On her way down, like it was a done deal. That was the familiarity of longtime friendship. Michael had been friends with Pearl's nephew Benny (Benito now that he had a high-end salon in Seattle) ever since high school. She'd gone with the boys to their first hair show.

Of course, it was sweet of Michael to think of her. But.

Why didn't you send her to Benny?

He could call himself Benito all he wanted but to her he'd always be Benny.

Got to be far away. Can't get much farther than where you are.

That was for sure.

You'll be good for her and she'll be good for you. Great with colors. She'll bring in younger clients. Guaranteed.

Well, and wasn't that what she needed? She texted her thanks to Michael and wondered how she was going to pay the girl. Obviously, someone would have to take a pay cut. Her.

She didn't have time to think any more about her unexpected new employee as her next client, Arlene Grayson, was walking in the door. Arlene was the sporty type, playing tennis and pickleball every chance she got. She was blessed with thick hair that loved to curl. She kept it short and battled to keep it from going crazy on those misty beach days when the fog rolled in.

More than once Pearl had expressed envy over Arlene's thick head of hair, to which she'd reply, "You don't want my hair. It's a pain."

"Trust me. It's good to have body," Pearl would assure her.

Arlene always had an answer to that, as well. She'd pat her hips and say, "You can have as much of my body as you want." Arlene was a curvy woman…another thing she didn't appreciate about herself.

What was it with women, anyway? Pearl had yet to meet anyone who said, "I like me just the way I am."

"Happy VD," Arlene joked and set a box of chocolates on Pearl's workstation shelf.

"You shouldn't have."

"Oh, yes, I should," Arlene replied. "Next to her gynecologist, a woman's hairdresser is the most important person in her life."

"How about her manicurist?" put in Chastity.

"That, too," said Arlene, who had brought chocolates for her, as well.

"That was so sweet of you," said Pearl. Who needed a man when you had friends to bring you chocolates?

"Better your waist than mine," said Arlene. "Donny is under strict orders not to buy me any candy. Of course, Shay is another matter. She can't resist the lure of Cindy's Candies and every time she goes in there, she winds up getting fat bombs for me, too."

"How is Shay?" Pearl asked. "I haven't seen her in ages."

"Oh, she's been busy," Arlene said evasively.

Pearl knew about the salon in Aberdeen, which was owned by a much younger woman who had her finger on the pulse of hair fashion. Some of Pearl's customers had stopped booking appointments with her, making the forty-minute drive to the next town to the new salon, and Shay was yet another defector looking for a hot hairstyle. Pearl had caught sight of her at Beachside Grocery the week before, sporting a fancy cut and teal-colored hair. Shay had seen her, too, blushed and ducked around the corner of the aisle and disappeared.

"Go ahead," Pearl said to Arlene with a sigh. "You can say she's going somewhere else. I saw the new color." No point taking offense. Shay was a cutie and she had every right to work that cuteness with the latest style.

"It's not that she doesn't like you, dear. You know that," Arlene said. "It's just that..."

Pearl gave her shoulder a pat. "I know. She's young and she wants someone young doing her hair."

"They all want these fancy styles and colors now," Arlene said. "What can you do?"

Adapt or die.

"Don't look now, Harry, but I think we found the end of the world," Moira said as she drove through the monolithic stone gateway that guarded the entrance to the town of Moonlight Harbor.

Harry, hunkered miserably in his cat carrier, let out a pitiful mewl. There had been a lot of twists and turns in the road the last part of their journey, and even though the highway had eventually straightened back out, he still hadn't forgiven her. She didn't blame him. She felt awful over having added to his misery. The poor little guy had yakked up and she'd had to pull over to clean the mess and reassure him.

But who was going to reassure her? This wasn't her scene. She was a city girl, always had been. She'd grown up in apartments and she liked being able to go to clubs and dance, to go downtown or run out to the mall and spend some of her tip money on clothes. Lang criticized a lot of what she spent her money on (not that she had much to spend once she kicked in for her share of the rent and bought groceries), but he never complained when she came home with something from Victoria's Secret.

There was sure no Victoria's Secret here.

And so what if there wasn't? She didn't have anybody to look hot for anymore. She sure didn't want the somebody she'd had.

Lang had texted her six times before she'd finally shut off her phone. At first the texts had been contrite—Baby, you know I'm sorry, followed by, Why aren't you answering? Then he got a little more anxious. Where are you? Then he got pissed. Damn, M, where the hell are you? The last two texts had been so full of cursing and f-bombs and threats of what he was going to do if she didn't quit ignoring him that she finally took Michael's advice and traded in her phone for a new one in a T-Mobile store in Olympia, going with the cheapest phone and plan she could find.

There was no turning back now. Even if they made up, even if he said he was sorry, he'd been mean to Harry—there would come another time when his temper would flare. Maybe she could have risked getting her jaw broken but she wasn't about to risk any more of poor Harry's ribs.

A bruised rib the vet she'd found in town had said. He'd given Harry something right there and provided her with painkiller meds for him.

If only there was something she could take to make herself feel better. She sure could have used some chocolate right then. What a mess her life was.

"It's not how you start," her high school English teacher, Mrs. Dickens, had once told her, "it's how you finish. Remember that, Moira."

Yes, she needed to remember that. She was going to finish well.

Here at the end of the world.

Okay, it wasn't so bad. "Look at those cute little shops," she said to Harry. Hard for Harry to do any looking from his cat carrier, so she went on to describe them. "They're all different colors. Green, not dark green like Christmas but green like an Easter egg, and orange like sherbet, and yellow like a sunny day. Oh, wow, and a go-kart track. I always wanted to drive one of those things. And there's an ice-cream place. It's so cute. Pink like a balloon at a baby shower. No, actually, darker than that. Like a sunset maybe. It's got a big old cement ice-cream cone in front of it."

Ice cream, sherbet. She parked in front of the Good Times Ice Cream Parlor. She still had a little cash left and she was hungry. Not simply for food but for hope. If a woman couldn't find hope in a cute place like this, where could she find it?

The lunch hour had passed and there weren't many customers inside—only two old women seated at a tiny wrought-iron table painted white, enjoying milkshakes. The woman behind the counter looked almost old enough to be Moira's mother.

The old ladies were staring at her like she had three boobs. Okay, so she had a nose ring and a tattoo of a butterfly flitting up her neck. Hadn't they seen anyone with a nose ring or tat? Maybe it was her hair that had them gawking. (Although the strange lollipop red of the one woman's hair was just as stare-worthy, and not in a good way.)

Moira's hair, on the other hand, was a work of art. A color that Michael had created, it was a gorgeous mix of pastels, silver and gold that he'd dubbed holographic opal because of the way it shimmered. Lang had thought it was hot.

What Lang thought didn't matter anymore.

The woman behind the counter smiled at Moira and said, "Welcome. What would you like?"

A new life. "What's your specialty?" She could have asked "What's good?" but anybody could say that. She liked the word *specialty*. It made her think of fancy French restaurants and TV celebrity chefs.

"How about some Deer Poop?"

Moira blinked. "Deer Poop?"

"In honor of all the deer we have around here—chocolate ice cream loaded with chocolate-covered raisins."

"Deer?" Just wandering around? The only deer she'd ever seen had been on TV or in pictures.

"Oh, yes. They're everywhere."

Wow. Now, that was cool. "Sure," Moira said.

"Sugar or waffle cone?"

"Waffle." *Live it up*, she thought.

"One scoop or two?"

"One," Moira said, deciding to limit the living it up. Who knew if things would work out here? Who knew how long that paycheck Michael was sending would last? With what she had in her bank account, even one scoop was a splurge.

"You're new to town," the woman observed.

"I am." Moira glanced over her shoulder to find the

two older women still checking her out. The freak show had arrived.

"I just got here," she said. "I'm hoping to find a job. Your town looks adorable." For the end of the world. Where were the people her age? Were there any?

Moira dug out a bill, but the woman waved it away. "On the house."

"Really?" *Wow.* The woman handed over the cone and Moira took a bite. "This is…" anyone could say *good* "…tasty."

The woman smiled. "All our ice cream is. What do you do?"

"I'm a hairstylist. My old boss sent me down here to meet a Pearl Edwards." Moira was suddenly aware of the two older women whispering behind her. She could almost feel their stares.

"Pearl, she's the best. She owns Waves," said the woman. "Everybody in town goes there. Well, everybody my age and older."

Old ladies and tight perms. This wasn't the end of the world. This was hairstylist hell.

You're here now. May as well check it out.

Now one of the women behind her spoke. "I have an appointment there. You can follow me if you like."

Moira could have found her own way there, but she thanked the woman and agreed to follow her. People at the end of the world were nice to you, even if they did stare.

"I'll see you later, Alma," the Good Samaritan said to her friend and pushed away from the table. Standing up, she wasn't much taller than she'd been sitting down. Moira was five foot five but she stood a good six inches above this woman. There wasn't much to her, either. She looked like she needed to go on a diet of daily milkshakes. Her sweatshirt was pink and it clashed with her hair and lipstick. I Got Moonstruck at Moonlight Harbor, it informed Moira.

"I'm Edie Patterson," said the old woman. "Everyone calls me Edie and you can, too. I own the Driftwood Inn."

The Driftwood Inn. Moira had a sudden vision of a cute little place with driftwood at its entrance. "That sounds charming."

"Oh, it is. It was one of the first motels here in Moonlight Harbor. My great-niece Jenna manages it and she's fixed it all up and brought it back to its former glory. It's one of the sweetest places in the whole town. Isn't it, Nora?"

"It sure is," agreed the woman behind the counter.

"If you need a place to stay while you're getting settled, I'm sure we can give you a room," Edie said as she led Moira out of the ice-cream parlor.

No way could Moira afford to stay at a motel indefinitely. No way could she afford to stay anywhere. She murmured her thanks and tried not to panic.

"Jenna doesn't like me to drive," Edie confided. "She's always worried I'll get in an accident. But she was busy giving someone a massage—she's a massage therapist, you know—so I just went ahead and took my car out when she wasn't looking," said Edie conspiratorially, pointing to an ancient car that maybe got fifteen miles to the gallon on a good day. "That's my car. You follow me."

It wasn't hard to follow Edie Patterson. A kid on a tricycle could go faster. They crept out onto the street and inched on down the main road.

It gave Moira time to finish her ice cream and check out the place. The buildings looked like they belonged in a movie from the sixties. And what was that? Some kind of store shaped like a giant shark. It looked like you entered through its gaping mouth, complete with long shark teeth. Now, there was something you didn't see every day.

And wow! Deer. There were two of them, grazing on the grass in the median. There was something you didn't see in Seattle.

Seattle. Lang. How many times had he tried to call her by now? He had to be really pissed.

Let him be. He didn't deserve her. And Harry sure didn't deserve the way Lang had treated him. She was glad she'd left. Glad.

Except she was sad, too. And she ached a little for what she'd had with Lang when they were first together and everything was good. And she half wished she could have that back.

She was a mess.

But she wasn't going to stay a mess. She was going to fix her head and fix her life. She and Harry would be just fine.

What if this Pearl Edwards didn't give her a job?

No, no. Don't go there. "We're gonna be fine, Harry. Don't you worry."

Harry let out another pitiful mew. *I don't believe you.*

She didn't blame him. She wasn't so sure believed herself, either.

Three

Arlene had left and Pearl had just finished trimming Jo's hair when the bell over the door of Waves Salon jingled and in walked Edie Patterson followed by a woman who was the image of young and hip and held a cat carrier.

"Whoa," said Jo, looking at her.

Whoa was right. The girl wore the latest style in jeans. Her jacket and gray sweater, while not high-end quality, were equally stylish. She had a tiny gold hoop threaded through one nostril, and when she flipped her hair aside, part of a butterfly tattoo showed on her neck. Her features were pretty and her makeup beautifully done. And that hair. She had glorious hair—long, shimmery and luminescent like a pearl or the inside of an oyster shell. The colors were magical.

This had to be the woman Michael had sent down. Either that or she was a gift from the hair gods. She looked around the salon, taking it all in.

Pearl saw the flash of disappointment in her eyes and suddenly knew how exposed Adam and Eve must have felt after they ate that forbidden fruit. *Adam, we're naked!* Looking at her little salon through the newcomer's eyes, she saw all the things that had become invisible to her over the years: the pink shampoo bowls, old Formica styling stations, posters on the walls showing dated hairstyles like mullets and feathered bangs. The walls were the same dull cream color they'd been when Pearl first bought the place. And the ancient linoleum floor... Ugh. The place looked tired and old. With the exception of Chastity and Tyrella Lamb, who was getting her nails done, so did the women in it.

The newcomer quickly covered her disappointment with an uncertain smile.

"Hello, Pearl," said Edie. "I met this nice young lady at Nora's. She's come here looking for a job."

The woman barely waited for Edie to finish before walking up to Pearl and holding out her hand. "Hi. I'm Moira Wellman."

Determined and polite. It made a good first impression. "I'm Pearl Edwards. Michael told me you were coming."

Insecurity surfaced. The girl caught her lower lip between her teeth. "Do you have an opening? I'm good with hair," she added.

"I'm sure you are or Michael wouldn't have sent you," Pearl said. She was aware of Jo seated in her chair, taking in every word. "I'll tell you what. I've got a Keurig in the back room. Help yourself to some coffee and I'll be with you in just a few minutes. Okay?"

Moira nodded, picked up the cat carrier and slipped through the curtain that separated the salon from the back area, where Pearl kept her supplies and washer and dryer, and a small break area.

"I didn't know you were hiring someone," Jo said as Pearl returned to finish with her hair.

Pearl hadn't known she was hiring anyone, either.

Before she could speak, Chastity said, "I love her hair. I wonder if she could do that to mine."

That decided it. "I think it's time I did some updating," Pearl said.

"She seems nice," put in Edie.

"The tattoo is a bit much," said Jo.

"Everybody under the age of thirty has them now," Pearl said in the girl's defense.

Jo frowned. "If you ask me, it's silly."

Nobody had asked her. Pearl gave Jo's hair a final snip and a quick dry.

"It's awfully short," she said, frowning at her reflection in the mirror.

"It's awfully damaged," said Pearl. "I'll sell you some product for it."

"Is that part of the Valentine's Day discount?" Jo asked.

"No, it's not," Pearl snapped.

"I hate paying for things I don't need," Jo said.

"Well, you need help with your hair," Pearl informed her. "Honestly, Jo, if you'd come to me in the first place, you wouldn't be in this situation now."

"All right, all right. Sell me your smallest bottle. I bet I can find a home remedy on the internet," she muttered as she followed Pearl to the cash register.

"Just like you did that perm," Pearl muttered back. But she did end up giving Jo a discount and even wished her a happy Valentine's Day before she left.

"That woman is such a leech," Edie said with a shake of her head. "Honestly, Pearl, you shouldn't let her take advantage of you like that."

"Stars in your crown," said Tyrella as she admired the job Chastity had done on her nails.

Any bonus points Pearl could rack up for the hereafter were fine with her.

"You ought to slap her until she sees stars," advised Edie. Edie was one of the sweetest, most generous women in Moonlight Harbor, but she did have a feisty side. "Ah, well, the customer is always right," she added. Something she knew firsthand since she was in the hospitality business.

And if Pearl wanted more clients, she needed to secure this newcomer before she got away. "Edie, you wouldn't mind waiting a few minutes while I speak to this girl, would you?"

"Of course not," Edie said.

"I'll be right back," Pearl promised and ducked into the back room.

Moira Wellman sat at Pearl's ancient little wood table, her hands clasped between her knees, looking around. She hadn't gotten herself any coffee.

"Wouldn't you like some coffee?" Pearl offered.

Moira shook her head. "No, that's okay." She bit her lip again and then said, "About that job. If you can't take someone on, I understand."

"What if I couldn't take someone on? Where would you go?"

"Harry and I would find some place." She gestured to the carrier where a black cat hunkered in the corner.

A women's shelter. Pearl donated beauty products to Hyacinth Brown, whose churchwomen collected them for a shelter in nearby Quinault but she'd never seen the inside of a shelter. She didn't think she wanted this woman to have to, either.

"Actually, I was just thinking that I need to modernize, bring in someone who's current with the new styles and colors."

Now Moira's eyes lit up. "Really?"

"Do you think you could be happy here?"

"I think I could be happy anywhere as long as Harry's okay."

Harry didn't look too okay at the moment. Maybe the ride down hadn't agreed with him.

"And as long as you're okay?"

"Me?"

The girl obviously didn't want to share, but if Pearl took her on, she wanted to know what all she was getting into. There would be no secrets.

"Michael said you're getting out of an abusive relationship."

Moira's cheeks flushed seashell pink. "I need a new start."

"Is he going to come here looking for you?"

The pink bled out, leaving her face ashen. She shook her head.

"He doesn't know where you are?"

Again, Moira shook her head.

"Because I don't want some man showing up here, tearing the place up."

Hard to believe the girl's face could get any more white, but it did. "No," she said, her voice barely above a whisper. Tears rose in her eyes. "I loved him, but…" Again with the lip biting, as if she was determined not to let any more confidences slip out.

"I know what it is to have to let go of someone you love. Good for you for realizing you have to move on."

"I had to. If it was just me, I don't know, maybe we could have worked things out. But Harry." Her eyes narrowed. "You shouldn't pick on a defenseless animal."

So that had been the tipping point. "Does he need medical treatment?"

"No. We found a vet here in town. Michael gave me some money. He's the best," Moira said, and a tear spilled. "He'll give me a good reference."

"He already did."

"I'm great with color."

"That's what he said. Let's try you out."

Moira looked at Pearl as if she'd just offered her a winning lottery ticket. "Really?"

"Really. I need some younger heads in chairs. I think you can help me with that. Would you like to?"

"Yes, I would."

"I can't pay you much."

"I don't need much."

"Then let's talk details."

"Thank you. You won't be sorry."

It didn't take long for them to come to an agreement, and when they returned to the salon floor, Moira was smiling right along with Pearl.

"Ladies, I'd like you to meet our new stylist here at Waves," Pearl announced. "Meet Moira Wellman."

"Welcome to Moonlight Harbor," said Tyrella. "I don't suppose you know how to do weaves."

"I do."

"All right," Tyrella said. "Now I can get my nails and my hair done here."

"Where did you come from?" Chastity asked.

"Seattle."

"Ooh, the Space Needle, Pike Place Market and Monkey Loft. And all those cool restaurants. I'd love to live in Seattle. Why'd you leave?"

Moira's face flushed pink again and her gaze dropped to the cat carrier at her feet. "It was time for a change."

"You're going to love it here," Tyrella told her. "We may not have as many slick clubs, but we've got great restaurants and line dancing at The Drunken Sailor on Sunday evenings. And we've got the beach, and it doesn't get any better than that."

Moira nodded. "Living at the beach sounds exotic."

"I don't know if we qualify as exotic," said Pearl, "but this is a great place."

"Where are you staying?" Tyrella asked Moira.

"Um."

"Haven't found a place yet?" Tyrella guessed.

Edie spoke up before Pearl could even open her mouth. "She can stay at the Driftwood Inn until she gets settled. We always have vacancies in the winter months."

"That's really nice of you, but I don't have a lot of money," said Moira.

"Don't you worry about that," Edie told her.

Moira was only momentarily relieved. She glanced down at the cat carrier she was holding. "Do you take pets?"

Edie eyeballed the cat in his carrier with disfavor. She had a parrot and was as far from a cat lover as a woman could get. "He does have good manners, doesn't he? We allow dogs, but cats are notorious for ruining carpets and eating birds."

"She's not going to sic him on Jolly Roger," Tyrella said to her. "And if the cat pees on the carpet, I'll donate the carpet cleaner. I carry a brand at the hardware store that works great."

"Harry's a good boy," said Moira.

"Then he's welcome, too," Edie said to her. "Just not

in the house. My parrot wouldn't like that. As soon as Pearl's done, you can follow me back to the inn and I'll introduce you to Jenna. She understands about starting over, believe me."

She certainly did. Jenna Jones had left behind a cheating husband and moved to Moonlight Harbor to hit Restart on her life, transforming the Driftwood Inn from a run-down eyesore to a charming vintage motel. Her sister, Celeste, had also found a new beginning at the beach.

Pearl herself had done the same thing back in 1980, when she, Glenn and their daughter moved to Moonlight Harbor after he lost his job. They'd built a good life here in this little beach town. Maybe Moira Wellman could do the same.

Victor King had made note of the new car in town following Edie Patterson. A fifteen-year-old Honda Civic, Washington plates. The woman at the wheel looked to be toward the end of her twenties.

She was hot. Just an observation. Cops had to be observant.

Cops had to quit falling for good-looking women, too. It never worked out. He'd learned his lesson with Celeste Jones. That had been a hot pursuit that went nowhere. Still, he couldn't help wondering who this new woman in town was.

He'd fallen in line behind her and Edie, mostly to make sure Edie arrived in one piece. Then, leaving his curiosity to be satisfied another day, he'd veered off when they pulled into the parking area at Waves. Nothing more to be done.

At least Edie had gotten to the hair salon safely without hitting anyone or anything. The woman drove slow enough to be a traffic hazard. He hadn't ticketed her for that particular offense yet but he'd gotten her for failing to yield when making a left-hand turn and for running a red light. *(I thought it was yellow. It's awfully hard to see in the fog.)* Victor wasn't sure she could see all that well even when the sky was clear and the sun was out.

He put in a call.

"You've reached the Driftwood Inn, where it's beach time all the time," Jenna answered, all happy and sunshiny.

"Jenna, it's Victor."

He didn't have to go any further. "Oh, no. Where's Aunt Edie? She sneaked out while I was giving the mayor a massage and I was just about to call Nora and see if she'd seen her."

"Don't worry. She's okay. She drove to Waves."

Jenna heaved a sigh. "I'm going to have to find a new hiding place for her car keys."

"Hide 'em in your tampon box," Victor advised. "She won't look there." He could feel his whole face burning. In the name of Dirty Harry, when was he going to get over embarrassing so easily? He had no fear of bullets or bad guys, but women almost always flustered him.

This time he'd brought it on himself. Tampons? Really? Except it was a good suggestion, one he'd read about on some online site about protecting valuables. Old ladies and men—neither had use for that stuff so it made the perfect hiding place.

"Great suggestion. Thanks, Victor. Are you blushing?" Jenna teased.

"Gotta go. I'm trusting you to get your aunt off the street," he said and ended the call.

That taken care of, his mind drifted back to the Honda with the Washington plates. Who was the new woman in town? Why was she here? No need to run the plates. He knew he'd find out sooner rather than later. News traveled fast in a small town.

He didn't have any more time to think about the newcomer as Nan, the dispatcher, sent him to deal with a complaint from one of the locals about a neighbor shooting at a deer. The population was out of control and a lot of people hated them, but it was against the law to shoot one inside the city limits.

The homeowner was a skinny middle-aged guy with only a few strands of hair hanging onto his scalp for dear life. He wore sweatpants, a University of Washington sweatshirt and a scowl.

The man was irate that his neighbor had called the police on him. "It's my property," he insisted. "And I wasn't even shooting a real gun, just a BB gun."

"Sir, you can't do that," Victor explained.

"Well, I don't see why not."

This guy was going to be difficult. "Because it's against the law," Victor said firmly.

The man frowned. "Okay, fine. I'll get a slingshot."

"You can't shoot them with a slingshot, either."

"Well, what am I supposed to do? Throw rocks at 'em?"

"Nope. Can't do that."

"They're eating everything."

"Buy deer-resistant plants," Victor suggested.

"I did! These deer have no resistance."

"Then get deer repellent. You can't shoot them. And you can't throw rocks at them. Are we clear on that?"

Victor was twice the man's size and half his age. The man was clear on it.

Yep, lots of high crime in Moonlight Harbor.

Victor didn't care if it wasn't a thrill a minute. He liked

the town, liked the people. He wanted to do his part to keep law and order but he wasn't an adrenaline junkie and he didn't have a death wish, so small-town life suited him fine. He hoped to grow old in the beachside berg, raise a family, coach Little League.

First he had to find a woman.

Did the Honda Civic babe have a boyfriend?

"Yow!" cried Courtney Moore as the box of dishes landed on her toe.

"Sorry," said Annie Albright. "I lost my grip."

And not only on this box. She felt like she'd lost her grip on her whole life.

"Hopefully, they're not broken," Courtney said.

Broken dishes, broken marriage. Annie plopped on the kitchen floor of her rental house—correction: former rental house—and began to cry. They'd already lost Swimmy the goldfish when Annie tripped carrying him out to Courtney's car and dropped the bowl, sending Swimmy bouncing off into the flower bed. By the time she'd gotten to him, Swimmy was crossing the rainbow trout bridge. She was going to have to run to the pet store in Quinault and replace him with a Swimmy look-alike before Emma got home from school.

First Swimmy and now her vintage Vernonware dishes that she hadn't wanted to leave behind. Of course, that was nothing compared to what else she was saying goodbye to.

"Hey, it's okay," Courtney said, kneeling next to her. "I didn't hear any crunch. They're probably okay."

If they were, they were about the only thing in her life that was. She'd finally had to acknowledge that her marriage was in shreds. Greg had gotten fired—a second time after his boss had taken pity on him and rehired him—and

-they were behind on the rent and the landlord was threatening eviction. Too embarrassed to ask her parents for money again, she'd gone to the construction site to talk to his boss. But this time no amount of pleading had convinced the man to give Greg another chance.

"He's drunk on the job most of the time, Annie. I can't have him working around power tools and climbing on ladders. It's too dangerous."

Meanwhile, Greg had gone to The Drunken Sailor to drown his sorrows and tell anyone who would listen what a jerk his boss was. And, in case they hadn't heard it that first day, he'd gone every day since for the last two weeks. She'd begged him to go back to AA. He'd told her to get off his case.

Well, now she was getting off his case. It was a sad aha moment when she realized he was going to do nothing but continue to bring her and their daughter down. She had to get out. Maybe, just maybe, if he came home and found her note, realized what he was going to lose, he'd come to his senses.

"Don't hold your breath," Courtney had said. "Move on. Trust me. There is life after divorce."

Courtney knew what she was talking about. She'd been through a divorce and survived to tell the tale. Now she was happy designing clothes and selling them at a small boutique shop in the Oyster Inn, the town's high-end B&B, and working part-time for Jenna Jones at the Driftwood. She had a sweet little rental on Butter Clam Loop with an extra bedroom she'd offered to Annie for her and her daughter.

Annie had taken her up on the offer. With possible eviction looming, most of her treasures were going into storage until she could sort out her life. If she didn't break them all first.

"It's not that," she managed between sobs. "It's everything."

"I know," Courtney said, and hugged her. "But everything's going to work out. You really are better off without him."

Tell that to Emma. "I don't want to be better off without him. I want to be better off with him."

"Maybe this will do it. But if not, don't keep giving him chances. You deserve more. So does Emma."

Which, of course, was exactly why Annie was moving out. Her ten-year-old daughter didn't need to lie in bed listening to her parents fighting at night, hearing her dad's drunken rages about how unfair life was to him. Courtney had been telling Annie for ages she was sending a bad message to her daughter putting up with his shit. Courtney was right.

"Come on, let's pick this up and try again."

Annie nodded, and together they hauled the box out to her car and stuffed it in the trunk. This was the last load. After that, she'd have to find a new Swimmy and then break it to her daughter that they were going to find a new life, one which might or might not include her daddy.

"You're doing the right thing," Courtney assured her.

Yes, she was. Enough was enough. They couldn't keep going on the way they were. She only hoped this would be the wake-up call Greg needed.

She also hoped she'd be able to find a Swimmy look-alike.

Four

Pearl put Moira Wellman to work filling out the paperwork necessary for a new hire while she gave Edie Patterson her shampoo and style. Edie's style consisted of tight curls—Pearl always used red rods on her for the tightest possible curl—and fairly short. She wished she could talk Edie into trying a softer curl, but Edie had been looking like a poodle for too many years and she had no desire to experiment. As for hair color, like Jo, Edie was a do-it-yourselfer. Which really only worked if you knew what you were doing. Pearl had tried to convince her to try something more subtle than the bright cherry red she loved, all to no avail. Contrary to popular belief, the customer wasn't always right. But the customer did have the final say.

Moira was done before Pearl, so she wound up chatting with Chastity, who had sent Tyrella and her fabulous fingernails on her way. It looked like the two of them were hitting it off, which made Pearl happy. Not only because it was important to her to keep a happy vibe in her salon but also because she was sure the newcomer was in need of friends. It had to have been hard picking up and leaving behind everything that was familiar to come to a place where she knew no one.

The good news was that people who came to Moonlight Harbor didn't stay strangers for long. Its citizens were supportive of each other, especially the women. Moira could find her feet.

She heard Chastity ask, "So how did you pick Moonlight Harbor?"

"It was time for a new start," Moira said. Obviously not ready to share details.

"Well, I'm ready for a new hair start," said Chastity. "Could you help me make my hair look awesome like yours?"

"Absolutely," Moira said, and Pearl could hear a new energy in her voice.

Yes, Moonlight Harbor was going to be good medicine for this wounded little gal.

"Why don't you take today to get settled," Pearl told her.

"We'll get you all set up in a room and you can have dinner with us tonight," Edie put in.

Moira promised to be back the next morning at nine o'clock, and then followed Edie out the door.

"Wow," said Chastity as the two women got into their cars. "It's going to be great having her here."

Pearl seconded that emotion. She had a good feeling about Moira Wellman. And suddenly her own future seemed somehow...fuller. She missed her husband, mourned her daughter and ached for the loss of the granddaughter who had vanished from her life. Sometimes it felt like so much had been taken away from her. But now, like treasure washed up on the beach, here was this young woman. Who knew what the future held?

Of course, she might not stay.

Then again, maybe she would. And for the moment, maybes were enough. Maybes were better than what she'd had for a long time.

Moira followed Edie Patterson back to the Driftwood Inn, inching along in slow motion. It gave her plenty of time to think. About her past, present and future.

The past was a montage of scenes—making what she'd thought would be lifelong friends in beauty school, going clubbing with those same friends, meeting Lang. Oh, yes, there was that first time she saw him, tall and muscled, with gorgeous brown eyes, dark hair, thick and luminous. (*Luminous*, great word.) She'd felt the electricity clear across the room when they first saw each other. She could still picture them dancing together, then, two weeks later, moving together on his bed, all murmurs and sighs at first, then groans and cries of pleasure like in a movie. She saw them when they were first together and she was falling under Lang's spell, the two of them seated at a restaurant table, holding hands, ordering coffee from Starbucks on a Saturday morning, biking around Green Lake. Then she saw him dissing her friends, complaining when she spent time with them. *Why are you hanging out with those losers?* turned into *You are such a loser.*

The first time he hit her also played out in her mind like a movie on the big screen. And reliving it was as horrible and unsettling as experiencing it had been, making her flinch.

Why had she stayed? Why hadn't she figured out earlier that things would get ugly? Why hadn't she been willing to acknowledge it when they did?

What was he doing right now? Was he missing her? Was he sorry he'd been so horrible to Harry?

Moira chewed on her lower lip. Could she ever go back? Would he change? If only he would, they could be so good together. If she went back, asked him to try again...

A new scene played in her mind—Lang yelling at her for leaving him and making a fool of him. Her heart rate picked up and she tightened her grip on the steering wheel as the scene played on to show Lang backhanding her and sending her flying.

He wouldn't change, no matter how hard she wished it. How could you change when you already thought you were perfect? She didn't know what her future held but she knew what it couldn't, if not for her sake, for Harry's.

She followed Edie Patterson into the parking lot of the Driftwood Inn and parked her car in front of the little office. The old motel wasn't large, only a one-story building. But it was welcoming, painted a slate blue with white trim. And it had a swimming pool! On the other side of the parking lot was a fast-food joint with a giant wooden clam of some sort on its roof. The Seafood Shack. It looked like the kind of place she could afford.

The Driftwood Inn's office was a separate building from the motel, also blue, with some fisherman's net artfully draped on one outside wall, holding a couple of flat metal fish. A cement seagull perched on fake wooden piers, standing guard outside the door.

"This is adorable," Moira said to Edie once they were out of their cars.

"It is," Edie agreed. "We've helped a whole lot of people make a lot of good memories over the years."

Moira hoped they'd help her make some, too.

"Come on in the office. Jenna will be in there by now, working the reception desk."

The inside of the office was as appealing as the outside. It was painted a lighter shade of blue. The walls were adorned with framed photos of beach scenes. One had been taken on a sunny day that looked almost too perfect to be real, just beach and driftwood and waves coming in. Another had caught a seagull in flight. Two were of a sunrise and sunset. And one picture had been taken at night, the moon beaming down on the water, making a path fit for a fairy princess. Or a dreamer.

The woman behind the desk looked to be somewhere in her forties. She was pretty, with blue eyes and blondish hair that looked a little neglected. Oh, what Moira could do with that hair. The woman had a nice mouth, too, although whatever lipstick she might have had on was long gone. She wore some mascara on her eyelashes and a hint of eyeliner and that was it. She didn't need more than that. But the hair could definitely use some attention.

She looked up and smiled at Moira. Her smile for her aunt looked a little strained. "Aunt Edie, I was worried about you."

"No need to worry," said Edie, waving away her concern.

"You know I would have taken you to the salon if you'd told me you had an appointment."

"You were busy, dear. I didn't want to bother you."

Jenna Jones did one of those things with her mouth that people did when they were trying not to look pissed in front of strangers. "It's never a bother." Then, her aunt dealt with, she turned her attention to Moira. "Hi there. Welcome to the Driftwood Inn."

"This is Moira Wellman," Aunt Edie said. "She's new in town and needs a room."

That inspired a genuine smile.

Until Edie added, "I told her we could put her up until she gets on her feet."

On her feet. Everyone knew what that meant. As in "no money." Jenna's smile looked strained again.

"That room next to Seth is free," said Edie.

Moira hadn't seen many cars parked in the parking lot. It looked like they had a lot of rooms available.

"I can pay," she said. "I just got a job at Waves."

Although so far she had all of one person who wanted her hair colored and Moira strongly suspected that Chastity didn't have a lot of money to spend and was hoping for a freebie from a fellow employee.

"Nonsense," Edie said briskly. "We believe in giving people a hand when they need it. Don't we, Jenna?"

Jenna Jones appeared to come to a decision. She nodded. "Of course we do." Then her smile turned genuine. "Welcome to Moonlight Harbor."

"Now, you plan to have dinner with us tonight," Edie said to Moira. "I'm making clam chowder."

"I've never had clam chowder," Moira said.

"Never…? Oh, my, we'll have to change that," Edie said. She picked up a plate of cookies from the reception counter. "You've never lived until you've had one of my sugar cookies."

Clam chowder, cookies…kindness. Had she died and gone to Heaven? Moira took a cookie and bit into it. Edie was right. She'd never lived. "It's…scrumptious."

"*Scrumptious*. I like that word," said Edie.

So did Moira. After watching a cooking show, she'd looked it up in the paperback thesaurus she'd bought at Goodwill. Sadly, in her haste she'd left the thesaurus behind.

"Well, now, I'm going to go back to the house and bake a cake. We're right over there," Edie said, pointing to a two-story house painted the same color as the motel. "Come on over anytime. Dinner's at six."

"Thanks," Moria said. Dinner. In a pretty house with a normal family. Yep, Heaven.

Jenna had a key in her hand. "I'll show you to your room."

"Thanks," Moira said. "Let me just get my cat."

"Cat?" Jenna stuttered.

"Edie said that was okay, but if it's a problem…" Then what would she do?

"No, no," Jenna said, sounding only half-sure. "If my aunt okayed it…"

"He's really well-behaved and he only uses his litter box." Although, who knew what Harry might do under stress, in a new place after being cooped up in his carrier all day? *Don't make a liar out of me, Harry.*

Jenna nodded gamely, and after collecting Harry, Moira followed her across the parking lot to room three.

It sure wasn't as big as the apartment she and Lang had shared, but it was hers alone, hers and Harry's. The carpet was orange. Not exactly Moira's favorite color, but you didn't get picky when you were getting something for free. The walls were painted a neutral cream, as if trying to make up for the carpet, and the decor was whimsical. The bed was clothed in a bedspread sporting seashells, starfish and seahorses. On either side of it sat simple wood nightstands painted white. On top of each one was a lamp with a base shaped like a sand dollar. Framed photographs of the beach at sunrise hung on the walls, along with a sign that said The Beach Is My Happy Place. The room itself said, "Welcome home."

None of the fancy words Moira had added to her vocabulary over the last year were good enough for what she was feeling. All she could manage was, "Wow."

"I'm glad you like it," Jenna said. "The rooms all have different themes. We did all the decorating ourselves. Not that I would have chosen orange carpet," she quickly added, "but we were on a pretty tight budget."

Maybe they still were. "About your aunt inviting me to stay for free," Moira began.

"It's fine. Really. Like my aunt said, we believe in helping people around here."

"I've got to admit, I could use some," Moira said.

"So could I when I first moved to Moonlight Harbor," Jenna told her. "I get it."

"I'll be happy to help out any way I can."

"Don't worry about it."

"No, really."

"We're in pretty good shape for workers right now. Unless you have handyman skills," Jenna added with a shake of her head. "Our handyman is the most unhandy man on the planet. But he came with the place and my aunt adores him so I'm stuck with him. He's definitely a character so if he says anything inappropriate at dinner, ignore him. I try to."

"I hate to take advantage," Moira said.

"It's not taking advantage if people offer to help you when you need it, and we're happy to do that," Jenna said and started for the door.

"I could do your hair."

Jenna stopped and turned around. "Yeah?"

"You'd look great with a blend of warm colors."

Jenna looked hesitant.

"I'm good with highlights, too."

That clinched it. "You know, I might just take you up on that," Jenna said.

Moira smiled. What woman could resist the offer of getting her hair done for free? And that would balance the scales at least a little bit so she wouldn't have to feel like a leech. It was important to her to pull her weight wherever she was. She might not have been the most well-educated woman on the planet or the richest, but she had skills. In fact, she liked to think of herself as an artist, and style and hair colors were her palette.

She'd always had a gift for being able to look at someone and analyze how that person could get the most out of her looks. In high school she'd done her friends' makeup, cut their hair and colored it. She loved being able to help women look their best and feel good about themselves. It was important.

When she'd graduated from high school with her beauty school scholarship, she'd figured that was her destiny and had embraced it, in spite of the teasing of some of the mean girls who were college bound.

"Half of them won't use those degrees, anyway," her mother had sneered. "Higher education is a bunch of BS."

Moira didn't think so. She'd have loved to get a college education. It was good to know things. But just because you didn't know things, it didn't make you stupid. Deep down she knew that. Sadly, it was buried so deep that she often had trouble finding it.

Still, when she was doing hair and transforming women from average to wow, her self-esteem rocketed. It was only when she got off work and entered the other part of her life that it plummeted. She'd leave work, a kite dancing on the wind, and then something would happen at home to pull her down.

Maybe here at the beach she could manage to stay up.

She let Harry out of his cat carrier and he began to cautiously prowl their new digs. "We're going to love it here, Harry," she assured him. "It's a new start."

What if she failed? Okay, so things weren't perfect with Lang but at least she'd had security.

Harry was moving slowly, like a little old man cat. Of course, he was moving slowly after how he'd been hurt. There'd been no security with Lang for Harry.

"We're gonna be fine," she said as much to herself as to her cat. "Okay now, I'm bringing in your cat box and litter. Don't pee on the carpet."

It didn't take her more than five minutes to bring in her few possessions. She was twenty-six years old and this was all she had. She really was a loser.

"You don't have to stay a loser," she told herself and hoped it was true.

She flopped on the bed and pulled out the book she was reading. *How to Be a Better You* by Muriel Sterling. She'd seen it on the book rack at a thrift store and bought it. Then hid it in her purse, knowing Lang would only make fun of her if he caught her with it.

She flipped to the back of the book with the author's bio and picture.

Muriel Sterling is the popular author of New Beginnings, Chocolate: Keeping It in the Family *and* A Guide to Happy Holidays. *She's happily married and makes her home in Icicle Falls, Washington.*

Moira had looked up Icicle Falls on the internet and learned it was a Bavarian-style town nestled in the heart of Washington's Cascade Mountains. It had looked like something out of a storybook and she'd been sure Ms. Sterling's life had been an idyllic one. Until she'd read the first chapter of the book and learned that Muriel Sterling had lost two husbands, not to mention nearly losing her family's business. Moira had often felt like she was the only one with a screwed-up life, but Muriel Sterling's story was a good reminder that nobody escaped problems.

Granted, some people did a good job of creating their own problems, and Moira supposed she fell into that category. Her girlfriends had tried to warn her about Lang. But she hadn't listened. In fact, she'd gotten downright angry when her friend Cara had said, "I'm sorry, Moira, but he's a douche bag. I don't get why you can't see that."

Because she hadn't wanted to. If she admitted she'd chosen a douche bag to hang out with, what did that say about her? Anyway, he wasn't. She'd kept on insisting that and pretty soon she'd believed herself. The one with the problem was her.

Moira studied the author's picture. Muriel Sterling looked like she was maybe in her sixties. She was fighting the whole aging thing and doing a pretty good job of it. Whoever did her hair was good. It was a flattering light brown, cut in a modern style. She wore a simple black sweater and a floral-print scarf around her neck to hide turkey-neck syndrome. She was still a beautiful woman with an air of wisdom about her. So far what she'd written had resonated with Moira.

She turned to chapter two and began to read.

"Acknowledging where you've gone wrong is the first step toward going right. Don't try to hide from your mistakes. Recognize them, say hello to them, admit where they've brought you and then say goodbye," Muriel advised.

That made sense. Moira read on. *"We all make mistakes.*

*That's part of being human. But God gave us brains. We can
figure out our problems and find a way to a better future."*

She reread that section aloud to Harry. "You hear that,
Harry? We can find a way to a better future. Maybe we
can find it right here."

In a motel in a small beach town at the end of the world.
Oh, boy.

Moira hadn't really taken time to figure out her problem. She'd acted on instinct and had been driven by emotion. Was that using her brain?

More than if she'd stayed in Seattle. Lang would be
coming home from work soon and finding her gone. Imag-
ining his rage was enough to give her the shivers. For a
moment the end of the world didn't seem far enough away.

Muriel Sterling assured her she could find a better
future. She'd already gotten a job and she had a place to
go for dinner.

"It's a beginning," she said to Harry. Then she shut the
book and walked next door.

Five

It had been a long time since Moira had been in a house. She'd grown up living in apartments and that was all she'd lived in when she was on her own, rooming with girlfriends. She and Lang had talked about renting a house but had never followed through.

She remembered how she'd loved hanging out at her best friend Heather's house when she was a kid. It had been small and cheaply built, not in the best neighborhood, but it had come complete with a big brother and a sister, a mom who baked cookies and a dad who played soccer in the backyard with the kids. Her own mom wasn't into baking, always watching her weight. (Unless she was depressed and bingeing, but Mom had always binged on store-bought cookies.)

Moira wasn't so great in the kitchen, either, although she tried. Not that Lang ever appreciated her efforts.

"Why don't you take notes when you watch a cooking show, for God's sake?" he'd demand.

Looking back on those times, she could imagine herself retorting, "Why don't you try cooking for a change?"

Except she knew where that would have gotten her. No place good.

Why had she stayed so long?

Edie Patterson met her at the door and ushered her into a house that made her think of the grandma she'd never known, the grandma who had cut off all ties with her daughter and baby granddaughter and then died before Moira was old enough to find her. This was what her grandma's house would have looked like, with cozy furniture in the living room, a knit blanket thrown over the sofa, a wood-stove in the corner with a fire burning in it. Moira could smell the aroma of a home-cooked meal wafting out to her from the kitchen.

And what was this? A real parrot! She wandered over to the cage where the bird was walking back and forth on his perch.

"That's Jolly Roger, my baby," Edie told her.

"Gosh, he's so pretty."

"Ask him if he's a pretty bird," Edie said.

"Are you a pretty bird?" Moira asked the parrot.

"Roger's a pretty bird. Give me whiskey."

Moira laughed. It felt good to laugh, to feel free to be herself.

"My husband taught him that," Edie said. "Ralph was such a character."

Was. As in… "He's not around anymore?"

"I'm afraid not," Edie said. "He was the love of my life. I died a little inside the day he passed."

To have a love of your life, what was that like? Moira had thought she knew. Turned out she didn't. *Oh, Lang, why did things have to go so bad between us?*

"We started the Driftwood Inn together," Edie said. "Built this house together. It hardly felt like home with him gone. But one has to carry on, especially when you have people who need you."

Moira didn't have anyone who needed her. No, wait. That wasn't true. Harry needed her.

"Now with Jenna and Sabrina living with me, it's given me a new lease on life," Edie said.

Sabrina. That was Jenna's daughter? What was their story? Edie hadn't mentioned a man. Was Jenna a single mom?

"Come on out to the kitchen," Edie said. "You can keep me company while I make the cheese bread to go with our chowder."

The kitchen was as cozy as the rest of the house, with a table set for four. The dishes looked vintage and had apples painted on them. A floral arrangement of red carnations and greens—a reminder that it was Valentine's Day—sat on the counter, next to a chocolate cake in a nine-by-thirteen pan.

"Flowers for my great-great-niece. Her boyfriend is away at college," Edie said. "Help yourself to a piece of cake if you like. It's one of my specialties. I'm sure your mother told you that you couldn't have sweets before dinner because it would spoil your appetite, but I don't hold with that."

Moira's mother had never told her any such thing. Her mom had concentrated on more practical advice like "You need to be on the pill so you won't get pregnant. If you do, it'll ruin your life."

Had she ruined her mother's life? Her mom had worked full-time in a department store and hadn't ever had much energy to play or do crafts or bake cookies like Heather's mom. She had found enough energy to date sporadically and Moira had seen a parade of "uncles" go through their lives over the years. When her mom was dating, she'd been happy and laughed a lot. When she wasn't, she'd cried in her bedroom late at night and sighed a lot during the day. That was when they did their mother-daughter bonding, sitting in front of the TV, eating cookies. In high school Moira had done her homework while they sat on the couch and watched *Grey's Anatomy.*

There was a knife and server next to the cake. And a little corner missing. It looked like someone had already sampled it. Moira cut off a bite and followed suit. "This is outstanding."

"I'm glad you like it. It makes me happy when people enjoy what I bake. Do you like to bake?"

"I've never done much," Moira confessed.

"Stick with me, my dear, and we'll make a baker out of you."

Sticking with Edie Patterson sounded like a good idea. "Is there anything I can do to help you?"

"No, you just relax and enjoy yourself."

It wasn't hard to do that here in Edie Patterson's kitchen.

Edie was just sharing the ingredients for her cheese spread when a pretty teenage girl with an amateur color job on her hair bounded into the room. "Is it cake yet?" she asked.

"It is," said Edie. "Help yourself, dear. Moira, this is my great-great-niece, Sabrina."

"Hi," Sabrina said and gave Moira a smile.

Lucky girl. She had a lot to smile about living in such a warm, happy place.

The girl's gaze fell on the flowers. "Ooh, flowers."

"Those came a few minutes ago," said Edie. "They're for you from you know who."

Sabrina danced over to the arrangement and picked it up. "He's so awesome."

Moira had thought the same thing about Lang when they first got together.

"Moira's new in town," Edie said to Sabrina. "She's a hairstylist."

Sabrina's friendly expression turned to awe. "Really?"

"Yep. I specialize in color," Moira said. She could do a lot with Sabrina's long hair, give her something a little more classy and sophisticated than the amateur blue she was currently sporting.

"Could you do my hair?" Sabrina asked eagerly just as Jenna Jones entered the room.

"Let's let Moira get settled in before we start bugging her."

"It's not bugging," Moira assured Jenna. "I'm happy to." With everything this family was doing for her, even if she did the hair of every woman in the family, it wouldn't be enough to balance the scales.

"It would be so awesome to have a real hairstylist color my hair," Sabrina said. "No offense, Mom."

Jenna smiled. "I know I'm no pro. We'll see," she added.

Sabrina rolled her eyes. "I know what that means."

"It means we'll see," said her mother, refusing to be guilted into a quick decision.

"Have some cake, dear," Edie offered.

"I'd better not," Jenna said. "I know The Porthole has got chocolate lava cake on the menu tonight and if I eat that and your cake, I'll be on chocolate overload. Of course, your cake is better," she hurried to add.

"Well, at least sit down and have a cup of tea," Edie urged.

"That I can do," Jenna said and moved to where an electric teapot sat.

The back door opened, and a new person entered the kitchen, a scruffy old man with gray whiskers. He was skinny and wearing stained jeans, boots and an ancient peacoat. He shrugged out of it to show off a flannel shirt that looked like it had been around since pioneer times.

"Something sure smells good, Edie, old girl," he said.

"Clam chowder," she informed him. "And cheese bread."

"All my favorites." He made a beeline for the counter and cut himself a piece of cake. "And my favorite cake, too. What's the occasion?"

"It's Valentine's Day, Pete," Sabrina informed him.

"Damn. I forgot."

How could you forget when candy was on sale in every store? Even Lang always remembered. He would have bought Moira that chocolate rose on his way home from work. His temper would have cooled down and his hormones heated up, and he'd have come home expecting sex, rough and quick. Except she hadn't answered any of his calls or texts, so the temper was probably boiling over by now. If she walked through the door at this point, she'd get no candy or flowers, only angry words and probably a slap in the face.

"We have company," Edie said to the old man. "Pete, this is Moira. She's going to be staying with us for a while. Moira, this is Pete Long, our handyman. He lives at the Driftwood."

Pete looked Moira up and down. "New in town?"

"I am," Moira said.

"Moira's the new stylist at Waves," Edie said.

"That explains the hair," Pete said, and not in a flattering way.

Moira wasn't sure she was going to like this man. He talked the way Lang probably would when he got old. She wanted to retort, *What would you know about hair, you grungy old Q-tip?* Instead she pressed her lips firmly together.

"Pete's an expert on hair," Jenna sneered, grabbing a mug from the cupboard. "And just about everything else, too."

"When you've lived as long as I have," he began.

"You should know when to shut up," Jenna muttered. "Don't pay any attention to him," she whispered to Moira. "He's a twit."

He sure was. As Edie sliced cheese bread and set it on a platter, Pete waxed poetic on women's styles. "You know, back in my day, women didn't fuss so much. They went au naturel. I had a girlfriend who never shaved her legs."

"That's gross," said Sabrina.

"That's nature. We got hair on our bodies to keep us warm. Women now all want to look like they're twelve, waxing places they shouldn't."

Sabrina's face turned red and Jenna scolded, "Pete, enough already."

"And all these weird hair colors."

Was Moira's hair weird? She loved it and thought it was pretty. Even Lang, who found fault with almost everything, thought her hair was hot.

"Pete!" Jenna barked.

He scowled and helped himself to a slice of cheese bread.

"It's artistic expression," Sabrina explained.

Pete let out a grunt. "You want to express yourself? Go paint a picture."

"Everyone likes to look their best," Moira ventured, making him grunt. "You know, Mr. Long, you've got great bone structure. With a good haircut, you could be a hunk."

That made Sabrina giggle and Jenna shake her head. Hopeless.

"I'm already a hunk."

"You could use some sprucing up," Edie informed him. He looked shocked. "Really?"

"Think Sam Elliott," Moira said. "Why don't you come in to the salon sometime? I'll cut your hair for free." Yep, at the rate she was going, she'd be fixing up everyone in town for free and never be able to afford rent anywhere. "First time's on the house," she added. Maybe she'd eventually get a paying customer out of the deal.

"I go to Joe the Barber."

"Once a year, whether he needs it or not," Jenna murmured.

Pete pointed his half-consumed bread at her. "I heard that."

"You've got nothing to lose," Jenna said to him. "You ought to take her up on her offer."

"I'll think about it," he said. But his tone of voice added, *Not.*

The chowder was now in a soup tureen and dinner was ready. "Are you sure you don't want a little?" Edie asked Jenna. "You know no restaurant in town makes chowder as good as mine."

"Okay, I'll have a cup," Jenna decided. "As an appetizer."

"She's going out for dinner," Edie explained.

Of course she was. Jenna Jones was a pretty woman and it was Valentine's Day.

Jenna pulled up a chair and after a quick blessing, which Moira squirmed through (Pete, too, she noticed), they dug in.

So that was what clam chowder tasted like—creamy and salty and delicious. Moira didn't turn down Edie's offer of a second helping.

After two helpings of chowder and three servings of cheese bread, as well as another piece of cake, Pete announced his intention to go to The Drunken Sailor. "You women are just gonna sit around and talk about hair, anyway."

"Drunken Sailor?" Moira repeated. This was the second time someone had mentioned the place.

"It's a popular pub here in town," Jenna told her. "They have line dancing on Sunday nights."

Moira's mind flashed on an image of rednecks and cowboys. She kind of liked rednecks. And everyone knew cowboys were sexy. Except...cowboys at the beach? What did they wrangle? Seahorses?

"It's fun," Jenna said.

"Line dancing," Pete scoffed. "You don't get to even touch a woman. Where's the fun in that?"

Jenna ignored him. "You can come with me and check it out sometime if you want," she said to Moira.

Some new friends, something to do. Life was looking up. "Thanks," Moira said.

Pete shoved away from the table. "You women have fun. I'll see you tomorrow."

"Don't forget I need you to go to the hardware store," Jenna reminded him.

"How can I forget? You won't let me," he retorted as he pulled on his coat.

"He's really a sweet man," Edie said after Pete had gone out the door.

Compared to what?

"He's a pain," Jenna said. "But he's been a good friend to Aunt Edie," she hurried to add, catching sight of her aunt's frown.

"Pete and I have known each other for a long time," Edie said. "He's practically family."

So that was the deal. Edie Patterson was gooey over the old guy, who was pretty much a leech, which was why Jenna didn't like him.

Moira vowed to make sure she didn't take advantage of the family's kindness and turn into Pete in drag. "Family's important," she said diplomatically.

"It certainly is. Tell us a little about yours," Edie said. "Do you have brothers or sisters?"

None that she knew of. Maybe someday she'd do that ancestry thing where you could find out whose DNA matched yours. Until then, family was… "It's pretty much just my mom and me. I haven't seen too much of her lately."

Not since the last time they'd fought about Lang. "He's bad news," her mom had said after the first time he hit her. "You've got to get out. Come back home."

"He's not like that," Moira had insisted. "He'd had too much to drink."

"He'll hit you when he's sober, too, if you give him a reason. And sooner or later you'll give him a reason."

"He said he was sorry."

"Your dad used to say he was sorry, but he never stayed sorry."

He sure hadn't stayed sorry enough to stick around very long after Moira was born.

"Don't be stupid, Moira."

Moira had opted for stupid and pretty soon it got awkward talking with her mother, having the same conversation over and over again. Finally her mother had said, "It's a waste of breath talking to you."

"Well, then, I guess you don't have to," Moira had retorted. "'Cause, really, what do you care? When have you ever cared? I don't need you in my life," she'd finished and ended the call.

That last shot hadn't been fair, but at the time it was how she'd felt. What did her mom know, anyway? She was never around when things were good between Lang and Moira.

Except things got increasingly less good. And Moira became shackled by shame. So many times she'd wanted to call and tell her mom she was sorry. Maybe now she finally could.

"Where does your mother live?" Edie asked.

"She lives in Seattle." And not one of the nicer neighborhoods.

"Well, she'll have to come down here and visit," Edie said.

Would her mom want to come visit her? Would she ever want to talk to her again? She hadn't tried to call Moira after that last conversation.

But Moira hadn't called her, either.

Shortly after Sabrina had gotten a text from the boyfriend and vanished up to her room, the doorbell rang and Jenna went to answer it. She was back a moment later with a tall blue-eyed supermodel of a man following behind her, who she introduced as Brody Green. It was a casual introduction, but obviously, if they were going out on Valentine's Day, there was something going on between the two of them. Maybe in the process of becoming a couple? He looked at home enough in this kitchen, helping himself to a piece of Edie's cheese bread and complimenting her.

To Jenna, he said, "We should get going. You know how crowded The Porthole will be tonight."

Jenna nodded, said a polite goodbye to Moira, and then they were gone and it was just her and a little old lady. She suddenly felt awkward. Should she offer to keep the old woman company? She hardly knew her. And what if Edie wanted to know more about Moira's life? She wasn't sure she was ready to share that she was running from an abusive boyfriend.

She picked up her dishes and put them in the sink.

"Just leave the dishes, dear," Edie said.

"Are you sure? I don't mind."

"I'll have plenty of time to wash them later."

"Okay," Moira said, but she did clear the rest of the table. Then it seemed like the right time to leave. "I should get back to my cat."

"Are you sure, dear? You're welcome to stay."

It was nice to be welcome to stay somewhere, but, "I'm sure. Thanks. And thanks for the dinner."

"You can join us anytime," Edie told her.

Moira and Pete, the twin leeches. She vowed not to make a pest of herself, even though it was tempting.

She was almost to her room when a truck pulled into the parking spot next to hers and the most gorgeous man she'd ever seen got out. He wasn't as tall as Brody Green but he was well-built and those jeans were hugging an awesome butt. He had dark hair like Lang's and a swarthy complexion and he made Moira think of Heathcliff in *Wuthering Heights*, her all-time favorite book.

He gave her a polite nod, then went into the room next to hers. Who was that?

Who cared? She needed to go on a no-man diet. She didn't know how to pick a good one.

Jenna obviously did. Brody Green sure looked like a keeper.

How did one go about finding a keeper? Maybe Jenna gave lessons.

Back in her room, Moira picked up Harry, who yowled in pain, and put him on the bed. "I'm sorry, baby. You'll get better, though, and so will our lives."

At least she hoped they would. Okay, so it was Valentine's Day and she and Harry were in a strange town all by themselves in a motel room. Nobody was getting insulted, smacked or kicked, and that was an improvement.

It was scary to start over all by herself so far from where she'd grown up, where she'd had friends. But she was also far away from Lang and that was a good thing. Maybe she could get her brain working again and make better choices for the future. No matter what Lang said, she wasn't a loser. She could make a good life for herself on her own. At least she hoped she could.

She contemplated the framed photo of a sunrise hanging on the wall. Sunrises were glorious. They represented new days and new beginnings. Only that morning she'd felt trapped in the darkest of nights. Maybe now sunrise was right around the corner.

When are we going to go home? had been the first words out of Emma's mouth when Annie told her they would be staying with Aunt Courtney for a while.

There was only one way Annie could answer that. Honestly. "I don't know if we're going to go back home. You know your daddy has some problems he needs to deal with."

"But he needs us," Emma had protested.

He needed help, and they couldn't give it to him unless he was willing to take that first step toward helping himself. How did you explain all that to a ten-year-old?

Annie had taken a deep breath and taken a stab at it. "Sweetie, the way Daddy needs to sort some things out, he'll be able to do better if we're not there."

What she'd wanted to say was, *Daddy treats us like crap. It's not okay that he's drinking all the time and not working. It's not okay for a man to punch walls and make his daughter have nightmares because he's yelling at her mommy.* But, as she'd done so many times before, she sugarcoated their ugly situation, pulled threadbare covers over their pathetic life, trying to shield her daughter from the ugly truth.

There was going to come a time when she wouldn't be able to do it anymore. Maybe that time had come, but if it had, Annie couldn't face it. She still had hopes of sparing her daughter from some of the ugly truth. If Greg would just get help and pull himself together.

Emma had cried all the way to Courtney's house.

Courtney rented a two-bedroom beach cottage that came complete with a long front porch and a path to the beach. She created and sold clothes for the little boutique in the nearby Oyster Inn and used the second bedroom as a sewing room, but she'd been more than happy to move her sewing supplies to a corner of the living room so Annie and Emma could have their own space. They'd found a trundle bed at a thrift store in nearby Quinault and Jenna's renter from the Driftwood Inn, Seth Waters, had brought it home for them in the back of his truck. A trundle bed, two dressers brought from home and Emma's toys and treasures were now crammed in the room. Annie had hoped that Emma's stuffed-bear collection would make it feel a little more like home. Emma loved visiting Aunt Courtney. If they were lucky, she'd enjoy staying with her, as well. The price was right. With sharing rent, Annie was only paying half what she'd been paying.

Emma hadn't exactly raced up the front steps of the house with its blue shutters and dormer windows. She hadn't exactly raved over the bedroom, either, even though Lula Bear and Mr. Brown, Teddy and Tilly were all sitting on the bed to greet her. She'd picked up Mr. Brown, the worn brown bear she'd had since she was three, and begun to cry.

Annie had knelt and hugged her. "It'll be okay, sweetie. We'll be okay." Was that a false promise?

Dinner was a solemn affair and Emma said little and ate less, even though Courtney had gotten her a package of those candy hearts with all the Valentine sayings on them and they'd made sure to have chicken strips and Annie's homemade mac and cheese, Emma's favorite foods, for dinner.

Annie didn't force her. She understood. She wasn't very hungry, either.

"Hey, I think we need to put on some music and dance," Courtney said after Emma had passed up ice cream for dessert.

Normally Emma loved dancing around the living room with Courtney when they came over to visit. Instead she shook her head and asked, "Can I be excused?"

"Of course," Annie said and watched sadly as her

daughter ran up the stairs to the tiny bedroom they were sharing.

"She'll adjust," said Courtney. "You gotta give her time."

"What if she doesn't?"

"Trust me, she will. I did when my parents split. Of course, I decided I hated my mom."

"Oh, thanks. I needed to hear that."

"Until my older sister told me Dad had cheated on Mom. With his secretary. Is that a cliché or what? Then I switched to hating my dad."

"I don't want her to hate Greg. I don't want to hate Greg. Although, sometimes I honestly think I do. He's ruining all our lives."

"He's not going to keep ruining them. You're seeing to that."

Annie sighed. If only she'd realized Greg had a drinking problem before they got married. He'd hidden it so well when they were dating. Yes, he'd loved his beer, but no more than anyone else in their crowd. Once they were together 24/7, it got hard to hide all those bottles piling up in the recycle bin. And the irresponsible behavior began to show. The hangovers, the missed days of work, the going out with the boys and coming home late, weaving into the house smelling like a distillery. Ugh.

She'd threatened to leave a year after they got married, and he'd cut back on the drinking. She'd thought that would be enough. But in the end it wasn't. The booze bottle population in the recycle bin started growing again. Then she got pregnant with Emma, and he'd been so excited. Once more he promised to change. He didn't, and now Emma was ten years old. How many chances did you give a man?

Greg chose that moment to call. Seeing his name on her cell phone screen shot Annie's heart rate through the roof.

"It's him." He'd come home and found the note she left. Confrontation time. She hated confrontation.

"Stay strong," cautioned Courtney.

It was hard to stay strong when you didn't want to, when you wanted everything to go back to normal. No, not normal. Better than normal. Back to what she thought she'd had when she first met Greg. He'd been so fun, so friendly, a perfect emotional rock for a shy woman to cling to. Greg had always been the life of the party. She just didn't realize until it was too late that he got all that energy from alcohol.

Annie managed a calm hello, even though she felt like her insides were in a blender.

He barely gave her time to get it out. "What the hell, Annie?"

"I told you I was going to leave if you didn't do something to prove you want to change. All you've done is prove you don't want to." What a hard truth to face. She wiped away a tear, but it didn't do any good. Another took its place on her cheek, and then another.

"Where are you?" he demanded.

"You don't need to know."

"Are you at Courtney's? Whose idea was it for you to leave? Hers?"

"It was my idea. And I'm staying gone. If you want me to come back, you know what to do." She could feel the adrenaline kicking in. She felt shaky. And sick.

"Come on, baby, don't be like this. Come home."

As if she were the one doing something wrong. "I'm sorry, Greg. I've had enough."

"This isn't fair to Emma."

He was bringing their daughter into this? Really? Anger stepped in and took over. "Oh, don't you dare go there," she half sobbed. "Scaring her with your drunken rages,

yelling at me, losing job after job—is that fair to Emma?"
Their daughter deserved better.

"Hey, that last job—"

Annie cut him off. "We both know what happened on
that last job so don't go there, either, Greg. Please."

"You can't make it on your own. You don't make enough
as a waitress."

Was he kidding? As if he was bringing in any income?
"Emma and I will be fine. I'd like us to be fine with you,
with a sober you. If you can't make that happen, we'll have
to move on without you."

And they would. She made enough to pay her share
of rent, and living with Courtney, maybe she could start
branching out and catering for parties around town, a great
first step toward getting that food truck she'd dreamed of
having for so long. Courtney would help her out and watch
Emma. Courtney was reliable, which was more than Annie
could say for Greg.

He was still sputtering when she ended the call. She
took a shaky breath and tossed aside her phone. She realized her hands were trembling and she wrapped them
together firmly.

"Good for you, Warrior Princess," Courtney approved.

Annie's cell began ringing again, demanded her attention. She shut it off. "Put on some music and let's dance."

After his shift, Victor King shed his uniform, safely
locked up his Glock and ammo, then donned his gym-rat
clothes and drove to the gym for a workout. There was
nobody in the gym on V-Day.

Good. He had the place to himself, one of the benefits
of not being in a relationship. Yeah, that was one way of
looking at it. Valentine's Day sucked when everyone else

around you was buying flowers and making plans for dinner. And sex.

On the way back home, he stopped by the grocery store and picked up some beer and a frozen pizza. Now he was in for the night, showered and comfortable in worn jeans and an even more worn flannel shirt, ready to stream something from Comedy Central. But first he had to build a fire.

He pulled on his heavy jacket, donned his work gloves and went out to fetch wood for the woodstove. The spring before he'd gone off to the forest with a buddy and they'd done the manly-man thing and cut down a tree. He'd split every piece of wood himself and was darned proud of his woodpile.

Since it got darker than Satan's pocket at night (no streetlights in most of the town's neighborhoods—better for stargazing), he'd installed a light on the side of the house so he could see what he was doing. But before flipping it on, he stepped onto his front porch and took a moment to enjoy the view of a starry night sky with no light pollution. Man, that was a view you couldn't get in the city. Orion, the Big and Small Dippers. Oh, yeah.

He walked around to the side of the house and there it was, his monument to self-sufficiency and testosterone. Also an enemy camp. He flashed the beam across the top row of stacked wood. It looked safe enough so he began to grab some chunks of fir.

He'd picked up his second one when, sudden as the killer in a horror movie, a wolf spider the size of a hatchet appeared right next to his hand. THE ENEMY!

"Ayeee!" Victor's heart seized and he stumbled backward, turning the air blue with every curse word his mother had ever soaped up his mouth for using, dropping the wood he'd gathered, tripping over a piece and landing on his butt. For the second time in one day. Small consolation that at least this time he hadn't landed in shit.

He swore again, got up and picked up a piece of wood. Then he crept back to the woodpile to do battle. Of course, the thing had buried itself deep in a crevice somewhere and now was lurking, waiting to strike.

Wolf spiders were venomous but their bite wasn't lethal. "You've got on gloves," he scolded himself. "Don't be such a wuss."

Okay, so he was a wuss. So what? He nudged a piece of wood with the one in his hand. "I know you're in there somewhere, you stinkin' thing. I will get you." If it didn't get him first.

Not lethal. You're fine.

Unless it came into the house. Where was it?

The monster refused to show himself. Victor gingerly picked up a piece of firewood. He poked at the pile again. Still no sign of the enemy. He snatched another piece. And another.

Then he grabbed the wood he'd already gotten and bolted for the house. It wasn't that cold, anyway. He didn't need to keep a fire going all night. He'd call the exterminator tomorrow.

Stinkin' spiders.

Of course, his older brother teased him mercilessly about his arachnophobia. But, unlike Victor, his bro had never been bitten by a spider and had the bite get infected. Or encountered one of these monsters close up. Victor still remembered the morning of that camping trip when he was six, snuggled into his sleeping bag in the tent with his brother, and he opened his eyes to see a massive spider right there in front of his nose. Luckily that one had been scared off when he bolted upright, but after encountering it he didn't have to go to the bathroom anymore.

Victor still hated camping. Who wanted to take a whiz in the woods or some smelly outhouse and freeze their ass off? And who wanted to stumble into nettles in their shorts? (Yeah, that had happened, too.) He didn't need to camp to prove he was manly, anyway. He'd done basic training in the army and if that didn't make a man out of a boy, nothing would. He'd played football in high school, run marathons and played on the Moonlight Harbor Blues baseball team, and that plus doing his own work on this fixer-upper he'd bought was enough to qualify him for nonwimp status.

Unless word ever got out on the force that he was afraid of spiders. Might as well turn in his balls if that happened.

He took a bad enough ribbing about his womanless state. Okay, so he didn't have a belt filled with notches. So what? And yeah, women tended to scare him. Not as much as spiders. But they had a way of making him feel tongue-tied.

Maybe that was because he'd had no sisters in his family and all his cousins had been boys. For him, women were an alien species, fascinating and desirable, but hard to understand. Victor was unafraid when it came to bullets or even getting the crap beaten out of him. (It hadn't happened much growing up, but he'd gotten his share of bloody noses and gut punches.) Bad guys? Bring 'em on. But women, they didn't deal in bullets and fists. They dealt in words, fast and cleverly delivered, and could cut a guy down to the size of a peanut with one look.

Girls had teased him and flirted with him in middle school and loved to make him blush. The first girl he'd tried to date had been shocked he didn't know how to French kiss and her mocking had mortified him. He'd passed on the offer of a lesson and taken her home and that had ended that. Luckily, his brother had fixed him up with a cutie from out of town, a friend of a friend of a friend, who'd been happy to tutor him with no judgments. His girlfriend in the army had been a wild one and great in bed, and had given him more confidence in his dealings with the opposite sex. She'd even given him hope that he'd found true love. But when he got out of the army and talked about becoming a cop, she'd ended things. The next girlfriend loved cops. And handcuffs. But she didn't love the idea of small-town life. Or kids. Finally, along had come Cecily Jones, who was hotter than jalapeños, loved Moonlight Harbor and had lots of personality. And, thanks to the loser who'd burned her, was determined to never date a cop. Victor had tried to snag her interest and failed.

He frowned as he crumpled old newspapers and stuck them in the woodstove. He had a career he loved, he was buying a house—so much of his life was on track. Why couldn't he get the relationship aspect of it on track, as well?

He reminded himself that he could have a woman if he wanted. Courtney Moore was more than willing. But Courtney was sassy and aggressive and made him feel like a hunted animal. If she ever kissed him, he was sure she'd suck the life right out of him.

Whatever happened to the idea of men chasing women? Yeah, it was old-fashioned, but he wanted to be the one to ask somebody out. He wanted a woman who wasn't such a smart-mouth that she made him feel like a dumb ass, and he wanted someone who wouldn't giggle when he blushed. (Like he could help that!) And he wanted to have sex, but with the right person.

He thought of the new woman he'd followed to Waves. What was her story? Maybe he'd have to find out.

Six

"I knew I'd find you," Lang said as he bent and looked inside the chicken coop where Moira was huddled.

She'd shaved off her hair and was bald and she and Harry were alone in the coop. No chickens. Only a bucket of Kentucky Fried.

"Leave it to you to find someplace like this to live," Lang sneered.

"I like it here," she insisted.

"Yeah, right. Look at you. You're covered in chicken shit."

So she was. Funny, she couldn't smell it.

"You left me to go live in a chicken coop? What were you thinking, anyway? I knew you couldn't make it without me." His expression softened and he held out a hand. "Come on, babe. Come back home. We'll forget this ever happened."

Harry came out first and snaked around Lang's legs and Lang bent to pet him. "See? Harry knows what's good. Come back. Everything will be perfect."

Out she came, and the next thing she knew she and Lang were in a small rowboat out on the open sea with no other living being around them, not even a bird in the air, and Harry was nowhere to be seen. She had hair again, tons of it piled high on her head like pictures she'd seen of Marie Antoinette but she was dressed in rags, like Cinderella.

Panic crashed over her like a giant wave. "Why are we here?"

"Because this is where you want to be. You like the beach so we're at the beach."

There was no beach. There was no land in sight.

Lang leaned toward her and his eyes narrowed. "It's just you and me now."

She pushed herself against the bow of the boat, trying to distance herself from him. "Where's Harry?"

"I'm Harry," he said, and then, like some cartoon character he began to change shape, his arms turning into legs covered in black fur. His face turned into Harry's face and his whiskers twitched. He grew in size until he towered over her. "Meow, baby," he said. Then he hissed and took a swipe at her with a giant paw, claws unsheathed, and she let out a screech and nearly fell out of the boat in her effort to dodge him.

"Did I scare you?" He bent his giant kitty face to hers and began to rub her cheek. His fur was so soft. He meowed in her ear and began licking her face with his sandpaper tongue.

And then he sat on her chest.

Her eyes popped open and she found herself lying in a strange bed with Harry sitting on her chest, staring at her, purring. A dream. She'd been dreaming. She took a deep breath, willing her heart to settle down.

She wasn't with Lang, thank God. And she wasn't stuck living in a chicken coop. She was in Moonlight Harbor, tucked safely away in a room at the Driftwood Inn.

But was she safe? Would Lang find her here?

Of course not. He had no idea where she was. He'd soon give up looking for her and find some other woman to terrorize.

There was an awful thought—Lang starting that whole cycle all over again with a new woman. Some unsuspecting, insecure woman who'd be taken in by his charm, who'd think he was so cool. Then the put-downs would surface, the angry outbursts, followed by the hitting. And, worst of all, the heartfelt, teary-eyed apologies. *I'll never do it again.* After a while he'd stop saying that and it would be "When are you going to learn not to disrespect me… make me so mad…be so stupid?" *Take your pick. But don't expect any option where it was his fault.*

"We did the right thing," she said to Harry, who meowed. "I guess you're hungry, huh?"

So was she. She wished she'd thought to bring along some food. Or buy some at the grocery store they'd passed coming into town.

At least she'd brought food for Harry. She dug a can of cat food out of her tote bag, along with Harry's dish. She filled the dish with water, broke up his medicine into his food and then gave him his meal. He fell on it like he'd been starving for days.

"I know how you feel," she said. "What I'd give for a donut." Maybe she'd have time to go to the store. She glanced at the clock on the wall—a funky vintage thing shaped like a miniature sun. "Oh, my gosh! Eight forty?" How had she slept so late? She was supposed to be at Waves at nine o'clock.

She grabbed panties and a bra and dashed for the bathroom. It usually took her fifteen minutes just to do her hair.

Now she had that much time to shower, dress, do her hair and makeup. She'd have to bag doing her hair.

She took a quick look in the bathroom mirror. Not an option. She needed to wash her hair.

She didn't have time.

She'd have to take time. She was a hairstylist. She couldn't show up at work looking like a greasy loser.

She showered in fast motion, got out of the shower and accidentally stepped into Harry's litter box. Eeew! Back into the shower to wash her foot. Eeew, eew, eew! Then into the bra and panties. She pulled on her cuffed skinny jeans and a top, then got out her hair dryer and raced back to the bathroom, willing time to stand still, blowing, brushing, curling, muttering, "Come on, come *on*!"

Okay, her hair was dry enough. She put on ankle boots and her favorite jacket, a stylin' thrift-store find. By that time Harry was by her side, wanting attention.

Even though she was beyond late, she took a moment to pet him. "You be a good boy and don't pee anywhere but your cat box," she said to him. Then she stuffed her makeup bag in her purse, grabbed her car keys and dashed out the door. She'd have to put on her makeup as she drove. No problem there. She was an expert.

She catapulted into her car, aware of the man in the room next to hers stepping out of his room. *Hot* registered in her brain, but she didn't even take time to acknowledge his polite nod.

Late. Late on her first day at her new job. Not that she had any appointments waiting yet, but it still made a sucky impression. She squealed out of the parking lot and headed down the main drag. The sky was gray and dribbling a fine mist. She flipped on her windshield wipers, then fumbled in her makeup bag for her foundation.

Late. Late, late, late! Why had she picked today of all days to oversleep? She never overslept. Even after a big fight with Lang, she'd always gotten up in time to get to the salon. She'd never even needed an alarm, her internal clock telling her to wake up and start a fresh day.

She slap dashed on her foundation, then took out the mascara. She was an expert at putting on mascara in the car.

Maybe she'd have to explain that to the cop in the SUV patrol car behind her, who had his you're-in-trouble lights flashing. *Nooo.*

She pulled over, barely avoiding hitting a deer in the process. Where had that come from? She let out a squeak, slammed on the brakes and Bambi bounded off into the tall grass of a nearby empty lot.

Moira's heart was now in overdrive as she took her wallet out of her purse. *License and registration, please.*

Anyone who watched enough TV knew the drill and that was the primary source of her knowledge. She'd only been stopped by a cop once in her whole life. She'd been nineteen then, and full of confidence. She'd also been wearing a low-cut top that showed off her boobs, which she was sure had helped. She'd flashed him her sweetest smile, promised to never speed again and had gotten off with a warning.

She wasn't wearing anything low-cut today and she didn't feel like smiling. In fact, she felt like crying. She was wearing waterproof mascara so why not?

She had her window down before the cop even got to it. "I'm sorry," she said, wiping at her eyes as she handed over her license and car registration. "I know I was speeding."

"And driving distracted," he added, looking at the license.

"What? No, I wasn't. My cell phone isn't on."

"You were putting on makeup."

"That's not distracted. I always do that." She was a woman. She knew how to multitask.

"You can't be watching the road if you're looking in the mirror."

"I saw you," she pointed out.

"You didn't see that deer, though, did you?"

"That wasn't because I was putting on makeup. I was looking back at you."

Okay, what the heck was she doing arguing with an officer of the law? Now he was going to give her a ticket for sure. She couldn't afford a ticket.

The precariousness of her new start hit her full force and she began to cry in earnest. "I'm sorry. That was inappropriate. This is my first day at work and I'm late. I'm broke and I don't even have any clients yet. And now I'll get fired. I've only been in town since yesterday and I'll get fired and have to leave and I don't know where to go," she finished in a wail.

She could go back to Lang. He'd take her back.

No. She couldn't, absolutely wouldn't do that to Harry.

"Where are you working?"

"At Waves."

He appeared to come to a sudden decision. "I'll give you an escort," he said, handing back the license and registration. "Don't put on any more makeup or I will give you a ticket for sure," he added sternly.

She swallowed hard and nodded. Then she fell in line behind the cop, speeding off down the road, thanking her lucky stars all the way that he hadn't ticketed her.

He sure could have. It was nice of him not to.

Nice. There was a plain word if ever she'd heard one.

He'd been more than nice. He'd been kind, gallant. Yes, gallant. He'd not only spared her, he was going out of his way to help her.

He sure was cute. There was another word that fell short. He was more than cute; he was appealing, with those broad shoulders and that manly chin. What was he like when he wasn't in uniform? Did he laugh easily? Could he dance? Did he have a girlfriend?

Probably.

Not that she needed to be looking for a man. She obviously had poor judgment when it came to men.

Still, it would be so nice—there was that ineffectual word again!—comforting to be with a man who would treat her with respect, who would protect her instead of beating her up.

Well, that was the old days. These days a woman protected herself. Maybe not by overpowering a bully, but by making sure she cut him out of her life. Moira had done that. It was something she could be proud of.

The cop pulled into the parking lot in front of the salon and she pulled in beside him. Two other cars were parked there, and out of the corner of her eye, she caught sight through the large plate glass window of her boss and a woman in the chair in front of her draped in a plastic cape, both gaping out the window. What a way to make an entrance on her first day. At least she was only ten minutes late. It could have been worse.

She hopped out of her car and ran over to the passenger side of the patrol car. The officer let down his window and almost smiled at her.

"Thank you so much," she gushed.

"Glad to help," he said. "But make sure you get up earlier from now on. You might not get a police escort next time."

She nodded. "I will. And if you ever want a free haircut…" *I'd love to get my hands in your hair.*

This time he did smile. "Bribing an officer?"

She smiled back. "No, thanking an officer. I know I shouldn't have been speeding. I just wanted to make a good impression on my new boss."

"Then I guess you'd better get in there," he suggested.

"Thanks again," she said, backing away with a little wave. Then she turned and ran into the salon, making sure the first words out of her mouth were "I'm so sorry I'm late."

"Is everything all right?" asked Pearl.

"Oh, yes. I'm afraid I…" Did she really want to confess to her new employer that she'd overslept? "I ran into a delay."

"Late on the first day, not a good sign," muttered the woman in the chair, middle-aged with thinning brown (bad dye job) hair and frown lines etched on the sides of her mouth.

"Things happen," Pearl said, making Moira glad Pearl was her boss and not this woman.

Chastity, the manicurist, came in the door. "I just saw Victor King pulling out of the parking lot. What happened?"

"He found out I was late on my first day and gave me a police escort," Moira told her.

"Speeding," muttered the woman as if she'd never gone a mile over the speed limit her entire life. Maybe she hadn't.

"I've been known to speed myself," said Pearl, and that shut her up. "Moira, I'm hoping you wouldn't mind running a load of towels for me. And if you could work the reception desk just until you get some clients, that would be great."

"Of course," said Moira, shrugging out of her jacket. "I'll be happy to."

"Chastity, Mrs. Parker called and said she's running late," Pearl continued. "She'll be here in about fifteen minutes."

"Good. That gives me time to get some coffee," Chastity said and followed Moira into the back room.

As they went, the thin woman's voice followed them. "Coffee breaks, coming in late—honestly, Pearl, you're entirely too lax."

"At least Pearl keeps her people," Chastity said in a hushed voice. "Susan Frank's gone through a dozen employees in the last two years."

"What kind of business does she have?" Moira asked.

"She sells ugly clothes. But she does offer the bonus of having to deal with her when you buy them. I went into the store once with my mom when she was visiting. That was enough for me. But never mind Susan," Chastity said as she got busy with Pearl's Keurig. "Tell me how you managed to get Victor King to give you a police escort instead of a ticket."

"I cried."

"Works every time."

"Not on purpose," Moira hurried to explain. She grabbed an armload of well-worn white towels from a basket and dumped them in the washing machine. "I really was upset. It's terrible to be late on your first day in a new job. I just didn't sleep very well last night, though, and I woke up twenty minutes ago. Anyway, you know how it is when you're late."

"Oh, yeah. I've bent the speed limit a few times myself. Good of him not to give you a ticket. By the way, he's single."

That answered that question. Moira shrugged. "Not really looking. I just got out of a relationship."

Chastity nodded, taking that in. "Better not to rush into anything. But if you were looking, you wouldn't find a better man than Victor. Well, except for my husband, of course."

"Of course," Moira agreed. Lucky Chastity, to have a good man and a happy marriage.

"But Victor is a sweetie. Tough on crime, soft on women. I saw him put on that scary cop face once with a shoplifter in Beachside Grocery. It was enough to stop me in my tracks and I've never taken anything."

Which was more than Moira could say. She wasn't proud of those few teen-girl-sticky-fingers episodes and could only be thankful that she'd never been caught.

"I've also seen him changing a flat tire for Edie Patterson," Chastity continued. "He's the whole deal."

How nice it would be to have a man who was the whole deal, who could be tough with bad guys but soft with a woman. That soft-with-a-woman thing sure wasn't in Lang's wheelhouse.

You're not ready to be with a man, she told herself as she dumped laundry soap into the washing machine. *You need time to screw your head back on straight.*

Who knew how long that would take? In fact, who knew if she'd ever be able to?

A free haircut. Victor liked the sound of that. Not because he was cheap. He just liked the idea of Moira Wellman having her fingers in his hair. He liked the idea of Moira Wellman, period.

He turned his mind back to when he'd stopped her and she'd burst into tears. A lot of women did that when you stopped them for a traffic infraction. Or else they tried to flirt their way out of a ticket. Victor had quickly learned to toughen up, ignore feeling like a bully, resist being manipulated by pouty lips or promises of eternal gratitude and concentrate on meting out justice. But this had been different. This woman had an air of brokenness about her that had made him want to gather her in his arms and tell her everything would be okay. What hadn't been okay in her life he had no idea, but he was sure there was something.

He hadn't gone far when the next call came in. Lost dog seen wandering on Sailboat Lane. He knew whose dog that would be, radioed in that he was on it and went in search of Dougal, Mrs. Burton's golden. Dougal had a gift for escaping his front yard, and upsetting his seventy-eight-year-old owner. Mrs. Burton was probably out looking for him, worrying that he'd been hit by a car.

It didn't take Victor long to spot Dougal, strolling down the street, stopping to sniff a tuft of grass to see if any other dog had left a calling card. Victor parked the car, got out and hollered, "Here, boy!"

You didn't have to call Dougal twice. He was happy to trot up to Victor, tail wagging.

"You know your mom's looking for you," Victor said as he gave the dog an ear rub.

Dougal whined and attempted to lick Victor's face.

"Yeah, you know you've been bad, dontcha? Come on, let's get you home."

Dougal was perfectly fine with Victor picking him up

and putting him in the dog cage he kept in the back of the patrol car—specifically for Dougal emergencies. "Be glad I'm not with Animal Control," he said, shutting the dog safely in.

Sure enough, when they turned onto Sunrise, where Mrs. Burton lived, Victor spotted her, a coat thrown over her bathrobe, feet shoved into boots, peering between two houses, looking for her wandering fur baby. She hadn't bothered to put a hat on and her white hair was already wet and sticking to her head, bits of pink scalp peeking out. At the rate she was going, her dog would be the death of her. Literally. If she didn't end up with pneumonia, it would be a miracle.

Victor let down his window and called, "I found him."

Mrs. Burton looked at Victor as if he were the patron saint of dogs. "Oh, thank God."

He pulled up next to her, got out and opened the passenger-side door. "How about I give you a ride home?"

"I'd love that," she said and climbed in.

He went around to the driver's side, thanking his lucky stars he'd found the dog right away. Mrs. Burton would have stayed out looking for him until she turned into a Popsicle.

"I'm so glad you found him, Victor," she said as he put the car into gear. She shivered and he turned on the heat. "The little mischief slipped away when I went to take out the recycling. I don't know what I'm going to do with him."

"Invisible fence?" Victor suggested. Obviously, the visible one wasn't doing much good.

"I may have to. I just hate to have him wear one of those shock collars, though."

"I understand. But that's better than having him get hit by a car."

"You're so right," she said solemnly.

Back at the house, he set Dougal free and made sure he got shut safely in his front yard. "Thank you so much," Mrs. Burton said from her side of the fence. "I don't know what we'd do without you. You stop by the house later when you're off work and I'll have some chocolate chip cookies for you."

"No need to do that," he assured her and hoped she wouldn't take him seriously. Victor wasn't so great in the kitchen, and he loved Mrs. Burton's cookies.

"I know, but I want to."

"Thanks," he said.

"I'm happy to," she told him. "Of course, one of these days you're going to find a sweet young thing to bake you cookies and you won't need me."

"I'll always need your cookies," he assured her.

"You are a dear."

Yeah, that was him. *A dear.* Too bad Mrs. Burton wasn't a sweet young thing or he an old geezer. He'd have it made.

His police radio was calling, so he said goodbye to Mrs. Burton and returned to his patrol car. Next stop: Sandy's restaurant, and not for food.

Frank was busy with a traffic stop, so Victor was on his own to handle Greg Albright. Not that dispatch had named him, but Victor knew. Simple deduction. Someone drunk and disorderly at Sandy's, where Annie Albright was waitressing. It had to be her boozer husband. Ten in the morning and already soused and making his wife's life miserable. It was what the guy did best.

Sure enough, when Victor walked in, there was Greg, unshaved and uncombed and probably unwashed, a scrawny-butt dude in jeans and a wrinkled flannel shirt under a camo jacket, following Annie as she walked with an armload of plates to where two older couples were waiting for their breakfast. He was waving his arms and shouting, and poor quiet Annie was red-faced and trying her best to ignore him.

"You gotta talk to me!" Albright roared.

Jerk. They had another Greg in town, a solid guy who'd moved his family to Moonlight Harbor a year earlier. Funny how people with the same name could wear it so differently. This mope might call himself Greg but everyone on the force called him Asshole.

Annie set down the plates, her face lobster red, said something quietly to the shocked people, probably an apology. Her loser husband kept waving his arms and yelling.

One of the older guys pointed a finger at him and snapped, "You watch your manners, young man."

Oh, boy, here was trouble for sure.

Yep. "You gonna make me, old man?" Albright demanded.

Probably not considering the fact that the man looked frail enough to blow away in a strong wind and had a cane leaned up against his chair.

"No. I am," Victor said, quietly, coming up behind him.

Albright whirled around, a belligerent look on his face, then blinked in surprise at Victor. Victor was only five eleven but he had plenty of well-toned muscles. That, combined with a uniform and a gun, was usually enough to bring people to their senses.

"I'm not doing anything," the loser protested.

"Come on," Victor said, pointing to the restaurant lobby. "We need to have a talk."

"I don't want to talk," Albright muttered, but he moved away from the table.

"I'm so sorry," Victor could hear Annie saying to the customers.

"Don't you worry. Not your fault," one of the women told her.

No, it wasn't. The only thing Annie Albright had done wrong was marry the guy.

The restaurant wasn't too crowded, but Victor led Greg through the lobby and then opened the glass front door, nodding for Albright to walk through it.

"I'm not leaving without my wife," he said and scowled at Victor.

"We need to talk out here where you won't be bothering the customers. You don't really have a problem with that, do you? The way you were acting in there put you right on the edge of getting hauled off for disorderly conduct."

Albright was sober enough to realize that he didn't have a problem with stepping outside, after all. He pushed open the door and then stopped, looking both mulish and embarrassed.

"You been drinking?" Victor asked. As if he couldn't tell. Albright smelled like the inside of a beer barrel. If Victor had caught him behind the wheel, he'd have been able to nail him.

"No. I swear I haven't," Albright lied.

The door opened and Annie joined them, shivering in her thin black waitress slacks and blue polo shirt. She was a delicate little thing with brown hair and pretty eyes. She'd served Victor and Frank many times, always efficiently and quietly. Even her smile was quiet. Victor sometimes wondered if she was just too beat down to find the energy for a real smile.

"Has he been abusive to you?" Victor asked her. As if he had to ask after the scene he'd just witnessed.

She looked miserable, like she wished she could fold up like a napkin and disappear. "No, he's...upset."

"There's upset and then there's out of control," Victor said. "Which do you think describes you right about now?" he asked Albright.

"I just want my wife. That's all I want," Albright said sullenly. "She's left me."

It was all Victor could do not to say, *Gee, I wonder why.*

"Where she works isn't the place to settle this. You need to go home and get sober."

"Fine," Albright said with as much dignity as his present condition allowed.

Victor held out his hand. "The keys to your truck."

"What?"

"Give me your keys. Unless you want to wind up with a DUI."

"I'm not drunk."

Victor leaned in closer. "Want to test that?"

Albright glared at him as he fished his keys out of his pocket. "This is police harassment," he said, handing them over.

"No, this is giving you a break you don't deserve."

"Annie, run me home," Albright said to his wife. "We can talk."

"I can't just leave work," she said.

"We have to talk!" Albright demanded, his voice rising again.

"You have to leave," Victor said in a tone of voice no sane man, drunk or sober, would argue with.

"It's five miles to our house," protested the poor excuse for a man.

"Then you better get going," Victor advised.

Albright pointed a finger at this wife. "This isn't over. We're gonna talk."

Victor stepped between them, the leather in his gun holster creaking ominously. "Are you threatening her?"

Albright blinked and took a step back. "No. Hell, no."

"Good. Because that would be a really stupid thing to do. Start walking. You can pick up your keys at the station tomorrow." If he could stay sober enough to get there.

Albright hunched his shoulders and slouched away, muttering.

"And don't you give him a ride, Annie," Victor said sternly.

Annie's face was still red. "I'm sorry," she said, her voice barely above a whisper.

"You have nothing to be sorry for," Victor told her.

She bit her lip. "He refuses to get help. I… It's not fair to our daughter."

It wasn't fair to his wife, either. "If you fear for your safety," Victor began.

Annie gave him a sad smile. "No. I'm mostly afraid of getting fired. If Greg keeps this up…"

"You can get a restraining order. And if he threatens violence, you need to."

She nodded and rubbed her arms. He could see goose bumps.

"Promise me you will, Annie," Victor said. "People can get out of control and then bad things happen."

"I will. I'll be fine."

"You have a place to stay?" Dumb question. Of course she did, since Albright was in there whining about her being gone.

"I'm staying with Courtney."

It stood to reason. She and Courtney were best friends.

If Albright went over there, Courtney would have no problem letting him have it.

Victor nodded. "Okay. You take care. Get inside before you freeze."

She nodded and turned toward the door.

"If he shows up again, either here or at Courtney's, call us."

"I will," she said.

"I mean it."

She nodded again, thanked him and then scurried back into the restaurant.

What a mess people made of their lives, Victor thought as he got back in his patrol car. Seeing this was a good reminder that it was okay not to be in a hurry when it came to getting with a woman. If there was one thing he didn't want in his life, it was the kind of drama that came with picking the wrong person.

Moira hated not having any clients, but she enjoyed being at Waves, greeting people and tidying up around the place. It was fun to eavesdrop as the parade of women came through, sharing their lives with Chastity and Pearl.

"This diet is killing me. I'd rather eat sand."

"I knew he had a woman on the side."

"I don't know why we have a clothes closet since he never hangs anything up."

"I'm going to be a grandma, finally."

The bits and snatches of conversation danced around her like music on the radio. (Actually better than the music Pearl liked to listen to, some kind of really old rock-and-roll stuff.)

One thing Moira had learned over the last few years was that hair salons were the perfect stage for drama. Someone was always having a relationship crisis, a diet crisis or a hair crisis.

Oh, boy, and speaking of crises, here came one.

"We need help," cried Sabrina Jones, bursting through the salon door, another girl in tow.

Seven

Sabrina was in total crisis mode as she raced into the shop, holding on to the other girl. Like Sabrina, this girl was fair-skinned and slender, with hair just as long but not quite as thick. They almost looked like sisters, except the other girl's face was a little longer, and she had a false eyelash dangling from the corner of a tightly closed eye. Her other eye was open so wide it was a wonder her eyeball hadn't fallen out. It wasn't hard to deduce what had happened.

Pearl, who was in the middle of shampooing an older lady, looked up. "Sabrina, what's wrong?"

"It's Hudson. Her eye's glued shut."

"I can't open it!" Hudson shrieked.

Moira hurried over to them. "Here, let me help you," she said and escorted them to a chair.

"I was doing her eyelashes," Sabrina explained, "and…"

"You glued my eye together! Oh, my gosh. I can't go to the party tonight looking like this," the girl named Hudson wailed. "I can't go anywhere! I'll never see again!"

"Don't worry. I can fix it and I promise you'll be able to

see again." Moira gave her shoulder a pat. "I've got this," she called to Pearl.

"Are you sure you can fix it?" Hudson asked.

"I'm sure. I've seen it before. Even did it to myself once."

"Am I going to lose all my eyelashes?" Hudson whimpered.

"You'll be fine. I promise," Moira assured her.

"See?" Sabrina said to her friend. "I told you she could help."

When it came to beauty, Moira was always prepared. She not only carried makeup in her purse, she carried makeup remover, sponges, a few cotton balls in a sandwich bag, nail clippers, files and extra nail polish. She didn't need much to fix this, though. She fetched the necessary tools and got to work, not an easy task since Hudson was fluttering her hands in front of her face and hyperventilating.

"Don't worry, we'll have your eye open in just a minute," Moira said as she soaked a cotton ball in makeup remover. "Take a couple of deep breaths. It'll be fine."

Hudson took a deep breath and then released it, along with a few words for her friend. "You told me you knew how to do this."

"I thought I did," Sabrina said. "I looked it up on Wiki-How."

"I tell you what," Moira said, "you guys find a night that works and I'll come over and show you how to apply eyelashes and give you some other tips, as well."

"Wow! Really?" Sabrina was looking at her as if she were the daughter of Santa Claus.

"Sure."

"That would be so awesome. Can you do our hair, too?" Sabrina asked eagerly.

"Anytime you'd like to come in to the salon. Doing color right takes time. We'd have to test your hair, do a consult, and the process itself takes a while. If you want it to look right," Moira added as she dabbed Hudson's eye.

"I just want to learn how to do my eyelashes," said Hudson. "By myself."

"Fine with me," Sabrina said, insulted. Then, switching gears back into happy mode, she said, "We could invite Jennifer and Kinley and Teagan."

By the time Moira had freed Hudson's eye, the girls had picked an evening for her to come over and Sabrina was already on her phone, texting her friends. It looked like Moira was going to be the hero of Moonlight Harbor High. Whether that would ever translate into any paying clients, who knew? But she was always happy to help women look their best and feel good about themselves. Everyone had a calling in life, and that was hers.

The girls left after hugging her and gushing gratitude.

"Well done," Pearl said. "I'm sure glad you're here. I am beyond the age where I want to deal with teen-girl drama."

"It was pretty funny," said Chastity, as she finished up with her client, a woman named Angie, who worked at the drugstore.

"It wasn't to them," Moira said.

"Although in a few years it probably will be," said Angie, admiring the finished nail job. "I remember when one of my friends offered to give me a haircut. We'd seen a picture in *Seventeen*. She kept trying to even out the bangs. Pretty soon I didn't have any bangs. Of course, we did this right before school pictures. My mom didn't buy any that year."

Moira had made her share of beauty mistakes, too, mostly with hair color. She remembered the year she decided to dye her hair green for Saint Patrick's Day—that had been a sure conviction, after seeing how it turned out, that she would be the freak of the school. She had been. But a couple of girls had thought it was cool, and soon she'd had friends asking her to dye or cut their hair.

"You've got a gift," her friend Heather used to tell her.

"You cut hair. It's not rocket science," Lang had once said.

Maybe it wasn't rocket science, but it made people happy, and surely making people happy was a gift. And being able to do that made Moira happy.

Maybe Lang's problem was that nothing made him happy.

"So when are you going to make my hair look fabulous?" Chastity asked after Angie left.

Moira had checked out the supply shelves in the back room. *Sparse* was the word that came to mind. "Not until I have more colors to work with."

Pearl, between clients, emerged from the back room with a cup of coffee in time to overhear. "I've been meaning to get to the supply store. Why don't you go for me this afternoon, Moira? I've got an account and you can get whatever you think you need."

Color was expensive. Actually, when it came to the tools of the trade, everything was expensive. Moira's Washi hair shears alone had cost her over two hundred bucks, and that had been buying them on eBay. But color was one of the biggest expenses of all for a salon, and while Pearl had clients, she wasn't exactly booked solid and turning people away.

"Are you sure?" Moira asked.

"I've been behind the times for too long," Pearl said. "I need to catch up."

Moira was glad to hear that. "What about catching up the salon a little, too?" she suggested. A new look would entice new customers.

Pearl's brows drew together as she looked around the salon. Uh-oh. Moira had overstepped her bounds.

"I was just thinking maybe a few little changes in decor," she said. There was an understatement. The place desperately needed a makeover. But who was she, a newcomer, to be pointing that out to a seasoned businesswoman? She wished she'd kept her mouth shut.

Until Pearl said, "You're right, of course. I know that. The place looks sad. And tired. Rather like me," she added with a smile that didn't quite reach her eyes. "I need a younger clientele, though. Maybe with a new look and you girls helping me, I can make that happen."

"For sure," Moira agreed, excited to be part of such a project. Just like Tabatha Coffey in the salon-takeover show she used to love to watch, gathering ideas for what she'd do if she ever had a salon of her own. She'd been sad when that show ended. "You could do so much with this place."

"I'd have to do it on a budget," Pearl cautioned.

"It wouldn't take much," Moira said. "Those pink shampoo bowls are retro and cool. You could go totally retro and maybe hang up posters of women from the fifties. You know, like you see on greeting cards and calendars. Since we're at the beach, have ones of women in old-fashioned bathing suits. We could repaint, even have an accent wall, a teal blue to remind people of the ocean, and hang some sort of fish decorations on it. That way it would all fit with the name of the salon."

Pearl nodded slowly. "I think you might have something there."

Chastity got on her phone. "Here's a site with all kinds of posters like that for sale." She hurried over to where Pearl was sitting and turned the phone so she could see, and Moira joined them, looking over their shoulders.

"Those are really cute," Pearl said.

"Pick out which ones you like and I can order them for you," said Chastity.

"Once we get the salon all fixed up, we can post pictures on your Facebook page and your website and Instagram," Moira said.

Pearl suddenly looked overwhelmed. "I'm not on Facebook or Instagram."

Moira blinked in surprise. A hair salon owner who wasn't using social media? "You do have a website, right?"

"Yes. I haven't done much with it, though."

Chastity brought it up on her phone and showed it to Moira. Pearl was right. She sure hadn't.

"We can fix that. One more thing," she ventured. "You might want to redo the floors—maybe with that gray wood laminate. That would make the place look really beachy." That would also probably be more than Pearl wanted to spend.

"I might have to call it good with paint and pictures," Pearl said. "I'm not sure I can afford to have that done."

"You don't need to hire someone," said Chastity. "Cole can do it for you. He's really good at that handyman stuff."

"It is a good idea," Pearl said. "Let me think about it. Meanwhile, Moira, why don't you go get us some product?"

"Is there a limit you'd like to stay under?" Moira asked, determined not to overspend. Fine time to be worried about that after all the costly suggestions she'd just made.

Pearl gave her a figure and Moira nodded, sure she could deliver.

"I can come with if you want," Chastity offered. "I don't have anyone else scheduled and Cole's working. I'd sure rather go shopping than stay home on a Saturday and clean."

Moira was happy to take her up on the offer and they left with the company charge card.

"Think Pearl will go for it and do the floors?" she asked Chastity as they drove to the town of Aberdeen, where the closest hair supply store could be found.

"I hope so. The place really is a dump."

"Yeah, but it's got great potential. She doesn't have a lot of clients, though, does she?" Moira ventured.

Chastity shrugged. "She does okay. A lot of the older women come in. But nobody our age."

"Where do they go?"

"There's a salon in Aberdeen that's pretty good and they're into the new colors."

Moira nodded thoughtfully. "People will go where they can get what they want."

"So maybe once people find out Pearl can give them what they want, they'll stay in Moonlight Harbor."

"For sure." And Moira knew she was just the person to make that happen.

"I hope so," Chastity said. "She's had some hard stuff in her life and I think it's about time she got a break."

"Like what?"

"Her daughter died a few years ago. Had an aneurysm."

"Oh, my gosh, that's awful."

"It gets awfuller. Her granddaughter couldn't cope. She got into drugs, then she ran away. Pearl hasn't heard from her in three years."

Chastity was right. It did get *awfuller*. Tragic. "I guess she doesn't have a husband."

"Nope. He's dead, too. All she has is her cat."

"And her friends," Moira suggested.

"I don't think she does much with her friends anymore. One of them, Arlene, is always trying to drag her off to something, but for the most part she's pretty much turned into a hermit. There's a bunch of women who meet at Mrs. Patterson's house on Friday nights. I know she used to hang with them because Mrs. Patterson's always inviting her to come back. But she never goes."

It was so easy to slip out of the habit of hanging with friends, Moira thought. And so hard to find your way once they were gone. She was in a new place and starting a new life. This time around she was going to keep the friends she made and not let a man come between them.

Shopping was always fun. Shopping for hair color products was especially fun. The store had a ton of Pravana, Kadus and Wella, and Moira stocked up. She also bought color accelerator and gray oxidizing drops, correctors, bleaches, bonders and lighteners. She felt like she'd suddenly found a fairy godmother with a credit card for a magic wand. *Fill your basket with goodies and then wave it at the cashier.*

But Moira was careful to stay within the budget Pearl had set. She hoped she could bring in enough new clients to justify both the purchases she'd just made and all the changes she'd suggested to her new employer.

"So, now we have color. When can we do my hair?" Chastity asked as they drove back to Moonlight Harbor.

"If you want, we can do it Monday when the salon is closed."

"Yes! I can hardly wait. I want it to look like yours, only with a little more green. Like a mermaid."

"I can do that," Moira said. "Then we'll take a picture. You can be my first Moonlight Harbor hair model."

"Cool. I always wanted to be a model."

"We can post the pics on Instagram and Facebook." As soon as Moira got those accounts set up.

"Once people start seeing what we've got to offer, they'll swarm the place," Chastity predicted. "I should start posting pictures when I do manicures, huh?"

"You haven't been?" Moira asked, shocked.

Chastity shrugged. "I've just sort of been dabbling at this. But I would like to get more clients. Cole and I want to get pregnant and I should be saving up for baby stuff."

Baby stuff. Moira couldn't even think that far ahead. She'd be doing well to take care of herself. And who knew if she'd ever even find a man? That had to be step number one because she had no intention of doing the single-mom thing like her mom had done. If she ever had kids, she was going to make sure she had a fabulous man to have them with.

They returned to the salon to learn that Pearl had ordered several posters and, in between clients, had run to the hardware store for paint samples. "What do you girls think of this one?" she asked, showing them a small deep teal blue card.

"Oh, yes," Moira said. "That will make a fabulous accent wall. I'll be happy to paint it for you." Living in apartments, she'd never had a chance to indulge in that kind of home improvement and the idea of getting to transform Pearl's salon with some color was exciting. But, "Are you sure you're okay with this?" She barely knew Pearl and here she was convincing the woman to spend money like she'd just won the lottery.

Pearl nodded. "I am. This is an investment in our future."

Our future. Moira loved the sound of that.

"Anyway, you have to spend money to make money. That's what they say."

The elusive "they" said a lot of things, like you'd know when you found the right one. The elusive "they" had sure lied about that, because for all Moira had thought she'd known when she met Lang, she hadn't known squat.

By the time she'd stocked the shelves in the back room, it was closing time. Time to go to her motel room and spend the evening watching TV. Alone.

No, no, she wasn't alone. She had Harry. And maybe even some new friends.

Chastity had left and Moira was about to follow her out the door when Pearl asked, "Moira, do you have dinner plans?"

"Not really." She'd appreciated Edie Patterson's standing dinner offer but she didn't want to make a pest of herself. At least not every night.

"I have some leftover stew I'm thinking of turning into a potpie. I'm wondering if you'd like to join me."

This from the woman Chastity had said was a hermit. Was Pearl just being nice?

"Of course, if you'd rather not…"

"No, I'd love to. I need to go home and spend a little time with my cat, though."

"I understand that. Why don't you come over around six thirty, then?"

"Okay. What can I bring?" Michael's wife had taught her by example that you never showed up at someone's house empty-handed.

"Nothing. You just bring yourself."

Herself didn't seem like enough. She'd think of something. She took Pearl's address and phone number.

Before returning to the Driftwood Inn to get in a little quality time with Harry and give him his medicine, she ran to the little grocery store to pick up something to bring to Pearl's house. The place was a mix of groceries and kitschy beach goods such as hot dog roasters, baseball caps with smiley-face moons on them and picnic supplies mixed in with food items. The aisles were small and packed with both goods and people.

Moira spotted a display of Valentine candy marked down. Everyone liked chocolate, right? Or maybe not. What if Pearl didn't like chocolate? Or what if she liked dark chocolate and Moira showed up with milk chocolate. Or vice versa?

Okay, flowers then, just as Michael's wife had done for her the one time she and Lang had invited them over for dinner.

It had been early in their relationship and things had been pretty good. He hadn't started hitting yet, only putting her down once in a while, and he'd still been open to having company. Michael and Heaven had arrived bearing a bouquet of tulips and Moira had been thrilled and then embarrassed that she didn't have a vase to put them in.

"I don't get flowers," she'd said. Boy, had she heard about that later. Not a good ending to the night.

"That's okay," Heaven had said. "I bet we can find something to put them in."

They had, a white ceramic pitcher Moira had bought at a thrift store. Perfect for frozen lemonade. It also turned out to be perfect for flowers.

"They look great in it," Heaven had approved.

Sheila Roberts

"Stupid," Lang had muttered, and after their company had gone, he'd asked Moira why she'd never bought a vase. Weren't women supposed to have stuff like that?

"Not if they don't get flowers," she'd said.

"Get a vase," he'd snarled, "and I'll buy you some damn flowers. God, you're so high-maintenance."

She didn't think she was, but with the mood he was in she hadn't said so.

She'd gone to a nearby Goodwill the next day and bought a vase, but he never bought her any flowers. Once she got settled, she was going to buy herself a new vase. And fresh flowers. Every week. Well, once she could afford them.

She bought a bouquet of red and white carnations from a bucket in the floral department. No need for a vase. Pearl looked like the kind of woman who'd have plenty. Then she picked up a bottle of white wine, as well.

Hmm. What if Pearl didn't drink? And what if she preferred red wine? Moira sighed. Indecision, another by-product of her life with Lang. What a mess he'd made of her head.

"Never mind him," she muttered. He was history.

And she was doing just fine without him here in the present. As for the future, who knew what that held. For sure it couldn't get any worse than her past had been.

She stuck with her wine choice, reasoning that it was the thought that counted.

"Looks like we're going to get some more sun tomorrow," the checker said to her as she rang up Moira's purchases. "It'll be a good day for a walk on the beach."

It was still frickin' freezing. "Isn't it a little cold for that?" Moira ventured.

"Nah. Put on a coat and you're good to go."

Maybe.

Moira pulled into the Driftwood parking lot just as her neighbor in the room next door was coming out. His dark hair was longish, and a breeze caught it and mussed it. Heathcliff on the moors. Sigh.

She told herself to quit drooling and managed a polite hello as she got out of her car.

"You must be the hairstylist," he said.

Boy, did word get around fast. "I am." She walked over and held out a hand to shake. "I'm Moira Wellman."

"Seth Waters. I rent the room next door," he said and took it.

Strong, sexy hands. Ooh.

"Jenna told me I had a new neighbor. I hear you're down from Seattle."

She nodded. *Think of something clever to say.* Nothing came to mind.

"It's not the big city down here, but it's a cool place."

"Have you been here long?" Moira asked.

"A while," he answered vaguely.

At that moment Jenna appeared, on her way to the motel office. She detoured to where Moira and Seth stood talking. Moira would have to have been blind not to see fire ignite in Seth Waters's eyes when he looked at Jenna. Mr. Muscle was obviously not in the market for a woman.

And Jenna Jones had two guys after her. Lucky her.

Jenna said a casual hi to Seth, then asked Moira how she was settling in.

"Great," Moira said. "I think I'm going to like it here."

"I know you will," Jenna assured her. "By the way, if you want to go line dancing tomorrow night, you're welcome to ride with me."

"Thanks."

And look at that, Moira had a social life. Sort of. If you could count having dinner with an old lady and painting a wall a social life. And line dancing with a bunch of redneck proles as her mother would have called them. But she liked Pearl, and she was excited about helping transform the salon. And line dancing was better than no dancing. And who cared what color somebody's neck was? Anyway, Jenna Jones was a confident, classy woman, and if she was going, it was probably worth checking out. Moira figured she could use some class. Maybe if she hung out with Jenna enough, it would rub off on her.

"You on your way to The Drunken Sailor?" Jenna asked Seth. She was as hot for him as he was for her. She tried to hide it, but Moira could sense it. Jenna had been quick to come over and now she suddenly needed to smooth her hair.

"Thought I'd go shoot some pool," he said.

Why wasn't he asking her to go with him? It was cold outside, but these two were creating their own weather system, a regular heat wave.

"Don't talk to strangers," she said. A little teasing… with a bit of a stinger attached.

"Gotta talk to someone," he replied, unfazed, and that made Jenna pout.

Yep, definitely interested.

"By the way, thanks for the rose," Jenna said, her voice going as soft as cat's fur.

"I suppose the house peddler gave you chocolates," Seth said.

Yep, a bit of a stinger there, too. What was with these two?

"I like chocolate. I like roses, too. You know that."

A very interesting romantic triangle here. But at the

moment Moira's presence was making it more like a quadrangle. Not that either Jenna or Seth seemed to remember she was with them.

"Nice meeting you, Seth," she said.

"Same here," he said and returned his attention to Jenna.

Jenna lowered her voice, but as Moira slipped into her room, she could hear her say to Seth, "Feeling a little jealous?"

"You know I am."

"Then do something about it."

If Seth Waters wanted Jenna, why wasn't he doing something about it? Very mysterious. And so romantic.

Speaking of romance, what was Lang doing right now?

"Oh, no," Moira scolded herself. "You don't care what he's doing."

But in a way she did. Even though she knew he was bad for her, a part of her—the stupid part—missed him.

Or maybe she simply missed the idea of him. The old him, the smooth-talking Lang she'd first fallen for. But that Lang had been a facade. The true Lang had been controlling and hurtful. She'd thought he was such a big man when she first met him but in reality he was small.

Harry came to greet her, rubbing against her leg. "You glad to see me, sweetie?" she said and bent to scratch behind his ears.

Yes, purred her sweet fur baby.

"If only I could find a human as nice as you."

The words were barely out of her mouth when Victor King, the cop, came to mind. What was he doing this weekend and who was he doing it with?

Eight

Pearl's house was easy to find. It was a small Cape Cod–style cottage sitting on a piece of land with a peekaboo view of the beach between the two houses on the other side of the street. Seagull Street. A fun name. All the streets in town seemed to have beachy names and Moira loved that. Seth Waters was right. Moonlight Harbor might not be the big city but it had a great vibe.

Pearl met her at the door, looking comfortable in leggings and a long pink sweater, leopard-print slippers on her feet.

"Thanks for having me," Moira said and handed over the flowers and wine. "I wasn't sure if you drank."

"I do, but you didn't have to bring anything."

"When you've been invited to someone's house, you should never show up with just your big mouth," Moira said, thankful that Heaven had filled in the cracks her mother had left in teaching her manners.

"Well, that's very sweet, but you don't need to make a habit of it. I do hope you'll make a habit of coming over, though."

Maybe Pearl wasn't as much of a hermit as Chastity thought. "It's nice to have someplace to go."

"You'll have plenty of places to go before long, I'm sure," Pearl said. "Here, let me take your coat."

She hung Moira's coat on an old-fashioned coat-tree and led her into the house. It was small, but tastefully decorated with old hardwood floors, a beige couch and a matching love seat in the living room. An end table sat on one side of the couch, its base a trio of wooden seahorses and a sign proclaiming Life Is Good at the Beach hung on one wall. The fireplace mantel held a collection of pictures and Moira drifted over to look at them.

"Is this your family?" she asked.

Pearl was already busy in the kitchen, pouring wine. "Yes. That one's of my husband and daughter and granddaughter on our last family vacation. We went to Disney World."

"Your daughter's pretty," Moira said. Was pretty. *Crap.*

"She was. She died way too young," Pearl added softly.

"I'm sorry." Sorry she'd gone anywhere near those photos. Pearl looked so sad.

Moira moved to the kitchen and parked at the breakfast bar. No granite or quartz countertops there, just some weird old-fashioned material made to look like wood, prettied up with a glass bowl filled with shells. The stove and fridge looked old, too—no stainless steel here.

"We all die," Pearl said philosophically, handing Moira a glass. "You just never think about that when it comes to your children, though. It's a hard thing to outlive a child."

"I can't even imagine," said Moira. "How'd you cope?"

"I don't know that I did. I just kept putting one foot in front of the other. I'm afraid my granddaughter didn't cope at all. She's... Well, I don't know where she is. She took up with the wrong people and…" Pearl sighed and took a sip of her wine. "I did my best to find her, even hired a private detective. I try not to think of where she might be now or what's she's doing or being forced to do."

Moira wished she could think of something wise and comforting to say. All she could come up with was, "I'm sorry."

"Life doesn't always go the way you planned. One moment everything is great and the next…" Pearl shook her head.

Boy, you could say that again. Moira took a healthy slug of her wine.

"It was so sudden," Pearl continued. "Jessica was a perfectly healthy young woman, and then, out of the blue, she had an aneurysm. You know, I'd been about to remodel the salon before I lost her. After that the salon seemed so unimportant. And then I was so busy with my granddaughter. I don't know what my excuse is now, other than I'm tired."

Tired from carrying around so much grief. And Moira had come into her life like a bulldozer. She took another drink. "I hope I haven't, like, pressured you into doing this."

"No. I think you've been a catalyst. So many times I've just wanted to curl up in bed and never leave."

"It's awfully brave to keep going when you don't want to."

Pearl cocked her head and studied her. "You're very wise for someone so young."

Moira gave a snort. "I know, right?" If she'd been so wise, she wouldn't have been so stupid about the man she'd picked.

"No, seriously."

"I guess it's easy to be wise when you're talking about

someone else's life." Moira found herself feeling suddenly ashamed. She studied her wineglass. Wineglasses and drinking meant partying, but this was no party moment.

Pearl reached across the counter and laid a hand on hers. "You got out of a bad relationship, Moira. That showed wisdom."

Moira did raise her face at that. "I don't want to screw up my life any more, and I'm not gonna be like my mom." Oh, boy. Why had she said that? She examined the contents of her glass, what was left of it. "She wasn't very smart when it came to men, either."

Except she'd been smart enough to see what a loser Lang was. Moira could have saved herself a lot of grief and bruises if she'd listened to her mom sooner.

"Well, you have a chance to change your family tree, and you're doing it."

"I hope so. I want to make something of myself. And you know," she couldn't help adding, "how you said remodeling the salon just didn't seem that important after you lost your daughter? I'm thinking she'd be proud of you for keeping on doing something and not giving up on life."

"I pretty much had. I was just going through the motions. Maybe I still am."

"You can't get anywhere without motion," Moira said.

Pearl smiled and raised her glass. "Then here's to motion. May it take us both somewhere good."

"To motion," Moira echoed, and they clinked glasses. "And to new friends. Thanks for being one to me."

"Oh, I'm purely selfish. You remind me a little of my daughter with your enthusiasm and zest for life. I'm enjoying having you around. You're a smart girl, Moira. You're going to succeed in carving out a good life for yourself."

She certainly hoped so. "Maybe we can carve out a good life together."

After two helpings of stew and three biscuits (home baked—how could you turn that down?), Pearl was still pushing food. "How about some ice cream? I have a pint of chocolate chip mint from Nora's ice-cream parlor."

Between Pearl and Edie Patterson, Moira would end up looking like the great white whale in *Moby Dick*.

"I'd better pass," she said. "I am stuffed like a Thanksgiving turkey." Not that her mom had ever stuffed a turkey. The kind of stuffing they ate came from a box mix. "Everything was great," she said. *Great.* Was that the best she could do? "Scrumptious," she added, taking advantage of an opportunity to use her new favorite word.

"Now there's a word you don't hear very often anymore," Pearl said.

"I like learning new words."

"I bet you like learning, period."

"I do," Moira said. "I always wanted to go to college."

"Maybe someday you will. What would you major in if you did?"

"Oh, I don't know. Literature. I like to read. Or business. Someday I'd like to have my own business."

"Someday I bet you will. Well, if I can't interest you in ice cream, how about some coffee? Or tea?"

Pearl seemed reluctant to let her go, and truth be told, Moira was reluctant to leave. "Tea would be good."

And so she drank some tea, met Pearl's big orange cat, Pumpkin, and spilled more about her life growing up.

"You're an amazing young woman," Pearl said when she'd finally finished.

"Hardly," Moira said. She'd like to be amazing. Maybe someday she'd get halfway there.

"No, you really are. You've had some strikes against you but you haven't let them take you out. You've got dreams and determination. That's a powerful combination."

"Yeah?" So uplifting to hear someone say something like that to her. Maybe she wasn't such a loser, after all.

"Some people would fold up and give up. I get the sense that you're not that kind of woman."

"I don't want to be, that's for sure," Moira said.

"Then you won't be," Pearl said as if that settled it.

Moira stayed a little longer, letting Pearl teach her how to play a word game she'd never heard of called Anagrams. It involved drawing letters, making words and stealing words back and forth by changing them into bigger and better ones. Moira even learned a new word that night: *zealous*.

"It means fervent or passionate," Pearl explained. "I get the impression you feel that way about what you do."

"I do," Moira said. "Zealous. I like that. I'm a zealous hairstylist."

"And once word gets out, they going to be fighting over you."

"I hope so."

Moira lost the game by two words but she left Pearl's house feeling like a winner. She had escaped an unhealthy relationship and she had a future.

Back in her room, she texted Michael to let him know how she was doing, closing with Big Thanx! Then she settled in to read more of Muriel Sterling's book with Harry curled up in her lap.

The best way to a new beginning is to have a plan.
Where do you want to be in your life in one year?
Three years? Five? List your goals and then list the
steps you need to take to reach them.

Good advice. Moira grabbed her phone and made some notes.

One year. I want to have a solid client base and be in a house instead of a motel room. I want to feel good about myself and I want new friends.

How am I going to do that? I'll start with line dancing tomorrow. And I'll see if Chastity wants to go for coffee after we do her hair. As for feeling good about myself, maybe I need to hang around Pearl more and ask her to pump me up every day. Pump me up until I explode.

Three years? By then I want to have a great man in my life—someone who doesn't put me down and tell me I'm nothing without him. SOMEONE WHO DOESN'T HIT ME!

And how am I going to do that? I don't know. I'm not going to rush into anything. I'll take my time and I'll figure it out. One thing I know for sure: the first time any man tells me I'm stupid, I'm gone.

Five years? Seriously? That's way far off. Okay, what do I want? I just want to be happy and stable. Maybe married. I love my mom but I don't want to turn out like her.

How to make that happen?

She had no idea.

Okay, she'd written enough for one night. "Let's see what's on TV, Harry. Maybe there're some reruns of *The Brady Bunch*."

That show had been on in the afternoons when she was a kid. All those Brady kids were grown-ups by then but she hadn't cared. Watching a normal family had been like being part of a cultural-exchange program, a revelation of how people lived. She used to fantasize about her mom finding a Mr. Brady who came with ready-made siblings.

Sadly, it never happened. Even now her mom was on

her own, resigned to her fate. "Being with no one is better than being with the wrong one," her mom had once said.

At the time that had sounded really pathetic. Now it sounded smart.

Moira returned to her notes and added, *"No matter what, I'm going to be wise. I'm not settling for another loser and I'm not going back to what I had. Not even if Lang tries to drag me back."*

Ha! Good luck with that. He had to find her first. And that wasn't going to happen.

Pearl sat up a little while longer after her guest left, working a crossword puzzle—one of the things she did to keep her brain sharp. Then she went upstairs to bed. She walked past what had been her granddaughter's room, which she still kept in readiness just in case the girl ever returned, and went into the bathroom to get ready for bed. The woman in the mirror looked tired and worn down—a shadow of what she'd once been. And old.

Of course, old happened if you lived long enough. But Pearl had always envisioned herself going into her golden years with verve, an example to the younger generation. *I want to be like Pearl when I hit my sixties.*

How differently that had played out. Pearl doubted anybody wanted to be like her. And who could blame them? She wouldn't wish her last few years on her worst enemy.

But did she want to carry this beaten-down version of herself into the future? Maybe like a hermit crab, it was time to dump that shell and move into a life that was bigger.

If only moving wasn't such hard work.

Courtney was down for the count, miserable with a cold and not wanting to do anything more than lie on the couch and surf the internet on her computer. Annie made her chicken rice soup, packed with carrots and celery and seasoned with sage, oregano and parsley. She accompanied it with homemade rolls.

"This is the best," Courtney had said, and sneezed. "You need to hurry up and get that food truck going."

"Maybe someday." When she was about a million years old.

How she'd love to be able to cook the food people ate rather than just serve it. At least Courtney and Annie's other friends appreciated her creations. Greg was usually too drunk to care.

"Daddy texted me," Emma announced after they finished dinner. "He misses me."

"I know he does," Annie said. Greg had texted her, too. He wanted his family back, right back where they'd been, with nothing changing. That wasn't going to happen.

"He could come visit us," Emma suggested.

Greg making a scene in Courtney's house. Wouldn't that be a ton of fun? Annie knew she couldn't deny him the right to see his child, but she was going to have to find neutral ground for them and those visits were going to have to be supervised by her. She couldn't trust Greg to come pick up their daughter for fear he'd be driving drunk. And his judgment sure wasn't the best when he was under the influence.

"We'll work something out," Annie promised. She could always drop Emma off at Beachside Burgers. And pay for Emma's meal because he probably wouldn't have any money. As if she were rich?

"When?" Emma persisted.

"Soon," Annie promised.

Soon was a very unsatisfactory answer, and Emma's sulking let her know it.

"Guess what I got today?" Annie said, determined to pull them away from the subject of Daddy. "A new puzzle." Emma loved puzzles as much as Annie did.

"What kind of puzzle?" Emma asked, not quite ready to let go of her frustration with her mother.

"An ocean-view puzzle with all kinds of fish." A five-hundred-piece one she'd found at Thrifty Babes, the local thrift store and favorite shopping destination of all the town's residents living on tight budgets. Customers ranged from seasonal workers to seniors on limited incomes.

"All right," Emma said, resigned to her no-Daddy status.

The puzzle was a hit, and it gave Annie something fun to do with her daughter. As they sat at the kitchen table and worked to fit the many blue pieces together, Annie couldn't help wondering how she was going to fit together the various pieces of her life. What did you do with all the pieces of a broken marriage? Was there ever a way to put them back together?

"It's so pretty," Emma said when they were finished.

"Yes, it is. Good job, baby."

"Let's leave it on the table so we can show Daddy."

Him again. No way did Annie want Greg in the house unless he was back in AA and sober. "We'll probably need the table at some point. But we can always put it back together again." Now, if she could only say the same thing about her marriage.

She put Emma to bed and tried not to clench her jaw as she listened to her daughter's nighttime prayer. "Please let us go back home to be with Daddy."

Ugh. There would soon be no home to go to and who knew where Daddy would wind up.

"You do remember our talk about how God answers prayers, right?" Annie asked her daughter as she tucked her in. "Sometimes he says yes, sometimes he says no and sometimes he says maybe."

"I think he'll say yes," Emma replied firmly.

Annie didn't. "Honey, Daddy and I have to sort out some things if we're going to go back home."

"Well, why can't you?" Emma demanded.

Because Daddy had to be willing to help with the sorting.

"We should go home."

"We can't right now, sweetie. I already told you. Daddy has to work some things out. You're just going to have to trust me on this."

Emma scowled and pulled the blankets over her head.

Annie scowled, too. Why couldn't Greg see the misery he was causing his family? "We'll get through this," she said, as much for herself as her daughter. The blanket still didn't come down, so she settled for kissing the lump under it that was her daughter's head and left the room.

Back downstairs she raided the junk-food cupboard where Courtney kept her snacks. Popcorn, nuts, chocolate. And what they both preferred, Doritos. Annie had recently made a contribution and she grabbed the bag and carried it to the living room couch.

Courtney's living room was a fun one, decorated with all kinds of funky decor—a painted cable spool for a coffee table, vintage fashion posters on the walls along with the requisite beach-themed sign, a cool bulb table lamp on a garage-sale end table filled with tiny lights made to resemble fireflies. A floor lamp with a fake Tiffany glass shade that Courtney had gotten at a garage sale sat by the couch, and it came in handy for reading. Now that Annie and Emma had taken over Courtney's sewing room, her work area with a cutting table, sewing machine and a dressmakers' form now occupied one corner of the living room.

Annie had often run to this house for solace when Greg was out of control, bringing Emma for sleepovers. It was great to have a place to stay and Courtney was the best. But it wasn't Annie's home. She was camping out here and she longed to be settled. Eventually, she told herself, she would be. With or without Greg.

If only he'd come around.

She grabbed the remote and turned on the TV, flipping to the Food Network in search of…anything to take her mind off her problems. Then she dug into the Doritos. Food truly was a comfort. A small comfort, but small was better than none.

She'd gone through two shows and finished the entire bag of chips when the truck pulled up outside the house. Then came the ringing doorbell, accompanied with strenuous banging and a drunken howling. "Let me in, babe. I need you."

Her heart rate picked up. If she didn't let him in, he'd fly into a drunken rage. But if she did let him in, she'd still end up telling him to leave and then the drunken rage would be in the house. She closed her eyes tightly, willing him to go away.

"Come on, babe, let me in." He was turning up the volume.

"I know you're in there, Annie! Let me in, damn it."

She held on to the edges of the sofa cushions, willing herself to stay put. *Go away.*

More banging.

Oh, God, make it stop.

Of course, it didn't stop. Annie ground her teeth. Should she call the police? She wanted to. But what if Emma woke up to find her daddy being hauled away in a patrol car?

What if Emma woke up, period?

"You can't keep doing this!" he bellowed.

No, she couldn't. What was she going to do?

Nine

Sunday morning was always pancake morning. At least that was something Annie could guarantee for her daughter. Made from scratch, served with butter and pure maple syrup. Emma ate four. A very good sign.

"We're going to see Daddy today, right?" she asked after she'd downed the last of her milk.

"I'm going to see if I can make that work," Annie said.

If he wasn't too hungover. Thank God her daughter was a sound sleeper and had slept through the commotion of the night before. Although she'd have wanted to see her father no matter what happened the night before. Children were so forgiving. So were grown-ups. Annie had forgiven and forgiven, looked for fresh starts time and again. They always came to nothing.

"Meanwhile, how about you put your dishes in the dishwasher and go take a shower?"

"Okay." Emma practically bounced up from the table. Such excitement for a man who was such a loser.

Annie had felt the same way once herself. When they were dating she'd get butterflies every time Greg roared up to her place in his truck.

She sighed and grabbed her phone. Of course, it went to voice mail. He was still sleeping in a cloud of beer fumes. She didn't bother to leave a message, opting instead for a text. *Emma wants to see you today.*

There. At least she could tell Emma she was working on getting her a daddy fix.

She cooked up the rest of the pancakes, piling them on a plate. Once they'd cooled, she'd pop them in the freezer for use later in the week.

She'd just taken the last batch from the pan when Courtney shuffled into the kitchen, still in her sleep T-shirt and jammy bottoms. "I feel like crap," she announced.

"You look like crap," Annie said. Well, as crappy as someone as cool as Courtney could look. Her eyes and nose were red and her long dark hair looked like a family of rats had been racing through it.

"Poor Jenna's stuck manning the office again," she said as she poured herself a mug of coffee. "And even sadder, I'll miss line dancing tonight. No Victor fix." She coughed and took a sip of her coffee. "I think he's hiding from me. I've been speeding all over town and not a single stop."

"You'll probably end up getting stopped by Frank," Annie teased.

"That would be about my luck. But I'm not giving up. One of these days Victor's going to realize how fabulous I am."

"As soon as he gets over being scared of you. I think he's afraid of man-eaters."

"Man-eater? *Moi?* I haven't had a good man since my divorce. Oh, yeah, I didn't have a good man before my divorce, either. So if that's what he thinks, he's got no evidence. Anyway, like there are that many men around here to eat." Courtney fell onto a chair and pointed to the plate of pancakes. "I don't suppose you'd like to play waitress on your day off and bring me a couple of those."

"Of course," Annie said and put two pancakes on a plate. She gave it to Courtney, then dished herself up one, got some coffee and joined her friend at the kitchen table.

"I see you finished the puzzle," Courtney said.

"We did." If only putting her life together could be so easy.

"You know, I could have sworn I heard banging last night. Or was I dreaming?"

"You weren't dreaming. Greg was here."

"You didn't let him in, did you?" Courtney asked in horror.

"No. It would have been too hard to get him to leave. He was drunk, of course."

Courtney shook her head in disgust. "Naturally."

"Emma wants to see him today."

"What are you going to do?"

Annie shrugged. "Find some neutral territory and meet him. I figure we can get a burger or ice cream or something."

"He's probably hungover. I hope you're not holding your breath."

"I'm not, but Emma is."

Courtney shook her head. "Why are there so many losers out there?"

"I don't know. Probably a more important question is why do we pick them?"

"I know why I picked mine," Courtney said as she forked up the last of her pancake. "He had a lot of money and he dressed great. What can I say? I was shallow."

That made Annie smile. Courtney had a gift for that.

"Why'd you pick Greg?"

"He was…fun. I wasn't very outgoing."

Courtney raised an eyebrow. "No. Really?"

"I guess I thought he'd somehow make my life better, more exciting."

"He has made it more exciting. Just not in a good way. Remember that and don't weaken," Courtney added, pointing her fork at Annie.

"I know. If he can't change for his family, he can't change. But he might. This could be the wake-up call he needs," Annie finished hopefully.

"How long are you going to give him to wake up?"

Annie bit her lip and stared at her empty plate. "I don't know."

"You can't hang in limbo forever. Not that I don't love having you here," Courtney added. "As far as I'm concerned, you can stay forever or at least until I marry my perfect man and move into an awesome beach mansion, which, at the rate I'm going, will probably be about a hundred years from now. But you have to start making some plans for a new life that doesn't have him in it. Dreams don't wait forever. What are you going to do about making yours come true?"

"Honestly, I don't know. The food truck feels like it's a million miles out of reach."

"Why don't you start small and build a nest egg? You could cater, you know. You already got your food handler license."

Annie's cell phone dinged with a text from Greg. Can't do today. Feel like shit.

"Of course you do," Annie muttered. Her fingers flew over the phone keys. Your daughter wants to see you. Get it together, Greg! Oh, how bold she could be by text.

Get off my case, came the answer.

Annie turned her phone and showed it to Courtney.

"Yep, there's a man who wants to change. You need to pack your emotional boxes and move on."

Annie felt the tears choking her, swimming up to her eyes.

"I'm sorry," Courtney said softly. "I really am."

Annie nodded and wiped at her eyes. "Why didn't I see this when we were first together?"

"I guess we all see only what we want to see," Courtney said. "But hey, you got a great kid out of the deal. That's more than I can say."

Annie wiped away a fresh brew of tears and nodded. Of course Courtney was right. But Greg could be great, too, if he wanted to try. "If only I could get him to change."

"Nobody can make anybody change. It's something you have to want to do for yourself."

"Maybe he'll decide he wants to." It could happen.

"If that permanent hangover ever goes away, maybe. Meanwhile, let's talk about you and your catering business. What do you want to name it?"

The last thing Annie wanted to talk about was her nebulous future.

"It'll take your mind off your troubles. And you need to move forward with your life."

Playing with names for a catering business was the front yard of foodie heaven, the only thing better than playing with new recipes. Except Annie wasn't sure she was in the mood to go to heaven. Not when Greg was keeping her in hell here on earth.

"Come on, let's toss around some ideas," Courtney coaxed.

Well, why not? She needed to think about moving forward with her life. "Okay."

Courtney grabbed her phone. "I'll play secretary and make notes," she said, then sneezed and let out a groan. "Somebody shoot me now."

"No shooting, not before you help me think of a name," Annie said, and that made Courtney smile.

"Okay, something beachy? The Best of the Beach."

Annie frowned. "That could be anything."

"Gifts from the Sea. No, never mind. That sounds like a gift shop."

They sat in silence for a moment, Annie drumming the table and Courtney tapping her chin thoughtfully. "How about Something Yummy," Courtney suggested. "Simply Yum. No, that's simply dumb."

"Simply Delicious," Annie said, piggybacking on her friend's last suggestion. Yes. That said it all.

"Oh, yeah, I like that. Simply Delicious Catering. Has a nice ring."

"It does," Annie agreed.

"Now you need a logo. Something beachy. And cute."

"Like what?" Annie could easily get creative in the kitchen but this was a whole other type of creativity and her mind was as blank as an empty plate.

"An octopus with a fork in each tentacle? A seahorse in a chef's hat. Ooh, how about a crab with a knife in one claw and a fork in another?"

"That does sound cute," Annie said. Only a few moments ago she'd been so miserable and discouraged. Suddenly she felt hope working to part those gray clouds.

"I bet we could get Jenna to draw it for you. She did the logo for the Seaside with Santa Festival."

"You think she would?"

"I know she would. She loves doing stuff like that. She's probably at church by now, but text her, anyway."

Annie had just finished her text when Emma came down again, scrubbed and ready to see her father. Ugh.

"Guess what?" Annie asked in the hopes of distracting her. "Aunt Courtney and I have just come up with a name for my new catering company."

"You're gonna do it?" Emma asked, dropping onto Annie's lap and picking up a crumb of uneaten pancake.

"I am. I'm going to call it Simply Delicious. And our logo is going to be a crab."

"With his knife and fork, ready to eat," added Courtney.

The idea made Emma giggle. "We can tell Daddy when we see him."

That again. "I hope we can," Annie said. "Right now he's not feeling real good."

Emma frowned and vacated Annie's lap.

"He'll let us know when he's feeling better. Maybe later today."

Her daughter glared at her. "You're making Daddy sick. It's your fault."

How on earth had Emma decided that it was Annie's fault her husband drank too much and got hungover? It was the other way around. Daddy made Annie sick.

Darn it all, why did she have to be the bad guy here? "Daddy is making himself sick, honey." It was logical and true.

And unacceptable. "I hate you!" Emma cried and ran out of the kitchen.

Annie could feel the tears starting again. She looked to where Courtney sat. "What am I going to do?"

Courtney frowned. "Tell him to pound sand." She sneezed, grabbed a napkin and blew her nose. "I feel awful."

So did Annie. Life was all about choices. Greg had

chosen booze and she'd chosen him. And so round and round they went. It was time to end that continuous loop.

"It'll get better," Courtney assured her. "No matter what happens. It won't ever be perfect but it will get better. Remember, I've been on all sides of this and I know."

"I should never have married him." She should have taken her time, paid attention, opened her eyes and seen the signs of trouble ahead. Choosing the wrong person was a mistake you paid for all your life.

"I'm going back to bed," Courtney announced. "Don't have a nervous breakdown until I'm well enough to help you, okay?"

"I'll try not to."

With Courtney in bed and Emma in the bedroom all afternoon, sulking, Annie was free to do some therapeutic cooking. She made a meat loaf, adding rosemary and sage, garlic and onions, then froze it for later in the week. She made marinara sauce and froze that, too. She baked shortbread cookies with chopped pecans and candied cherries embedded in them and chocolate chip cookies for the freezer. Those would get doled out in Emma's lunches. She finished up with a chicken stew, which she'd turn into potpie if they had any leftovers. And that took care of cooking for the week. Now what?

Answer her cell, even though she didn't want to.

"What are you guys doing?" Greg asked.

Your daughter's not speaking to me and I'm trying to cook away my troubles. "Just waiting to hear from you. Emma really wants to see you."

"I'd be able to see her anytime I wanted if you hadn't moved out," he said, at his surliest.

"Greg, I'm sorry. She doesn't need to keep seeing you drunk." When things had started getting out of hand, it had been difficult for Annie to address the issue. It had been easier to let the elephant keep roaming around the room, creating chaos. These conversations still made her stomach clench, but the elephant was no longer welcome.

"I don't get drunk that often," he insisted.

"And we're always fighting." More him yelling and her crying. Her daughter didn't need to be around that.

"We wouldn't fight if you didn't rag on me all the time."

Ragging on him about silly little things like not being able to hold down a job, putting them in a financial mess, wasting his unemployment checks on beer and whiskey. Yes, shame on her.

"Greg, there's really only one reason we fight and you know what that is. If you'd just go back to AA, maybe we'd have a chance."

Silence. She held her breath, hoping he was thinking, really taking in what she was saying.

He finally spoke. "I've tried that. It's not me. Anyway, I don't drink that much."

How could you change when you didn't want to acknowledge you had a problem? Even a family intervention hadn't done the trick. He'd felt bad, promised to go to the rehab his brother offered to pay for and then backed out. AA attendance had only lasted until one of his buddies wanted to go out for a beer. Greg was a partier, and he was of the opinion that you couldn't party without alcohol.

"So, I guess I'll come on over," he said.

"We'll meet you somewhere," she said, determined to keep Courtney's house a Greg-free zone. "How about Beachside Burgers?"

"I'm tapped out."

Of course he was.

"I'll pay," she said. It seemed like she was paying for

him in so many ways. At least she'd earned some good tips on Friday and had cash on hand. "See you at five?"

"Okay. Then we can talk."

"I think Emma's going to want your attention," Annie said and ended the call before he could say anything more. As far as she was concerned, she and Greg were done talking.

As expected, Emma was ecstatic about seeing her father. When they entered the restaurant, she practically ran into another kid in her haste to get to him and jump into his arms.

His shirt was rumpled and he hadn't shaved. Annie wondered if he'd even bothered to brush his teeth. Emma didn't care. He scooped her up and she hugged him as if he were a soldier returning from battle.

The look he shot Annie said, *See how much she misses me? You need to come home.*

She sighed and went to the order counter. Like most of the businesses in town, the place paid homage to its locale with blue plastic chairs at the tables and colorful paintings of smiling sea creatures on the walls. The order counter was strung with fishing nets and the servers all wore blue polo shirts and sailor hats.

They were all smiling and happy to serve. The customers in line were happy, too. So was Emma. And Greg. Everyone was happy but Annie.

She ordered hamburgers for all of them, along with milkshakes—vanilla for Emma, who loved to mix it with root beer from the pop dispenser, chocolate for her and strawberry for Greg. She ordered fries for Emma. None for herself. She didn't need the extra calories. Certainly none for Greg. He didn't deserve the extra kindness.

Emma had led him to a table and was already sitting

next to him, chattering away. He nodded absently, pulled out his cell phone and checked it, instilling in Annie an urge to deliver his food…right over his head.

"Order number fifteen," called a perky teen girl behind the counter and Annie stepped up to claim it. "Enjoy your meal," the girl said to her as she slid the blue tray piled with food at her.

Annie knew she wouldn't.

At the table, she sat down opposite her husband and daughter, and watched while they both eagerly reached for their burgers. He was smiling as if they were a happy, well-adjusted family. Annie's appetite walked out the door.

"All right, fries," he said.

Oh, no. She'd paid for his burger and shake. He wasn't getting their daughter's fries, too. Annie set them in front of their daughter.

"Those are for Emma." *You freeloader.*

"I'll share, Daddy," Emma said and moved the fries between the two of them.

Greg took one and smirked at Annie.

Emma removed the lid from her shake, took a gulp and then announced, "I'm going to make a root beer shake."

"She said she's missed me," Greg informed Annie as Emma made her way to the drink station.

"Of course she does. You're her father."

"We need to be together. Come home." He reached across the table for her hand.

She pulled it back. "Please, don't."

"Come on, Annie. I'm trying here."

Was he kidding? After the night before? "No, you're not, and I wish you would, more than anything."

He sat back and frowned. "What happened to us?"

"Jack Daniels and Michelob."

The frown escalated to a glare. "You knew I drank when we got together."

"I didn't know you drank so much. And it's only gotten worse over the years. Our life is chaos. I can't live like this, Greg. And Emma shouldn't have to."

It hurt having to say those words, hurt both her heart and her stomach. She wrapped her arms around her middle. Was she getting an ulcer?

"You think she's happy where you've got her now?"

"I think, if you don't change, in the long run she'll be better off."

He threw up his hands. "Why is it always about me?"

"Because you're the one who's ruining our lives," Annie said, and just like that there were the tears, back for a return engagement.

"Oh, no, don't do that crying thing. I don't need you guilting me up the ass."

"I'm not trying to guilt you," she said earnestly. "I just want you to see what you're doing to us."

"I don't need this shit," he snapped and slid his chair back, its metal legs screeching against the tile flooring.

"Greg, please."

"I'm out of here."

Emma returned just as he gave his chair an angry shove. "Daddy?"

Greg was too enveloped in his haze of anger to even see her. Swearing, he stormed out of the restaurant, opening the door with an angry shove and causing the people he'd passed to turn and stare. Annie could feel their curious gazes shifting to her. Her face felt like she'd stuck it under a broiler.

"Why is Daddy mad?" Emma wanted to know.

"I don't know," Annie said. She honestly couldn't understand how someone could so deliberately fail to see the part he was playing in his own misery.

Emma plopped onto her seat and stared at her hamburger. Her lower lip began to tremble. "Is he mad at me?" she asked in a small voice.

"No, of course not," Annie said, reaching across the table to pat her arm. "He's still not feeling well." She was doing it again, covering for him. Like she'd done so often over the years. Enabling him. She had to stop doing that.

Emma began to cry, big tears falling onto her lap.

And in that moment, Annie knew she no longer loved her husband even the smallest bit. She hated him.

You're not in the city anymore, Moira thought as she and Jenna walked into The Drunken Sailor. The clubs where she and Lang used to dance were slick and expensive, with fancy bars and hip decor. This place was… What was it?

Two carved wooden lady pirates with boobs spilling out of their pirate vests greeted them. Off to one side was an eating area with a floor littered with peanut shells. She watched in shock as a couple of patrons, enjoying their beers, shelled peanuts from a plastic bowl and dropped the shells on the ground. She might not have had the most high-class childhood but even she knew you shouldn't throw stuff on the floor.

Jenna saw her gaping. "It's part of the charm."

"Okay," Moira said dubiously, not sure if Jenna was being serious or facetious.

A couple of pool tables sat across from the dining area and adjacent to the bar, both in use. Moira saw Seth Waters standing by one, leaning on his pool cue and waiting his turn to play. She gave him a tentative wave and he smiled and lifted a hand from the top of his pool cue. She was sure Jenna had seen him, too, but she didn't wave. What was *with* those two?

They moved farther into the place, stopping at the bar to pick up sodas and say hi to Brody, who was comfortable with a beer and some nachos.

"I see you brought a recruit," he said, smiling at Moira. The man sure had a high-wattage smile.

"I did," Jenna replied.

"Are you going to dance?" Moira asked him.

"No," Jenna answered for him. "He's too chicken to get out there and make a fool of himself."

"Cluck, cluck," Brody said and lifted his beer in salute. "I'd rather watch. Jenna's worth the price of a beer," he added with a grin.

She shook her head at him. "Thanks." She picked up her Coke and said to Moira, "Come on. I'll introduce you around."

There were plenty of people to meet, including their teacher, Austin Banks, who was dolled up in tight jeans, elaborately embroidered boots and a Western shirt. She'd finished off her outfit with pink earrings shaped like miniature cowgirl hats.

Great hair, thought Moira as they were introduced. Thick and long and highlighted. Where did Austin get her hair done? At Waves?

"Austin and Roy own the kite shop," Jenna explained.

Moira had never in her life flown a kite. What would that be like? Maybe she'd have to find out.

Tyrella Lamb was there, wearing jeans and a T-shirt, her dreadlocks clacking with colorful beads. "You're going to love this," she promised Moira.

Moira's heart did a little giddyap at the sight of a certain good-looking man who was just stepping onto the dance floor to join the dancers. "I think I am," she said.

Nope, this sure wasn't some club in the city. It was better. Way better.

Ten

Moira had thought the guy looked sexy in his police uniform, but now, in boots, jeans and a black T-shirt that hugged those impressive pecs, he looked ready for the cover of a romance novel. She caught a glimpse of a tattoo peeking out from one of his sleeves. Tats on guys were so sexy. Hazel eyes, square jaw. He was the whole package. With all that thick hair, he'd probably never have to worry about going bald. And it had some body to it. Oh, yes, she'd like to get her hands in his hair.

He seemed to be walking in their general direction, so Jenna called him over. "Victor, have you met Moira Wellman?" she asked him. "She's staying with us at the Driftwood until she can get settled."

"I'm betting he's wanting to," Tyrella said, and her words made a pink tide rise up his neck and onto his cheeks.

A man who blushed, that was adorable. "We did meet, sort of," Moira said. "He gave me a police escort to work."

"Our tax dollars in action," Jenna teased, and the pink grew deeper.

"I don't like to ticket newcomers if I can help it," he said in his own defense.

"We're just giving you a hard time," Jenna told him. To Moira she said, "Victor is one of our best cops and we're lucky to have him here in Moonlight Harbor."

Moira suspected any woman would be lucky to have him. Period.

"Are you settling in okay?" he asked her.

She nodded. "I am. Everyone here is…" *not nice, so much more than nice* "…so kind." It wasn't a very fancy word, but *kind* truly said it all.

He nodded.

Tyrella and Jenna both suddenly saw other people they needed to talk to and left Moira and Victor to themselves. Hardly obvious at all. Now Moira could feel her cheeks getting a little warm.

"I've never done this before," she confessed. She looked down at her suede half boots. "I don't have any cowgirl boots."

"You don't need 'em. You'll be fine," he said. "Ask me if you need any help with the steps."

Their teacher took her place in front of the dancers and spoke into her mic. "Okay, everybody, are y'all ready to shake it?"

"Oh, yeah," said several people.

"We've got a couple of newbies with us," Austin said, "so you experts be sure to help them out. And just so our newcomers don't feel too lost, let's all demonstrate a couple of steps, starting with a grapevine. You just step with one foot, put your other foot behind and then land back on your starting foot. Easy, right? Let's all try it. You ready? Here we go, to the right."

That was easy enough. Moira managed to keep up.

"We'll often do a triple step. It looks like this," she said and demonstrated. "Okay, let's all try that."

Moira triple stepped right along with the best of them.

"All right. And a kick-ball-change."

Kick-ball-change. It was getting a little harder.

"Good," said Austin. "I think we're ready to learn a new dance. Let's start with 'Dirty Boots.'"

Dirty boots, dirty dancing…sex. *Okay, slow down*, Moira told herself.

Speaking of slowing down, was there a remedial line dancing class? "Is this a beginner's class?" she asked Victor.

"This first part is pretty much. She gets more complicated after the first half hour."

If this was beginner level, Moira sure didn't want to see the more advanced stuff. By the time Austin had walked them all the way through the first dance, Moira's brain was on the verge of exploding.

"Now, let's try this with the music," Austin said.

"Don't worry, you'll pick it up," Victor assured Moira.

The steps didn't want to be picked up. It seemed at every turn she was either facing the wrong way or running into someone. Wow! Who knew line dancing was so hard?

And it only got harder with the next three dances.

Moira was more than ready to take a break by the time the dance lesson ended.

People were moving toward the bar to get drinks. Jenna was busy talking to Brody, and Moira was busy feeling like the proverbial third wheel when Victor came up to the bar where they were standing and asked Moira, "Can I buy you something to eat?"

She was broke. And hungry. And he was friendly and

interested and had her hormones hopping. But did she need to be hopping into anything?

"Never turn down a free meal," Jenna said to her with a wink.

It was only something to eat and she wasn't going home with him. "Okay."

"We'll save you a place by the dance floor," Jenna promised and left.

"I see a free table over in the corner," Victor said and led her to it, their feet crunching on peanut shells as they went. "So, what do you think of Moonlight Harbor?" he asked, once they'd settled at the table.

"It's really charming," she said. "Sure different than where I lived in Seattle."

"Yeah?" he prompted.

"You know what cities are like—lots of traffic, people, high cost of living." And not just in terms of money.

"Oh, yeah. Here there's no such thing as rush hour."

"Or crime?"

He shrugged. "We have some break-ins, some people living on the edge, doing drugs. No place is crime-free. But Moonlight Harbor comes close."

"Have you always lived here?" Moira asked.

"No. I'm from Portland. Wound up in Seattle after the army—I was an MP and police work seemed like the next step. I got hired by the Seattle PD. My family's there so I tried it for a while, but then this job opened up. I always wanted to live by the beach. This works for me. How about you? What brought you here?"

Fear. She gave him her standard line. "It was time to move on." That was what she'd done: she'd moved on, not run away. Okay, she'd run away, and she was glad she had.

Their waitress came over to take their orders and that

put a halt to the conversation. But after they'd ordered burgers, he returned them to it.

He took a drink from his water glass, then casually asked, "Did you leave a lot of friends behind?"

"Some good ones." She was going to miss hanging out with Michael and his family.

"Anyone special?"

Of course he wanted to know. He was obviously interested in her. And she certainly was attracted to him. Still, she wasn't going to tell all to someone she'd just met. "There was someone, but he turned out not to be special at all. How about you?"

"Nope. But I'm thinkin' I might have found someone here," he said and smiled.

Dimples. He had dimples when he smiled.

"I like your ink," he said, pointing to her neck.

She'd put her hair up and the butterfly was on full display. "Thanks."

"Any reason you picked a butterfly?"

Lots of women picked butterflies because they were so pretty. Moira had had a different reason.

"I like the symbolism," she said. "Breaking out of a cocoon, flying free. That was how I felt after I finished beauty school and moved out. Like I could go anywhere and do anything."

He nodded. Then he pulled the sleeve of his T-shirt up to give her a full view of the tattoo on his forearm of a police badge.

"I guess I don't need to ask what that symbolizes," she said.

He told her, anyway. "Commitment, care, peace and justice."

He was not only gorgeous, muscled, sweet, but noble, as well. Where was the catch?

"Okay, what's wrong with you?" Oh, no. Had she really just said that out loud?

His eyebrows shot up. "Huh?"

Someone had lit her face on fire. Oh, yeah. Her. "That didn't come out right. I guess what I meant is, everyone's got flaws. I'm not seeing any in you." She hadn't seen any in Lang, either. Not for a long time.

Victor shook his head and smiled. "I've got flaws."

"Well, you can't do drugs." They tested for that kind of stuff, right?

"No way. Seen too much of what that does. Not a big drinker, either. I like a beer once in a while but that's about it. I'm competitive. Don't like to lose at anything." He shrugged. "I don't know. I'm pretty boring. Did all my wild stuff when I was a teenager—sneaked out after curfew."

Oh, yeah, pretty wild. Moira thought back to her shoplifting phase and cringed.

"I got in some fights—a lot of 'em with my brother," he added with a grin.

Fights. The word triggered an uneasiness that had her ignoring her hunger and her burger when the waitress set the plate in front of her. "I read somewhere that police have a bigger domestic abuse problem than the NFL."

Victor's dimples disappeared. "Bullshit."

"Sorry?" she said in a small voice.

"The cops I've known are good guys, just trying to do their job."

"Of course. I didn't mean to insult you," Moira said, backpedaling. Something she'd gotten very good at doing, thanks to Lang.

"You didn't. It's just…cops aren't all that popular these days. I guess I'm a little sensitive about it."

"People are fearful."

"Are you?"

She hesitated. Was she? Still? Yeah, probably a little. She shrugged. "Not of cops. Really. Just violence in general."

His brows pulled together. "I know we just met, but… were you around someone with a violence problem?"

She bit her lip and stared at her burger.

"A man?"

No point denying it. She nodded.

"That's why you're here, in Moonlight Harbor?"

She nodded again.

"I'm sorry, Moira. I really am."

"It's behind me now. I'm making a new start. But I'm starting slowly. They say it's not good to jump into a new relationship when you've just gotten out of one." There was the nebulous *they* again.

"I get that," he said. "And you should take your time. People rush into stuff and then they're sorry later."

She was so done being sorry. "Thanks for understanding."

"I get the whole not-wanting-to-be-burned-again thing. I met somebody a while back who'd been with a cop who cheated on her. After that, she didn't want anything to do with cops." He shrugged like it was no big deal and took a bite of his burger.

"Not even you?" Moira guessed.

"Hard to imagine, huh?" he joked and his cheeks took on a rosy hue.

"Yes, it is," she said and felt her own face heating up again. "I guess when it comes down to it, we all just want to be loved and treated well." *And sometimes we fall for somebody and let him walk all over us because we're so desperate for love.* No more, though. She refused to ever be that desperate again. Lang had convinced her that he was the best she could do. But if she couldn't do better than him, she'd rather do without.

"Guess so," Victor agreed. He seemed so kind and honest. Could she take a chance on another man, on this man? Could she ever trust her instincts again?

Victor King sure appeared to be the opposite of Lang. Lang had been charming, bombastic, full of himself. He'd been the equivalent of white-water rafting, fun at first, then dangerous. Victor, on the other hand, was calm waters—easygoing and self-effacing. His voice took on energy when he talked about the old log cabin he'd remodeled, had her laughing about how he'd almost fried himself mastering the mysteries of house wiring and left her longing to see the place.

But he didn't brag. She was coming to realize that people who were emotionally healthy and confident didn't need to shine a spotlight on themselves. You couldn't help but notice and admire them. She was sure noticing and admiring Victor.

They finished eating and then joined Jenna and Tyrella and Brody, who'd claimed a table next to the dance floor. "How was your dinner?" Jenna asked Moira.

"It was delicious." The conversation had been equally satisfying.

"The food here is good," Tyrella said. "But they don't take out the calories." She patted her hips. "I've gained five pounds from their garlic fries alone. And it was worth every one," she finished.

"You'll be able to work some off in a minute," Jenna

said, nodding to the front of the dance floor, where Austin's sidekick was fiddling around with the sound equipment, a sure sign that the music was about to start.

"I'm about to give up on ever making that happen," Tyrella said with a flick of her hand, which showed off Chastity's manicure skills.

Austin had the mic and was talking. "Okay, y'all, we're gonna get started, and for our newbies, we're starting with one of the dances we learned earlier, so come on out on the floor."

All the tables around the dance floor had filled up and a lot more people were streaming onto the floor now, people who hadn't been at the class and who obviously already knew what they were doing. Jenna and Tyrella got up and so did Victor. Moira hung back.

"You looked pretty good out there," Brody said to encourage her.

Victor held out a hand. "Come on, Moira. I'll help you."

Well, why not? Even if she looked stupid, no one here was going to put her down.

"Okay," she said and took his hand. It was big and warm and comforting—a hand to protect and not to hurt. Yes, she liked Victor King.

And she liked him even more later in the evening when a hefty, greasy-haired tool wearing jeans and a torn T-shirt that said Chicks Love Dicks came up next to her between dances and proceeded to hit on her.

"You new around here?" he asked, and the beer fumes ran up her nose.

"Sorry, not interested," she said and tried to boot-scoot away.

"Aw, come on. Get friendly," coaxed her new admirer.

The music started and he got behind her and attempted to turn their line dance into dirty dancing.

Creepy and controlling. She needed to tell him to back off in no uncertain terms. But after Lang, her spine had grown soft. Diplomacy and subtlety were the two skills she'd worked on mastering. Here in a public setting that was best, right? She tried to edge away, but the tool followed her like a shadow. Diplomacy and subtlety were not going to work on this man. *Okay, spine, time for a growth spurt.*

She was working herself up to barking at him to back off when Victor grabbed him by the neck of his tacky T-shirt and pulled him away and growled, "Lay off her, Rufus."

"Hey, that's police brutality," protested Rufus.

"I'm not on duty, so don't push me."

"You think you're so great just 'cause you're a cop? You think every girl wants to fu—"

Rufus didn't get to finish his sentence. Victor gave his T-shirt a twist, bunching it into a cotton noose and making him squeak. "You don't keep hitting on women when they tell you to back off. And you watch your mouth."

There they all stood, like a boulder in the river with dancers flowing around them. But hardly anyone was paying attention to their steps. One woman finally stopped to gawk and another ran into her, pushing her into a third, who went careening off to the edge of the floor. Victor hauled Rufus away and Moira decided she should leave the chorus line as well before someone got hurt. Actually, the way Victor was looking at Rufus, it was a sure bet he would get hurt.

They reached the edge of the dance floor, Victor's chin set in granite, Rufus red-faced and sweating and choking.

Victor let go of the shirt and Rufus stepped back, gasping for breath.

"You didn't need to do that, man," he panted.

"The lady told you she wasn't interested. What part of *no* don't you understand?" Victor demanded.

"Women say no all the time. They don't always mean it."

He was a greasy, gross Lang the Second. Adrenaline started off-roading through Moira's veins, making her shake.

"I guess you never heard the phrase 'me, too' under that rock where you've had your sorry ass," Victor snapped. "I better not see you bothering her anymore."

"Fine," Rufus said with false bravado. "She's not that hot. You can have her."

"Sour grapes," Victor said to Moira as Rufus marched away.

"Thanks," she managed.

"You want to sit this one out?"

Actually, she was now done for the evening. "I don't think I want to dance anymore."

"Don't let Rufus put you off. He doesn't come that often and everyone else here is cool."

She bit her lip and nodded. There would always be Rufuses and Langs. She'd run away once. She didn't want to make a habit of it.

Victor sat at the table with her for the rest of the evening, buying her sodas and garlic fries. Rufus stayed on the far side of the room, pouting and drinking beer.

Victor finally pulled out his cell phone and made a call. "Watch out for Rufus. He's a DUI tonight for sure."

It wasn't hard to figure out whom he was calling.

"You're on duty even when you're not on duty," Moira observed.

"You can't let potential problems slide," Victor said. "It's too easy to go from drunk to dead, and often it's not the drunk who dies."

"This town really is lucky to have you," Moira said, and Victor shrugged and tried to hide his pink cheeks behind his glass of Coke.

Around ten, Jenna was ready to go home. "I've got massage clients in the morning and a ton of work to do in the office," she said to Moira.

"If you want to stay longer, I can take you home," Victor offered.

Part of her did want to stay longer. Hanging out with him was like a balm for her wounded soul. But she was determined not to rush into anything, and the longer she stayed, the more tempted she'd be to rush.

"I'd better go," she said. "I've left Harry too long."

Victor's eyebrow went up again. "Harry?"

"My cat, Harry Pawter."

That made him smile. "Harry Pawter, huh?"

"I'm a big J. K. Rowling fan."

"I read those books when I was a kid, too," he said. "She got me into reading."

A cop, a sweet guy and a reader—Victor King looked like the perfect man. But looks could be deceiving.

"Thanks for the burger," she to him. "And for taking care of Rufus."

"Glad to," he said.

She wanted to say more, wanted to remind him he had a free haircut coming. She didn't. She had to figure out who she was and where she'd gone wrong with Lang before she could hope to go right with anyone new.

* * *

"Looks like you and Victor hit it off," Jenna observed as they walked to her car.

"He looks like the quintessential perfect man." *Quintessential*, that almost made her sound like a college professor or something. Maybe that word was a little too big.

"He is a great guy," Jenna agreed.

"But I'm not interested in a relationship right now. I'm taking my time," Moira said once they were in the car. "Looks like you've got some great guys interested in you."

Fishing, fishing. Well, she was a people person and people persons could get nosy. Anyway, if she hadn't been nosy before, being in the hair business certainly had made her that way. The salon chair was gossip central.

Jenna didn't pretend not to know whom Moira was referring to. "They are. Like you, I'm taking my time and not rushing into anything. Been there, done that. I want to be sure the second time around."

"I get that. My ex was a nightmare with legs. Your men both seem pretty cool, though."

"They are. But...it's complicated."

"Love shouldn't be so hard," Moira said. It should be easy to find somebody who was the one. Why had she made such a mess of it?

"No, it shouldn't," Jenna agreed. "But maybe it's a little like learning a new language. You make a lot of mistakes before you become fluent. My sister sure did. But she finally got it right and found a great man. I think things work out with the right one at the right time."

Was Victor the right one? And was this the right time? Moira hoped so.

Eleven

"This place is going to look great," Chastity said as she and Moira walked into Waves on Monday to color Chastity's hair.

Pearl had finally picked a color for the rest of her walls, a pale apricot, which Moira had assured her would beautifully complement the accent wall, and they'd made plans to paint the following weekend. The posters would be coming by the end of the week, and once they got those framed and up, along with the collection of chalkware fish Moira had found online at a vintage decor site, the salon was going to scream, *This is the hottest salon around. Come here if you're somebody.* Moira could hardly wait to start hanging everything.

"In two weeks you won't even recognize it," she predicted. Although she wished Pearl had decided to update the flooring. Budget constraints had left her opting to do that at some later date.

"Pearl's gonna end up having to turn away customers," Chastity predicted.

"Or hire more stylists," Moira said. She could already

see the little salon packed with people and humming with the sound of hair dryers and laughter.

"That, too. Especially once everyone starts seeing what you can do."

"You'll be a walking ad for the salon," Moira said with a smile.

"I can hardly wait. And I sure would like to have the colors you've got, but I don't want to be a copycat."

"I don't have a problem with that, but Michael has a bunch of pictures on his site of what I've done. Let's look at them and see if you find something you like better."

She brought up the site, which was loaded with pictures of hair models all sporting a variety of hair lengths, styles and colors. Chastity forgot about wanting to look like a mermaid when she saw a model with hair that started with a pearlescent white at the roots and blended into pink.

"It makes me think of roses," she said. "Let's do that one."

The decision made, it was time for a strand test.

"As in cutting off my hair?" Chastity asked warily as Moira settled her in a chair.

"Don't panic, I'm only going to snip off a strand," she said and lifted Chastity's long hair. "It won't show. Anyway, you've got plenty and you won't even notice it's gone. I promise."

She snipped and secured the hairs with some superglue, then mixed the colors they were testing. "We'll have to do global lightening before we apply the color."

"What's that?"

"That's code for full-head bleach."

"Yuck," said Chastity.

"It has to be done if the color's going to turn out,"

Moira told her. "There's so much more to hair now, especially with pastels. People buy box color and they think if they put the product on their hair, it will be the same as the woman pictured on the box. But it won't because that woman's color was done over white hair."

"But bleach. Aren't you going to fry my hair?" Chastity fretted.

"Don't worry. I'm a professional."

Chastity watched as Moira got busy. "Cole is going to love this."

"Yes, he is. Great hair always turns guys on."

The strand test and sensitivity test took time, with Moira checking the hair every fifteen minutes, but at last they were ready to start. "How did you end up in Moonlight Harbor?" Moira asked as she worked.

"I came with Cole. His family used to come down here in the summers a lot. His parents finally decided to move down and we followed them. I'm glad we did. I love the beach."

"I've never spent much time at the beach," Moira said. Situated on Puget Sound, Seattle had plenty of water. She just hadn't happened to live near it. A few trips to Golden Gardens with her childhood friend Heather's family during summer vacations when she was a kid had been a treat, but when she got old enough she started working during the summers, babysitting, then, as a teenager working at the nearby grocery store, earning money for school clothes and car insurance. It hadn't left much time for beach excursions.

"You'll love Moonlight Beach," Chastity assured her. "I walk there at least three times a week, even in winter. Of course, in summer it's really pretty when the sky's blue and the water's all sparkly. I love to look for agates and beach glass. But winter is fun, too, and you can find all kinds of cool stuff after a storm, like glass floats."

Glass floats sounded like an exotic find. And beach glass. Moira had a necklace with a piece of beach glass. In her rush to leave, she'd left it lying on the dresser. She'd never see that again.

"Of course, we get a lot of rain this time of year, but summers are great. It doesn't get much above seventy-five. Some people can't take the gray skies in winter, though."

"I'm from Seattle so the rain doesn't bother me," Moira said. "The gray is what brings the green."

"How come you left Seattle?" Chastity asked.

"It was time to leave."

Chastity wasn't the type of woman who would let an evasive answer stop her from digging. "What does that mean?"

Moira lifted a section of hair and concentrated on applying product. "It means I had a rotten boyfriend."

"Rotten…like he cheated on you?"

"No."

"Then what?" Chastity's eyes suddenly got big. "Oh, my gosh, did he hit you?"

Moira bit her lip. It was horrible to have to admit that she'd been with such a man. She nodded.

"That's awful. Good for you for leaving, though. No woman should have to put up with that."

"For sure."

"Did you call the cops on him?"

Shame heated Moira's cheeks. "I should have but I never did."

Chastity was looking perplexed and Moira wished she

could explain more about her choices. But how could she explain them to someone else when she couldn't explain them to herself? It was such a tangle of love and fear and insecurity.

"Gosh, that's so awful."

Was awful. Past tense. History.

"How'd you end up here?"

"My boss knew Pearl and recommended me."

"He must have been psychic or something because you're just what Pearl's been needing."

It was nice to be just what someone had been needing.

Chastity had great hair and features, which made her a perfect model. After Moira had finished they were both smiling, Chastity happy with her new shimmery pink rose look and Moira pleased with her work of art. She turned the chair and held up a hand mirror so Chastity could see the back.

"Wow," Chastity breathed. "This is amazing."

"We need to take a picture," Moira said and fetched her ring light from the supply room.

She positioned Chastity in the corner by the front window, shining the light just so, then took several pictures with her cell phone from different angles. "Your picture will be the first to go up on Pearl's website. And on Instagram."

"I'll be famous," Chastity said with a giggle. "Actually, you'll be famous."

"I don't need that." Feeling good about what she did, helping women feel good about themselves, that was enough for Moira. "But I won't complain if I can make Waves famous." It would be a great way to pay Pearl back for taking a chance on her. Payback didn't always have to be a bitch.

* * *

Annie had forced herself to shrug off the gloom that had descended on her after meeting with Greg and spent Monday online, applying for a food-catering permit and requesting a field plan review. Tuesday, after she finished her morning shift at Sandy's, she drove to the Moonlight Harbor Evangelical Church to talk to Pastor Paul Welch about possibly renting the church's kitchen. They'd often worked side by side at the food bank, and she was hoping that, even though she didn't go to the church, their volunteer connection would earn her enough points to use the facilities.

"I'll have to run it by the trustees," he said, "but I can't imagine there being a problem. It's a good first step toward getting that food truck you've been talking about for the last two years. What does Greg think about all this? Is he behind you?"

At the rate they were going, he soon would be, but not in the way the pastor was thinking. "Right now we're not together."

Pastor Paul didn't comment, merely nodded, taking in the information.

"I moved out," she continued. "I'm hoping it will be a wake-up call for him."

"I'll be praying things work out for you two," he said.

She murmured her thanks and then drove home. Her new home at Courtney's.

If only Greg could free himself from his alcohol addiction. They could have such a good life together.

But if he chose not to, so be it. She was going to do something with her life. She'd been hanging in limbo way too long and her dreams had been fading. Now they were coming into focus and she was determined not to lose that focus.

* * *

Moira felt like she was finally really beginning to live her life, the one she'd been meant to live. She was making friends and settling in. Harry was healing up nicely and seemed content with his new digs. Jenna Jones and her family kept insisting she eat dinner with them and she was becoming very attached to all of them. Well, except for the obnoxious Pete.

Sabrina was her new best friend, happy with the results of her spa party. Moira had given them all a lesson in the proper attachment of eyelashes, and some makeup lessons as well, helping each girl find the best colors for foundation and eye shadow.

"You can use your shadow to enhance the eyeliner," she'd said as she demonstrated on Sabrina's friend Hudson, and the teen beauties had all oohed and aahed.

"That was so great," Sabrina had said after her friends had left. "And Mom says I can come to you and get my hair done."

"Whenever you're ready," Moira had said.

"Tomorrow?"

"Sure. We'll do a strand test and go from there."

So Wednesday afternoon brought Sabrina in right after school. It took Moira the rest of the afternoon to color her hair and it was past closing time by the time she gave the last few locks of Sabrina's hair a final gentle curl. With Pearl looking on, she handed Sabrina a mirror and turned the chair so she could see the back.

"It's so pretty," Sabrina breathed, checking out the dip-dye job Moira had done, giving her a gold tone at the roots growing out into a pale rose gold at the ends.

"You look stunning," said Moira. The girl was already

beautiful, and her hair was great. She made the perfect hair model. "Let's get a picture."

Out came the ring light again, and Moira posed Sabrina in the same place she'd posed Chastity the day before. That was two styles photographed now. Maybe she could convince Jenna to come in and let her play with her hair. Then she'd have three pictures—a good beginning for the Facebook page she'd set up for the salon. And those, plus the pics she was going to take once they'd given the salon its makeover would really make the website appealing. Facebook, Instagram, the website and new styles showed off on all of them—Pearl was going to be current now and that was bound to help her business grow.

Moira took several pictures from different angles, then showed them to Sabrina.

"I love my hair so much!" Sabrina gushed and hugged her.

All in a day's work for Super Colorist. "I'm glad," Moira said.

This was why she enjoyed what she did: seeing women leave the salon smiling and happy made her happy. It gave her such satisfaction to help women feel good about themselves.

She was starting to feel good about herself again, too. The last few days she'd felt like she was in a hot-air balloon, drifting above the rest of the world, no worries, nothing to bring her down.

"You are a color genius," Pearl said as Sabrina skipped out the door.

"Yes, I am," Moira agreed with a grin.

They were about to close up when a woman—probably in her late fifties, wearing a jacket and jeans—dashed in. She let down the jacket hood and announced, "It's raining cats and dogs out there." Then she turned to look at Moira. "So, this is the new girl. My goodness, are you pretty or what? And look at that hair. It looks like something right out of *Vogue*."

"Moira, this is my friend Arlene," Pearl said.

"The bossy one who's taking you out to dinner tonight. She doesn't get out nearly enough," Arlene said to Moira.

"Arlene, I've been on my feet all day. I just want to go home and sit in front of the TV."

"You can sit at a table at The Porthole. Bring this sweet thing along, too. You don't have plans for dinner, do you, darling?" Arlene asked Moira.

"Well..." Moira hesitated. If she said yes, then Pearl would be stuck going out when she wanted to go home and relax.

"Give up and say yes," Pearl told her. "Once Arlene gets an idea in her head, there's no stopping her."

"That's because Arlene is always right," cracked the woman. "Come on, grab your coats. Donny's waiting in the car."

And so that settled it. Moira was going out for dinner with two old ladies. She could imagine how some of her old friends would scoff if they could see her now, those friends who went to Grandma's for Thanksgiving and enjoyed big family gatherings at Christmas. Those friends who took so much for granted.

"Can I meet you there?" Moira asked. "I want to let Jenna know I won't be showing up for dinner."

"Ah, Edie's already taken you under her wing," Arlene surmised.

"She has."

"Well, that's fine. We'll save a seat for you. You know where it is? It's on the main drag. You can't miss it."

Moira thanked her, then drove to the Driftwood. She went into the office to tell Jenna she wouldn't be coming over for dinner, but instead of Jenna, she found a striking brunette with long thick hair, strong features and a flair for makeup behind the check-in counter. She was leaning on the counter, checking something on her cell phone, giving her jaw a good workout with a piece of gum.

The woman looked up and smiled. "You must be Moira. Jenna was telling me about you. She's right. Your hair is fabulous. And I just saw what you did with Sabrina. Genius."

Genius. Moira's smile began deep in her heart and worked its way to her mouth. "Thanks."

"I don't suppose you can do something like that with my hair. I love to make a statement."

Moira could tell by the woman's outfit. She wore a deep turquoise shirt with a frayed collar and beach glass buttons under a bright red jacket with frayed cuffs. She'd accessorized with geometric-shaped, shoulder-grazing earrings and a thick pink-and-green enamel bracelet.

"I bet I could do something you'd like," Moira said to her.

"Something awesome, just like me," the woman said with a cheeky grin. "By the way, I'm Courtney, part-time helper here at the Driftwood and future famous fashion designer."

"Did you design that?" Moira asked, pointing at the shirt. "I love the buttons."

"I did," said Courtney, looking pleased with herself. "I sell my clothes in the gift shop at the Oyster Inn."

"I'll have to check it out," Moira said, although she suspected the price of Courtney's creations would be further than she could stretch her current budget. "I was looking for Jenna."

"She's over at the house with a massage client."

"Massage?" Oh, yes, it seemed Mrs. Patterson had said something about that when Moira first met her.

"She's a massage therapist. And an artist," Courtney added. "She designed the logo for our Seaside with Santa Festival."

"A lot of creative people down here," Moira observed.

"It's that fresh beach air—good for the brain," Courtney said with a wink. "Anyway, go on over. She's giving Frank Stubbs, one of our local cops, a massage and I know she'll be happy for an excuse to get him gone. He's got the hots for her and she always has a hard time getting him out the door."

Jenna Jones was a regular man magnet, Moira thought as she crossed the parking lot to the house. But that was hardly surprising. She was a pretty woman, both inside and out.

Moira knocked on the front door and heard a faint "Come in." She opened it and stuck her head around it. "Hello?"

"Hello?" echoed a birdie voice from the living room. "Hello? Hello?"

Well, the parrot was home. "Anybody here?" she called.

"Anybody here? Give me whiskey," demanded Jolly Roger.

"In here," Jenna called from a room off the front hall.

"In here," said the bird. "In here. In here."

Moira heard a male groan followed by "Oh, yeah. Right there." Just what kind of massages did Jenna Jones give?

Moira opened the door to a dimly lit room scented with

sandalwood. Jenna stood at a massage table, working over a mound of male flesh, who let out another groan.

"Hi, Moira. What can I do for you?" Jenna asked.

The Mound had a head. It lifted, and there was a round face with a snub nose and eyebrows that needed trimming. "Whoa, who's this?" asked the Mound.

"This is no one for you," Jenna informed him.

"Ha! You're jealous. I knew you liked me," said the Mound.

"You know I'm with someone else, Frank," Jenna said.

"So introduce me," Frank demanded.

"Moira, this is Frank Stubbs, one of Moonlight Harbor's finest."

"Just finished my shift," Frank said. "Jenna's working out the kinks. If you ever need a massage, she's the best."

"Also, the only," Jenna said.

"I've never had a massage," Moira confessed. Massages were for rich women. Richer than her, anyway.

"We'll have to fix that," Jenna said to her. "Are you coming for dinner tonight? Aunt Edie's out in the kitchen making lasagna. She probably didn't hear you knock."

"No, that's why I stopped by. I've got a date."

"Taken already?" Frank lamented.

"I can guess who with," Jenna said to Moira with a wink.

"Actually, I'm going out with Pearl and one of her friends to The Porthole."

"Can't go wrong there," Frank said. "We got lots of good restaurants here in town. Been to Sandy's yet?"

"No." She'd barely been anywhere yet.

"I'll take you there sometime," Frank said.

Jenna rolled her eyes and mouthed, *God's gift*, then dug into a shoulder.

"Uh, thanks," Moira said, and made her escape.

The Porthole was the kind of restaurant she could never afford, with expensive-looking decor, a fish tank in the lobby, soft lighting and long windows that would allow people a view of the ocean beyond on a summer evening. She hoped Pearl's friend was footing the bill. Otherwise, she'd have to settle for water and a cup of soup.

They were at a table by a window, along with a short gray-haired man dressed casually in slacks and a polo shirt. Arlene caught sight of her and waved. "Sit down, sit down," she said when Moira got to the table. "When it starts staying light longer, we get a beautiful view of the ocean from here. Donny, this is Moira, Pearl's new stylist."

"Hi, Moira," Donny said and smiled at her. There was something about his smile that made her think of Santa and his elves. It was the kind of smile that promised fun, which probably made him a good match for his wife.

"Donny, darling, order us all crab cocktails," Arlene instructed. "And I need a cosmo. What would you like to drink, Moira? Order whatever you want, of course."

Okay, that had to mean they were paying. "Iced tea?" Moira ventured.

"Live it up," Arlene said to her. "Order a drink. Sex on the beach, that's what you need."

That would be nice. Oh, right, she was talking about the drink.

"In fact, I think I'll have that instead of a cosmo. Give all of us girls one," Arlene said to the waitress when she came. "Donny, too. He likes sex on the beach. Don't you Donny?"

"You bet I do," Donny said with a wink.

"Now, tell us how you wound up in Moonlight Harbor," Arlene commanded once they'd given their orders.

"It was time to leave Seattle, and my boss happened to know Pearl," Moira said.

"Well, good for your boss for sending you our way. You're just what we need here. Isn't she, Pearl?"

"Yes, she is," Pearl said and smiled at Moira.

Moira couldn't help but smile back.

"I'm thinking Shay might want to give her a try," Pearl said, and Arlene's cheeks suddenly got pink.

"I'm sure she will," Arlene said. "Ah, here are our drinks. Let's toast to our newcomer." Once they all had their glasses, Arlene raised hers. "To Moira. May you find your happy place here at the beach."

Moira could easily drink to that.

Pearl had been more than ready to go home and curl up on the couch with Pumpkin and watch a movie. Sometimes, smiling and being social felt like such an effort. But being out with friends, old and new, felt good.

She had to admit, ever since her new stylist had arrived, the dark cloud that had hovered over her for so long seemed to be lifting just a little. She was even looking forward to seeing her salon updated. She'd love to have done that fancy flooring, as well as paint. Maybe in a few months, if her business picked up. Which it very well could now, thanks to this new young woman in her life. Moira Wellman was a breath of fresh ocean air, something Pearl had been needing for a long time.

She stuffed herself with clam chowder, fresh halibut wrapped in bacon and chocolate-silk cherry pie. By the time she got home, she was in a food stupor.

"I ate too much," she informed her cat, who'd run to greet her.

Pumpkin didn't care how much her owner ate. She

only cared about getting some more in her food bowl. She wound around Pearl's legs and yowled.

"I shouldn't give you any more. You're getting fat," Pearl said. But she caved and gave her kitty a second helping. "I'm a bad mom," she murmured, shaking her head in disgust.

To her cat, maybe. But to her daughter she'd been a great mom, there for Jessica when she lost her husband, helping her as she struggled financially. If only she could have found a way to get her granddaughter through the rough waters.

The very thought of Allie made the tears well up. If only Pearl had done more. But what more was there to do? She'd taken her granddaughter in to live with her after Jessica died, done everything she could think of to keep Allie in school—bribes, pleading, stern lectures. She'd even tried to get Allie into a program when she'd discovered her drug problem, but nothing had worked. Allie had abandoned school in her junior year, stolen fifty dollars from Pearl's purse, along with her watch and the gold charm bracelet that had been Pearl's mother's, and run off. It was the final crack that broke Pearl's heart.

Her heart could never be completely whole again, she knew that. But somehow, this woman who'd landed on her doorstep was managing a patch job.

Thinking about someone else really did do the heart good, she thought the next day as she watched Moira working on Natalie Bell. Natalie was in her midforties. She insisted on wearing her hair shoulder-length, which only accentuated her slightly long face, but Pearl never argued with her clients.

Moira hadn't argued, either. Instead, she'd raved about Natalie's eyes and suggested trying a style that would show them off. She'd done a little demo, lifting Natalie's hair to her chin and saying, "Look how it draws attention to your eyes. So sexy."

Just like that they were on to a new style.

"I don't even look like me," Natalie said, looking awed by her reflection in the mirror. "And that's a good thing."

"No, you do look like you," Moira corrected her. "Your best you."

"My husband's going to love my new look," Natalie said. "Pearl was right. You are amazing."

Moira looked at Pearl and beamed, and Pearl found herself smiling right back—a happy smile, not just a polite one or the smile you dragged out for friends when all you wanted to do was burrow into the sand like a mole crab.

She wore that same smile a few minutes later when the posters arrived.

Natalie was handing over her credit card to Moira. Jenna had dropped Edie Patterson off for a shampoo and style and Pearl was just about to start working on her.

Moira unfurled one of the vintage posters and turned it so Pearl and then Chastity, who was busy with Cindy Redmond, could see. "Look how cute."

"That is darling," said Natalie, who'd lingered to check it out.

Moira pulled out another two and showed them off.

"Too cute. Where are you going to hang them?" asked Cindy.

"All around," Moira said. "We have some other things coming, too. It's going to look really cute in here when we're done, like a whole new place."

"You should have a grand reopening," Natalie suggested. "A good way to bring in business."

"That's a great idea," Moira said. "We could make it

a real party. Maybe even have a hair model show. Would you come show off your new style?" she asked Natalie.

"You bet. And I'll be happy to sing your praises to the sky," Natalie said.

"I think that's an excellent idea," Edie said as Pearl rested her head on the shampoo bowl. "I'll bake cookies for you."

A grand reopening. It sounded like work to Pearl. But it also sounded rather fun. She looked at her sad old floors. Should she run up her credit card and go all the way with this remodel thing?

"Run an ad in *The Beach Times*," advised Natalie. "And send out invites to all your clients. Make them RSVP. That's what we did when we opened Beachside Burgers."

"How much fun!" declared Edie. "I love a party."

"Everyone loves a party," Moira said. "Can we do it, Pearl?"

If she wanted to grow her business, she needed to. New paint and decor, a party…on the sad, old, dated floors.

"We should," she said. "Before we do, though, we'd better replace this floor."

"Are you sure?" Moira asked, looking worried.

"Yes, I'm sure," Pearl said. And a little nervous, a little worried about spending the money. But if she was going to do this, she should do it right. She was giving her salon a new face, and what was the point of getting a face-lift if you only lifted half of it?

"I think that's wise," Natalie said.

"Go big or go home," added Cindy.

"Cole will do it for you," Chastity said. "Victor did the floors on his house and Cole helped him. They can probably get it done in a couple of days."

She'd have to close for a couple of days. But maybe

the boys could help her out on the weekend. The salon was closed on Sundays and Mondays so at most she'd only lose one day of business. And if she wound up with more women coming in, it would more than make up for a short closure.

"Talk with Cole and ask him if he'd be interested," Pearl said to Chastity. "Tell him I'll pay him."

"He loves you. He'll do it for free," Chastity said. "I'm texting him right now. And he can text Victor. This is going to be awesome!"

"We'd better get our painting done this weekend, then," Moira said to Pearl. "We only have a couple of people coming in. I'll call them and reschedule."

"I'm helping paint," Chastity said.

And I'm actually excited, Pearl thought. She couldn't remember the last time she'd felt excited about anything.

"You really should come over Friday night and tell the girls all about your new project," Edie said to Pearl later as she waited for Jenna to come pick her up. Chastity and the other clients had all left and it was only her, Pearl and Moira.

"Oh, I don't know," Pearl hedged. A new employee, a new look to pull together for the salon—everything was coming at her so fast. All good things, but she suddenly felt a little overwhelmed. She also felt more than a little silly coming back to the Friday night gathering of local businesswomen that happened at Edie's place every Friday night.

"They'd like to hear what you're up to. They'd like to see you, too. We've missed having you with us."

More than one of the local women had urged her to come back, but she'd been too miserable to socialize. It had felt wrong to even try to have a good time after the losses she'd endured.

"And bring Moira. It will give her a chance to meet some of the younger women. Would you like to join us Friday night, Moira? We have these gatherings every week, just the girls."

Moira stopped sweeping her station. "Who all comes?"

"Oh, everyone who's anyone," Edie replied airily. "A lot of our local businesswomen—Cindy, for one. Courtney, who I believe you've met, and her friend Annie. Jenna, of course, and Tyrella Lamb, Patricia Whiteside. It's a nice mix."

"Sounds fun," Moira said.

"Good," Edie said as if that settled it. "Oh, here's Jenna. I've got to go. Moira, you come on over for dinner tonight. I'll show you how to make pie."

"Great," said Moira and waved a cheery goodbye to Edie.

"See you Friday," Edie called over her shoulder.

"Friday," Pearl repeated. It looked like, ready or not, she was going to have a social life again.

Moira spent some time playing with Harry, then walked to the blue house next door. Jolly Roger was muttering to himself as Edie let her in. "Edie, old girl. Edie, Edie. Jenna's gonna work me into the ground."

"He's been listening to Pete," Edie explained. "I'm afraid he and Jenna don't always get along."

Moira suspected Pete and a lot of people didn't get along.

"He has a rough exterior," Edie continued, "but he's really a dear."

If you say so. Moira just nodded and followed her into the kitchen.

"I enjoy having him around. Every woman should have a man in her life. It's the way things were meant to be. We balance each other out, don't you think?"

It depended on whom you were trying to balance with. "I guess so," Moira said. "I haven't found the right balance yet."

"You will," Edie assured her. "It takes time. Just look at Jenna."

Yes, Moira wanted to look at Jenna.

"Her husband was a crumb. He cheated on her and then had the nerve to demand spousal support."

"Didn't he have a job?"

"He's a struggling artist." Edie's tone of voice showed what she thought of that struggle. "So he's never made much money. The poor girl worked like a dog to support him so he could follow his bliss. That's what they call it these days, isn't it? In my day we'd have called it being a lazy loafer. Anyway, things are working out for her down here. She's with Brody Green now and he is sterling silver through and through."

Moira remembered seeing her with Seth Waters. If Brody was silver, Seth was the gold standard. "What about Seth Waters?" she asked.

"Oh, he is a dear. He's been such a help to us."

"So there's nothing between her and Seth?"

"Not that I can see," Edie said, taking down a can of shortening from the cupboard.

Moira wondered how good Edie Patterson's eyesight really was.

"I'm sure Jenna and Brody will wind up getting married. I just hope they hurry up and do it while I'm still around to attend the wedding. I'm not getting any younger."

Edie had a serious collection of wrinkles. She had to be in her eighties. Still going strong, though. Moira hoped she'd be like Edie Patterson when she got old.

"Now," Edie said briskly, "wash your hands and let's get started on this pie. I'm making cherry. It's Pete's favorite."

From the few times Moira had watched Pete gobble up whatever was on the table, it looked like everything was his favorite.

She washed up and Edie put her to work, supervising as she made the crust. "Lots of flour on the board and on your rolling pin," she instructed. "You don't want the dough to stick. Roll from the center out. Yes, just like that. You want to try and get it in one take because the more you fool with piecrust, the less flaky it gets."

Moira's first attempt came out in pieces but Edie helped her patch it. Then, with the bottom layer in the pie pan, they moved on to the filling.

"I always add a little dab of almond extract," she said, handing the bottle over to Moira. "It's a nice extra touch."

This was what it would have been like to have a grandma, someone spending time with you, watching over you, teaching you simple skills, sharing simple pleasures. They finished assembling the pie and put it in the oven. Then Edie set Moira to the task of peeling carrots for a tuna salad she was going to make, all the while chatting about life in Moonlight Harbor, and life in general.

After half an hour the timer went off and they took the pie out of the oven, a beautiful golden-brown work of art. "I can't believe I made this," Moira said, looking at it. "Thank you so much for teaching me."

"I'm happy to. I love sharing my cooking secrets. You

know, even with all those cooking shows on TV, it seems so few women have time to be in the kitchen anymore. And that's a shame, because it really is an art."

The pie certainly was. But by the next day it would probably all be gone.

"Yes, but the sad thing is, everybody eats what you make and then that's the end of your art," Moira said. When you did a woman's hair, it lasted longer than five minutes. Walking art.

"Ah, yes, but the smiles remain, and so do the memories. One of the best things you can do in life, Moira, is make memories, good ones."

"Thanks for helping me do that," Moira said. She wanted to make good memories, a whole avalanche of them to bury the bad ones. Edie and Pearl were an integral part of that. Who else would be?

She flashed on an image of Victor King in his police uniform and smiled. Maybe, just maybe.

Twelve

Friday was a busy day. Pearl was off ordering flooring so Moira was in charge. By the time Pearl returned, she'd done three haircuts, written up an ad for the paper and was putting in a load of towels. And she'd earned twenty dollars in tips. Not the kind of tips she'd gotten at Michael's salon for sure, but she could live with it. Leaving his salon, she'd felt adrift. But more and more Waves was coming to feel like a safe harbor, a place where she could thrive.

"I knew you could handle it," Pearl said.

Yes, she could. The old Moira, the confident Moira who Lang had buried, was coming back to life. It wasn't just Waves Salon that was going to be new and improved.

"Did you get the flooring?" she asked Pearl.

"I did. And I stopped by the grocery store and firmed things up with Cole. He's going to come in and tear out the old floor on Sunday, his day off. And he's going to get Victor to help. Then they'll lay the new flooring on Monday. That gives us Saturday to paint. Think we can do it?"

"Absolutely," Moira said. "What do you think of this for your ad for the grand reopening?"

Pearl took the piece of scratch paper Moira had written

on and read. "'We are ready to make you beautiful. Come to Waves Salon for our March Madness Grand Reopening and let us show you what we can do for you.'"

Moira held her breath, waiting to hear Pearl's opinion.

"I think this is perfect."

"All we need is a date," said Moira. She pulled up a calendar on her phone. "I thought you might like to have the party on the Saturday before Saint Patty's Day. Everyone who wears green could get her name put in a drawing for a grand prize."

"What kind of prize did you have in mind?" Pearl asked, sounding leery, and Moira was sure she was thinking of the money she'd already spent.

"A free hair color? I'd be happy to do that. And we can give away some smaller prizes, too. Chastity and I could buy some nail polish in hot colors at the beauty supply store and put them in those little organza bags. Maybe give one to every tenth guest who comes in? We can call them Lucky Leprechaun Bonuses."

"You are a clever girl. Yes, let's do that."

Approval and a party to plan. This day couldn't get any better.

Or could it? She was just finishing a color consult with one of Sabrina's friends when Victor King walked into the salon, still in his police uniform. Her heart gave a little skip at the sight of him.

"Victor, it's nice to see you," Pearl said. "I guess Cole's bamboozled you into helping lay down our new floor."

"Happy to help," he said.

"I can't imagine you're coming to take measurements since you're still in uniform."

"I'm off now. Actually, I, uh, need a haircut."

Really, he barely needed a trim but Moira would be happy to oblige.

"We can do that," said Pearl.

She started to move toward her station when he blushed and said, "Uh, Moira offered to give me one."

Moira knew she was blushing, too, under Pearl's assessing gaze.

"Of course," Pearl said. "Have a seat. She's almost done."

"I'll be ready for you in just a few minutes," Moira said. After the loser she'd been with, she was more than ready for him. *No rushing, remember?*

"I'm glad you took me up on my offer," she said once she had him in the chair with a plastic cape around his shoulders and was snipping away.

"I sort of am. I'm gonna pay."

"Oh, no. That's not the deal we made. You'd better not welch or I'll stop right now with your hair only half-done."

"Kind of stubborn, aren't you?" he teased.

"Sometimes." Perhaps that was what had kept her with Lang even when things got scary. Stubbornness sounded less pitiful than stupidity.

"Okay, then. How about after you get off I take you out for pizza?"

Oh, boy, was that tempting. So was the thought of getting her hands on more of him than his hair.

"I'm afraid I've got plans tonight," she said.

"How about tomorrow, then?"

"We have to paint the salon. I'll be pretty pooped afterward." Okay, she didn't want to rush but she didn't want to send out signals that she wasn't interested, either. He was starting to look a little uncertain, so she added, "But I'm planning on going to The Drunken Sailor on Sunday." Actually, she hadn't been. She sucked at line dancing.

He perked up. "Yeah?"

"Maybe you can coach me so I don't suck abysmally this time."

"I think I can."

Okay, line dancing with Victor. And lots of other people. It wasn't rushing if she waited until Sunday to see him, was it?

She finished with his cut and sent him on his way with a smile.

"Looks like you've made a conquest," Pearl observed as they closed the salon. "Victor's a real catch."

Nobody had ever said that to her about Lang. She was moving up in the world of relationships. She, too, was smiling as she walked out the door.

But that smile was a little nervous as she entered Edie Patterson's home along with Pearl on Friday night.

"You'll love these women," Pearl told her. "They're all smart and accomplished and good businesswomen."

Most of the faces she recognized—Nora Singleton from the ice-cream parlor; Tyrella, who ran the hardware store; Courtney, the fashion queen; Cindy Redmond, who owned Cindy's Candies and had been in to the salon. And, of course, she knew Jenna and her great-aunt. But there were some new women to meet as well, such as Patricia Whiteside, a stylish older woman who owned the Oyster Inn. There was also a woman seated next to Courtney who looked to be somewhere in her thirties. Courtney introduced her as Annie Albright.

Annie said a shy hello, followed by "I like your hair."

"You should. She's the new color specialist at Waves," Courtney said. "I so want you to make me gorgeous."

"You're already there," Moira said.

Courtney grinned. "Oh, yes, we are going to be friends for sure. Make me gorgeouser."

Moira wasn't sure that was a word, but she promised to deliver, and looking at Courtney, inspiration hit. "You know, I think I have the perfect colors for you." She could see it now. Courtney was already striking. By the time Moira was done with her, she'd be stunning.

"Oh, yes," Courtney said happily.

"I wish I could do something with my hair," Annie said softly.

"I can think of plenty of things we could do with it," Moira said to her.

Annie shook her head. "I could never afford it."

There was something about this woman, something tired and beaten, that made Moira want to give her a hug. "We're going to be having a grand reopening at Waves and I could use some hair models."

"As in we wouldn't have to pay?" Courtney asked. "If that's the case, we're both so in."

"What would we have to do?" Annie wanted to know.

"Show up at the party and look awesome," said Moira.

"Piece of cake," Courtney said with a flick of her hand. "Right?" she asked Annie.

"I guess," Annie said dubiously. Annie was obviously not the kind of woman who looked for the spotlight.

"It's painless, I promise," Moira said to her.

"Perfect timing, too," Courtney said. "Getting a new look is a great way to celebrate your new business."

"You have a new business?" Moira asked.

"I'm starting a catering business," Annie said. "Down the road I want to have a food truck."

"What kind of food will you serve?" Moira asked.

"Breakfast and lunch food—lattes, muffins, wraps, sandwiches. That sort of thing."

"And cookies. Don't forget the cookies," put in Courtney.

"Sounds good. I'd sure be your best customer," Moira said. "I can't cook worth squat. But Edie's teaching me," she added, looking in Edie's direction and waving.

"You can't get a better teacher," Courtney said. "Those cookies she makes for us to give people when they check in are to die for."

And speaking of, here came the cute little old woman now. "Moira, dear, I'm glad you could join us," she said. "Now, come get some wine and some shortbread."

Shortbread. What on earth was shortbread?

Spectacular, that was what it was. And the wine was excellent. So was the conversation.

"We're so glad to have you with us tonight," Edie Patterson said to Pearl after the women had gotten their refreshments and crowded into her little living room, settling in for a group visit.

"It's good to see everyone," Pearl said. "And I think you've all met my new stylist now, right? She's helping me with our grand reopening at Waves."

"A reopening?" asked Patricia.

"Yes, we're giving the place a face-lift and we decided to debut it with a party."

"Does that mean party favors?" asked Courtney.

"Absolutely," said Pearl, and she let Moira tell the women a little of what they had planned.

"I'll be there," Nora said. "I want a change. I've got a birthday coming up and we're going to have a party to console me. I want to look hot. Can you make me look young and sexy?"

"Girl, you're already sexy," Tyrella told her. "But young? Don't push it," she finished, which made the other women laugh.

"I can help you with a new look," Moira said.

"You going to cater your party?" Courtney asked Nora.

"I'm thinking about it."

"I know just the caterer," Courtney said and pointed to Annie. "Ta-dah! Meet the face of Simply Delicious Catering."

"You did it!" Tyrella cried and clapped her hands together. "Good for you!"

Annie's cheeks turned pink and she nodded. "It's my first step toward getting my food truck. I just got my business cards today. Jenna designed the logo."

"Show 'em," urged Courtney, and Annie pulled out some cards from her purse and passed them around.

"So darling," murmured Patricia. "And I love the name."

"I'll be your first customer," Nora said. "You can cater my birthday party."

"There you go. You're on your way," Courtney said, smiling at Annie. Obviously, these two were close friends.

"You could use some good things happening in your life," Jenna said. "I'm glad."

Later, as the women broke into smaller groups to help themselves to more food and wine, Moira asked Jenna, "Has Annie had something bad happen to her?"

"More like someone," Jenna replied. "She's been dealing with an alcoholic husband for years. She finally left him in the hopes it will be a wake-up call. So far, though, he doesn't seem to want to wake up."

So Moira wasn't the only one with man troubles.

"What brought you to Moonlight Harbor?" Patricia Whitehead asked, settling on the couch with Moira as everyone drifted back into the living room. Moira was aware of Edie Patterson on her other side, Tyrella across from her, all listening intently.

The question was bound to keep coming up. She should just make an announcement to the whole group and be done with it.

"I was in a bad relationship. It was time to leave."

"If it was bad, it certainly was," Edie said with a vigorous nod.

"Certainly was what?" Nora asked, settling down in a nearby chair.

"Time to leave a bad relationship," Edie answered for Moira.

Courtney and Annie were back in the living room now and Moira was aware of Jenna hovering in the archway between the living room and the little dining area along with Cindy, the candy lady. Suddenly she had an audience.

Announcement time. "It was bad. He was abusive. I left." All those complicated, miserable years summed up in three short sentences.

"You're not the only one here who's had to deal with a scoundrel," Edie assured her. "My first husband was a real villain, a wife beater. Thank God I met dear Ralph."

"My first was a loser, too," Courtney said. "Leaving him was the smartest thing I ever did. Sometimes you have to hit Restart."

Annie sighed at that, and Courtney put an arm around her.

"I'm happy to be hitting restart here in Moonlight Harbor," Moira said. "Everyone has been so welcoming."

"We watch out for each other here," Nora told her. "We have to, especially when it comes to business. Right, ladies?"

"Right," echoed the other women.

"And we'll all be at that grand reopening," said Edie. "When is it going to be, Pearl?"

"The Saturday before Saint Patrick's Day," Pearl replied.

Moira felt she needed to tout the event just a little more, so she added, "Be sure to wear green. We'll have some fun prizes."

"Prizes. Count me in," Tyrella said.

"Me, too," echoed several others.

The gathering broke up a little before eleven o'clock, and as the women were leaving, Moira exchanged phone numbers with Courtney and Annie.

"It was a lovely evening," Pearl said to Edie as she and Moira headed out the door.

"We're glad you're back with us," Edie said to her. "Friendship is the best balm for a hurting heart."

Moira had to agree. She was pretty sure Pearl had had a good time. She knew she had. Edie Patterson and Jenna Jones had served more than cookies and wine. They'd served hope and encouragement.

Back in her room, Moira set Harry on her bed and then made a phone call, her heart fluttering as she thumbed the call icon. It went to voice mail, which was a little disappointing in light of the fact that she'd had to screw up her courage to make it.

She left a message, anyway. "Mom, it's me. I just wanted you to know, I left Lang. And I'm not in Seattle anymore. But don't worry, I'm doing great."

Yes, she was.

Thirteen

On Saturday Moira and Chastity arrived at the salon, ready to paint. Pearl was waiting for them wearing a pair of ancient gray sweatpants and a black top that looked like a leftover from the eighties. Her hair was covered with a bandanna. Chastity was in faded jeans and a ratty sweatshirt she said she'd had since she was seventeen. Moira, in a pair of cuffed jeans and a shirt she hoped wouldn't get too paint splattered, didn't quite match the other two.

Pearl looked at her and frowned. "You don't want to paint in those clothes. You'll wreck them for sure."

"It's all I have." It was either her jeans or her bra and panties, and she preferred to get paint on the jeans.

"I've got something you can wear. Don't even go near a can of paint until I come back," Pearl commanded.

"You don't need to sacrifice your clothes," Moira protested.

"And you don't need to be giving up a Saturday," Pearl said, "so I guess that makes us even. Don't start without me, girls."

"No painting," Moira promised. "We'll get the mirrors down, though."

Taking down the mirrors was nerve-racking. "Seven years bad luck if you break a mirror. That's what my grandma once told me," Chastity said as they moved one into the storage room.

Moira had already had enough bad luck. "Then let's be super careful."

"At least we don't have to take up those salon chairs," Chastity said as they returned for another mirror. "I'm glad I'm not the guys."

"Same here. It's going to be a lot of work pulling up this old floor, too," Moira said. She could already see Victor King wielding a crowbar, pulling up chunks of the old floor with his bare hands. Bare. With all that hard work and sweating, he'd be shirtless, of course.

"I'm glad Pearl decided to redo the whole place instead of going halfway," Chastity said.

"It is going to look awesome," Moira agreed, and then thought of Pearl herself. She was an attractive older woman who dressed nicely enough. But her hair, drab gray, straight and in that ponytail—it didn't exactly project an image of style. Could they do something about that? Preferably before the grand opening?

Pearl returned with some ancient drawstring pants and a long-sleeved top like the one she was wearing, only this one was a dingy white. "They're ancient and ugly," she said, holding them out to Moira, "which makes them perfect for painting."

The top was snug through the bust—Moira was definitely curvier than her boss—but it fit well enough. "How do I look?" she joked when she came out of the back room where she'd changed.

"Like a serious painter," said Pearl. "Let's get to work, girls."

The work should have been tedious but Moira found it pleasant and satisfying, visiting with the other two women, watching the wall begin to glow with its new color.

"This is going to be gorgeous," she said, taking a step back to admire it.

"The whole place is going to be gorgeous," Pearl said. "I'm so glad you girls convinced me to do this."

Here was an opportunity. Should she take it? Pearl had loved the idea of redoing the salon but maybe she wouldn't love the suggestion of redoing herself quite as much. Well, nothing ventured, nothing gained.

"I was just thinking," Moira began. She could almost sense Pearl bracing herself for yet another idea that would cost her money.

"You were?" Pearl didn't exactly sound eager to hear what she had to say.

"I was thinking you might enjoy a new look, too."

"Oh, no." Pearl shook her head. "I don't want to turn my hair purple."

"No, something more sophisticated." Moira could already envision it—metallic, shimmering silver and gold highlights to enhance what Pearl already had. She would look stunning. Moira had done something similar for one of Michael's older clients. "I did a really interesting color on someone when I was at Michael's." Moira wiped her hands off on a rag, then dug her phone out of her purse. She brought up the image and hurried to where Pearl stood painting to show her.

"Oh, my," Pearl said, almost in awe.

"With those highlights and in a basic black dress, you'd look like a movie star," Moira promised.

Chastity had joined them to check it out. "Oh, my gosh," she breathed. "Pearl, you'd look so hot. You should do it."

"Yes, because Pumpkin wants me to look hot," Pearl joked.

"Think of what great advertising it would be for the salon," Moira said, taking a different approach.

"Oh, yeah," Chastity agreed. "Every woman in town will want to look like you."

"I'll think about it," Pearl said.

From the little smile on her face, Moira knew they had her hooked. She was a smart businesswoman. She'd make the change, if not for herself, for her shop. Color, both on a woman and in a business establishment, made all the difference.

Once they were done painting, the three women stood admiring their handiwork. "The apricot really warms the place up," Pearl said. "And it goes beautifully with our accent wall. Good color choices, Moira."

"I know my colors," Moira said. Not bragging. Just sayin'. It was one area where Lang had never been able to shake her confidence.

"A job well done. Why don't you girls come over to the house and I'll give you some of my leftover quiche lorraine."

"I should get home," Chastity said. "I need to clean the kitchen before Cole gets off work. And myself," she added. "I'm a sweaty mess."

"How about you, Moira?" Pearl asked.

Moira didn't have a man to get back to or a house to clean. Her cat probably wouldn't care if she was gone one more hour.

"Sure," she said. "I'd like that."

* * *

Back at the house, Pearl's cat, Pumpkin, jumped down from the back of the couch, gave a stretch and then wandered over to Moira to get petted.

"Hi there, Pumpkin," she said, kneeling to greet the kitty. "She's so sweet," Moira said to Pearl.

"She's my baby," Pearl said as she went into the kitchen. "I don't know what I'd do without her. These days she's all I've got left."

The words resonated with Moira. She knew how Pearl felt. Animals brought their own special comfort. It seemed like humans so often let you down, but animals were straightforward. You always knew what they wanted and really, they didn't ask much. They didn't make unreasonable demands and they didn't play games.

Still, as difficult and heartbreaking as those human relationships could be, who wanted to go through life without them? Much as Moira loved her cat, their conversations were pretty one-sided.

She cozied up to Pearl's kitchen island and watched while Pearl heated the quiche in the microwave. "I've never had quiche."

"Never had quiche? Really?" Pearl looked shocked.

"My mom wasn't much of a cook." Why hadn't her mom called her back yet? Was she still mad? Mom could hold on to her hurts tightly.

In all fairness Moira had sliced her up pretty good the last time they'd talked. If only she could take back those heated words she'd blasted at her mom.

"Your mom worked, right?"

"Yeah."

"Cooking can feel like a chore if you have to come home and do it after a full day's work. But I found it relaxing and a good creative outlet. I couldn't always do what I wanted when I was working on the women who came into the salon, but in the kitchen I was free to create." Pearl took a piece of quiche out of the microwave, got a fork and set it in front of Moira. "Let's see how you like this."

She took a bite. "Mmm, delicious. I'd like to learn how to make this."

"It's easy. I'll show you how."

"Thanks." It felt good to be with this woman, almost like finding a grandma.

Imagine that. After growing up with none, finding two grandma figures in the same town. Both Pearl and Edie probably simply thought they were being nice, offering meals and sharing treats they enjoyed. They were doing so much more—filling in a hole in Moira's heart, a hole much bigger than she'd realized.

"And thank you for all your help today," Pearl said. "I'm so pleased with the new colors."

"Just wait until the new floor's in and we get those posters on the wall."

"It is going to be something. It was definitely time for a change."

It had been time for a change for Moira, too.

"Speaking of change, I want you to get started setting us up on social media next week."

"Already on it," Moira said with a smile.

"I'll pay you, of course," Pearl said, setting a mug of tea in front of Moira.

"Oh, no. I'm happy to do it."

"I know you are, but you're probably happy to pay your bills, too."

"You've already given me a job. I don't want to be a mooch."

"You're not mooching if I offer. Anyway, I suspect your clientele is going to build in a hurry, so I want to take advantage of your youthful internet skills before you get too busy."

"I won't let myself get so busy that I can't help you," Moira promised.

"I certainly owe Michael a debt of gratitude for sending you my way."

"Same here," Moira said. Sending her to the end of the world was opening up a whole new world.

She stayed another hour, visiting with Pearl, then went back to the Driftwood. Courtney was working the reception desk so Jenna could go out, and Moira visited with her for a while. It felt good to have a friend to visit with, another lost piece of life falling back into place.

A motel guest came into the office, wanting suggestions for where to eat, so Moira pushed off and went to her room to shower and tuck in for the evening with her cat. Sitting at home on a Saturday night—what you did when you had no social life.

Except she had a social life. And so what if she was in a motel room? It was a funky, homey room and she was safe. What more could she ask for?

A man, a place of her own.

She'd get there.

She'd just showered and settled in with Harry and her Muriel Sterling book when her cell phone rang. She knew that number. Her heart stalled out and she answered with a wary "Mom?"

"Are you sure you're all right? Where are you?"

"I'm in Moonlight Harbor."

"Where on earth is that?"

"It's on the coast. At the beach."

"Oh, Moira." Her mom sounded both worried and disgusted. She might as well have added, "What have you done now?"

"It's all good, Mom. I'm starting over down here. I've got a job at a salon and I'm helping the owner make it over. And I've met some really nice people."

"Men?" Mom sounded suspicious.

"I'm taking my time on that," Moira said.

"Good. You don't have the best judgment."

Like her mom was one to talk. "I'm doing fine, Mom," Moira said, irritated.

"Okay, okay. That's good. I just don't want to see you jump into anything."

"Once I get a place, you can come down and visit and see for yourself."

"Once you get a place? Where are you?"

Okay, she should have worded that differently. "I'm staying in a little…" *Crap. How to explain this.* "A cute little motel. I'm friends with the owner and she's letting me stay here in exchange for doing her family's hair." That was sort of true. If she'd told her Edie Patterson had offered her a room for free, her mom would have been instantly suspicious. According to her mother, no good deed came without a hidden agenda.

"You be careful down there," Mom said.

"I will. Don't worry."

"And, whatever you do, don't call Lang."

"I have no intention of doing that, trust me."

"Okay. Let me know if you need anything."

"I will," Moira promised. "I love you, Mom."

"I love you, too," her mother said, but she might as well have added, "Even though you make me nuts."

"And, Mom?"

"What?"

Moira could envision the frown on her mother's face. *What now?*

"I'm sorry I was a shit." No need to mention when. Her mother had to remember their last conversation as vividly as she did.

"We're all shits sometime or another," her mother said. "Be careful," she added, then ended the call.

Moira sighed. They did love each other. But often that love felt prickly. She wondered if that was what happened when there were only two of you, growing up together, trying to figure out life and butting heads in the process. There'd been plenty of headbutting over Lang. Her mother had taken it as a personal affront when Moira refused to take her advice and stuck with him. At the time, her mother, with all her past mistakes, had hardly seemed like the font of all wisdom. Looking back, Moira realized her mother had gained a lot of wisdom the hard way. Hopefully, somewhere down the road, things would smooth out more between them. For now it was enough that they were speaking again. And if she wanted soft and sweet, she had Edie Patterson right next door.

She opened her Muriel Sterling book. *"Always remember, it takes time to evolve. You may not see it yet, but even now you are becoming the best version of yourself."*

"I think I see it," Moira said to Harry. "Just a little. What do you think?"

Harry purred in agreement.

Pearl studied herself in the mirror. "You look like a crone," she informed herself. Her faded gray hair was a fact of life she'd been living with ever since her granddaughter took off. What was the point in bothering to dye it? You couldn't turn back the clock. But, darn, she looked so washed-out and ghostlike.

Which was what she'd become. Even more than her once-vibrant hair, she missed her old self, the Pearl who laughed a lot and enjoyed hosting parties and going out with friends. She had to admit, it had felt good to ease back just a little into that old life, to have someone to visit with and share a meal with, to see friends. Could the old Pearl come back?

Not the youthful Pearl, but maybe a new and better, mature Pearl, a woman who was starting a new phase of life. The salon was getting a makeover. Why couldn't she? She should let Moira do something with her hair. If she didn't like it, she could always grow it out. Hair grew.

She lifted it off her neck. Maybe she'd have Moira cut it, too, go a little shorter. It looked heavy. Like the emotional load she'd been carrying for so long. She was tired of feeling old. It was time for a new look and a new outlook.

Sunday morning Moira put on her coat and went for a walk on the beach. It didn't last long as the gray clouds soon started spitting rain, and that, coupled with the brisk air, was enough for her. But she found a pretty shell and a piece of green beach glass before the nasty weather drove her back inside. Come early evening, she was back in Edie Patterson's kitchen, learning how to make chicken and dumplings.

"Perfect for a rainy day," Edie said. She handed the bowl of batter and the big mixing spoon to Moira. "Drop it into the gravy, one spoonful at a time." Moira did as she was told and then Edie put the lid on the pan. "All right, now we leave the lid on for twenty minutes. And don't peek. Otherwise, they'll fall."

The dumplings, along with the baked chicken, were a new and appreciated treat. "These dumplings are so tasty," Moira said when she joined the family for dinner. "It's like eating clouds."

"Eating clouds. I like that," said Edie.

"Good as always, Edie, old girl," said her friend Pete.

He really wasn't a bad-looking older man. "Pete, when are you going to let me cut your hair?" Moira asked him.

He frowned. "Never. Real men don't go to women's hair places."

"I just had a policeman in my chair on Friday," Moira said.

"Give it up," Jenna said. "He's hopeless."

"He probably wants to boink you," Pete muttered.

"Boink?" Sabrina repeated, looking confused.

"You're too young to know about that," Pete told her.

"Oh," she said. "Sex."

"Too young," said her mother firmly.

Sex, boinking, boinking with Victor. Moira's hormone encampment started a bonfire.

"It couldn't hurt to give Moira a try," said Edie.

"I look fine the way I am," Pete insisted.

"Well," Edie said, a world of doubt in that one word.

He looked shocked. "Edie?"

"I'm just thinking how handsome you'd be with a shave and a haircut."

"I shave," he insisted. "Not every day. It's a waste of time."

"Looking your best is never a waste of time," Edie said sternly. "You could use some sprucing up."

Pete was the picture of wounded male pride. "Well, I like it like this," he said irritably and took a big bite of a dumpling.

Edie changed the subject. "Are you girls going dancing tonight?"

"I'm going to give it one more try," Moira said. "It's definitely harder than I thought it would be."

"You'll pick it up," Jenna assured her.

And once they got to The Drunken Sailor, Victor was on hand to help her with her steps. Thankfully, Rufus did not show up.

"So," Victor said casually as they stood at the bar, waiting to order Cokes, "how about that pizza tomorrow?"

"Don't you have to finish working on the floor at Waves?" she reminded him.

"We'll probably knock off by six. What do you say?"

She knew what she wanted to say. But, "I'm trying not to rush into anything."

"Getting pizza isn't really rushing," he said. "You have to eat."

Not with a man. Not even you. Not yet.

Still, she'd already eaten with him once, so wasn't it a little late for that resolution? "I do love pizza," she said. "It's my idea of a perfect food. Plus if you add salad, that's a bonus."

"We can do that. The Pizza Palace has a great salad bar. What do you say?"

Say no. "Thanks. I'd like to." Oh, boy, what was she thinking? Out of the frying pan into the fire.

What a stupid staying. What did that mean, anyway? Whatever it meant, it couldn't apply here. There was nothing wrong with eating pizza with a new friend.

"Just as friends, though, right?"

"That's the best place to start."

"Okay," she said. "I'd like that."

He smiled. And there were those dimples. "All right,

then. I'll pick you up at seven. You still staying at the Driftwood?"

"Yep." It was weird to be living in a motel, but she was thankful to have a roof over her head.

Monday evening she informed poor Harry that she was leaving him for the night. He let out a yowl and rubbed against her leg.

She sat on the floor and let him crawl into her lap for a good chin and ear scratching. "I'm not paying much attention to you, am I? And there's not much to do in this little room. But don't you worry. Once I have a steady paycheck coming in, we'll find an apartment or maybe even a house. You won't be here forever."

Not at the motel but maybe in Moonlight Harbor, which was quickly coming to feel like home. Not the slightly off-tilt home she'd had growing up or the temporary home she'd had with girlfriends. Definitely not the nightmare caricature of a home she'd been in with Lang, but a warm, happy home, like those ones she'd seen in TV reruns growing up.

She gave Harry some more affection, then put his evening meal in his bowl and got busy fixing her hair and makeup. A date. She had a date.

No, not a date. Just going out for pizza with her new friend. Her great-looking friend. Her sexy friend.

She smiled at her reflection in the bathroom mirror after she'd finished. "You look fabulous," she informed herself. "And you deserve to be happy." That last line was a direct quote from Muriel Sterling. Muriel Sterling was a wise woman.

She'd forgotten to give Victor her room number, so she decided to wait outside the room. It was cold, and she pulled her jacket collar more tightly around her and stamped her feet to stay warm. Across the parking lot a car pulled up and unloaded a middle-aged couple. Other than the guest who'd come into the office when she was visiting with Courtney, they were the first paying guests she'd seen at the motel since she arrived. Hopefully, the place did better during tourist season. Otherwise, she didn't know how Jenna's family managed to pay the bills.

Then she remembered Frank the Mound and Jenna's side business as a massage therapist. It was good to have a plan B to fall back on when times got hard. Moira didn't know what she'd fall back on if women ever stopped wanting their hair done. Hair was all she knew.

But it would have to be the end of the world before women stopped caring about how they looked. As long as the apocalypse stayed away, she'd be working.

A black truck pulled into the parking lot and stopped in front of her. Of course Victor would have a truck. He seemed like a truck kind of guy: steady, ready to haul wood or help you move furniture. Lang, on the other hand, had driven a black Mazda and loved to brag about how great his car was. As if it were a Ferrari or something. She decided she preferred trucks.

She was hurrying toward the passenger side, but Victor hopped out from behind the wheel and beat her there, opening the door for her. Lang had never opened a door for her. She'd never even thought to ask him.

"I should have gotten your room number," he said. "Sorry you had to stand out in the cold."

"I didn't mind." But it was nice to be inside the cab with the heater going. "How are the floors looking?"

"Great," he said. "We just have to put in the baseboards

tomorrow night after work and the place will be good to go."

"Awesome."

And there the conversation faltered momentarily, leaving them in silence. Not a comfortable we've-been-together-for-years kind of silence, but an awkward where-do-we-go-from-here silence. Working in a hair salon required people skills, as well as hair skills, and good conversation. Moira had thought she had both. Until now. Conversation starters were suddenly playing hide-and-seek.

He found some words first. "You look nice."

"So do you," she said, then had to laugh. "Pretty lame conversation so far, huh?" Oh, no. Now she'd made him blush. "I didn't mean you. I meant…" *Both of us?* "Well, who knows what I meant."

"I suck at small talk," he confessed.

"I don't. People expect their hairstylist to talk to them. But I'm usually talking to women." *Not men I want to make an impression on*. And with Lang, well, she'd never had to say a lot. He loved to talk. About himself.

"I'm usually talking to guys."

"Didn't you have any sisters?" she asked.

"Just a brother and lots of cousins, all boys."

"But I bet you flirted with girls."

He shook his head. "Not really."

"Seriously? I bet they flirted with you."

"They tried to make me blush," he said, looking straight ahead. And even though it was dark, both outside and in the cab, she could tell that was what was happening even as he spoke.

"That's mean," she said.

He gave a snort. "High school girls. They can be monsters. But then, so can guys," he said, making her think of Lang.

"Yeah, they can. But hey, that was then, and this is now, right?"

He smiled. "Right."

"And I'm sure you've had girlfriends since high school."

"A couple."

A succinct answer. There would be no swapping horror stories of exes. Maybe that was for the best.

"So, a brother," she continued. "Any pets growing up?"

"A dog. I wouldn't mind getting another one someday."

Dogs were smelly, and they bit. She knew that from experience. She'd been bit as a child and she'd steered clear of the animals ever since, even the cute little ones.

"I'm a cat person," she said. From now on, any man who was interested in her needed to know that and be cool with it. Lang had never really liked Harry, and after they moved in together, poor Harry hid behind the couch whenever Lang was home. Heaven knew there had been times when Moira had wanted to join her cat there.

Victor shrugged. "Cats are okay. Kind of snobby, though."

"Not Harry," she hurried to say. "He's a love, a real snuggle bug."

"Yeah?"

He was just pretending to be convinced. She could tell. "If you met him, he'd convert you into a cat lover."

"I guess I'll reserve judgment," Victor said. Then, "So what about you? Brothers or sisters?"

"No. Mom didn't want any more kids. I guess I can't blame her since my dad was never in the picture. She didn't have it easy being a single parent."

"No grandparents to help?"

Moira shook her head. Her life growing up sounded pathetic.

"That sucks," he said.

It had. But it hadn't been all bad. At least her mom had kept her and hadn't stuck her in foster care. "I guess you can't control what you have growing up."

"Nope. You can control what you have once you're grown-up, though," he said, and she liked the sound of that.

"I plan on it," she said, as much to herself as him. "You know, we got pretty good at small talk, didn't we?"

"That we did," he agreed. "Although not all of it was so small. You're easy to talk to, Moira."

"I guess the hairstylist gene kicked in," she joked.

They pulled up in front of the restaurant and she started to open her door.

"Stay there," he commanded and went around to open it for her.

"That was really chivalrous of you," she said once she was out of the truck.

"I guess it's kind of old-fashioned, but my mom always says 'equal pay for equal work and extra nice so you don't look like a jerk.'"

Moira smiled. "Your mom sounds pretty cool."

"She is," he said and led the way into the restaurant.

It was a small restaurant, only a dozen tables, but obviously popular since most of them were already taken. The aroma of tomato sauce and spices greeted them as they walked in. The atmosphere was as inviting as the smells. Tables all had small pots of rosemary on them and red-checked tablecloths protected under glass tops. The side of the restaurant held a long salad bar that offered everything from spinach to sprouts. The order counter sat over stacks of wood, round ends facing out. And behind that was the kitchen, sporting a brick pizza oven.

"This is so…" Moira paused, searching for the best word to describe what she was seeing "…atmospheric."

"Great pizza, too, just like Mama Mia used to make."

She smiled. Victor King was a clever man.

"What do you want on your pizza?" he asked as he picked a menu off the counter.

"Anything and everything but anchovies."

"Agreed," he said. "Those things are gross."

The pizzas were all named after kings, and Victor ordered drinks for them along with salads and a Theoderic the Great. "It's their supreme, which basically has everything you could imagine on it. I told them to hold the anchovies."

"This is really nice of you," she said as they filled their glasses with soft drinks.

"I'm not being nice. I wanted to see you," he said.

"So you're not normally nice?" she teased.

"I'm nice *and* I wanted to see you. How's that?" he said and took a drink of his pop.

"That's a good answer."

They staked out a table and then hit the salad bar. "This all looks scrumptious," she said, piling iceberg lettuce on her plate.

"Some vocabulary you've got there," he observed.

"I like words."

"Big ones. I should have brought a dictionary."

She didn't think that was funny. Lang used to make fun of her obsession with improving her vocabulary.

"Seriously, do you have a fancy degree or something?" Victor asked.

She concentrated on spooning black olives over her pile

of lettuce. "I wanted to go to college but that wasn't something my mom could afford." She shrugged. "That's okay, though. I love what I do. And we can't all be smart."

"Who says you're not smart?"

Lang. She shrugged.

"A degree doesn't make you smart. It just means you got to learn a lot. I only got as far as an associate degree."

"It's more than I have."

"Yeah, but I don't have all those fancy words," he said. His smile was kind, not the sneer Lang was so good at wielding.

"Someday maybe I'll go to college."

"It's a long life," he said. "You've got plenty of time to do everything you want. And you should."

The pizza was tasty and the conversation easy. Unlike Lang, Victor didn't scoff at her dream of getting that college degree and someday owning her own salon. "Why not?" he said.

Why not indeed.

They spent two hours eating pizza and talking. She learned that Victor liked action movies and books by Lee Child. She preferred her romance novels and biographies but she might enjoy reading about Jack Reacher. He liked puttering around his house. She confessed that she'd never gotten beyond apartments but would love to have a house someday. He liked to fish and kayak. She'd never done either.

"I don't know about the fishing, but I'd sure like to learn how to kayak," she said.

"I'd like to teach you," he said.

The pizza vanished and so did all the other customers. Closing time.

"I guess we should get out of here," Victor said.

"I guess you're right," she said, but she hated to see the evening end.

"You probably want to get back to your cat."

"I think he'll be fine for a little longer." She did want to check on Harry, but really, he would be all right on his own for a bit more and, deep down, she knew Harry could do without her a lot better than she could do without him.

"Want to see my place?" Victor asked.

She shouldn't be in a hurry to do that. Seeing a guy's place led to seeing his bedroom and no way was she going to move that fast no matter how much she wanted to. Still, this man seemed so different from Lang. So…safe.

Let up on the brakes already, screamed the mayor of Hormone Town.

Okay, she could say yes to seeing Victor's place. It didn't have to include a tour of the bedroom.

"I'd like that," she said. "I've only seen log cabins in pictures and on TV."

"You won't be able to see much of the outside in the dark, but I've got the inside fixed up nice."

He did indeed. Plank flooring, a woodstove in one corner, with the last of a low-burning fire dancing behind the glass, a big leather sofa and matching chair. Of course, he had a fancy flat-screen TV. She could envision the two of them curled up on that couch watching movies. They could alternate—an action movie one night and a romantic comedy the next.

The kitchen was impressive, too, with some kind of fancy countertops. Not granite, though.

"My brother came down and helped me do the counters," Victor said, seeing her looking in that direction. "Quartz. I hate granite. It always looks like somebody puked on it."

"I love the pine cupboards," she said. "It all looks like something out of a magazine."

He nodded, a satisfied smile on his face. "It turned out good. Make yourself at home," he added, motioning to the couch.

She could easily make herself at home here with this man.

"Want something to drink?" he asked, moving toward the refrigerator. "I've got beer, Sprite and Coke. And milk."

"Milk's only good with cookies," she said. "Oreos."

He grinned. "I've got Oreos."

"Well, then, bring 'em on."

He did, along with two big glasses of milk that he set on a long wooden coffee table.

"My mom bought these all the time. We'd eat them and binge-watch *Gilmore Girls*," she said.

"I didn't have these much growing up," he said. "My mom always baked."

Of course she did. Moira wished her mom had always baked. Or even sometimes baked. But Oreos were good.

"I don't get up to Seattle that much now, though, so these have to do."

"Good thing you like 'em, then," she said.

She was on her third cookie when a huge spider that looked like it was on steroids made an appearance on the arm of the couch. Moira was not fond of spiders. "Eww, spider," she said, pointing.

And that was when she discovered one of Victor's imperfections.

Fourteen

Victor looked to where she was pointing. He let out a strangled yelp and jumped up from the couch, sloshing his milk on the floor and sending the package of cookies they'd had resting between them flying. Moira had no desire to get close to the thing, either, but when it came to a race to safety Victor was the clear winner.

"Don't worry, I'll get it," he said. He went to the kitchen and came back with a gigantic frying pan. Was he going to cook the thing or kill it?

"If you want, I can get a glass and capture it and take it outside," she offered. "That was what my mom and I always did."

Everything deserves the right to live, her mother had once said. *Even spiders.*

"No, no, that's okay, I'm on it," he said and took a couple of tentative steps toward the uninvited guest. Sneaking up on it.

The spider began to scuttle along the arm of the couch and Victor let out a war whoop and banged the frying pan down. Whacking it once wasn't enough. He made it worth his while, letting the thing have it two more times. *Poor spider. Talk about overkill.*

"I guess you got it," she said.

He blushed. "Uh, I don't like spiders."

"No kidding." She found a roll of paper towels on a spindle on the counter and brought them to the living room. "You want milk patrol or burial duty?"

"I'll take care of the corpse," he said and took some towels from the roll. Then, without another word, he collected the remains of Mr. Spider and dumped them in the kitchen trash.

Moira mopped up the milk, then returned to the kitchen with the glass and sodden paper towel. "Arachnophobia," she said as she threw the mess in the garbage. "A lot of people have it."

"It's a dumb thing," he muttered.

"No more dumb than being afraid of heights," she said. "Is that you?"

"No, but I guess I could be if someone tried to push me off a mountain." Her fears centered on more concrete things like a man's swinging fist. "People are afraid of all kinds of things."

"I'm not really afraid of spiders," Victor insisted as they returned to the living room. "I just don't like 'em."

"I don't, either." Except she hadn't bolted off the couch like someone had lit her pants on fire. Well, someone had, but not in that way.

He picked up the package of cookies and took one. "I guess they're my Achilles' heel."

"Or your kryptonite."

He smiled at that. "I'm not a superhero."

"I don't know. Look what you do for a living."

"Haven't had to use my superpowers yet," he said with

a smile, then leaned over and inspected the back of the couch.

"Looking to see if he had a wife?" Moira teased.

"You never know."

"If you ever want a spider wrangler, let me know. I'm good with an empty glass."

"I think I'd rather call pest control."

"All those chemicals. If it comes down to pest control, I'll bring Harry over. He likes to catch spiders. Although I do try to get to them first."

"I'm with your cat," Victor said. "I'm already starting to like him."

And she was already liking Victor. So much.

"Speaking of Harry, I should probably get back now."

"Sure." He took her coat from the closet and helped her into it. "Uh, nobody at the station knows that I'm not into spiders."

"None of their business," she said. Then couldn't help adding, "Even the bravest of men are afraid of something. Take Indiana Jones, for example. You've seen those old movies, right?"

"Oh, yeah."

"There you have it. He faced all kinds of dangers but he was afraid of snakes. And, anyway, you didn't run away. You faced your fear. Which is more than I can say," she couldn't help adding. "I ran away."

"Staying in an environment where you're getting hurt isn't brave, Moira. It's dangerous. You did the right thing. You got out. And doing that takes courage."

She wasn't so sure about that, but she was glad she'd done it. Really glad. If she hadn't left Lang she'd never have met Victor.

Every nerve was aware of him right next to her when

he dropped her off at her door. She opened the door and turned to say good-night and the way he was looking at her sent the adrenaline rushing through her body, leaving her jittery with excitement.

"I know you don't want to rush things," he said.

No, she didn't.

He braced an arm on the doorjamb and leaned down. "Does one kiss count as rushing?"

"Probably," she said.

She could smell his cologne and it smelled like temptation. *Eau de pheromone*. He was looking at her lips. She swallowed. Hard.

He pushed away and straightened back up. "Okay. Everything good is worth waiting for."

"You are too nice," she said.

He smiled and shook his head. "No, I'm not. I just don't want to blow it."

"Maybe one kiss wouldn't be blowing it," she said.

"Yeah? You think so?"

"I'm pretty sure."

"Just one," he promised and leaned back down, slipping his arms around her and pulling her up against him.

Every nerve ending in her body was dancing before he'd even kissed her.

His lips on hers. The dancing went to jumping and running, high fives. Ooh, this was… What was the word for it? Oh, who cared?

She slipped her arms around his neck, kissed him back for all she was worth and luxuriated in the sensations produced by two bodies so close together.

"That was some kiss," he said when they'd finally parted.

"Mmm," she said, her eyes still closed. "But we're not rushing this."

"No rushing."

No rushing, but a tiny bit of hurrying couldn't hurt.

"Thanks for coming out with me tonight," he said. His voice was a soft caress. "Good night, Moira."

It certainly was, she thought as she watched him walk back to his truck. He stopped, then turned and came back. "Give me your phone number?"

Gladly.

Harry was still curled up on the bed where she'd left him when she slipped back into their room, feeling all gooey and sappy. "Did you miss me?" she asked, coming to sit next to him and pet his head. He leaned into her hand and purred. "I had a good time with Victor," she said. "I think you'll like him. He's not at all like Lang."

Harry stopped purring.

"You're right. We don't need to ever mention him again. He's history." Thank God, because the idea of ever seeing Lang again was scary. Those who didn't learn from history were bound to repeat it. She hoped she'd learned her lesson.

Just the thought of Lang did bad things for her subconscious because that night it dredged him up and put him in another dream. This time he was a giant spider, twice her size, chasing her down the beach.

"Where are you going?" he called after her. "I thought you wanted to walk on the beach."

"Not with you!" She was trying to run but the sand kept sucking at her feet. She couldn't get any traction.

He finally caught her in a furry spider arm. "You're not leaving me. Ever," he said and scuttled off down the beach with her. He turned down a path that led to a wooded patch, and there, in a fir tree, was a giant spiderweb. "You'll like it here," said Spider Lang.

In the distance she could see a log cabin and she tried to cry for help, but nobody came because all she could get out was a strangled gurgle.

"He's afraid of spiders, babe. It's just you and me. Here you go. Welcome home," he said and pitched her like a baseball toward the web.

She woke up before she hit, gasping for breath, heart hammering.

A dream. It was just a dream. She'd never see him again.

But what if she did? Would she be able to face him, tell him off? What if he showed up ready to kill her? She was such a wimp. She hadn't even been able to stand up to Rufus, the dance floor pest.

"You'll get stronger," she told herself and hoped she was right.

She wasn't able to get back to sleep again. She tossed and turned until five in the morning, then gave up, grabbed her Muriel Sterling book and read some more. *"You may have days when you feel like you're making no progress in reaching your goals, when old attitudes and habits you're trying to change don't seem to be changing at all. Don't give up. Change takes time. Look for those small accomplishments and celebrate them."*

Helping Pearl remodel her salon, that counted as an accomplishment, didn't it? Starting a new job in a new town, that counted for sure. She was making progress.

Victor still had to put in the baseboards that evening and there was nothing to do at the salon, but Moira went to Waves, anyway, anxious to see how the new floors looked.

Pearl had beaten her there and was standing in the middle of the salon with a mug of coffee, taking in her new and improved domain.

"I can't get over how great everything looks," she said. "It doesn't look like the same place."

"It is," Moira said, "only better."

Pearl sighed and took a sip of coffee. "My daughter would have loved this."

"I wish I could have met her."

"You'd have liked her."

"For sure. I like her mom."

That made Pearl smile. "Thank you for talking me into doing this."

"I didn't have to talk very hard. I think you were ready."

"Maybe you're right. I think the salon was ready for a new beginning and so was I."

"Me, too. Thanks for giving me one."

Pearl smiled at her. "If ever a woman deserved a new beginning, it's you. Now, go find something fun to do with yourself."

A good suggestion. Moira started by checking out Books and Beans, a local coffee shop.

The shop was inviting, with a tower shelf of books for sale in one corner and a collection of coffee-related goodies in the center of the store. Half a dozen tables and chairs lined up along the plate-glass windows and the requisite glass display case of edible treats sat toward the front, along with the cash register.

Rita Rutlege, the owner, was probably somewhere in her forties. She was thin and a casual dresser, wearing jeans and a brown T-shirt that said Coffee and Books— Can't Run Out of Either. She had nice-enough features but her hair was unremarkable, both in color and style, long, straight and neglected. Her nails were short and plain. No wedding ring. Divorced? Never married? Who knew? Not that it was any of Moira's business, anyway, but she was always curious about people.

"How did you come to have a business down here?" she asked as they chatted.

"I had some money to spend, wanted to invest in a business. I saw this coffee shop for sale and thought I could do some fun things with it."

And she had. She might not have worried about her own appearance, but she'd taken care with her coffee shop, with burlap coffee-bean bags hanging on the walls along with framed posters of authors. One especially called out to Moira, a picture of Oscar Wilde with a quote that advised, "Be yourself. Everyone else is taken."

"I love that poster," Moira said, pointing to it.

"Good advice to follow," Rita said. "Sometimes it takes you places you don't expect, but that's okay. I think we all eventually end up where we're supposed to be, doing what we're supposed to be doing."

"I think so, too," Moira said. She'd certainly wound up doing what she was supposed to be doing. It was looking like she even had the where part sorted out, as well.

She got a small latte but passed on the temptation that was calling her from the bookshelf. Instead, she found her way to the local library and got herself a library card, along with a copy of *A Room of One's Own* by Virginia Woolf (because you had to read something by Virginia Woolf to be truly educated) and Robyn Carr's latest novel (because you also had to be uplifted and entertained). Those she would alternate with Muriel Sterling's book to round out her reading for the next couple of weeks. Also, she wouldn't have to panic when she was done with the Muriel Sterling book because she had nothing to read.

She splurged and bought fish and chips at the Seafood Shack, the fast-food restaurant across the parking lot from the Driftwood and took a selfie standing outside it, making sure she included the giant clam on the roof in the picture. She sent it to Michael, captioning it, Keep Clam. Ha ha. A tribute to Ivar's restaurant in Seattle.

Back at the Driftwood, she called Courtney Moore to see when she'd like to schedule a hair transformation.

"Jenna didn't need me and I'm done creating for the day, so how about coming on over now?"

Now worked fine for Moira and Courtney gave her the address.

Moira fell in love with Courtney's rental the moment she saw it—a two-story cottage with a long front porch, a flower bed waiting to come to life and a path to the beach.

She loved the inside as much as the outside, with its fanciful decor. She smiled at the rough wood sign on the wall. Life's a Beach.

"Cool place," she said as she walked in with her bagful of beauty supplies.

"I like it," Courtney said. "And it's fun having Annie and Emma staying here. Reminds me of my college dorm days."

Moira wished she'd had some college dorm days and felt a moment of jealousy.

"What are we going to do with my hair?" Courtney asked.

Oh, yeah. Hair. "Here's what I was thinking," Moira said and brought up the picture from Michael's website on her phone. It was a color she'd done and was one of her favorite artistic accomplishments. The woman had dark hair like Courtney's and Moira had accented it with a combination of deep violet and blue and crimson.

"Wow," breathed Courtney on seeing it. "Yes."

They got to work, bonding as they went by talking about their favorite movies: *Me Before You*, every version of *Jane Eyre* ever done. *"Miss Congeniality,"* Moira said, "because they made Sandra Bullock's character look so fabulous."

"Like that's hard to do," Courtney said with a snort. "And talk about fabulous. Do you remember *Ocean's 8*? I wanted Cate Blanchett's whole wardrobe."

"Me, too. Maybe someday she'll be buying your designs."

"From your lips to God's ears. How about this? I'll do her clothes and you can do her hair."

"I like that," Moira said.

That moved the conversation from the art of dressing to looking good in general.

"I don't think you need a lot of money to look good, just a lot of good taste," Courtney said. "I mean, look at us, right?"

"Right," Moira said with a smile. Hanging out with Courtney felt like being with the sister she'd always wanted and never had.

She felt the same way about Annie, too, who came in later after a consult with a local boy about designing a website for her new catering business. She was all enthusiasm and plans and Moira admired her determination to make a go of her business.

"I need to take pictures of some of my specialties," she finally said.

"We'll help you," Courtney told her. "And I'll be happy to help consume those specialties afterward," she added with a wink.

"What are some of your specialties?" Moira asked.

"Oh, my gosh, her bruschetta is to die for," Courtney said. "So's her penne salad. And her lemon sugar cookies. I think we should make some of those when Moira's done with my hair."

"I'm already a step ahead of you," Annie said, and started pulling ingredients from the cupboards.

So the afternoon continued with Moira working on Courtney's hair transformation and Annie baking. Women to hang out with—how Moira had missed that. Why had she ever let Lang separate her from her friends?

It could be summed up in one word: *deceived.* Somehow, she still wasn't quite sure how, he'd convinced her that she hadn't needed her friends. All she'd needed was him. How romantic. No, how controlling. But she'd been insecure enough to believe him. That had been step one. Then he'd programmed her to believe that, since he was all she needed she couldn't do without him.

Stupid her. She'd fallen for that lie and, like the famous fable of the frog in the pot of water, she'd stayed, ignoring the fact that the water was getting hotter and hotter. Slowly but surely, threat by threat, slap by slap, head game after head game, he'd hemmed her in until she came to the conclusion that she deserved what she got.

Now that she was away from him, she was coming to a different conclusion: she deserved to be happy. Once upon a time she'd thought she needed him. Funny. She was doing just fine without him.

"You look incredible," Annie said after Moira had finally blown out and styled Courtney's hair.

"You are a hair goddess," Courtney said to Moira.

She never got tired of hearing such praise. "I'm glad you like it. For the open house we can French braid it and that will show off the colors and look really elegant."

"Elegant. That's me," Courtney said and did a model's

glide around the room. "You're next," she said to Annie as Moira took pictures of her.

"Not today," Annie said. "Emma will be home from school soon and I have to help her with her homework. Plus I want to stage these cookies."

"We can help with that," Courtney said. "After all, we're all artists, right?"

"I'll take all the help I can get."

"We can stage cookies, do homework, then get pizza and watch a movie," Courtney said, obviously in a party mood.

"Sounds good," Moira said, "but I should probably get back and check on my cat."

"You have a cat? My daughter would love to have a cat," said Annie.

"You can get one while you're staying here if you want," Courtney offered.

Annie shook her head. "No. We're still in flux. I don't want to add one more worry to my list."

"I'll share," Moira offered. "Your daughter can visit Harry Pawter anytime she wants."

"Harry Pawter? That's his name?" Annie asked.

"A tribute to J. K. Rowling. Her books got me into reading," Moira said.

"Emma's a big reader," Annie said. "And she's reached the point where she loves playing with her hair and putting on fingernail polish."

"Boy, is she going to love you," Courtney told Moira.

"Good. I like kids. I'd love it if you shared." Maybe Moira would never have any of her own. She sure wasn't going to do the single-mom thing. She'd seen how hard it had been for her own mom.

"Emma's a great kid," Courtney said and helped herself to a cookie.

She handed one to Moira. It practically melted on her tongue. "This is incredible."

"She's good. Here," Courtney said, and began clearing the table. "Let's stage these. Too bad it's not summer. We could put them out on the table on the front porch along with a pitcher of lemonade."

"Let's use my teapot and a cup and saucer," said Annie. "Like we're getting ready for a tea party."

"Good idea," Courtney agreed.

"It's already like a regular party around here," Moira said as Annie disappeared to fetch her teapot.

"Pretty much," said Courtney. "Feel free to come over and party anytime you want."

"I'd like that."

Courtney studied her. "Have you thought about where you're going to stay once things get busy at the Driftwood? In another month or so it'll really start filling up."

Then it wouldn't be right to be taking up a room for free, and Moira sure wouldn't be able to afford to pay for a nightly rental. She shook her head. Hopefully, she will have earned enough money for first and last month's rent before things got busy.

"I'm hoping Jenna will let me stay a little longer."

"She will. She's got a big heart."

"But I don't want to take advantage of that big heart. She also needs to run a business. I'm sure I'll find a place somewhere."

"You could stay here if you want," Courtney offered. "Of course, you'd be stuck on the sofa bed since Annie and her daughter are in the second bedroom until she gets her life sorted out, and at the rate she's going that could be about a million years. I guess it's not much to offer..."

It was plenty. "I'd love it," Moira said, jumping at the chance. "But are you sure?" She'd be in the way, camping out in the living room.

"Yeah. Why not? I like having people around. When we had a big storm a couple winters back, the power went out and I wound up taking in a bunch of people. It was great."

"If Annie wouldn't mind."

"Someone to play with her daughter? Are you kidding? How do you feel about having a third roommate?" she asked as Annie returned to the room. "I'm offering Moira the fabulous opportunity to sleep on the sofa."

"It's fine by me," said Annie. "Anyway, it's your house."

"Yeah, but you're paying rent."

Rent. Uh-oh. "How much—" Moira began.

Courtney didn't let her finish. "Don't even think about it. Like I'm going to charge rent for my sofa."

"It's only fair."

"You do our hair and we're even," Courtney told her. "I've been where you are. After my divorce I wound up living in my parents' basement for a year. So humiliating. But so necessary. Anyway, we all need help hitting Restart once in a while. Go get your stuff and come on back. We can watch a movie later after Emma's in bed."

A house to live in, roommates, a little girl to play with Harry and help keep him company—it was a win-win situation. Moira hurried back to the Driftwood to turn in her key.

"Aunt Edie's going to miss you," Jenna said to her when she handed it over, along with the promise of hair care for life and eternal gratitude. "We're all going to miss you."

"You'll still be seeing plenty of me. I want to keep coming to your Friday night group. And I hope you'll come to Waves and let me do your hair."

"I might have to take you up on that," Jenna said. "I'm ready for a change."

"Change is good," Moira said. *More than good*, she thought, thinking of her own life. It was sensational.

"Won't you stay for dinner, dear?" Edie urged. "I'm making tuna roll-ups."

"Tuna roll-ups?"

"Very easy to make and very tasty. I've had the recipe since the 1970s."

It was older than Moira. "Well…" She hesitated.

"And apple pie for dessert."

That clinched the deal. Moira let Courtney know she'd be along later.

"I wish you weren't moving out," Sabrina said as they finished their dessert.

"Everyone has to move on at some point," Pete said and helped himself to a second piece of pie. It didn't look like he was planning on going anywhere. The guy was such a sponge.

"You'd think so," Jenna murmured.

"I wanted to have another party," Sabrina said and pouted.

"You can always come to the salon. And I know you'll want to come to our grand reopening party before Saint Patty's Day. You can be one of my hair models if you want."

"Awesome," said Sabrina.

"Pete, if you want to come to the party with Edie, I can get you all fixed up, too," Moira offered.

"The token sex symbol," Jenna cracked and Pete scowled at her.

"Bah," he said in disgust. "But I'll take you if you want, Edie, old girl."

"I'll see," Edie said, playing coy.

Pete frowned and pushed away his plate.

Moira helped clean up after dinner, then said her good-byes, collected her cat and her belongings, and drove to her new home.

"This is our new roommate I was telling you about," Courtney said, introducing her to Annie's daughter.

"Do you know how to braid hair?" Emma asked. "My mom sucks at it," she added, making her mother roll her eyes.

"I sure do," Moira said.

"Cool," said Emma. She knelt in front of Harry's cat carrier. "What's your cat's name?"

"Harry Pawter."

Emma giggled. "Is he friendly?"

"Once you get to know him." Moira knelt and took the cat out, cradling him in her arms.

Emma reached out a tentative hand and he squirmed away and jumped out of Moira's arms, trotting to the far side of the living room.

"He'll warm up," Moira promised as Harry began to inspect his new surroundings.

"He's so pretty," Emma said.

"If you sit on the couch he'll probably jump in your lap before the night's over," Moira told her.

Sure enough, an hour later, as they watched a Disney movie, Moira got up for a refill on soda pop. Harry, find-ing himself lapless, paraded over to Emma and settled on her lap.

"He's sitting on me!" she announced, all smiles.

Annie came into the kitchen to make more popcorn. "I haven't seen her this happy in a long time," she said to Moira. "I'm glad you're here."

Later, after Emma was in bed and the three women had switched from soft drinks to white wine, Courtney echoed Annie's sentiment. "It's great to have you here. Now we can have a regular slumber party every night. Well, except for Sundays, when I'm at The Drunken Sailor. That's when I'm out with my future husband."

Future husband? This was the first Moira had heard of a man in Courtney's life.

"Not that he's asked," Annie teased.

"He will," said Courtney. "Have you been to The Drunken Sailor yet?" she asked Moira.

"I've been there line dancing a couple of times," Moira said. "Not that I'm any good at it," she added.

"You'll get good," Courtney assured her. "Anyway, it's the closest you're going to get to any nightlife down here. We can go together this weekend if you want. Oh, damn, I forgot. I won't be here Sunday. My cousin's getting married and I have to drive to Bellevue for a bridal shower. I won't get home until late. Oh, well. After that. It'll give Mr. Wonderful plenty of time to miss me. Absence makes the heart grow fonder, they say. Or was it abstinence? Oh, well, either way."

"So, who is this Mr. Wonderful?" Moira asked. "Would I have met him?"

"You probably saw him at The Drunken Sailor," Courtney added. "Best-looking man there."

Best-looking man. So far Moira had seen only three men who qualified for that title and two of them were crazy about Jenna Jones. That left… No. It couldn't be. A feeling of uneasiness began to creep over her.

"Had a traffic violation yet?" asked Courtney.

"Traffic violation," Moira repeated. The uneasiness went from creeping to stomping.

"Yeah. He's a cop."

There were lots of cops in town, right? It couldn't be...

"Victor King," said Courtney.

Nooo.

Fifteen

Great. Moira was into the man Courtney was crazy about. If she kept seeing Victor when the woman who'd just taken her in and been kind to her wanted him, what kind of an ingrate did that make her? The quintessential ingrate, that was what kind.

Surely, though, if Victor were interested in Courtney, he wouldn't be wanting to hang around with Moira. "Have you been going out with him?" she asked.

"We've mostly hung out at the pub," Courtney said.

So, not dating. Just friends. But one of them wanted to be much more. She'd called him her future husband. *Don't stand in Courtney's way*, Moira advised herself. Courtney was emotionally solid and ready for a relationship while Moira was still finding her feet. Courtney was a better match for Victor.

But darn, Moira liked him so much. Still, the girlfriend code demanded that you didn't go after a man your friend wanted. Especially when your friend was offering you a place to stay.

Courtney continued to rave about Victor, Annie fretted about the messed up situation with her ex and Moira listened and felt sorry for herself.

Everyone finally went to bed and, with blankets and sheets Courtney had given her, Moira settled in on the foldout. It was actually really comfortable.

She hardly slept.

Annie and Emma were up bright and early, Emma ready for school and Annie ready for her morning shift at the restaurant where she worked. Moira's eyes felt full of sand but she gave up on sleep and got up and made coffee and, on Emma's request, braided her hair in a French braid for school.

"Thank you," Emma said and hugged Moira.

Love and gratitude—the best breakfast ever. "Anytime you want something done with your hair, just let me know," she told the girl.

"Can you color my hair to look like yours?" Emma asked eagerly.

"When you're sixteen," her mother said firmly, making her pout. "Go brush your teeth, baby. We've got to go."

"It's tough being a kid and wanting to be a grown-up," Moira said as Emma slouched out of the room.

"Being a grown-up isn't all it's cracked up to be," Annie said.

"You can say that again. But I get the wanting to play with hairstyles. I sure did when I was a kid."

"Me, too. But she's way too young for something so permanent."

"How about something more temporary and fun?" Moira suggested. "I could get some hair color wax. It's fun to wear for parties or special occasions but it washes right out."

"That's an idea," Annie said.

"We could get her all fixed up for the salon's grand re-opening."

Annie nodded. "She'd like that."

"Then she can be all fancy like her mom."

"I just don't know about doing the hair color thing. I'm not as…out there as Courtney."

"I wouldn't put you as out there," Moira promised. "Something more subtle."

"I'll think about it," Annie said.

Moira wondered if she really would. She had so many big changes on her plate, probably even something as small as doing her hair felt like a huge leap. Moira decided not to push it.

Anyway, she had other makeovers to think of. She showered quickly before Courtney got up so the bathroom would be free, then, after fixing herself some toast, went to the salon to check out the finished product and help Pearl hang their posters and chalkware fish and put the mirrors back up.

Thoughts of Victor kept trying to intrude as she drove but she pushed them firmly away. At least they hadn't gotten further than one date.

And one kiss.

But what a kiss.

Enough already! Push, push.

Once again, Pearl had beaten Moira to the salon and was sweeping the floor. "I can't believe they got this done so fast," she said, looking around. "The poor men worked like dogs. They were here Saturday night until ten and then back again at eight on Sunday. Poor Victor here on his day off Monday, then back again putting in baseboards

as soon as he was done with his shift at the station yesterday. I don't know how I'll ever repay them."

"Haircuts for life," Moira said with a grin. "But I bet you don't have to." Pearl appeared to be one of those women everyone loved and was happy to help.

"Probably not," Pearl agreed. "Men enjoy a project. My husband did. And there was nothing he loved better than to swing a sledgehammer and wreck something. Still, I'll have to get busy and bake those boys a batch of cookies."

"Victor would love that for sure," Moira said. All this talk about Victor dropped a seed of sadness in her heart. *Don't go there.* "Hey," she said briskly, "let's get started on the rest of our decorating. And then we can do your hair. You have decided to let me color it, haven't you?"

"Yes, I think I'm ready for a new look. After all, it's a little silly to update my salon and not update myself."

"You'll love it, I promise," Moira said.

"I'm sure I will. I love every suggestion you've made for this place. You have excellent taste, Moira."

"Except in men."

"Oh, I think Victor's pretty special."

The little seed of sadness began to sprout. "I don't think that's going to work out."

"You know that already?"

"Pretty much."

Pearl didn't press her for details, for which Moira was grateful. "You have time to figure out your love life. Meanwhile, let's get the mirrors back up and hang some posters."

The posters and the vintage fish were the perfect finishing touches. Moira took pictures and posted them on the Instagram account she'd set up for the salon and on

the Facebook page. Once she had more hair models, she planned to make a gallery for the website.

They had only a few clients scheduled, which left the women with the afternoon free. It was time to transform Pearl.

She was a pretty woman waiting to be turned into a silver fox. Moira's metallic touches did the trick.

"Now it's time to style it," she said once she'd finished with the color. "Can I go short? Would you be okay with that?"

"I was thinking of going a little shorter."

"How about a lot shorter?"

Pearl hesitated and Moira kept quiet, determined not to press her. Yes, hair grew, but if a woman didn't like what had been done to hers, that growing time could be miserable.

"All right," Pearl said with a decisive nod. "Why not? In for a penny, in for a pound."

"I think you'll like what I have in mind. Do you have some great earrings?"

"I have some gold chandelier ones."

"This will show them off."

"Just don't buzz cut me. I don't want to be quite that cutting-edge."

"No buzzing," Moira said and got busy.

Half an hour later Pearl was looking like a star with a short cut combed sleekly forward, the bangs hanging low over her brows. The color was luminescent and Moira gave herself a mental pat on the back.

"Oh, my," Pearl breathed, staring at her reflection in the mirror when Moira was finished. "This is so glamorous. I don't even look like me."

Funny how women always said stuff like that. They were always wrong.

"Yes, you do—the new you," Moira told her.

"I love the new me."

"And people are going to love the new Waves," Moira predicted.

"I think so, too. Now, why don't you come over to the house for something to eat?"

"You talked me into it," Moira said.

As she sat at Pearl's kitchen counter, sampling crab dip, she couldn't help marveling at the great new life she was getting in Moonlight Harbor. And to think she'd been so afraid to leave the city. And Lang. She didn't miss her old life at all.

Well, other than Michael and his family. But they'd been texting and she'd been enjoying showing off what she'd been doing.

You landed on your feet. Good for you, he'd texted. Now get out there and find somebody great.

She had. Just her luck that someone else had found him first.

There were other fish in the sea, she kept reminding herself. Other men in Moonlight Harbor.

Like Frank Stubbs.

Oh, well. She'd find another man. Eventually. Maybe.

Meanwhile, she had to avoid the one who could have been right. Not easy to do.

He called her the next night, which was awkward since she was in Courtney's living room, watching a movie with Courtney and Annie, asking what she was doing. Her cheeks felt a little warm, as she moved to the kitchen, saying, "I'm hanging out here with my new roommates."

"Roommates? You found a place to live?"

"I moved in with Courtney Moore. I think you know her?"

"I do," he said but didn't add anything to indicate he was interested in Courtney. "Are you all settled in? Got time to go out?"

She wished. "I'm still busy settling in. In fact, I'd better go."

"Oh." He sounded surprised. "Okay. Guess I'll talk to you later."

"Okay, bye," she said, not making any promises.

"Who was that?" Courtney asked when she came back into the living room.

"Nobody," Moira said and plopped back onto the sofa. Nobody for her now, that was for sure.

She decided she wasn't into line dancing and skipped the next Sunday. Courtney wouldn't have been there so she could have hung out with Victor. But not with a clear conscience.

Later that day he called her on her cell and she resisted the urge to take the call, letting it go to voice mail.

"Hi, it's Victor," said his recorded voice. "Thought I'd, uh, say hi. So, hi. Thought I'd see you tonight. How about giving me a call?"

That would not be a good idea.

Late the next afternoon he stopped her for a traffic violation. Five miles over the speed limit.

Five miles? Seriously?

"I'm not going to give you a ticket," he said, "but you should be careful. The deer make a habit of strolling out in front of cars."

"I will be," she promised and wished he'd go away. He was such a temptation in his uniform. Out of it, too, darn it all. And it was almost seven o'clock. Why was he still cruising around in his cop car?

"Isn't it kind of late for you to be working?" she asked.

"I'm on evening shift now."

"I guess I won't see much of you, then," she said. Thank God.

"I've got mornings free."

"I'm working."

"I guess I'll have to come in for another haircut."

She didn't want to encourage regular visits to the salon. All that maleness up close and personal. "Oh, I think you're fine for a while." He was fine, period.

"Okay, well, I guess I'll be seeing you at The Drunken Sailor. Where were you Sunday?"

"I wasn't feeling good." No lie. She'd been sick at heart.

He nodded. "You feeling better now? Interested in a lunch break at Beachside Burgers tomorrow? My shift doesn't start until three."

"You know, we're so busy getting ready for the salon's grand reopening I can't get away." Not even for lunch. Did that sound lame or what?

He looked confused, and he had a right to be, considering how well they'd hit it off. Now she was sending him mixed signals. She should come right out and tell him to go away, go hang out with Courtney.

He didn't give her time. "Okay, then," he said brusquely. "Drive carefully."

She wanted to call him back, longed to explain that she really did want to see him. But how would that help matters? Best to let him think she was the queen of the flakes. They'd barely started anything so, really, what did it matter?

It mattered a lot. Her poor vulnerable heart had latched onto him and didn't want to let go. Why did it have to be Courtney of all people who wanted him? Why couldn't life go smoothly?

"Life's a bitch," her mother used to say. Moira hated to admit it, but she was beginning to think Mom was right.

Victor was frowning when he got back behind the wheel of his patrol car. What was going on with Moira? He'd thought they'd hit it off great, thought she was interested. She'd sure kissed him like she was interested. Now it looked like she was trying to avoid seeing him.

What was with women? Why couldn't they send out clear signals?

Okay, who was he kidding? That had been a pretty clear signal. *No time for you, Victor.*

But why? What had he done?

He drove down Harbor Boulevard toward town and pulled off on a side street to run radar. It didn't take him long to catch a speeder. Willie Winkle in his souped-up truck was going fifteen over the limit. Willie was into cage fighting, cars and speeding—maybe trying to compensate for his name?

No matter. You didn't get to compensate by breaking the law.

Victor pulled him over and gave him a ticket.

"Man, this sucks," Willie complained.

Yeah, well, life sucked. *Welcome to the club.*

Life wasn't all bad. Moira was happy with how well things were going at Waves. Clients had already been coming in to check out the salon's new look, and everyone was excited to attend the grand reopening party. No surprise. It was going to be a major event.

Moira did get one surprise, though. Pete Long showed up at the salon. He entered like a man stepping from a spaceship onto a foreign planet, looking around cautiously, waiting for something to get him.

"What can we do for you?" Pearl asked him.

"Edie sent me to see Moira," he said, sounding half-resentful. "I'm Pete."

"Oh, Edie's wonderful Pete. She's told me so much about you. And she's right. You are a handsome devil." Pearl really knew how to lay it on thick.

"Well." Was that embarrassment Moira saw on the crusty old guy's face? "I don't know about that. I was something in my day."

"Your day's not over yet. Moira's almost done. She'll be with you in a minute."

"Good luck with that one," murmured Cindy Redmond, who was in Moira's chair.

"I know, right?" But Moira could see beyond the scruff. Pete probably had been something when he was young. A decent haircut and a shave, some nice clothes and he'd look pretty good. She intended to do her best, for sure.

She finished up with Cindy and sent her on her way, then turned her attention to the ugly duckling she intended to turn into a swan prince.

"Pete, come on over," she called.

He came, dragging his feet all the way. "Edie said she won't go to this party with me if I don't have you fix me up," he said sourly. "I don't even want to go," he muttered. "Just offered to take her to be nice."

"It's very chivalrous of you," Moira said. Another favorite word. She'd sure never used it to describe Lang.

"You're not gonna do some weird hair color thing, right? Just a haircut. I don't want to look all prissy."

"Just a haircut," she promised. "And I imagine you can do your own shave."

"I can."

She led him to the pink shampoo bowl and he frowned and shook his head. "Never thought I'd see the day."

"I won't tell," Moira said.

"Just a trim," he said once he was back in the chair. "Trust me."

"I don't."

"Well, you're going to have to," she said, and began to snip.

"You know, I was damn good-looking in my day," he said again as she worked.

"I'm sure you were," Moira said diplomatically.

He fell silent a moment, then said, "Edie wants me to dress up."

"Would you like me to go shopping with you?" Moira offered.

He frowned. "I draw the line at women picking out my clothes for me. Anyway, I've got a suit. Had it for years. Still fits."

Who knew? Maybe enough time had passed that Pete's suit had cycled back into fashion again.

"Used to wear it when I went dancing at the disco."

Or not. Edie wouldn't care. She'd simply be happy that he'd dressed up and cleaned up. And who knew what she'd wear?

Twenty minutes later Moira was finished. She watched

as Pete checked himself out in the mirror. He nodded slowly. "Not bad."

It was the highest praise she'd get. "Edie will like it," she said, and he smiled.

"Once he's scraped off the gray bristle and is in some nice clothes, he'll look pretty good," Pearl said to Moira after he'd left.

"Not quite Sam Elliott."

"Who told him he'd look like Sam Elliott?"

"Me."

Pearl snickered. "Whatever it takes. In his mind, I'm sure he looks better. Unlike us, men always look in the mirror and see what they want to see."

"Just so long as Edie likes what she sees," Moira said.

"She already does. This will be a bonus." Pearl smiled as another car pulled up in their little parking lot. "And here comes another customer. At the rate we're going, everyone will have seen the salon's new look before our party."

"We're the hot new thing," Moira said.

"Let's hope we stay hot. I have to pay off that flooring."

Flooring Moira had talked her into getting. She sure hoped the party would be a success and that their business would grow.

The party was definitely a success. Waves was packed with women enjoying white wine, the cookies Edie Patterson had made and an appetizer Annie Albright had contributed, one of her specialties—cucumber slices topped with a dab of goat cheese and a green olive slice.

Annie had finally worked up the nerve to let Moira color her hair and the pastel green with lavender lowlights worked beautifully with her delicate skin tone. She'd allowed Emma to enjoy a temporary new look via colored hair wax. Moira had mixed in green and blue and then braided her hair in a mini-version of the elegant braid she'd done for Courtney and the little girl was enjoying being with the grown-ups, preening and collecting compliments.

"I'm next," Nora said. "I want to start experimenting now so I'll look great for my party."

Susan Frank, the sourpuss Moira had encountered when she first walked into Waves, was standing nearby with a plate filled with cookies. She did an eye roll and shook her head. "Don't you think you're a little old for that, Nora?"

She said it just as Pearl joined them. "Since when is there an age limit on looking good?" Pearl demanded. With her classy new haircut and color along with the basic black dress, heels and a green scarf, she was the picture of sophistication.

"I'm just saying," Susan began, then stumbled to a halt.

Pearl cocked an eyebrow. "Yes? What were you saying?"

"We should leave some of these styles to the younger women."

"Why should they have all the fun?" Nora demanded. "I'm not in my grave yet."

"Me, either," said Pearl. "Don't be such an age bigot, Susan."

Susan shut up.

"How much do you charge for one of those fancy hair colors?" asked a woman who'd introduced herself as Jo. Moira told her and Jo, also, shut up.

Arlene was there with a slender woman around Moira's age, who she introduced as her daughter, Shay.

The woman wore her hair chin-length, styled in beachy waves. The color was a solid purple—not much subtlety or artistry there.

"I'm really happy Pearl's brought in somebody who can do colors," she said to Moira.

"It's my specialty," Moira told her.

"I think I'd like to try something different."

A good idea.

"Shay's such a pretty girl," said her proud mama. "I can hardly wait to see what you come up with for her."

She was indeed pretty. And kindhearted, having shown up with a hostess gift of wine for Pearl.

"Maybe I'll have to try something different," said Edie, who was standing nearby. She'd dug out a green sheath from the sixties that smelled strongly of... What was that?

"Mothballs," Pearl whispered.

Well, at least she looked cute. She'd accented her dress with vintage rhinestone jewelry and a corsage that Pete had given her, and was beaming like a debutante. Pete, at her side, looked dated but almost debonair in his John Travolta–wannabe suit.

"I think a change would be good," Pearl said. "What do you think, Moira?"

"Not silver," Edie said firmly. "I don't want to look like an old lady."

"You shouldn't change a thing," Pete said. "You look good just the way you are, Edie, old girl."

She beamed at him. "Really?"

"Really. I like the natural look."

As if there was anything natural about Edie Patterson's hair. But Moira could tell by the smile on Edie's face that she wouldn't be coming in to make any hair color changes.

Jenna Jones hadn't made the leap into a new hairstyle. "But I'm thinking about it," she said.

Moira suspected that, like her aunt, she wouldn't make any radical changes. She'd stick to her blond highlights. And that was okay. Moira did those, too.

"Even if you want to keep the style and color you've got, I can maintain it for you," she said to Jenna. "And I really want to be able to pay you back for how you helped me when I first got here."

"No need. We were happy to. But I might take you up on your offer. By the way, you did a nice job on Pete."

Their conversation was interrupted by the approach of two women; one, with gorgeous long dark hair, was dressed to kill in a black twist-front jumpsuit accented with a green silk scarf. The other was a woman with unremarkable brown hair and big brown eyes. She wore leggings and a long, loose-fitting top that did nothing to show off what curves she had.

"I'm Bethany," announced the stylish one. "I dragged Hyacinth here. She needs help."

Hyacinth's face bloomed red.

"Hyacinth owns the quilt shop here in town," Jenna said.

"She's brilliant at quilts," put in Bethany, redeeming herself. Then she added, "But she needs major style help. If she wants a certain someone to wake up and see her."

Jenna, for some reason, suddenly looked a little uncomfortable. "Oh, there's Tyrella," she said and slipped away.

"What can you do for my friend?" Bethany demanded.

"We can do anything you like," Moira said to Hyacinth.

"Never mind what she likes. Make her hot," said her bossy friend, and Hyacinth's face got even more red.

"How about coming in for a consult?" Moira suggested.

Hyacinth nodded and Moira suggested a day. "You can come in after you close your shop."

"I can't come that late. Tyler's got a game," Bethany lamented.

"Does that day work for you?" Moira asked Hyacinth, ignoring Bethany.

Hyacinth nodded.

Moira had a feeling she and Hyacinth would make much better progress without her overbearing friend along. "Good. See you then."

Pearl was summoning Moira, so she excused herself and left the two friends. As she moved away, she could hear Bethany saying, "I wish you'd picked a time when I could come with you."

Moira was more than willing to bet that Hyacinth had been delighted to pick a time when her friend couldn't come with her.

She joined Pearl, who was standing with Courtney and Annie and a cute thirtysomething guy with glasses. He was wearing a casual shirt, expensive jeans and flip-flops.

"Moira, this is Aaron Baumgarten. He writes for *The Beach Times*. I've been telling him about you and we're talking about featuring you in an article."

"Me?" Moira had never been featured in anything. She could feel her head swelling like a balloon under a good blast of helium.

"We can call it something like 'Bringing New Colors to Moonlight Harbor,'" Aaron said. "How about it?"

"It will be great promotion for the salon," Pearl added.

"Sure," Moira said, beaming. She was all about helping the salon.

Aaron happened to have a photographer with him and

they posed Moira in the middle of the women whose hair she'd colored, including Pearl.

"How long have you been in Moonlight Harbor?" Aaron wanted to know.

"I came in February," she said.

"From?"

"Seattle."

"You're a pretty long way from the city," he observed. "What made you choose Moonlight Harbor?"

As if she'd even heard of the town. "A friend recommended it." God bless him.

"Are you liking it here?"

"No. I'm loving it here. I think I've found my forever home."

"I bet a lot of people will be happy to hear that," he said.

He was awfully cute. And a journalist, so obviously smart. No ring on his left hand. But Moira didn't really care if he had a girlfriend or not. She told herself that was because she was taking her time, but she knew it had more to do with a certain cop.

"Just think," said Courtney after Aaron left the party, "you're going to be famous."

Famous. Wait a minute. Famous, as in Lang could hear about her?

"Oh, no," she said faintly.

"What?" asked Courtney. "What's wrong?"

"I don't want my ex to see that article."

"It's only a small-town paper," Courtney said.

"But they have an online edition," Annie added, and the three women exchanged concerned looks.

"Pearl will call Aaron and tell him not to do it," Courtney said.

Pearl had been so excited, though. And really, after a month, would Lang even be looking for her? He'd have moved on, already found some other woman to make miserable.

"I'm probably being paranoid," Moira decided. "I mean, really, who's going to pay attention to a small-town newspaper?"

"Right," agreed Courtney.

Still, Moira couldn't help feeling uneasy. She forced herself to smile through the rest of the afternoon and get into the spirit of the thing when it was time to draw a name for the grand prize.

"And the winner is Susan Frank," she announced after drawing Susan's ticket from the giant fishbowl. The announcement got a half-hearted smattering of applause. Susan was obviously not the most popular girl in town.

"I thought you weren't into colors," Nora said to her. "Why on earth did you put your name in the drawing?"

"Why not?" Susan retorted. "I can always give it away at the shop."

Giving away a giveaway.

"Tacky," whispered Pearl after she'd handed Susan the certificate.

The grand-prize drawing pretty much signaled the end of the event and people began to drift away, many making appointments with Moira for haircuts and color consults before they left. Pearl was ecstatic.

Moira was happy for her boss, of course, but that happiness was tarnished with worry.

Back at the house that night, she barely paid attention when they all watched a rom-com Courtney had guaranteed would make them laugh. Courtney and Annie laughed. Moira did a little. When her attention wasn't wandering. It was hard not to look back at how scary her life had been. Now that she was away from it, she marveled that she'd been able to downplay her situation in her mind, at how she'd hung on to a bad relationship like it was a life raft in a stormy sea. The relationship itself had been the stormy sea. She didn't want to reenter it.

But Lang had his smooth lines down pat. He wouldn't have sat around waiting for her to come back. He'd have moved on. He was good-looking and he made good money. He'd have no trouble luring another woman into his web.

Where he'd then devour her soul. Moira couldn't help but feel sorry for whoever came after her. She should have reported his abuse, at least the physical abuse. Now maybe some other woman was suffering all because she hadn't stood up to him and stopped him.

They were almost to the end of the movie when someone banged on the door. Moira jumped and let out a squeak, making Harry jump off her lap onto the floor. "Who's that?"

"Annie!" bellowed a male voice. "Annie, you need to come home."

"Here we go again," muttered Courtney. She went to the window and twitched the curtain a crack. "His truck's not out there. He must have walked. Or staggered. Can't get him on a DUI."

The doorbell began an incessant ringing. "Annie!" This was followed by more banging on the door. "Let me in. We need to talk."

"Can the police arrest him for being drunk and out of control?" Moira suggested.

"We don't have a drunk-in-public law in Washington," Courtney said.

"Annie, you bitch! Let me in or I'm breaking down this door."

Annie was shrinking in on herself, hugging a pillow. "There's no controlling him when he gets like this," she said, her voice agitated.

"Oh, yes, there is," Courtney said and grabbed her phone. "He just crossed the line into disorderly conduct, and we do have a law against that. I think it's time for Greg to spend a night in jail."

Sixteen

In a matter of minutes they could see the flashing lights outside, and then heard the voices.

Especially Greg's. "I'm not doing anything!" he yelled. "My wife won't let me in."

At that, Courtney yanked open her front door. "That's because this is my house and I don't want you in it. He threatened to kick the door in," she told Victor King, who was standing next to Greg and looked like he already had everything well in hand.

"You need to butt your big nose out of this, Courtney," Greg shouted, pointing a finger at her.

"And you need a time-out," Victor said and started leading him to the patrol car. All the while, Greg was protesting that he only wanted to see his wife.

"Thanks, Victor," Courtney called.

"That's what we're here for," he called back.

"He's the best," she said as she shut the door.

Yep, thought Moira, girlfriend code firmly in place.

Annie hadn't moved from the couch. She was looking ready to cry. Now she stood and murmured, "I'd better go check on Emma."

Courtney returned to the living room, plopped back on the couch next to Moira and shook her head. "I swear, that man is the biggest loser."

"I can think of a bigger one," Moira said and drained the last of her white wine. "Why do we pick men like that?"

"Fantasy," Courtney said. "We like to think whoever we fall for is perfect for us. Once you do that, it's pretty hard to unthink it."

"You don't always see behind the mask," Moira said. In her own defense or Annie's? Maybe both.

"True. I mean who says on a first date, I'm a shit and I'll make your life miserable. Wanna hook up?" Annie came back into the room. "How is she?" Courtney asked.

"She slept through the whole thing, thank God. I swear, she could sleep through an earthquake." Annie frowned. "Of course, she'll want to see him tomorrow and he'll pretend everything's fine and I'll look like Bad Mommy."

"Hard stuff," Courtney said. "But you've got to stop giving him chance after chance. Pull the Band-Aid off quick and be done with it."

Annie sighed. "Then if he does finally get straight and we're not together, Emma will never forgive me."

"You're not exactly together now," Courtney pointed out, making her friend frown. "I don't see him coming around."

"I can't give up. Not yet," Annie said. "When he sees I'm not coming back until he really changes…"

She hesitated and Courtney completed her sentence. "He'll still be a selfish jerk."

"It's hard," said Moira. "You keep hoping things will be different."

"People don't change," Courtney said.

Moira sure hoped that wasn't true. She liked to think she

was becoming stronger, more her own person. She liked to think if she ever saw Lang again, she'd stand up to him and tell him what a pool of puke he was.

Annie heaved a sigh and dug a handful of M&M's out of the bowl on the coffee table. "I hate my life."

"Don't go there," Courtney said firmly. "You are doing good things with your life. Don't let his screw-ups overshadow that."

Good advice, thought Moira. Past mistakes didn't have to mean future mistakes. Lang had been a bad dream, but the dream was over.

Try telling that to her subconscious. Once she fell asleep, there he was, finding her on the dance floor in the club in Seattle where they'd first met. She was all by herself in the crowd, looking around for…someone. Whom she wasn't exactly sure. And then he appeared at her side in his expensive shirt and designer jeans.

He slipped an arm around her and drew her close. "You've missed me, haven't you missed the good times we had together?"

"We haven't had a good time together in a long time," she informed him.

"That can change. Come back, Moira." He started them slow dancing. "Haven't you missed this?" he whispered.

She woke up before she could answer. She had missed being close to someone, having a man's arms around her. But not him and not his arms.

Harry had been sleeping at her feet, but when she stirred he stretched and walked up the couch to sit on her chest, assuming that, of course, if she was awake, she wanted to pet him.

Because she was a well-trained cat owner, she obliged.

"We're so much better off where we are, aren't we?" Even if they were sleeping on a living room sofa.

Harry purred in agreement.

Moira went back to sleep and didn't dream about Lang again. Maybe her subconscious was finally getting the message.

By the time she awoke the next morning, Courtney had gone off to pull her Sunday morning shift at the Driftwood Inn. As she and Annie enjoyed a leisurely breakfast with Emma, she couldn't help feeling grateful for the positive turn her life had taken and the good place she'd landed in.

Emma was upstairs, brushing her teeth, and Annie and Moira were lingering over a second mug of morning coffee when someone knocked on the door. Moira hadn't been expecting anyone. She shot a look Annie's direction in. *Your husband?*

Annie shook her head.

Right. It was too early for a hungover man to be up, especially if the police had hauled him off to spend the night in jail.

Moira went to the door and discovered Victor standing on the front porch, wearing jeans, sneakers and a windbreaker. "I'm stopping by to see how Annie's doing," he said.

"That's really kind of you. Is that part of the job?" Moira asked, stepping aside to let him in.

"We go above and beyond here in Moonlight Harbor."

Moira led the way into the kitchen, aware of him behind her with every step and wishing she'd be line dancing with him that night. "Someone to see you," she said to Annie and couldn't help wishing Victor had been there to see her.

"I just wanted to check on you and make sure you're doing okay," he said to Annie.

"I'm okay. Where's Greg?"

"Back home now. He spent the night in jail and we ticketed him."

"Is he going to need a lawyer?" Annie asked. She looked ready to cry.

"When we left, he was threatening to get one and sue the police department."

"I'm sorry," she said.

"It's not your fault, Annie. You shouldn't be the one apologizing."

She bit her lip and didn't say anything.

"Why was it Courtney who called us last night and not you?" he asked.

"She acted faster than me," Annie said.

"So, would you have called us?" Annie hesitated and he frowned. "You can't let him get away with this stuff. It doesn't help anyone. It especially doesn't help him."

"I know," she said, her voice barely above a whisper.

"Let him hit bottom, hard. It might be enough to make him want to change."

She looked at him hopefully. "Do you think so?"

"People are different," came the nonanswer. "All I can tell you for sure is I'd better not catch him behind the wheel in that condition. We don't put up with drunk driving."

There was an uncomfortable moment of silence in the room before Victor cleared his throat and said, "Guess I'll be going."

"Thanks for coming by," Moira said and walked him to the door.

"You coming to line dancing tonight?" he asked.

Just tell him. "I'm not sure. We've got a lot going on here."

"So, really that means no, huh?"

"It's just that—"

"Just that what?"

Emma chose that moment to bound down the stairs, hairbrush in hand, obviously wanting Moira to help her style her hair. At the sight of Victor she said a shy hello, then parked on the bottom stair, waiting for Moira. It wasn't the right time for the kind of conversation she and Victor needed to have.

"Come tonight," he urged. "Annie will be fine without you."

"Thanks for stopping by," she said, determined not to commit herself.

Victor left but thoughts of him remained in Moira's mind as she styled Emma's hair. She wished she was the kind of woman who had no boundaries, who could easily rationalize cutting another woman out of a relationship. But she wasn't and she couldn't, and that was that.

She finished with Emma's hair, then went back into the kitchen to load the morning dishes in the dishwasher, although she suspected Annie would have beaten her to it. Annie didn't like a messy kitchen.

Sure enough, all signs of breakfast had already been removed and Annie was now busy putting together an appetizer plate for another website photo.

Emma got her mother's phone and took a selfie, then sent it to her dad, along with a text. "We are going to see Daddy later today, right?" she asked her mother.

"If he can make it," Annie said evasively.

Moira doubted he'd make it.

"Meanwhile, how about getting your math homework done?" Annie suggested.

Emma looked far from thrilled at the prospect of homework, but she took herself off to the living room to plop on the couch with Harry to help her with her math assignment.

"Victor's right," Annie said in a low voice after she left. "I need to let Greg fall hard. I'm giving him an ultimatum. He has until May 1 to get checked into rehab. If he can't pull himself together by then, I'm filing for divorce."

Moira didn't know what to say other than "I'm sorry."

Annie sighed. "Me, too. But I've had enough. If it wasn't for Emma, I'd cut him completely out of my life. He's a psychic anchor."

"That was my ex, too. I'm glad I'm free of him. I don't have a kid, though."

"That complicates things, but I sure don't regret having Emma. She's the one good thing that's come out of my marriage." Annie sighed. "I wish we could give her the kind of family she deserves."

"She's got a good family. You."

Annie did smile at that. "Thanks. I'm going to do the best I can to give her the security she deserves. I'm going to launch my catering business at Nora's party and then I'm moving forward with getting my food truck. I'm going to apply for a Blue Moon grant."

"What's that?"

"It's money from a special fund set up by the local business owners. It's meant to help people who are trying to set up a new business here in town or who are struggling to stay in the black. The deadline to apply is the end of this month. I'm downloading the forms and filling them out today."

"I think that's great," Moira said.

"I've waited too long. Victor's right about letting Greg hit bottom. Maybe if he sinks low enough, he'll figure out that he's drowning. But I can't afford to drown with him. Someone has to give Emma the kind of life she deserves."

Where had this Annie come from all of a sudden? Magic. Instant Warrior Princess. The Annie of the night before, of only a few minutes before, had been shy and a little timid. This Annie was determined.

Moira realized that was how it had happened for her. One minute she was afraid to leave Lang, the next she was packing her things. Everyone had a tipping point.

"If I get the grant, I can maybe open my food truck by the Fourth of July," Annie said.

"I think that's a great idea." Muriel Sterling would approve.

"How are you doing with your goals?" Moira read later when Annie and Emma were at the grocery store and Courtney was off at The Drunken Sailor.

Good. Her life was on track. All except her love life. She frowned, shut Muriel's book and dug out her romance novel.

She was still reading when Courtney finally came in that night and plopped onto a chair, stretching her legs out. She wore a frayed denim shirt with buttons shaped like clams—one of her designs. The buttons didn't show up to do their job until they met with the top of her lacy black bra. Her hair was still braided and she wore dangly geometric-shaped earrings. Her legs were wrapped in tight jeans and red cowgirl boots. Call that style Urban Beach Ranch. No, call it sexy. Courtney had the kind of long, lean legs men loved and women envied. Knowing where she'd been and who she'd been with, Moira felt a disloyal stab of envy.

"That was fun," Courtney announced with a satisfied smile. "You should have come."

And tortured herself watching Courtney flirt with Victor. "That's okay. I was fine here."

Annie, who'd been out in the kitchen whipping up hot chocolate, came out bearing mugs for herself and Moira.

"Want me to make you some?" she asked Courtney, handing Moira hers.

"No. I'm too hot."

Yes, she was. How could any man resist a woman who looked that good? Moira took a sip of her hot chocolate. It didn't taste as good as she'd thought it would. She set the mug on the coffee table.

"How'd it go?" Annie asked. "Has Victor fallen at your feet yet?"

Courtney made a face. "Ha ha, so funny."

"I take it that's a no," Annie murmured.

"He will," Courtney insisted.

"If he was going to, don't you think he would have by now?" Annie reasoned.

Good point. Give it up, Courtney. Please.

"It takes some men a while to figure out what they want," Courtney insisted.

It hadn't felt like that when Moira was with him. He'd made it pretty clear what he wanted when they'd kissed.

"Maybe he's not the one for you," she ventured. No hidden agenda there.

Courtney's brows pulled together and she frowned.

"There are other men in Moonlight Harbor," Annie said.

"None like Victor," Courtney said. "He's one of a kind."

He sure was.

"Anyway, we're already friends. It's only a matter of time until chemistry takes over."

It was a very disloyal thought, she knew, but Moira hoped Courtney would flunk chemistry.

* * *

Moira had no love life, but at least she had the distraction of work. And that was a pretty big distraction. Ever since the grand reopening, the phone at Waves Salon had been ringing off the hook with women wanting their hair done. One of Moira's first new clients was, surprisingly, the cranky Susan Frank.

"I thought you were going to give away your prize," Pearl taunted her.

Susan frowned and shrugged. "Figured I might as well use it. But I'm not doing anything crazy," she was quick to add.

"What would you like me to do for you?" Moira asked her.

"I want to look like Marilyn Monroe."

"Marilyn...Monroe?" Moira stuttered.

"You can do that, can't you?" Susan dared.

"Sure, no problem. I mean, I can make your hair look just like that." The body and face were another matter.

"Well, then, do it," Susan commanded and settled in for an afternoon of transformation.

The hair turned out perfect. There wasn't anything Moira could do for the face under it. Susan Frank simply wasn't a Marilyn Monroe look-alike.

But she gave Moira a five-dollar tip and left wearing something very unusual for her. A smile.

"Now I've seen everything," Pearl said as Susan got into her car. "I guess we'll have to start calling her Marilyn."

Next came Hyacinth Brown.

"I think we can do a lot with your hair," Moira had told her when they had their consultation. "You've got a really pretty face. We just need to bring it to life."

They needed to bring Hyacinth to life, too. As Moira

worked on her, she struggled to keep their conversation going. Yes, Hyacinth liked Moonlight Harbor. Yes, her quilt shop was doing well.

"I admire anybody who can put together all those colors and come up with a work of art," Moira said.

"It's not that hard," Hyacinth demurred.

"So, when you're not quilting, what do you do for fun?"

Long pause. Was *fun* a foreign word to this woman?

"I like to read," Hyacinth finally offered. "And I garden. I do the flowers for church."

Church. That was something Moira hadn't done. As for flowers, she wasn't quite there yet. But reading. Okay, they had just stepped onto common ground.

"Me, too. What do you like to read?" she asked.

Hyacinth's cheeks turned pink. "I like to read romance novels," she said, her voice lowered. Her gaze darted to where Pearl was working on Arlene's hair. They were absorbed in their own conversation.

"Me, too," Moira said. "Especially the ones with lots of hot sex."

Hyacinth's cheeks went from pink to red.

"You don't do sex?" Moira guessed.

"I'd like to." Okay, judging from how deep the red had just gotten, that was top secret information. "With my husband," she added. "If I was married."

"Are you seeing anyone special?" Moira asked.

Hyacinth looked down at her lap. "No."

"Well, the right man will come along. Once we get your hair done…"

"I don't think he's into hair."

So there was someone.

"I mean…" Hyacinth stopped and chewed her lip.

"There's someone you're interested in?"

This triggered a huge sigh. "It's hopeless."

Moira knew how she felt. That was the word that came to mind whenever she thought of Victor.

"It's never hopeless," she lied.

"This is. I don't even know why I'm bothering."

"Because you want to look good. Nothing wrong with that. So, this man, is he someone I might have met?"

Hyacinth clamped her lips together, determined not to say another word.

"You don't have to tell me if you don't want to, but you should know I don't gossip."

"You're the only woman in town who doesn't, then," Hyacinth said, sounding bitter. "I can't believe no one's told you about me and Pastor Paul." A fresh red tide swept up over her face.

"Oh, it's your pastor? That sounds like a good choice," Moira said diplomatically, as she applied more color.

Hyacinth shook her head, nearly pulling free the strand of hair Moira held. She looked ready to cry.

"It can't be that bad," Moira said gently.

"Yes, it c-c-can." Hyacinth was half sobbing now.

"What the hell happened?" Moira demanded, then realized she was talking to a church chick. "Sorry."

"I said something at his wedding."

"He's married?" This was so confusing.

"He was trying to get married. You know that part where the minister asks if anyone knows a reason why the people shouldn't be together?"

"Oh, no," Moira said. "Were you the one?"

"She wasn't right for him," Hyacinth said, a sudden fire in her voice. "She didn't really love him. Otherwise she'd have stayed."

"She left?"

"Ran back down the aisle. He was so mad at me."

"Whew! That had to be hard."

"I didn't want to do it. But I didn't want to see him miserable for the rest of his life, either."

"Is he still mad at you?"

"No. He forgave me. But he still doesn't want me. I guess I can't blame him. I ruined his life."

"Sounds to me like you saved it," Moira said.

"He doesn't even see me. He never really has."

Maybe you haven't given him anything to see. Moira decided not to voice that thought.

"I shouldn't have told you all this," Hyacinth muttered.

"People tell their stylists all kinds of things," Moira said. "Don't worry. I'm on your side. And wait till you see how great you look when we're done here."

"It probably won't make any difference." This woman was a regular Eeyore.

"Don't be so sure. If there's one thing I've learned over the years, it's that men like women who look good."

"Paul's a pastor," Hyacinth said, as if that made him exempt from the temptations of lesser men.

"He's still a man and he's got hormones and eyes."

"He's not that superficial," Hyacinth insisted.

"And I'm sure he appreciates you for you. But you want him to do more than appreciate you, right? So doing something to grab his attention might be just what you need. Hair, makeup, maybe a new outfit. He'll appreciate that. And so will you. When we look good, we feel good about ourselves and we even act different."

"I'm not that pretty," Hyacinth said, determined to be down on herself.

"Yes, you are. You'll see."

Moira not only turned Hyacinth's hair a mix of lavender and pink, she also showed Hyacinth how to update her makeup. When they were finished, Hyacinth stared at her reflection and smiled.

"Wow," she breathed.

"Yeah, wow," agreed Moira. "Look, I don't go to church and I don't know anything about pastors, but I know about beauty. People are attracted to it. You seem like you're already beautiful on the inside. You just had a disconnect with the outside. Now they both match. I think your pastor might appreciate that."

Hyacinth cocked her head and studied her face. "Even if he doesn't, I do. Thank you so much."

"Hey, it's what I do," Moira said. "I'm into clothes, too, if you ever want to go shopping."

"I'm not much of a shopper."

Moira could tell. "I am. How about a run to Aberdeen one day this week? I saw a Ross Dress for Less there, and I've been meaning to check it out."

"Oh, I don't know."

"It'll be fun." Hyacinth hesitated and Moira, determined to help her, pushed. "How about tomorrow? I don't have any clients until two. Close your quilt shop for lunch and I promise I'll have you back by one thirty. What do you say?"

Hyacinth said a reluctant yes.

The next day Moira drove Hyacinth to the nearby town of Aberdeen to hunt for the perfect outfit to go with her new hair. They found a dress with vintage flair that made her look like a heroine from a fifties movie—sweet and innocent but still a little bit sexy.

"Wear that to church," Moira suggested.

Hyacinth looked doubtful. "It's kind of short."

"It's just right. Trust me. Wear it this Sunday and see what your friends think. I bet nobody will say it's too short."

But it was flirty and Hyacinth looked killer in it. Moira also talked her into buying a coral-colored sweater to go with it and some attention-grabbing heels. Pastor or not, this guy she was crazy about was still a man. And men thought with their eyes. (Not to mention other body parts.) Hyacinth was a sweet woman. She deserved a second chance.

Everyone deserved a second chance.

On Friday Nora came in for a hair makeover before her big birthday party. She also brought a copy of the newspaper to show to Pearl and Moira. "Look, you're famous."

They sure were. There was a picture of the salon and the one the photographer had taken of Moira and Pearl and the other hair models. Large as life.

It's only a little local paper, Moira assured herself. *Nobody in Seattle's going to see it.*

But what if somebody did?

Seventeen

Moira decided she was being paranoid. She couldn't keep looking back over her shoulder. Lang was miles away and a lifetime ago. This was a new life and the road to happiness was clear. Well, clear except for the detour sign hanging over her love life.

There had to be more good men out there besides Victor King. Annie had said as much. Moira would find one eventually.

Although, really, she'd probably never find one who measured up to him.

At least things were looking up for Hyacinth. Moira had just finished a late-afternoon color consult with Cindy Redmond when Hyacinth slipped into the salon and took a seat.

"Hyacinth, what can we do for you?" Pearl asked, coming over to greet her.

"I just wanted to see Moira for a minute. When she's done."

It wasn't hard to tell why. She had good news written all over her face. Sure enough, after Cindy left, Hyacinth pulled Moira outside the salon and announced, "We went out for coffee."

"That's awesome. How'd it go?"

"Great. He'd said he wanted to talk to me about helping with the flowers for the church anniversary, but then we got to talking about other things."

"Like what?"

"Church in general and how hard it can be to do the right thing. He actually admitted I was right when, um... Well, that I was right about him and Celeste."

"Celeste," Moira repeated, trying to place the name with a face.

"Jenna's sister. She doesn't live here. She just comes down to visit."

Jenna's sister. That explained Jenna's sudden desire to adios across the room when Hyacinth's friend had made mention of a certain someone at the salon's grand reopening party. The certain someone had almost married the man of Hyacinth's dreams. Awkward.

"What did you say?" Moira asked, returning them to the main topic.

"I said what I'd said to him before, that I was really sorry and I'd only been trying to save him from making a horrible mistake."

"And he said?"

"That I was probably right and things had worked out the way they were supposed to. Then he asked me what kind of woman I think he should be with." Hyacinth's face turned pink.

"I hope you told him you."

She shook her head. "No, I told him that he needs someone who shares his vision for the church and who would work by his side and always support him. And that he should have someone who really, truly loves the same things he did, like baseball."

"I take it he likes baseball."

"Yes."

"And you like baseball, too?"

"Of course I do." Hyacinth said, shocked at the implication that she'd fake liking something to get a man.

"Did he say anything about your hair?"

"He did say he liked it."

Moira grinned. "Told you."

Hyacinth shook her head. "I don't think it was just about a new hairstyle, though. Not for him, anyway. I think this was about, well, a new me. Maybe making some changes gave me the courage to let more of my real self show." She took a sudden interest in her feet. Those shoes. They needed to expand her shoe wardrobe. "I'm kind of shy. It's hard for me to put myself out there. I think maybe doing something crazy with my hair gave me permission to be a little more brave."

Like standing up at someone's wedding and announcing it was a mistake didn't count as brave. Maybe that wouldn't be a good thing to point out. Moira could tell Hyacinth still felt awful about what she'd done, even though she'd been convinced she'd done the right thing.

Doing the right thing sure was hard sometimes.

"I'm glad," Moira said. "Did he ask you out?"

"Not exactly. But he was impressed by how many baseball stats I know."

"That's a good beginning." At least Moira hoped it was. She'd done all she could. The rest was up to Hyacinth. "At least you're in the game," she said, deciding a baseball metaphor would be appropriate. "So keep swinging."

"I will," Hyacinth said. "Thank you for all your help. It's a little scary stepping out of your comfort zone."

"But so worth it, right? And no need to thank me. Just name your first child after me," Moira quipped, making Hyacinth blush.

Good heavens, Moira didn't know anyone who blushed as much as Hyacinth.

Except... *No, don't go there.*

The whole Victor thing had been short-lived. He didn't come back in for a haircut and she stayed away from The Drunken Sailor. *All for the best,* she kept telling herself.

Her stupid heart wasn't getting the message, though, and went all googly wonkers when he stopped to help her change a flat tire on a rainy Sunday afternoon. The very sight of him started it skipping. *Zippity woo-hoo!*

She was on her way back to the house with a quart of Deer Poop ice cream from Good Times Ice Cream Parlor when her tire blew. She'd gotten as far as getting out the car jack and staring at it, trying to give herself a mental refresher course on tire changing when his truck pulled up behind her.

"Need a hand?"

"That would be great. I haven't changed a tire since driver's ed."

"Not much to it, but lug nuts can be hard to get off," he said and took the jack from her. "You don't want to be standing out in this rain."

He was right. She didn't. She was already shivering. But it probably wasn't the nippy wet air that was causing those shivers.

"Why don't you wait in my truck?"

She nodded and hurried to his truck and got in. It smelled like pine from the air freshener hanging on the rearview mirror and aftershave. She wished she could just stay in the truck, drive back to his rustic log cabin and snuggle up next to him on that comfy couch of his. Darn it all, he still hadn't asked Courtney out. Maybe he never would and all this nobility on Moira's part would be wasted.

She watched as he worked, the rain pelting him. He was wearing a jacket, but his jeans were getting wet. He'd have to go home and get out of those wet clothes. Take 'em all off.

Stop that!

Moira sighed. She didn't want to stop that. She wanted to go home with Victor and help him strip off those pants and whatever was underneath. Boxers? Yes, he probably wore boxers.

Another sigh. If only Courtney would hurry up and get together with him and put Moira out of her misery.

Like that would help.

Why weren't there more Victor Kings in the world? Why couldn't they clone him? Courtney could have the clone.

He finished his job and she hopped out of the truck, getting back to her car as he was putting the flat tire in the trunk. "Thank you so much. You saved me."

"I'm happy to do it."

Do it. Oh, yes, she'd like to do it with him. *Stop it, stop it, STOP IT!*

He put the jack back in the trunk and shut it.

"Well, thanks again," she said. "If I was a decent baker I'd bake you cookies."

"I don't need cookies from you. What I need to know is what happened."

She played dumb. "What happened?"

"I thought we were at least friends."

"We are."

"Then how come you stopped coming to The Drunken Sailor? How come you've ignored my phone calls? How come I'm getting these weird vibes?"

"I'm sorry if I'm being weird. I just can't start something."

"Every guy isn't out to mess you over, Moira."

"I know."

"Then why don't you at least give us a chance?"

"I can't. I just can't."

"But why?"

"Trust me. I've got my reasons. Look, I need to get going. My ice cream's melting."

He frowned. "Okay, fine. But I'm not giving up. It felt too right between us to do that."

Oh, great. If he was so fixated on her, he'd never go for Courtney. What a loss all the way around.

"There are other women in Moonlight Harbor, you know."

"Yeah, but they're not you."

Well, shit. "I've got to go," she said and got in her car and shut the door. Then she drove off, not even waving at him because that would look too friendly.

Darn it all. She wanted to be friendly with Victor.

By the time she got to the house the ice cream was soup and she was feeling cranky. Then guilty when Courtney, who'd just gotten in from her shift at the Driftwood Inn, said, "Ice cream! I am so glad you're living here."

In a house instead of a motel room—a house where almost every day felt like a party. And that was thanks to Courtney's generosity. Moira would be the bitch queen to betray that generosity.

She held up the bag with the ice cream. "I had a flat tire on the way home. I think it's soup."

Annie was parked on the sofa, working out her menu for Nora's upcoming birthday party. She got up and held out her hand. "We can make a shake out of it."

Moira handed over the bag. "I think it already is."

"I can fix it," Annie said, and Moira had no doubt that she could.

"Poor you," said Courtney. "I'm impressed you could change it. If that happened to me, I'd be calling Triple A."

"I didn't need it. Turned out someone stopped and helped."

"Good deal. Who was it?"

Shit. She should have kept her big mouth shut. "Victor King."

"So you finally met him. Is he fabulous or what?"

"He is." If only he was just "or what." It would be so much easier to give him up.

Emma had heard Moira come in and was now hanging on her, wanting to do manis and pedis. "Sure," she said. Anything was better than talking about Victor with Courtney.

Emma hauled her out to the kitchen, where Annie had the blender whirring, making their milkshakes. "Chocolate syrup, crumbled peanut butter cookies and we're good to go," she announced as she stopped the blender.

"Yummy!" cried Emma.

Milkshakes and nail polish, good distractions from the fact that Emma hadn't seen much of her daddy, who was avoiding them. Annie was hopeful that he was busy trying to get himself back together. Courtney had said she wasn't holding her breath. Moira hoped, for Annie's sake, that Courtney was wrong.

Annie poured her creation into glasses and handed them over. Courtney joined them at the kitchen table. "Oh, yes, this is sooo good," she said after sampling hers. "Good thing I'm going dancing tonight. I'll maybe be able to work off some of this." She turned to Moira. "When are you going to shed your chicken feathers and come with me?"

"Not tonight," Moira said. "Emma and I have to do our nails."

"That won't take long. You can go if you want," Emma offered.

"It's okay. I'd rather stay home and watch a Disney movie with you," Moira told her.

"You need to get a life," Courtney lectured.

"I have a life, a great one."

"I guess, if you want to go forever without se…" Courtney, aware of Emma's presence, switched gears "…seeing anyone."

"She sees us," Emma said.

"And that's plenty of seeing," Moira said and took a big gulp of her milkshake. Sex was overrated.

Yeah, and chocolate tasted nasty.

"I'm not taking no for an answer," Arlene said to Pearl. "Just sitting at home on a Sunday evening is a waste of a makeover. You look sexy. It's time you started showing it off."

"I have been showing it off," Pearl protested.

"To the women who come into the salon? Big deal."

"It is a big deal. My business has nearly doubled since our reopening."

Thanks to Moira. She not only had an eye for color and a gift for working social media, she was also good with the women who came in and her clientele was growing to the point where she was booked out two weeks in advance. In addition to the regulars, Pearl was seeing new, younger faces in the chairs. At the rate they were going, she'd have to hire another stylist come fall.

"There's more to life than work, you know that," Arlene said. "Now, come on, don't be a stick-in-the-mud. This will be fun. Anyway, it's only dinner and you have to eat. Why not eat with us and a nice man?"

"You know I like being with you, but this is silly."

"Meeting new people is never silly. And I promise you'll like Donny's cousin. He's a sweetie."

"I'm not in the market for a man." Romance was for young people. They were the ones who dated, mated and had kids. That was how the cycle of life worked. Once you were old, what was the point?

"Since when is there an age limit on love?" Arlene argued. "Or just plain enjoying life? Come on, girlfriend. This will be good for you."

Since when is there an age limit on looking good? Pearl's words to Susan Frank came back to haunt her. If a woman should be able to enjoy looking good at any age, shouldn't she also be allowed to feel good, too? Did she want to spend the rest of her life feeling bad over the people she'd lost? She had some years left in her. Maybe it was time to follow up that style makeover with a life makeover. Anyway, this wasn't that big of a deal. It was only dinner out.

"All right," she said.

"Good. We'll pick you up at seven."

Seven o'clock. Pearl had two hours to decide on an outfit.

It took the whole two hours. She tried on and discarded so many clothes she had a mini mountain on her bed by six thirty. She finally settled for leggings, boots and a long sweater that she accented with a multilayered boho seashell necklace. A little mascara, some lipstick and she was good to go.

"Not bad," she told her reflection in the bathroom mirror.

Not bad, she told herself when she met Donny's cousin, Devlin Patrick. He was a large man with only a small bit of belly hanging over his belt. He'd dressed casually in jeans and a shirt with a sports coat worn over. His hairline was receding but he still had plenty left—a rusty red, slightly faded by age—and he reminded of her of James Spader with that full mouth and those gorgeous big eyes. Yes, why shouldn't you enjoy life even when you were older?

"Well, hello," he said appreciatively as he opened the car's back door for her to get in.

"Well, hello yourself," she said back, all flirty and silly.

"Donny, you didn't tell me I was going to be meeting a former Miss America," her date said as they made their way to the restaurant.

Oh, brother. What a line. Pearl smiled in spite of herself.

Donny's cousin turned out to be good company. He'd lost his wife a couple of years ago and had a grown daughter who'd married a man almost good enough for her, and they had a son and a teenage daughter who would love to have hair as cool as Pearl's.

"You might have to bring them down here to Moonlight Harbor so we can give your daughter and granddaughter a new look," she said to him as they waited for their appetizers.

"I might at that," he agreed.

As the dinner progressed, she found herself hoping that he would, indeed, make a visit to town with his family.

It certainly looked like he intended to when he asked for her phone number at the end of the evening. Maybe life could be good again. Never what it once was, but better than what it had been for the last few years.

Moira got lots of positive comments from her clients about the article in the paper, and a text from Michael, who'd read the online version, but Lang never showed up at the salon, and she allowed herself to breathe and start really enjoying her life in Moonlight Harbor. Her client list kept growing and she was quickly turning into the go-to fixer for beauty mistakes.

One of Pearl's clients, Jo, who Moira quickly learned was a cheapo, switched to her after coming in with a major beauty crisis.

"Oh, my gosh," Chastity exclaimed the day Jo slunk into the salon, her hair hidden under a scarf. "Your hands are purple."

"I keep telling you not to do this stuff yourself," Pearl said sternly, showing no mercy.

"I know, I know," Jo said miserably.

Edie Patterson, whose hair Pearl was trimming, began singing an old song in her reedy voice about a one-eyed purple people eater.

"Ha ha," Jo said irritably. Then, "Somebody help me!"

"I'm on it," Moira said and led her to a shampoo bowl. "Wait here." She ducked into the back room, grabbed some liquid soap detergent and baking soda, and mixed them together in a bowl, then returned to her purple-handed patient. "It's set in a little so we might not be able to get it all out."

"Don't tell me that," Jo said miserably.

"It's okay. Hair dye doesn't last on the skin as long as it

does on hair. It will completely disappear after a week or two," Moira assured her as she mixed the soap and soda together to clean Jo's hands.

"A week or two? We're going on a cruise next week."

Pearl began picking up the lyrics to the song Edie had started.

"That's not funny," Jo snapped. To Moira she said, "It gets worse." She slipped off the scarf to reveal bright purple hair. And ears.

"It serves you right," Pearl scolded. "We've had this conversation before, Jo. If you'd come to us in the first place and let Moira do something, you wouldn't be having this crisis now."

Moira had never heard Pearl speak like that to any of her other customers. "I think I can fix it," she said.

"For the full price," Pearl said. "No discounts."

"Fine friend you are," Jo muttered.

That really set Pearl off. "I could say the same about you, Jo. How many years have you been coming here, always after a deal, never wanting to pay full price. No one else does that."

"There's nothing wrong with wanting a bargain," Jo retorted hotly.

"And there's nothing wrong with paying people what they're worth. I'm running a business here. If you don't like my prices, you can drive to Aberdeen. But I can guarantee they won't be any cheaper. Or, of course, you can keep doing things yourself and making a mess of it."

"I don't do things myself that much," Jo insisted.

"Only the pricey things. But there's a reason perms and hair colors cost more. They involve more and take more time."

"Okay, okay," Jo said, "I get it. Can you fix this?" she asked Moira.

"I'll try," Moira said.

"No discount," Pearl repeated.

Jo frowned but she didn't argue.

It took a good two hours, but when Moira finally finished the wild purple had settled into a soft lavender with gold highlights, and Jo was smiling.

Until she heard the price. "That much?" she protested.

"Aberdeen," Pearl said.

"Okay, okay. It really is nice," she said to Moira. "I love it." But not enough to leave a tip.

"I knew she wouldn't," Pearl said after she left and they began to close up. "I've been dealing with her for years. She's the cheapest thing on the planet."

"I guess she really got to you," Moira ventured.

Pearl scowled. "She's been getting to me for years. Today was the final straw. I'm tired of being taken advantage of and I'd love it if she'd been insulted enough to find another salon. Sadly she liked what you did so she'll probably be back."

"At least she's a good advertisement for the salon," said Moira.

"We're already getting enough of those and they don't try to mess us over," Pearl said. "Ah, well, that's business, isn't it? You can't love everyone who walks through the door. And, I admit, I wasn't very professional. Maybe I'm getting burned-out. Maybe it's time to retire."

And close up the shop? What would Moira do? "I hope you don't for a while."

"Yes, that would be silly, wouldn't it? Especially after all the money I've sunk into the place. Don't mind me,

I'm having a cranky day. I guess I'm just wanting more time to play."

Moira knew she'd found someone to play with thanks to Arlene coming into the shop under the guise of wanting her eyebrows waxed and pumping Pearl for details on what she'd thought of Donny's cousin.

Only the day before Pearl had gotten a call on her cell phone that made her smile, say, "Hello yourself," and disappear into the back room.

Moira had been in the middle of doing highlights for Jenna. Both had stopped talking. Both had heard a giggle come from the back room.

Jenna wasn't a snoop. She didn't ask for deets and Moira didn't share any, but their reflections smiled at each other and Jenna had murmured, "Go Pearl."

"Anytime you want to take a weekend off, I can manage the salon for you," Moira offered that evening when she and Pearl settled in for a game of Anagrams, supervised by Pumpkin.

"That's really sweet of you. Maybe I'll take you up on the offer one of these days."

Maybe someday Pearl would make her the manager. Managing a salon would be almost as good as owning a salon. Almost. At least it would be a step in the right direction, and Moira was all about steps in the right direction.

Annie was, too. And the day she got her Blue Moon grant, she celebrated by cooking lobster for her roommates and giving them all chocolate lava cake for dessert. Later, after Emma was in bed, they brought out the champagne.

"This and Nora's party next week," Courtney said. "You're on your way."

"I am," Annie said, beaming. Her sunny smile dimmed a little. "With or without Greg."

Moira and Courtney stopped smiling at that, as well. Greg was talking about going into rehab, something that was going to cost his parents a bundle. Whether he'd follow through was still anybody's guess, but Annie was determined not to wait any longer for him to get his life together.

"I'm moving on, with or without him," she kept saying, maybe as much to herself as to her friends.

"You can't wait for him forever," Courtney said.

"He has until May 1."

"Are you going to stick with this deadline?" Courtney demanded.

"I am. If he hasn't checked into rehab by then, I'll know he's not serious and he doesn't really care about us." She stared at her half-empty glass of champagne a moment, then set it on the coffee table. "I don't even like this stuff," she muttered.

"Good thing, since you'll never be able to have it around him," Courtney said.

"I never have. You know that."

Courtney held up a hand. "Hey, don't bite my head off. I'm just sayin'." She picked up the bowl of chocolate kisses. "Here, have some chocolate. We're celebrating, remember?"

Annie forced a smile. "You're right. We are." She helped herself to one.

"So, here's to success," said Moira.

"To success," echoed both Annie and Courtney.

Success. What a heady drug it was. The day of Nora's party, Annie felt like she was on a sugar buzz as she replenished the refreshment table that was loaded with silver platters holding crab cakes, fruit kabobs and her brûléed goat cheese log and crackers. She'd also made her penne with artichoke and bacon, which was going over well. She'd been off the hook for the cake as Edie Patterson had insisted on baking Nora's birthday cake. Nora had opted not to serve alcohol, and Annie had come up with a perfect nonalcoholic punch.

"This is all so good," said a woman who was on her second helping of treats. "Do you do entrées, as well? My son's getting married in September and I'd love to have a catered dinner."

"I do," Annie said. She reached inside her white chef's jacket and pulled out a business card. "I'll be happy to meet with you."

"Great. I'll be sure to call you."

Of course, calling her and actually using her weren't the same. Many people loved the idea of having a catered dinner until they saw the price. Still, looking at the size of the diamond on this woman's hand and the diamond studs in her ears, Annie suspected she wouldn't balk at the cost.

"You're a success," Courtney said to her. She filled a plate, removed the gum she was chewing and set it on the edge so she could sample a crab cake. "Yum. How come you don't make these for us?"

"Catch me some crab and I will," Annie replied.

"I think I will. I saw those crab traps you can put on the end of a fishing pole. It looks pretty easy."

Moira joined them now, and she, too, filled a plate. "This all looks so good."

"It is," Annie said proudly. She knew her food.

Nora's husband tapped his glass for everyone's attention. "A toast to the birthday girl," he said. "You may be sixty-nine now but you don't look a day over—"

"Sixty-nine," inserted Tyrella, making everyone laugh. "But that's okay. You're rockin' it."

"Yes, she is," said Nora's husband. "And I don't think she looks a day over fifty. Everyone, let's toast to the prettiest woman in Moonlight Harbor. To Nora."

"To Nora," the guests echoed, and everyone drank.

"Thanks everybody for coming and helping make this birthday a little less painful," Nora said. "Instead of counting the years, I'm going to count the memories and all the good friends I have."

"Here's to many more," said Edie Patterson. "And don't worry about those years. You're still a baby compared to some of us."

Jenna produced the cake, a huge creation alight with candles, and the guests sang "Happy Birthday." Nora blew out most of the candles, then Jenna moved the cake to the counter, where dessert plates had been set out, and Nora followed her and started cutting it.

Annie watched as Nora worked, her husband standing by her, a hand on her shoulder, and felt a moment of intense longing. By the time she was that age, would she have a loving husband standing next to her as she cut her birthday cake? What was the rest of her life going to look like?

Her work life, she knew, was going to be great. Her marriage was still up in the air. Way up in the air. One thing she knew: she was going to stick with her resolve. She wouldn't wait forever for Greg. She couldn't. Not if she wanted to be in the same happy place Nora Singleton was. She wanted to find that recipe for a good relationship but if he didn't want to look for it with her, it would be his loss.

coffee. Panic put every cell in her brain to sleep, and instead of quickly walking away like any sane person would do, she ducked behind the giant cement ice-cream cone outside the shop, photobombing a mom's attempt to take a picture of her daughter, who was perched on top of it.

"Excuse me, we're trying to take a picture here," the woman said, glaring at Moira.

"Sorry. I'll just be a minute," Moira promised and peeked out around the cone to see which way Victor was walking.

"What are you doing?" the little girl asked.

"I'm playing hide-and-seek," Moira improvised.

The woman continued to glare. "Aren't you a little old for that?"

"Who are you playing with?" the child wanted to know.

"That nice policeman. Don't tell him."

"Are you hiding from the law?" the woman demanded.

"No. Just someone I can't see. It's…complicated."

"Complicated? Right. Officer, over here," the woman called.

"No, don't," Moira begged and tried to play ring-around-the-ice-cream-cone. Sadly she ringed the wrong direction and made contact with Victor's knees.

"This woman is hiding from the law," the mom said. Tattletale.

There was no hope for it but to stand up and pretend to be a mature adult rather than some idiot character in a movie. Both Victor and Frank were looking at her like she'd slipped a cog.

"I was just, ugh, checking this out. It's very clever." Moira said and then scatted, a three-alarm fire on her cheeks. Ridiculous. She was ridiculous.

But the worst happened on Monday, her day off. She'd

Eighteen

May arrived, bringing sunshine and blue skies. It also brought a call for Annie from Greg, who was checking himself into rehab and promising to find a job as soon as he got out.

"I'm optimistically cautious," she told Moira and Courtney. "I'm still moving forward with my own plans, though."

Those plans were going well. She'd already catered another party and was booked to do a wedding in August.

For Moira, May brought beach walks with Chastity and Friday night fun with the gang who gathered at Jenna's place. She continued to avoid Victor—not an easy thing to do in a small town—and it seemed the harder she tried, the more Victor sightings she had.

One day she spotted him lurking on a side street of Harbor Boulevard, running radar and had immediately slowed to one mile under the speed limit. Just driving by the patrol car and seeing him in it set her heart racing.

Next came the almost encounter at the ice-cream parlor. She'd been about to go in when she saw him and Frank the Mound inside and coming toward the door, Frank carrying a double scoop of ice cream, Victor holding a cup of spent the day at Chastity's and had stopped at the grocery store on her way home to pick up a couple of things. She'd gotten some bananas and a can of tuna fish and some deodorant when, on impulse, she decided she needed cookies, as well. Oreos. She needed Oreos.

As soon as she turned down the cookie aisle, she saw Victor, positioned right in front of them.

At least it was easier to escape down a grocery aisle than to hide behind a cement ice-cream cone. She whirled about and raced around the corner, running into the grumpy Susan Frank, knocking her off balance enough that she dropped her shopping basket and careened into an endcap display of chips.

"I'm so sorry, Mrs. Frank," Moira said, racing to grab a can of black olives before it rolled into the cookie aisle.

"You should be," snapped Susan, pushing her Marilyn Monroe hair back in place. Growing out. It needed a touch up. "What do you think this is, a racetrack?"

Moira grabbed a loaf of bread and an avocado. "I had…" A hair emergency? A panic attack? A heart attack. That last one was no lie. She had a heart attack of sorts every time she saw Victor. She gave up on her search for an excuse. "My bad," she said, putting the escaped groceries in Susan's basket.

"It certainly is," Susan informed her.

Moira knelt and began frantically stuffing bags of chips back onto the display tower. She was probably turning half those potato chips to crumbs. Oh, boy.

"Need help?" asked a low voice.

Double *oh, boy.* There he stood, muscled and gorgeous, wearing his civilian clothes. He bent to help her all the while sending a telepathic message. *What is your problem? What is our problem?*

She wished she could tell him, but that wouldn't be fair to Courtney. They weren't exactly in grade school passing notes. *My friend likes you. Do you like her back?*

"My avocado's probably bruised," Susan announced, not making a move to help Moira and Victor. "Honestly, you millennials are so irresponsible."

"No one was hurt," Victor said in his solid policeman voice.

"Someone could have been," Susan retorted.

Moira dug her wallet out of her purse and pulled out a five-dollar bill. "Please, take this and buy some chips on me. If the avocado's bruised you can make guac."

Then she shoved the last chip bag back into place, grabbed her own shopping basket, muttered a thank-you to Victor and bolted, barely dodging a woman with a full grocery cart.

"Irresponsible," Susan called after her.

Grocery store shaming. Moira speed walked up to the front of the store, gave her basket to a bagger and said, "Sorry, I have to get out of here." Then she ran for it. She could do without the tuna fish and bananas, and she could pick up deodorant at the drugstore. She definitely needed to buy that because she'd just worn out what she had on for sure.

After the grocery store encounter, Cupid finally took pity on Moira and spared her from any more Victor encounters. She began to breathe easy again, and, with Mother's Day approaching, turned her attention to a different relationship, inviting her mother down for a visit. Surprisingly, her mom accepted the invitation.

"That's great your mom's coming down," Chastity said. They had a rare lull between customers and were visiting with Pearl, who was enjoying a midafternoon cup of tea.

"I reserved a room for her at the Driftwood Inn," Moira said. "I hope she'll like it."

"She will," Pearl assured her. "Those rooms are all adorable. Jenna did a great job of fixing them up. What do you have planned?"

"I'm not sure yet. I want her to meet Jenna's family, but I know her mom and sister and brother-in-law are all coming down so this probably isn't a good time for that. I'm going to take her for a walk on the beach, for sure."

"Why don't you bring her over to my house for brunch on Sunday?" Pearl suggested. "I'd love to meet your mother."

"Really?" Moira loved the idea of introducing her mother to Pearl. Pearl was the grandmother Moira never had, but also the understanding mother Mom never got. Plus she was proof that Moira didn't have such bad taste in people, after all. "That would be spectacular. Will you make your quiche?"

"If that's what you'd like, of course."

"I wish we weren't busy," Chastity said. "I'd like to meet your mom. You need to have her down again."

Hopefully, if Mom had a good time, she'd want to come down again. Maybe she'd even quit her job at Macy's and move to Moonlight Harbor, get a job at one of the little shops. They could both be making new starts in Moonlight Harbor.

Her mother's first words after they'd hugged hello in the Driftwood Inn parking lot didn't bode well for that. "This is where you stayed?"

"It's really cute and retro," Moira assured her, and let her into the room she'd reserved. It was one of the Seaside rooms, its walls painted a pretty sky blue and sporting pictures of the ocean. The bedspread on the queen-size bed was blue as well, and on the nightstand sat a lamp with a base that looked like a blue crab. "Isn't it cute?" Moira prompted.

"It's dinky," her mother said with a frown. "I'm glad you're not staying here anymore."

"It was only Harry and me. We didn't need a lot of room."

"Well, you didn't get a lot."

Oh, no. Mom wasn't getting the last word. "I'm not here now and the house is perfect," Moira said. She and Courtney had agreed there would be no mention of sleeping on the couch.

"Anything's better than this. I'm glad you left Lang, but, Moira, you're in the middle of nowhere."

"Moonlight Harbor is somewhere."

"There's not much to do here."

As if her mother ever did much, anyway. She worked, she watched TV, she surfed dating websites, trolling for winners and always finding losers.

"There's plenty to do. I've made some good friends and I'm busy all the time."

"Where do you shop?"

"We have a grocery store."

"No mall."

"We have lots of cute shops. Didn't you see them when you first drove in?"

"Tourist traps," sneered Mom. "Where do you go when you need a bra or shoes?"

"There's Quinault, and Aberdeen's not that far. They've got plenty of places to shop there. Even a Walmart. And I can always order things online."

Her mother didn't say anything, just nodded.

"And wait till you see the salon. It's really cute."

That got another nod. Moira had sent her mother a copy of the newspaper article about her and Mom had been impressed that she'd made the paper, but hardly blown away by where she was working. A little salon in a little town—it was a far cry from a trendy salon in the city. At least Mom had been able to brag about her daughter working in such a high-end salon even she couldn't afford to go there. Moira's new job hadn't come with bragging rights.

Only a lifeline and an advocate.

"Let's take a walk on the beach," Moira suggested.

The sun was out, the seagulls wheeling in an azure sky over sparkling blue water coming toward shore in majestic waves. Her mother looked at it and smiled for the first time since she'd arrived.

"It's stunning, isn't it?" Moira said softly. *Stunning* wasn't even a good enough word.

"It is beautiful," her mother admitted. They walked a ways in silence before Mom asked, "Are you really happy here?"

"I'm totally happy." As long as she didn't think about Victor.

"It seems like it doesn't have enough action for you."

That was the old Moira, the excitement seeker who couldn't get enough of clubbing and fun drinks that cost way too much. Who'd read more books than all her friends put together yet hadn't been so smart in choices. The Moira who had dreamed of a glamorous life with the perfect man. The silly, unrealistic Moira.

"I've got friends here, real friends, not just party friends. And wait until you meet Pearl. She's been like a grandma."

That made Mom frown. Her mother had been a disappointment to them both, and Moira was sure Mom felt responsible for the relationship that never had happened for her daughter.

"She's having us for lunch tomorrow."

"What did you have planned for tonight?"

"I'm going to take you over to the house. Courtney will be there for a while before she has to go help out here, and Annie will be there and her daughter, Emma."

"So there's three of you staying in this house plus a child? It must be pretty big."

"Not really. But we manage," Moira added, hurrying on before her mother could ask for too many details about the house.

"It is cute," her mother said as they pulled up in front of the house.

Yes, it was. The flower beds were in bloom, showing off azaleas and Shasta daisies, and Courtney had put a couple of Adirondack chairs on the front porch, which made it look inviting.

Both Courtney and Annie welcomed her mother and told her how much fun they were having with Moira. Her mother looked around the living room approvingly, checking out the beachy decor and admiring the latest fashion creation on Courtney's worktable, a shirt with a blue ribbon trim and fringed with tiny seashells.

"I'm creating a whole line," Courtney explained. "I call it Beach Dreams."

Mom nodded her approval. Then her gaze drifted toward the stairs.

"How big is this house?" she asked. *Uh-oh.*

"I don't know the square footage," said Courtney, sidestepping the issue of bedrooms. "But it's plenty big for all of us. Right, Moira?"

"Oh, yeah," Moira agreed just as Harry Pawter strolled

into the room. "Look who's here, Harry," she said, hurrying to pick him up and bring him over to her mother.

That was enough to distract Mom from the size of the house and Moira and Courtney exchanged relieved looks. *Dodged that bullet, at least for the moment.* Hopefully, Mom wouldn't ask to see Moira's bedroom.

Fortunately, she didn't, and once they sat down to dinner, Moira and Courtney managed to keep the conversation going. Moira was glad she was there as Annie wasn't a big talker and Emma had turned suddenly shy with the stranger among them.

Annie could talk plenty, though, when it came to food, and loosened up once Moira's mother asked her about the cioppino. "Of course, you need the clams and the shrimp and fish, but it's the red pepper flakes and the fennel that really make it pop," Annie said as she offered her a second helping. "The cheese bread is my own recipe," she added.

"Practically everything we eat is her own recipe," Courtney said. "Annie's a caterer."

Mom's eyebrows went up in surprise. *Yes, Mom, your daughter is hanging out with some talented people.*

After dinner cleanup, Moira drove her mother around for a tour of the town. The little cabana shops were all closed for the evening but Good Times Ice Cream Parlor was still open and doing a brisk business, filled with a boisterous mix of young families, teens and couples. The go-kart track next door was doing a roaring business and the arcade was packed. Moira's mother turned up her nose at the offer of Deer Poop ice cream, but was very happy to accept a single scoop of the huckleberry.

"What do you think so far?" Moira asked when they finally drove back to the Driftwood.

"It's a little isolated," Mom said.

"But the people are great," Moira countered. "It's a tight-knit community, and the women here really help each other."

"Is that why your friends are sharing a house?" Mom asked. "Do they need help?"

Moira could hear the hint of disapproval in her voice. Really? As if Mom had managed her life so perfectly.

Moira frowned. "There's nothing wrong with being there for each other."

Mom backpedaled. "No, there's not. And they seem very nice. Who owns the house?"

"Nobody. Courtney's renting it. Annie's staying with her and sharing the rent until she can get her life sorted out."

Mom frowned. "I take it she's divorced."

"Not yet. Her husband's an alcoholic and she finally moved out. But he's in rehab and it looks like they'll get back together."

"It sounds like they already had a houseful before you came," Mom observed.

"They did, but they took me in until I can save up enough to get a place of my own. Emma loves Harry."

"You never showed me your bedroom."

"I didn't know you wanted to see it."

"It doesn't look like that big of a house. How many bedrooms does it have?"

"What, Mom, are you suddenly in real estate or something?"

"No, I just want to know." Mom's voice got stern. "Where are you sleeping, Moira?"

"They're not making me sleep on the porch if that's what you're thinking."

"Moira."

She never let up. "Does it matter?"

"So, you don't have a bedroom. Are you on the couch?"

"Okay, so I'm on the couch. So what? Would you rather have me back with Lang? I had a bed there." *Snotty daughters of the world unite.*

Her mother's lips pressed together in a tight line.

"Mom, it's okay, really," Moira said earnestly. "Courtney isn't even asking me to pay anything toward rent."

"I should hope not," Mom said in disgust. "What's her story?"

As in, what was her problem? "She's single, Mom." This whole conversation was getting irritating. Being with her mother was getting irritating.

"Never married? I'm surprised. She's nice-looking."

Courtney was more than nice-looking. She was striking. But that was a word her mother would never use. Mom had never been into expanding her vocabulary.

"She's divorced," Moira said.

Her mother frowned. "So, three women with men problems."

Really, Mom? What was with her mother, anyway? And since when was she in a position to judge?

"All trying to figure things out. You should get that, Mom. You've had enough men problems." Okay, maybe she shouldn't have pointed that out. Moira braced for an argument.

"Yes, I have. I wish I'd had some friends to help me get through them. Your situation isn't ideal but your roommates seem really nice."

Moira blinked in surprise at the softness in her mother's voice. And the regret.

"I guess maybe you've found a good place to start over, after all."

Here was a choice her mother approved. Mark that on the calendar.

"Even if they are making you sleep on the couch," Mom added. What was it about moms that they always had to get the last word?

They pulled into the motel parking lot and her mother surprised her again by saying, "That was fun today."

"Wait till you meet Pearl. I know you'll love her," Moira said.

Her mother didn't make any promises.

"I'll come back in the morning and we can do another beach walk before we go over there if you want."

"That sounds good," Mom said. "I really liked the beach."

The beach walk had been something they'd both enjoyed. Amazing how well they got along when Mom wasn't disapproving of her choices. Moira reminded herself that many of their past arguments had been as much her fault as her mother's. It was hard to approve stupid and dangerous choices.

She arrived at the Driftwood the next morning bearing lattes from Books and Beans as well as cinnamon rolls from Sunbaked, the local bakery she'd recently discovered. "These are a pound of fat just waiting to happen," Mom said, but Moira noticed she ate hers, anyway.

Mother Nature had brought out the perfect day with another cloudless sky and only a light breeze to play with their hair as the two women walked the beach.

"I used to love going to the beach when I was a kid," Mom said.

Sometimes it was hard to think of her mother as a child, and it was especially hard to think of her mother enjoying much of anything. "Your grandma used to take me."

Mom looked out at the sparkling water. "Before Daddy died and things got hard." She bent and picked up a round white stone.

"I'm sorry your life's sucked so much," Moira said and meant it. As a child she hadn't given any thought to what her mom felt. She certainly hadn't as a teenager. She'd been too obsessed with what she thought about her own life, and those thoughts hadn't been exactly filled with gratitude for a perfect childhood.

Her mother shrugged. "Life sucks sometimes. You have to keep moving forward. I hope that's what you're doing, Moira."

"Definitely, that's what I'm doing," Moira said.

"I don't want to see you making the same mistakes I made."

Moira didn't want to ask it. She did, anyway. "Was I a mistake?"

"Your father was a mistake."

It was an answer but not a complete one.

Before Moira could press her further, Mom said, "Let's not talk about it. It's too nice a day."

Moira hoped their visit to Pearl confirmed that she was making good life choices. How could her mother possibly think otherwise? Pearl was the epitome of a class act.

She had her table set with a blue tablecloth and white plates with blue napkins. She served them quiche and scones and a tossed salad with shrimp in it. It made Moira think of magazines with glossy photo shoots of perfect people enjoying gathering in a perfect setting. Now, here she was, living a magazine moment.

Pearl spoke about her to her mother in glowing terms, and when she concluded, "You've raised a lovely daughter," it was sweeter than the lavender cookies she served for dessert.

"Thank you," Mom murmured and looked almost uncomfortable. Hardly surprising since Moira had pretty much raised herself.

Back at the Driftwood it was time for her mother to check out and drive back to Seattle. Courtney was at the check-in desk about to end her Sunday morning shift, working a piece of gum, which Moira had learned she'd used to break a smoking habit.

"You'll have to come back and visit again, Mrs. Wellman. The Fourth of July here rocks the dock," she said.

Mom's smile fell on Moira like summer sunshine. "I might have to do that," she said.

Before she got in her car, she hugged Moira. "I'm glad I came. It looks like you're doing great and I can stop worrying about you."

Worry equaled concern and concern equaled love. And love covered a multitude of sins—mother sins and daughter sins.

"Thanks, Mom, for caring," Moira said, feeling suddenly teary.

Her mother looked almost surprised by those words. "I've always cared."

"Yeah, you have."

She hadn't been like Moira's friend Heather's mother, but then Moira hadn't been a Heather. They'd been all the other had and they still were.

She hugged her mother, not a casual-hello hug or a goodbye-see-you-around hug, but a real happy-Mother's-Day hug. Mom hugged her back, and in that moment Moira felt a shift in their relationship. The top layer of frustration with each other and the discontent had fallen away, so had the tenseness that came along with changing roles when a young woman fought to establish her independence, even if she was staking out that independence in dangerous territory. They parted, not as adversaries calling a truce, but as two grown women forging their way toward a new relationship.

"Happy Mother's Day," she murmured.

"It has been," Mom said.

Moira watched her drive out of the parking lot through teary eyes.

The rest of the week hurried by and Moira was almost too busy to think of Victor King. Almost.

Until the following Sunday when Courtney came home from The Drunken Sailor and shared that she and Victor had danced a cowboy cha-cha together. Okay, she'd had to drag him out on the floor, but he'd enjoyed himself once he got out there. What was not to enjoy, after all? He was with her. Ha ha ha.

Yeah, ha ha. Moira's muscles balked at smiling and it was a battle to get them to cooperate. "So, is he ever going to ask you out?" she demanded.

"Never," put in Annie, who was parked in a chair, calculating how much chicken to buy for a dinner party.

"Oh, thanks," Courtney said irritably.

"Seriously, if he was into you, he'd have asked you out by now," Moira said. *Sounding a little pissy here. Feeling a little pissy, too.*

So what? She had a right to feel pissy.

Courtney dropped onto the couch opposite Moira. "He's just so frickin' shy."

Moira hadn't thought he was shy.

"I think I'm going to have to move things along and ask him out."

Yes, please. Put us all out of our misery.

"Good idea," Annie said. "Once he turns you down, you can get him out of your system," she added, and Courtney scowled at her.

Moira couldn't have agreed more.

"Okay, so maybe I will next Sunday." Courtney gave Moira a jab in the leg with her toe. "How about you come along for moral support?"

"Like your morals need supporting?" Moira replied.

"Yeah, they do. Come on, it'll be fun."

"I'll see," Moira said. *Not.*

But when the Friday night gang assembled at Edie Patterson's house, it looked like Moira was going to be swept along with the tide because Jenna's sister, Celeste, was in town for the weekend with her husband. Celeste was even prettier than her sister, with full wavy hair that Moira would have loved to play with and a life-of-the-party personality. She and Courtney together were impossible to refuse when they demanded Moira join them on Sunday night.

"It'll be fun," said Celeste.

Not for Moira, but Sunday night Courtney was not taking no for an answer. "I don't know what your problem is," she said as she practically dragged Moira out the door.

"I'm just not into it," Moira lied. Even if the evening didn't turn out to be awkward, it would feel awkward.

The minute they walked into The Drunken Sailor, she knew she'd been right. Celeste and her husband and Jenna were already at a table along with Jenna's friend Brody. And there at the bar stood Victor King buying a soft drink.

"Is that a gorgeous man or what?" Courtney demanded.

"And they don't come any nicer. Come on, let's go over and say hi."

Moira's heart was on red alert and her feet had turned to cement. *You shouldn't have come*, chanted her brain.

The whole saying-hi thing was as uncomfortable as Moira had thought it would be.

"I guess you've met Moira," Courtney said.

"I have," Victor said stiffly.

He wasn't blushing this time but Moira knew she was. Someone needed to take a fire extinguisher to her face.

"I think I'm going to go over and say hi to Jenna," she said and made her escape.

"You came!" Celeste greeted Moira as if they were old friends. "Come on, pull up a chair."

"I'm surprised," Jenna said. "I thought you'd sworn off line dancing."

"I had. I have." Moira shot a glance to where Courtney stood talking to Victor. He was looking in her direction and frowning. She bit her lip and looked away. Then she was suddenly aware of Jenna studying her and quickly shifted her attention back to the group at the table, pinning on a smile.

"This is my husband, Henry," Celeste was saying, hugging the arm of a man with glasses who actually looked a little bit like Stephen King, a young version. "He's brilliant."

"Of course I am," Henry said. "I had to be to convince you that you wanted to marry me."

Along with a little help from Hyacinth, Moira thought. Her rebellious eyes insisted on turning toward the bar again and that was when she saw Courtney headed her way, dragging Victor. Shit.

"Excuse me a minute," she said. "I…" *have got to get out of here.* "Little girls' room."

She fled to the bathroom, locked herself inside a stall and took several deep breaths. Okay, this was silly. There was nothing between her and Victor King and she was being ridiculous. She'd go back out there and pretend to have a great time. No, she'd go back out there and buy the biggest beer she could find.

The bathroom door opened. "Moira?" called Jenna.

"I'll be out in a minute."

"I'll wait."

Double shit.

Moira flushed the toilet and stepped back out.

"Is it my imagination or is something weird going on?" Jenna asked.

"I don't know why you'd think that," Moira hedged.

"Maybe because of the way you and Victor are looking at each other coupled with you running away like a burning bunny the minute he and Courtney started walking toward us."

"It's nothing," Moira insisted. "I don't feel very good."

"So that's your story and you're stickin' to it?" Jenna asked.

Moira bit her lip again. At the rate she was going, she was going to have tooth dents in it as deep as the Grand Canyon.

Jenna leaned against the sink and waited.

"Courtney really likes him."

"Courtney's really liked him for a long time. He doesn't feel that way about her, though. Never has. Was there… something between you and Victor?"

"Not really. We went out." *And we kissed.*
And then I moved in with Courtney.

Jenna nodded slowly, a love detective, putting together the clues. "So, now you don't want to go out with him again because Courtney likes him."

"She took me in."

"Well, I'll say this. You are a selfless friend. But trust me, if something was going to happen between those two, it would have happened long ago."

"Maybe. But I'm not going to be the one to mess it up for her."

"Okay," Jenna said. "I get that. Relationships can sure be complicated, can't they?" She appeared to know that firsthand.

Moira nodded.

"Come on, let's go back out. The lesson's about to start."

Moira followed her out of the bathroom but she didn't get far as Victor was standing outside in the hallway, waiting for her.

"I'll see you out there," Jenna said and left Moira to fend for herself.

"I'm kind of surprised you came tonight," he said. "You've been avoiding me like the plague."

"I didn't want to."

"Then why did you?"

"Because Courtney was insisting. She's crazy about you, you know."

"What does that have to do with anything?" he demanded. "Do you like me or not?"

"Of course I do."

"No, not the friend thing. Are you into me? I thought you were when you kissed me. Or were you just messing with me?"

"No, I wasn't," she said earnestly.

"Okay, then, do you want to take this somewhere or not?"

"I do, but..." Oh, what to say? Whatever inspiration she was looking for ran away and hid behind the woman standing behind Victor, staring at them in shock.

Nineteen

Disastrous, that was the word that came to mind as Moira looked at the expression on Courtney's face. How much had she heard?

Enough, obviously. She looked both shocked and hurt. And then angry. Really, really kill-my-friend angry.

"Well, this explains a lot," she said, her eyes narrowing to slits.

No, it didn't. It didn't even begin to explain.

"I'm leaving," Courtney announced, each word a chip of ice. "You can probably find a ride home."

Home? Did Moira have one now? Oh, this was bad. "This isn't what it looks like."

"Oh, yes it is," Courtney snapped. Then she whirled around and started to march off.

"Courtney, wait," Moira called.

She started after her friend but Victor caught her by the arm and stopped her. "Let her go."

"I have to fix this or she's never going to speak to me again."

"What?" Now he was looking perturbed.

"She's in love with you—you have to see that."

"I'm not in love with her so what's that got to do with you and me?"

"She's been hoping that would change, and now here you are with me and she probably overheard everything we just said."

"So now she'll move on."

"Now she'll never speak to me again." Moira was ready to cry. She couldn't have the man and now she was losing the friend.

"Courtney and I were never a couple."

"It doesn't matter. She wanted you and it looks like I just stepped in and took you away."

"Is this why you've been avoiding me? I don't believe it."

"I've got to go make this right."

"What? No, you don't. That's just stupid. There's nothing to make right."

Stupid. The word hit a nerve and made her wince. "I'm not stupid."

"I didn't say you were."

"Yes, you did. You know, that's what Lang used to tell me all the time, but he was wrong. And so are you."

"Come on, Moira, I really didn't mean it that way."

"Let me go."

"Moira, listen to me."

"No, I need to go make things right with my friend." Who had never, ever called her stupid. "Let me go!" she demanded, giving his hand an angry shake.

He obliged, but he begged, "Come on, don't be like this, please."

As if it were wrong to want to make things right with a friend? She shook her head at him and hurried back to the dance floor.

A lesson was in progress but Courtney wasn't one of the dancers. She already had her purse and was steaming her way toward the exit. Feeling sick at heart, Moira ducked in and out of the rows of dancers until she got to Jenna's table.

Her sister and brother-in-law were out on the dance floor but Jenna was seated at the table next to Brody. She looked at Moira in concern.

"I need a ride home," Moira said to her. "Can you help me?"

"Sure," Jenna said. To Brody she said, "Tell Celeste I'll be back." Then she grabbed her purse and walked with Moira out of the pub. They were barely outside before Moira started to cry.

"I know, stuff like this is awful," Jenna said, putting an arm around her as they made their way to Jenna's car, "but maybe it's for the best to get this all out in the open and clear the air."

The air was anything but clear. Relationship pollution.

"We were becoming such good friends," Moira said between sobs. "Now she thinks I'm a traitor. And I'm not. I stopped seeing him as soon as I found out she was into him."

"Don't beat yourself up too much. You didn't know. And it's not like they were married."

"The girlfriend code still applies."

She didn't have to explain the girlfriend code. Jenna nodded. "I get it. But you were already seeing him before you found out. The girlfriend code can't apply to something that happened before you were friends. Keep that in mind."

What Jenna said was perfectly reasonable. But when emotions were involved, people weren't always reasonable.

"I think I may need to move out," Moira said miserably once they were on the road.

"If it comes to that, we'll find you a room at the Driftwood. Just stop by the house and Aunt Edie will get you a key."

By the time Moira got to the house she'd come to consider home, Courtney was already in her bedroom.

Annie was on the couch with Emma. They were multitasking by watching a Disney movie and doing a small puzzle on the coffee table. She left her daughter to keep looking for corner pieces and motioned Moira into the kitchen.

As soon as they were out of earshot, she asked, "What's going on? Courtney came in here with steam coming out of her ears, announced she needed some time to herself and went right upstairs."

The writing was on the wall. Moira would be headed to the Driftwood Inn. Three women, one little girl and a cat all in one house was probably overload, anyway. It still broke her heart to leave.

And to lose a friend. "She hates me," she said miserably and wiped a tear from the corner of her eye.

"She could never hate you."

"Oh, yeah, she could," Moira said, and told Annie about the love triangle she'd unwittingly created. "I've been acting like the town fool trying to avoid him, and then tonight… Oh, I knew I shouldn't have gone," she said with a groan.

Annie frowned, then got up and poured them both a glass of lemonade. "She's been delusional about him for ages," she said as she set one in front of Moira. "She'd better not let this ruin a friendship."

"I hate her thinking I'm an ingrate. She's been such a

good friend to me. But I don't know how to fix this. I don't know if she'll believe me."

"All you can do is try," Annie said.

There was no time like the present. Moira took a fortifying drink of lemonade, then made her way up the stairs to Courtney's bedroom. Was this how the French noblewomen felt when they had to climb to the guillotine?

She knocked on Courtney's door but got no answer. "Courtney, I didn't know, honest. I stopped seeing him as soon as I found out you were interested." There was still no answer. "I'm so sorry." No answer. *Sorry* didn't cut it.

Okay, it looked like she'd be moving out. The good news was that it wouldn't be long before she could afford to get a place of her own, maybe another month. The bad news was that she had to get a place of her own and she wouldn't be with the two women who had become such good friends. She'd not only enjoyed her time with Annie and Courtney, she'd also enjoyed hanging out with Emma. This felt like leaving a family.

What would Mom say when she heard about this? Nothing, because Moira vowed not to tell her.

She waited until after Emma had gone to bed, then packed up her things. It didn't take long.

"I wish you wouldn't go," Annie said, watching her.

"It's for the best."

"Not really. We're going to miss you. Emma's going to miss you."

"You can still bring her into the salon to get her hair braided."

"That won't be the same as having her own personal stylist in the house." Annie got serious. "I'm going to miss you. And even if Courtney stays mad, that won't affect our friendship."

Moira was both touched and depressed by her words.

Well, you made friends, you lost friends. That was how much of her life had been. Friends moved away, they gave up on you when you picked a loser boyfriend. This was life.

Life sucked.

"But I can't imagine her staying mad. She's not like that."

Not normally, unless your friend turned out to be an ungrateful sneak. Even though Moira was innocent of that charge, she sure looked guilty. Would Courtney give her a chance to explain? Ever? Some people collected hurts like squirrels collected nuts. Maybe Courtney was one of those people.

Edie Patterson was more than happy to help Moira get installed in a room again. "It's lovely to have you back, dear," she said. "You come on over tomorrow and get breakfast with us. I'll show you how to make French toast."

Moira could have hugged her for not asking why she was back. Not all friends gave up on you.

The next morning, over French toast, Edie said again how nice it was to have Moira with them.

"I thought you moved out," said Pete, who had turned from Prince Charming back to Scruff Man, sporting a dingy, worn shirt over stained jeans and gray stubble on his face.

"I'm only back for a while," Moira said. She was getting close to having enough money for first and last months' rent somewhere plus a pet deposit. "And I'll pay for my room," she told Edie.

"You're practically family. You'll do no such thing," Edie said.

"You can't keep giving away rooms for free, Edie,

old girl," said Pete and Moira wanted to kick the crusty old coot.

"Moira will earn her keep," Edie said. She smiled at Sabrina, who was just entering the kitchen. "I bet Sabrina's ready to do something more with her hair."

"Hi, Moira," Sabrina said cheerfully. "Can we try a different color on me?"

"Sure," Moira said. "Text me later and we'll set up a time."

"Sweet," Sabrina said happily.

Jenna, too, made her feel welcome. "Things will work out," she said before she left to go do paperwork.

"They always do," Edie added.

Yeah, just not the way you wanted.

Moira went to her room and settled on the bed with her cat and her Muriel Sterling book. She was two-thirds done with it and she thumbed ahead to see if the wise Ms. Sterling covered sorting out new friendships. Sadly, she didn't.

"What am I going to do?" she asked Harry.

Harry had no idea. He stuck out a hind leg and began cleaning it. Life was so much simpler when you were a cat.

Muriel Sterling couldn't offer any wisdom, and a walk on the beach didn't help, either. Moira sat on a piece of driftwood and looked out at the waves. They were so powerful, so constant. Normally she found that view so comforting. There was order in the world.

This morning, waves hurling themselves on the sandy beach, pulling at pebbles when they retreated, made her think of chaos. And loss. Was her life always going to be like this, one step forward and two steps back? She wished it wasn't her day off, wished she had something to do and people to talk to. Except she really wasn't up for making small talk.

Afternoon found her conveniently in Pearl's neighborhood and then knocking on Pearl's door. "I was just driving by," she said. *Haven't seen you in ages.* So lame.

"Come on in," Pearl said, swinging the door wide. "I was about to pour myself some iced tea. Would you like some?"

Moira nodded and followed her into the house, taking her usual place at the breakfast bar.

"How have you been filling your day off?" Pearl asked.

"Reading. And…stuff."

Pearl set the glass in front of her and studied her. "Stuff?"

"I moved back to the Driftwood Inn for a while."

"The Driftwood. Why? I thought you were happy with Courtney and Annie."

"I was. But…" She should not be dumping her troubles on Pearl. The woman had gone through enough shit without having to dodge someone else's.

"Are you okay?"

"I'm fine," Moira insisted. She should not have come here, but her mom was working and wouldn't have time for a shrink session—not that Mom excelled at those, anyway—and Pearl was the closest thing to a grandma she'd ever had.

"You don't look fine."

Moira sighed. "I've got a problem."

"Let's see if we can solve it," Pearl said and came around the counter to take a stool next to Moira.

Moira spilled everything. Yep, doing a great job of not dumping her troubles on Pearl.

Pearl sighed. "Women should never be rivals, but that's in a perfect world. I hope Courtney comes around. She's got a big heart."

That was beating only for Victor.

"But she's also a bit of a firecracker so you'll just have to wait and see."

Wait and see. Moira hated waiting and she was afraid of what she'd see.

Victor spent his day off working on expanding his back porch, sawing and banging nails into wood. He even banged a spider to death with great glee. Moira would have put the thing in a glass and carried it to safety.

Moira. He could bang on things all he wanted but it wouldn't take the edge off the frustration simmering inside him. After he whacked his thumb with the hammer and turned the area a nice deep dark blue, he gave up on trying to find an outlet for the way he was feeling and determined to track Moira down and talk to her.

Rationally. Like two intelligent people. How could she have thought he was calling her stupid? What kind of tool did she think he was?

He showered and got in his truck and drove to the salon. Oh, yeah. Closed on Mondays.

They both had Mondays off. Darn it all, why weren't they spending those Mondays together?

He cruised by Courtney's place. Moira's car wasn't there. Courtney's was, though, so he didn't stop.

Where was Moira? He drove into town, checking out the grocery store for some sign of her. Maybe she was there, buying cookies. Nope. He drove back to Courtney's place. Still no sign of Moira's car. He cruised by Pearl's house. No sign of her there, either. She couldn't have left town. She had nowhere to go.

Okay this was dumb. He was dumb. With a frown he went back to the grocery store and bought a giant bag of chips, a supersize box of cookies and a gallon of milk. He wasn't going to keep stalking her. He wasn't a creep and he wasn't that desperate.

He'd go to the salon the next day.

At six o'clock there was a knock on Moira's motel room door. She opened it to find Courtney standing there with a pizza box. "Come on over to the office and join me for dinner."

If this was a peace offering, it sure was a fragrant one. Moira followed her across the parking lot, hopeful and nervous.

Courtney plopped the box on the reception desk and opened it. "Have a slice. Or, if you prefer, shove the whole thing in my face. I guess I deserve it."

Moira blinked in surprise.

When she didn't move to take any, Courtney said, "Help me out here. I can't eat this all by myself." She picked up a slice. "And tell me what you're doing here."

"Living?"

"You bitch."

Okay, she deserved that.

"Running away without even talking to me."

"Um, pretty obvious you didn't want to talk last night," pointed out Moira.

Courtney scowled and took a bite of pizza. "I needed time to process, okay?" She dumped the rest of her slice back in the box. "But I'm done processing now, and Emma wanted to know where you were this morning. She wanted her hair braided."

"Annie can bring her to the salon."

"Or you can come back home."

"I figured I'd overstayed my welcome."

"Yeah, that was what I thought. But that was last night and this is today. Look, I should have been more mature, more noble, but darn it all, Moira, I didn't want to be noble. I wanted Victor. I really thought he was coming around." She frowned at the pizza box. "Annie told me I was delusional. She was right."

"I wouldn't poach, honest. I stopped seeing him the minute I knew you wanted him."

Courtney sighed. "It's hard to poach when there's no relationship to poach. And how old am I, anyway, thirteen?"

"I'd be mad, too, if I thought my friend had tried to cut me out," Moira said.

"Yeah, but you didn't. And there was nothing to cut out. Look, I'm crazy about Victor, have been ever since I moved here. He's just so…perfect. And I wanted to get my love life all lined up. You know, good man, family—of course, we'd have a little girl who would love wearing the clothes I designed for her." She frowned and shook her head. "I guess I got addicted to my own fantasy."

"Finding a good person to share your life isn't really a fantasy," Moira said. "It's a goal."

"It's a fantasy when nothing's happening and you keep trying to make it happen."

When you tried to convince yourself the loser you'd picked was a good choice, that, in spite of the awful things he did, he loved you. And that, in spite of the awful things he did, you should stay with him.

"To keep wanting a man when he wants someone else is crazy. And I'm not that nuts," Courtney said. "And I'm not so small as to put out the fire on another woman's love life. If Victor wants you to go out with him, then you should. And you should get your clothes and your cat and get your butt back home."

"Really?"

"Really. I'm sorry, Moira. Sorry I jumped to conclusions, sorry I misjudged you. Forgive me?"

"Of course," Moira said, relief and happiness washing over her.

"You're a good friend. I wouldn't want to lose you."

"Same here," Moira said.

"And if Victor decides he doesn't want you, then he can come crawling to me. Maybe, if he's lucky, I'll go out with him. Or maybe I'll really make him suffer and find someone else."

"That'll show him," Moira said, and Courtney smiled and picked up her pizza slice and took another bite. "This is so good."

"Yes, it is," Moira agreed, but she wasn't talking about the pizza.

Moira was glad her relationship with Courtney had been restored, but she wasn't so sure about restoring what she'd started with Victor, not after what he'd said to her Sunday night. If there was one thing she'd learned from her rotten relationship with Lang, it was to be on the watch for clues to the real man behind the mask. Maybe Victor wasn't as perfect as she and Courtney thought.

It was pushing toward noon on Tuesday when he showed up at the salon. Moira had just said goodbye to Hyacinth, who'd stopped by to give her an update on how things were going with her pastor, and she had time to kill. No clients until one o'clock.

So she really had no viable excuse to dodge him when he came in looking for a haircut, especially when Pearl, who was working on Patricia Whiteside, one of the women from the Friday night group, called to him, "You're in luck. Moira's in between clients."

Moira could feel her whole body stiffening as he approached. "I really need a haircut bad," he said as he slipped into the chair. "Please?" he added.

There they were, reflected in the mirror, her with her lips pressed tightly together, him looking like the picture of humility. "All right, fine," she said, her tone of voice failing to match her words.

"And I need to talk to you."

"Really, Victor, I don't think there's anything to talk about," she said as she put a cape around his shoulders.

"Yeah, there is."

She didn't say anything as she led the way to the shampoo bowl.

"Don't drown me. Okay?"

She didn't laugh.

"I really wasn't saying that you were stupid. Hell, you're smarter than me. I'm sorry it sounded like that. I just think the idea of not giving yourself a chance to be happy is stupid. Why would you want to do that?"

"You obviously don't understand anything about friendship. Or women."

"Hey," he protested, jerking his head away as she raked the shampoo through his hair. "Are you trying to scrub out my brains?"

"Sorry," she muttered.

"I know I don't understand women," he said. "Maybe I never will. But I want to understand you."

"Here's something you need to understand, then. I don't want to lose a friend. I've been there and done that. My ex did a good job of weeding most of my friends out of my life. And I let him. I won't do that again."

"Okay, I get that. But I still think it's stupid to miss out on having something good with somebody on the off chance that a friend would be mad at you. What kind of friend would act like that?"

She put his chair up and began to towel off his hair.

Again, he pulled away. "I think maybe I'd better do this cut before you rub every hair off my head," he said and took over.

They walked back to the chair and she removed the towel and grabbed her scissors.

"Please don't cut my ear off."

"I'm not violent," she snapped.

"Me, either," he said.

"And I'm not into put-downs."

"I wasn't trying to put you down, really," he said earnestly.

"It sure felt like it," she said.

"Look, I was frustrated and I didn't think."

"Yeah? Well, Lang used to get frustrated a lot and it never turned out well for me."

"I told you that when we first met, I've never hit a woman in my life and I never would. I can prove that to you over time, if you give me a chance." He looked at her, pleading, "Come on, Moira, give me a chance to prove I'm not a shit. Courtney won't stay mad at you forever."

"She didn't," Moira admitted and started snipping.

"You guys worked things out?"

"We did."

"That's great. Then can't we try to work things out?"

Pearl had just turned off her hair dryer, and his question echoed around the room like an announcement on a PA system.

"For heaven's sake, give the man a chance," Pearl said.

"Give yourself a second chance, too, Moira," she added with a smile.

"There. See? Even your boss thinks you should give me a chance," said Victor, smiling. "We can take it slow. And if you want, I can provide references. My mom will vouch for me."

"If a man treats his mother well, he'll treat you well, too," Pearl added.

Moira kept snipping. She'd patched things up with Courtney. Victor was being as sweet as a man could be. She hadn't appreciated what he'd said, but he obviously hadn't meant it the way she'd taken it. Maybe she was still seeing things through dark glasses that colored everything in a negative light. What could it hurt to remove them and see if her vision didn't improve, as well as her life?

"You got time for lunch?" he asked.

She looked at their reflections in the mirror. There was no superior smirk on Victor's face like the one Lang favored, no angry frown, nothing negative. He looked earnest and sincere. And trustworthy. And she wanted to trust him.

More than that, she wanted to trust herself, wanted to know that her instincts weren't trashed beyond repair. Her instincts told her to go ahead and go for it.

"Please?" he added.

"I think lunch is a good idea," she said.

He grinned. "Great. I'm glad."

So was she.

"Isn't that sweet to see?" Patricia said in a hushed voice as she handed her credit card to Pearl.

"It is," Pearl agreed. "I'm hoping what's starting with

them will bloom into something nice. She deserves to be happy."

"Every woman deserves to be happy, Pearl. Even you."

Even her. Sometimes she wondered. There had been many times over the years she'd wondered what she'd done to make God so mad at her.

As if God was so easily offended? And why was it that people always blamed Him for the bad things in their lives and never gave Him credit when something good came down the pike?

She and Devlin had enjoyed several phone conversations since their date, and he'd come down to spend time with her on the Saturday of Memorial Day weekend. "I'd really like you to meet my family," he'd said before he left.

Family. She'd missed those days so much. It was like a phantom pain from a lost limb. Even though the limb was gone, you still felt it and it ached. Having Moira in her life had helped fill the void, but it had also made Pearl greedy for more. Maybe she could have that more.

Patricia left, followed by Victor and Moira, on their way to Beachside Burgers and smiling. That left Pearl alone with her sandwich.

She went into the back room, took her cell phone from her purse and went to the contacts section and brought up Devlin Patrick.

He answered on the second ring. "Well, hello there," he said. "I was just thinking about you."

"Were you really?"

"I was. And thinking about that great beach of yours."

"I think the weather's looking good for this Sunday," Pearl said, "and I was considering making a Crab Louie. All I need is someone to share it with me."

"I hope no one else has applied for that job."

"You're the first applicant I've called."

"I hope I'm the only applicant," he said. "You make me Crab Louie for lunch and I'll take you to dinner. How's that sound?"

"That sounds fun."

"But don't tell Arlene. She and Don will want to come along. Love 'em but I want you to myself."

That really sounded fun.

Pearl was smiling when she finally ended the call and dug out her sandwich. That ache for what she'd lost would always be there, she was sure, but maybe it didn't have to hurt so badly.

Twenty

June brought tourists and nice weather. The little cabana shops were beehives of activity with shoppers swarming in and out of them. Every other person on the sidewalk was eating ice cream from Good Times Ice Cream Parlor and the buzz of go-karts hummed in the air. People stood in the entrance to Something Fishy with its giant shark's mouth, posing for pictures, and bought hot dogs to eat at the beach while flying their kites. Merchants were happy and it seemed like everyone in Moonlight Harbor was smiling.

Except Annie. Any hope she'd had that she and her husband could put their marriage back together died the night she was driving home from catering a party and saw him weaving out of The Drunken Sailor. Only days after he'd returned to Moonlight Harbor and they'd talked about getting back together. So much for rehab. She'd called his brother and learned that he'd lied to her. He hadn't completed the program, had insisted he didn't need to. He was good.

So good that he'd chosen his party friends over her. It was past time to take the painful step and cut herself free from him. With help from her parents, Annie hired a lawyer.

"I just have to have to find someone to serve the papers to him," she said when she met on a Friday night with the group of women who had become both friends and support group. "One more expense for my parents to help with," she added miserably.

There had already been many a time when they'd sent money to pay her utilities, and many a gift card that had shown up in the mail. There'd also been many pleas to leave him before he completely ruined her life.

"I doubt they mind," said Pearl, who had over the last few months become a regular attender again. "In fact, I'm sure they're so relieved that they're more than happy to do whatever it takes to get you away from him."

It was true. In addition to helping financially, they'd offered to come down and take Emma back to their home in Seattle for July and August so Annie could work on launching her new business. So many people were willing to step in and help her. She was grateful, but in the way a person mourning a loved one would be grateful. She appreciated the support but how she wished she wasn't in a position to need it.

"You don't have to hire someone to do that," Jenna said. "In the state of Washington, anyone over the age of eighteen, other than your child, can serve divorce papers, even a friend. One of my mom's buddies from the grocery store did that for me."

"I don't know who I'd get," Annie said.

"I do," Jenna told her. "Seth Waters. He's buff and tough and he can be intimidating if he needs to be."

"Oh, I couldn't ask Seth," Annie began.

Jenna didn't let her finish. "I could. Trust me, he'll be more than happy to do it."

It turned out that, indeed, he was. He made the delivery on Monday evening and had no trouble getting Greg to sign the Acceptance of Service paper.

Courtney was working at the Driftwood and Emma was at a friend's house, so it was just Annie and Moira at home when Seth called to let Annie know the deed was done.

"How'd he take it?" she asked.

"Let's just say he wasn't happy and leave it at that," Seth replied. "By the way, he was already buzzed."

Annie bit her lip. She could only imagine the venom Greg had spewed. "I tried. I really did," she said, as much to herself as to Seth.

"Everyone knows that."

"Everyone but him," she said miserably.

"Oh, he knows. He just doesn't want to admit it. There are people in this life who take responsibility for their problems and people who don't. You know which one he is."

"Alcoholism is a disease." So should she have stuck with him until he was well?

"It's not incurable. You have to want to cure it, Annie. He doesn't. Not yet. Maybe never."

Maybe never. With those divorce papers, she'd pointed them to a fork in the road, a fork that led one way for her and another for him. She had no idea where his road would take him but she knew her destination, knew it could be a good one. She would have to cling to that knowledge. Maybe at some point he'd find his way back to her, the old Greg, the fun-loving, happy Greg—not the embittered, angry Greg who was mad at the world and everyone in it, including his wife; the Greg who blamed everyone but himself for his problems.

"Thanks for doing this for me," she said to Seth.

"Happy to help. And remember, when you find that food truck, I want to go with you and check out the engine."

"That's so nice of you."

"Not really. I like cars and trucks. And cookies," he added.

Seth Waters was a gem. "I can do cookies. I'll let you know," she said. Then she ended the call and sat with her phone in her lap, trying to decide if she felt anything but numb.

"So it's done. How'd he take it?" Moira asked.

"Not very well, I guess. I can only imagine what he said to Seth. I'm sure he called me every rotten name he could think of."

"Why is it always us who are the bad ones and never them?" Moira wondered.

"Do you think I did the right thing?" Would Emma ever come to think she'd done the right thing?

"I know you did. How many chances have you given him over the last couple of years?"

"I've lost count."

"Maybe this will really do it. Maybe after this he'll join AA and stay in."

"I don't know. All I know is I can't ride that roller coaster anymore."

Whether she could or not, Greg didn't want to let her off it. He showed up at the house at ten o'clock that night, blaring his truck horn, then banging on the door and shouting insults. Annie sat on the couch with Moira, her jaw clenched and her eyes squeezed tightly shut.

"I should call Victor," Moira said, reaching for her cell phone.

Annie put a hand on her arm. "Please don't. Greg's already miserable enough. I don't want to make him even more miserable by calling the police on him. He'll give up and go home eventually."

Moira nodded and put her phone back on the coffee table, then grabbed the remote and turned up the volume on the TV.

Greg did finally go away and Annie did finally get to sleep. Somewhere around three in the morning, after she'd lain awake second-guessing her decision not to call the cops. He'd plainly been drunk, which meant he'd been driving drunk. He could have hit someone, killed someone, and it would have been her fault.

She woke up feeling heartsick and gritty-eyed. She had to be at work at seven o'clock. It was going to be a long day. Maybe she should have waited until the weekend to have those papers served. At least she could have slept in Saturday morning.

But no. She'd waited long enough.

"You've waited long enough for everything," her mother assured her when she called home. "Stop feeling guilty for things that are his fault and get on with your life."

Her mom was right. She had waited long enough for everything.

The very next day, after completing her morning shift at Sandy's, she started scouring the web, checking out food trucks for sale. By the end of the week she'd found what looked like the perfect one for sale in Long Beach, another town farther along the Washington coast. The truck was eighteen feet long, complete with a flattop grill, refrigeration, a three-compartment sink, prep space and a toaster.

And it even had AC. She could get it for nineteen thousand, which would leave her with just enough left from her grant to buy supplies.

Courtney, who was taking a break from a sewing project, joined her at the kitchen table, and Annie turned her laptop so her friend could see it.

Courtney looked at the picture and wrinkled her nose. "Kind of blah. Reminds me of my parents' old camper."

"I could paint it and it would look really cute," Annie said.

"Correction. We could paint it," Courtney said.

"The price is right, and it's only eight years old."

"So why is the person selling it?"

"I don't know," Annie said.

"Maybe whoever it is couldn't make a go of it," said Courtney.

Annie sat back in her kitchen chair. What if she couldn't make a go of it?

"You can, though," Courtney quickly added. "Long Beach is only a couple hours' drive from here. Call Seth and get him to go with us to look at it. We can go tomorrow after you're off work. Meanwhile, call the owner and tell him not to sell it to anyone else."

Seth was willing and ready to go check out the food truck, so the next morning she, Emma, Courtney and Seth climbed into her car and set off for Long Beach.

"Can I help cook?" Emma asked as they drove along.

It was good to see her finally excited about something. And speaking to her mother again, something she hadn't done for two days after Annie broke the news to her. All the assurances in the world that she'd still get to see her daddy hadn't been enough to buy forgiveness. Courtney had finally intervened with some very hard truths about

Emma's daddy, which had left Emma not speaking to either of them. Fortunately, this new adventure had provided a temporary truce.

"When you get a little older, if you still want to," Annie promised. "Meanwhile, though, I'm going to need someone to stand nearby and help hand out fliers when we open."

If all went according to plan and she could get the permits she needed in time, she hoped to have a soft opening the last weekend in June. Then, hopefully, she'd be ready for the Fourth of July. Her parents would be coming down for the day and then planned to take Emma back to Seattle with them the next day, which would give Annie the rest of the summer to work her food truck on the weekends and take advantage of tourist season. If she bought the food truck, she planned to cut back to part-time at Sandy's.

Scary thought, especially with her catering business getting off to a slow start. But she knew she'd have to scale back on something. In the end, being her own boss and having her own business was bound to make her more money than serving up eggs and pancakes at a restaurant.

But what if the food truck bombed?

It wouldn't. She'd done her research. She'd plan carefully and be frugal. It took time to build any business. She could be patient. She wanted this badly enough. She'd make it work.

They followed the directions to an old house that looked like it had been built in the early 1900s. It sat on a large lot and had a long driveway. Parked on that driveway was the possible future home of Simply Delicious...on wheels.

"Is that it?" Emma asked eagerly.

"Oy," Courtney said and gave the gum she was chewing a snap.

"It's got potential," Seth said. "Could be a good deal if the engine's sound."

Courtney pulled up the drive and parked behind the food truck and they all got out, Emma running ahead.

The seller had seen them coming and was already on the front porch. He looked to be somewhere in his fifties with long brownish hair pulled back into a ponytail. The size of his gut proclaimed him a lover of food.

"He probably ate all his profits," Courtney said to Annie as he hurried down the porch steps.

"Hi, I'm Joe," he said, shaking hands with all of them.

"I'm Annie, and these are my friends."

"And this is Julia," he said, motioning toward the food truck. "Named after Julia Child. We had some good times together, Julia and me."

"Do you mind my asking why you're selling?" Annie said.

He shrugged. "The wife. She's tired of it. Thought it would be fun at first, you know. And it was, for about a month. Then reality set in. Long hours, man. And if you hire people to work it, there goes your profits."

Joe obviously wasn't a natural born salesman. As he talked, Annie began to feel the urge to run back to the car before she could drive off the food truck cliff.

"We got grandkids and we don't want to work this hard anymore," he continued. "I ain't getting any younger. You're still young, got lots of energy, dreams."

Dreams. Yes, how could she have forgotten for even a moment?

"You gotta follow those dreams and catch 'em. Otherwise you end up with regrets."

Joe wasn't a salesman but he was a good philosopher.

"Can we take a look under the hood?" Seth asked.

"Sure. She's not in bad shape." To Annie, he said, "She's unlocked. You can go inside and take a look around if you want."

That was all it took for Emma, who was the first one in the door. Annie and Courtney followed.

"This is kind of cool," Courtney said, looking around.

It was more than cool. It was perfect. Annie stepped over to the work space. Yes, she could see herself putting together shrimp croissant sandwiches here. The grill was perfect. So was the sink.

"I can make this work," she said. Yes, she could. "I want this truck." No, she needed this truck like a fish needed water.

"It looks dumpy. We absolutely have to paint it," Courtney said.

"Can I help?" Emma asked, forgetting she was mad at Courtney.

"Absolutely," Courtney answered for Annie.

They stepped back outside to find the two men poking around the engine. *Please don't find anything wrong with it.*

Seth went from the engine to looking around underneath the truck. Then he came back out from under it and he and Joe stood and talked another five minutes.

"The suspense is killing me," Courtney said to Annie.

Finally, Seth strolled over to them and nodded. "Spark plugs need cleaning, got a frayed wire connecting the battery to the starter, but those are nothing. I've got a friend who can help with that. You'll need new tires."

"And a paint job," added one-note Courtney.

"If you were me, would you buy it?"

"I'm not you," he said. "I can tell you, though, owning your own business is a lot of work."

He knew whereof he spoke. Seth owned a mold removal business and spent his days removing rust and mold from houses and business buildings around town.

"I'm not afraid of work," she said.

"No, I guess you're not. Then buy it."

That cinched it. She got out her business checkbook and took the first step toward making her dream come true.

"My friend Devlin wants to come down tomorrow and bring his daughter," Pearl said to Moira. "She wants me to cut her hair." She might as well have added, *I hope I get an A on the test.*

Moira knew that Pearl and her *friend* were now talking on the phone every day, and Pearl's Saturdays were rapidly getting booked with a lot more than Waves clients.

"She's going to love you," Moira predicted.

"I hope so. I hope she's not one of those possessive women who doesn't want to see her dad with anyone."

"If she is, you'll change her mind."

Moira had yet to see the mysterious Devlin in person and was anxious to meet him, along with the daughter, who had Pearl more nervous than a mouse in a cage filled with mousetraps.

The following day Pearl came into the salon wearing slacks and a modest white blouse accented with a gold necklace and simple earrings. Classy and conservative—trying to make a good impression on the daughter. As if Pearl simply being her kind and generous self wouldn't make a good impression on anyone.

Promptly at two in the afternoon, a large man with faded red hair walked into the salon. He wore jeans and a shirt rolled up at the sleeves and looked like what he was: an older man aging well. With him came a slender woman with the same large eyes and hair still a vibrant red. It hung to her shoulders and probably didn't need more than a trim. So maybe this was a test. Or simply an excuse to meet the other woman in Dad's life.

Moira was giving Jo the Cheapo a haircut so she forced herself to pay attention to what she was doing. But Jo had no problem watching the newcomers.

"Who's that?" she whispered to Moira.

"New customer, I guess," Moira replied. If Pearl wasn't inclined to talk about the man in her life, Moira sure wasn't going to.

"This is my daughter, Molly," Devlin was saying.

Molly said hello to Pearl, a reserved hello.

"Your father's told me so much about you," Pearl almost gushed.

Moira gave her a psychic nudge. *Play it cool.*

"Really?" The daughter sounded as if Pearl had just shared some suspicious information.

"He tells me you have your own consulting business."

"I do. It's hard to get away."

"I hope we can make it worth your while," Pearl said.

"Daddy wanted me to meet you." Molly looked around the salon. "This is cute."

An observation more than a compliment. Moira tried to think of a descriptive word for this woman. *Aloof* came to mind. Or maybe just *territorial.*

"Did you want a haircut?" Pearl offered. The woman almost pulled back. A miscommunication there. She was obviously proud of her long hair.

"I guess I was wrong about that," said her father.

"I tell you what, then. Why don't we go on over to my house? I've made some clam dip I think you'll both enjoy," said Pearl.

Molly of the long red hair nodded and so did her father.

"Moira, will you close up for me?" Pearl called.

"Of course. Anything for you," Moira added in an attempt to let the woman know how deserving of loyalty her boss was.

As soon as they'd left, Jo asked, "Is Pearl dating?" Fortunately for Moira, she didn't wait for an answer. "Well, good for her. It's about time she got a life."

As Pearl ushered her company into her house, she tried to see it from Molly's perspective. Relatively small, dated kitchen cabinets and counter. But decorated nicely, surely that had to count for something.

"Sit down," Pearl said, gesturing toward the living room. "Make yourselves at home."

They settled into matching armchairs. The arms were a little faded with wear. Pearl vowed to put her charge card to use and replace them.

"Have you visited Moonlight Harbor before?" she asked Molly.

"Of course," Molly said as if Pearl had just asked the stupidest question ever.

"We came down to see Donnie and Arlene a lot over the years," Devlin added.

"I don't have time now," Molly continued. "Between the kids and my business, I'm too busy." As if to prove it, she checked her cell phone.

"Of course," Pearl said politely.

"She's almost too busy for her old man," said Devlin.

"Oh, Daddy, I'm never too busy for you," his daughter insisted.

Pearl handed them both glasses of iced tea, then returned to the kitchen for clam dip and crackers.

She was on her way back to the living room bearing a tray with plates and napkins, crackers and dip when Pumpkin put in an appearance. The greeting committee.

Pumpkin sauntered up to Molly and tried to rub against her leg, but Molly used that leg to nudge Pumpkin away. "I'm allergic to cats."

"Oh, sorry," Pearl said. She set the dip on the coffee table and hurried to pick up Pumpkin the Allergen.

"I wish I could have one, though," Molly added. Sharing a little about herself. Now they were getting somewhere.

"Do you have pets?" Pearl asked.

"We've got a Labradoodle. Pixie."

"Cute name," Pearl said and Devlin's daughter offered the beginnings of a smile.

"Would you like to try this clam dip?"

"I'm not much into clams," Molly said.

"You used to like them when you were a kid. Give it a try," coaxed her father, and Pearl wondered if he was talking about more than clams.

She took a plate, put a cracker on it and a microscopic dab of dip, then raised it to her mouth. She wore the same expression Pearl's daughter used to wear when Pearl insisted she try some new food she didn't want to eat. Suddenly Pearl found herself tearing up.

Devlin saw it. "What's wrong?"

Pearl shook her head. "Nothing," she said. "You reminded me of my daughter just now."

"Your daughter?" Molly asked, setting the cracker back down. "Daddy didn't tell me you had a daughter."

"I lost her a few years back. She died of an aneurysm."

Here was the way to have a cheerful get-to-know-you chat. Except now Pearl didn't feel like being cheerful or chatting.

"I'm so sorry," Molly said earnestly.

"I didn't know," Devlin added, sounding shocked.

Of course he didn't know. Their friendship was still new. He'd shared about losing his wife and she'd shared about losing her husband, of course, but she hadn't felt comfortable laying out the rest of her losses. Not when she was beginning to move on into a happier frame of mind. She'd had no desire to smother something good with that heavy dark blanket.

"This is life," she said with her usual attempt to be philosophical. "I shouldn't have mentioned it."

"Of course you should have," Molly said. "It's hard losing someone you loved. I still miss my mom."

Now her eyes were full of tears, too, and so were her dad's. This was not going to go down as a good first meeting.

"I still miss her every day," Molly said in a small voice.

"Of course you do," said Pearl.

"No one will ever take her place." It hadn't been said as a warning, only a simple statement of fact.

Pearl had no intention of taking anyone's place and was about to say so when Molly checked her phone. "I need to get back."

"We just got here," Devlin protested.

"I know. But it looks like Jimmy's ride to the game tonight fell through and he's pitching."

"I thought Carl was taking him."

"He's got to work late."

Had a text just come through? Pearl hadn't heard a ding to signal a notification. Maybe something had, though. Or maybe Molly was making it up.

She stood, announcing an end to all strategizing.

"Thanks for having us over," she said to Pearl. "I'm sorry I've got to go."

Pearl doubted it.

So did her dad. "Me, too," he said, his lips pulled down.

"I hope you'll come again," Pearl said to Molly. "Maybe you can bring your kids."

"Thanks," Molly said, then, looking self-conscious, she scooted for the door.

"That went well," Pearl murmured as the screen door shut behind her.

"It takes her a while to warm up to people," Devlin explained.

If ever, Pearl thought. If only she hadn't served clam dip. And had a cat. And had met the daughter before she met the father. Maybe they would have started off as friends and then Molly would have been willing to share her father. Too late now.

It had been good while it lasted.

Twenty-One

Moira called Pearl later that night wanting to know how the meeting with Devlin's daughter had gone.

"Horrible," Pearl said. "She's allergic to cats, she doesn't like clams and I'm pretty sure she doesn't like me."

"She doesn't know what she's missing."

That was Moira, always encouraging. "Oh, well. At this point in my life I don't really need a man."

"Who says?"

"Me."

"He might think different."

"No. At our age, a parent's first loyalty is to the child. I get that. My daughter might have felt the same way about me dating if she was still alive."

"I don't think so," Moira said. "I think your daughter would have wanted you to be happy."

She could have been with Devlin. But, "I can be happy just as I am."

And really, she could now. She was rebuilding her life one day at a time, one dinner out, one gathering with friends. And her business was doing great. Really, why complain? And why mourn something that had barely come to life. No sense in crying over spilled clams.

She said as much to Devlin when he called half an hour later. "I don't think this is going to work out."

"Oh, yes, it is," he said, his voice steely. "You didn't see Molly at her best."

Did she have a best? Oh, yes, she liked dogs. And she missed her mother. Two points for Molly.

"She really did have to get back, but she wants to come down again and get to know you better."

"Devlin, be honest with me, are you trying to force your daughter to like me?".

"No," he insisted. "But I did point out that she could have been a little more friendly. Like I said, it takes Molly a while to warm up to people."

It took a long time for glaciers to melt, too. Pearl wasn't sure she had that many years left. "I'm sure she would," Pearl said, trying to sound polite rather than sarcastic. "No hard feelings," she added, then, when he asked about seeing her the next weekend, gave him an excuse why she couldn't.

"I'm not giving up on this," he said. "I loved my wife, Pearl, but I don't want to be alone for the rest of my life. I want to spend it with someone kind and fun. And I like clam dip."

She couldn't help smiling at that, but it was a wistful smile.

Three days later, however, she was surprised when she got a thank-you card in the mail. The handwritten note in it was simple. *"Thank you for having us over. Sorry we couldn't stay for dinner. I hope we can get to know each other better in the future."* It was signed simply, *"Molly."*

Molly, who missed her mom and knew no woman would

ever take her place. Just like nobody could ever take the place of Pearl's daughter, or the granddaughter she'd tried so hard to find. But maybe, if things worked out with Devlin, Pearl and Molly could each provide some comfort to the other. They'd never be mother and daughter no matter what happened with Pearl and Devlin, but maybe they could become friends.

Pearl fished her cell phone out of her purse and called him.

"Well, hello there," he answered, his voice a smile.

"Hello there yourself," she said. "I'm making some fresh clam dip later this week."

Moira's life was the best it had ever been. She not only had a great job and good friends, but the grandmother she'd always wanted, as well. And she was with a man who was as close to perfect as a man could get.

Even though they'd barely begun hanging out, that man was already hinting about her leaving Courtney's couch and moving in with him, but she was determined not to rush into anything. She'd already been there and done that and once was enough.

"I keep forgetting," Victor said when she reminded him of her determination not to jump into any kind of commitment. "But you're right. We don't need to be in a hurry. Guess I just don't want anybody to come along and steal you."

"From a cop? Who would do that?" she joked.

"I think a lot of guys would risk it. You're something else, Moira."

Lang had said that once, too, but in a very different tone of voice.

Lang. Every once in a while he would sneak up on her

in her dreams and she'd wake up gasping and trying to still her racing heart, but she reminded herself that she'd been gone for months, and if he hadn't tracked her down by now, he never would.

"If he ever shows up, I'll beat the crap out of him before I let him hurt you," Courtney promised as they painted Annie's food truck.

Seth and his friend had given it a tune-up and brought it back better than new. Moira had helped her pick out a deep teal blue for the color and, now, even only half-painted, the little truck was already transforming into something übercute. Thanks to Brody Green, who had a friend at city hall, all the necessary permits were being expedited.

"Me, too," said Annie.

"Right," Courtney scoffed. "Miss Wimp."

"I'm not a wimp anymore," Annie insisted, although every time Greg showed up at the house wanting to talk to her, she folded in on herself like a snail retreating into its shell. Still, she'd stayed determined to move on without him and her friends were proud of her.

To prove how unworthy he was, Greg was nowhere in sight the day of the soft opening for Simply Delicious. Some men supported dreams, others ruined them. Moira knew which kind of man Greg was. It still hurt Annie that he hadn't cared enough about her and Emma to wrestle his addiction to the ground, but Moira hoped the excitement of finally getting her food truck was helping to ease her friend's pain.

It certainly looked like it. Annie was beaming as she handed out shrimp or ham-and-cheese croissant sandwiches accompanied by a fat dill pickle in red-and-white-checked paper serving dishes. She'd kept her menu small and simple and in addition to the croissant sandwiches, which were going to be her signature specialty, she offered grilled cheese sandwiches, veggie burgers, a cookie of the day and lemonade or iced tea. Moira, Courtney and Emma had been gratuitous with their flyers as it seemed half the town had turned out for the big day. All the Friday night gang and their families showed, along with members of the Moonlight Harbor Chamber of Commerce, which Annie had recently joined.

"This is great stuff," said Brody Green, who was president of the chamber. "I'll be a regular customer, you can count on that."

"I think you're going to have a lot of regular customers," Jenna Jones told her.

"I hope so," Annie said and waved to Seth Waters, who was standing at the edge of the crowd. "Moira, will you remind Seth that anything he wants is on the house?"

"Sure," Moira said.

It took her a while to swim through the crowd to where he stood and deliver the message.

"I'll get something later. Let her take care of the paying customers first," he said.

"I think she wants to make sure you know how much she appreciates you helping her."

"I know it," he said. "Nice color, by the way. Really makes the truck stand out. Who picked that?"

"Both of us," said Moira, determined not to be a spotlight thief.

"Good job, both you," he said, then melted into the crowd.

Annie ran out of food an hour before she was supposed to close. "I didn't plan that very well," she said after they'd followed her truck back to the house to celebrate her success.

"How could you have known the whole town would show up?" Moira said to stop her before she could beat herself up.

"I should have known," Annie said softly. "The people here are amazing."

"Yes, they are," Courtney agreed. "And at least you have a better idea how to plan for the Fourth."

Plans. Everyone had some for the Fourth of July, and the salon hummed with activity as women came in getting their summer cuts and refreshing their hair colors. Hyacinth was helping Pastor Paul get ready for a church picnic, coordinating the food. Nora's family was coming down for an overnight, and Pearl's new man was coming for a visit and bringing his family. His daughter, Molly, had volunteered to bring cupcakes.

"I barely have room for them all," Pearl said as she styled Arlene's hair.

"You know we're happy to take the overflow," Arlene said. "I'm sure happy this is working out. Dev is one lucky man."

The way Pearl was smiling, it was plain to see she felt like one lucky woman.

Edie Patterson was issuing invitations for the annual bonfire she and her great-niece threw every Fourth of July. "I hope you'll come," she said to Moira. "Celeste and her husband will be down and I know she'll want to see you. She has a big announcement to make and I think I know what it is," Edie added with a smile. "Bring Victor."

"He's working an extra shift but I'll be happy to come on my own," Moira said. She loved that her man was so dedicated to his job and the community, but she was also a little disappointed. She'd hoped they'd be able to hit the beach and watch the fireworks together that night. Everyone had been telling her how crazy it was. Thousands of people came to town to set off fireworks on the beach.

"Not a city in the state can compete with the show people put on down here," Chastity had told her. "Everyone brings their fireworks and has bonfires. It's my favorite holiday."

"Oh, yeah," Courtney agreed when Moira got home from work and was sharing what she'd heard. "This place rocks. And Jenna's beach party is the best. You don't want to miss it."

Moira took in the pile of chicken breasts and legs, the bowls of flour and eggs and then looked at the large pan of sizzling oil. Courtney was a genius with fabric but she wasn't the world's best cook.

"Uh, what are you doing?" she asked.

"I'm making fried chicken to bring to the party tomorrow. I found a recipe online. Pretty easy."

"I guess," Moira said dubiously. She half wished Annie was around to supervise but she'd gone shopping for supplies for the food truck and had taken Emma with her. Well, how hard could it be to fry chicken?

She'd just helped herself to a glass of the lavender lemonade Annie had made and settled on the porch with a biography about Coco Chanel that she'd found at the library when she heard a screech coming from inside the house. She bolted out of her chair and ran in, colliding with Courtney, who was bolting the other direction.

"Quick! How do you put out a grease fire?" Courtney demanded.

How was Moira supposed to know? Her mother had never fried anything.

Courtney didn't wait for an answer. She raced back

into the kitchen where a happy little bonfire was dancing on the stove top.

"Shit!" cried Moira and grabbed her cell phone to dial 911.

"What is your emergency?" asked the dispatcher.

My roommate thinks she can cook. "Our stove's on fire," Moira cried.

Courtney was screeching and pulling things out of the cupboard. "What do I use? Baking soda, right? Or is it flour?" She found a five-pound sack of flour and heaved its contents toward the stove top. The flames found it delicious and grew bigger and Courtney let out a fresh shriek.

"The stove," Moira said to the dispatcher. "What should she use to put out the fire?"

"Not flour," said the woman. *Too late for that.* "Baking soda."

"Baking soda," Moira called from the edge of the kitchen.

Things were now flying from the cupboard. "Where *is* it?"

"What do we do if we can't find the baking soda?" Moira asked the woman. *Besides panic.*

"Fire needs oxygen. Put a lid on the pot."

"Put a lid on it," Moira reported.

"Are you nuts? It'll burn my arm off." Courtney yelled, frantically hauling things out of the cupboard, dropping them on the counter. Cans were bouncing everywhere. A box of baking soda bounced off the counter and fell to the floor.

"It's too late for that," Moira said to the woman. "We need help."

"What's your address?" the dispatcher asked, still calm. Easy for her.

Moira told her. Then, "Shit! There goes the wall."

Courtney had found another small box of baking soda. Standing far from the stove and leaning away, she shook it in the direction of the fire. The flames just laughed. She yelped and jumped back, dropping the box.

"If you don't have a fire extinguisher, get out of the house," said the dispatcher. "Someone's on the way."

"We have to get out," Moira called, heading for the door.

Courtney should have been right behind her. She wasn't. Moira poked her head back inside to see where she was. There wasn't that much smoke yet. She couldn't have keeled over from smoke inhalation.

She looked to the right. No Courtney in the kitchen. Only an early Fourth of July bonfire on the stove. Moira looked to her left. There in the living room was Courtney, gathering up a pile of fabric.

Moira rushed back in. "What are you doing?"

"I don't want this jacket to burn."

"*You're* going to burn," Moira snapped. She helped grab some more sewing supplies and then towed her friend out of the house. They were barely out when Moira remembered her cat. "Harry Pawter!" she cried and dashed back into the house.

There was no Harry in the living room, which meant he was upstairs, sacked out on Emma's bed, one of his favorite places. Moira dashed up the stairs. Yep, there he was.

"Come on, Harry," she said, grabbing him. "We've got to get out of here." She ran back down the stairs, Harry protesting over all the bumping, and raced back out of the house.

She got out just as a collection of firefighters, all suited up, carrying axes and fire extinguishers came up the front porch steps. "You need to get out of the house, ma'am," one barked.

They didn't have to tell her twice. She ran down the steps and stood next to Courtney, who was hugging her half-completed jacket and swearing.

The firefighters had the problem under control in only a matter of minutes. "Not too much damage," said one when they came back out. He was cute enough to light some fires himself. Cute enough for Courtney?

"Are you okay, Courtney?" he asked.

"Yeah, now that you guys saved me from burning down the house." She cocked her head and studied him a moment. "Do I know you?"

"Jonas Greer. We've only met once. I've come a few times to The Drunken Sailor. Line dancing."

"Line dancing," she repeated as if trying to place him.

He frowned slightly. "You were always too busy with Victor King to notice me."

Courtney had to have really been obsessed not to notice him. It looked like she did now, though. Moira smiled.

"Anyway," he said, back to business. "You should always have a fire extinguisher handy. Kitchen fires can get out of control in a hurry."

"I guess so," Courtney said. "This is the last time I ever fry chicken."

"You just have to keep a watch."

She sighed and shook her head. "I'm a fire hazard."

"I teach a fire safety class," said Jonas. "Why don't you come?" He had a smile almost as great as Victor's.

"Maybe I will," Courtney said. "Thanks for getting here so quickly."

"It's what we're here for. Call us anytime."

"I hope we don't ever have to again," Courtney said fervently.

He nodded. "Maybe I'll see you at the station. I'd be glad to teach you about fires."

Courtney was getting the message. "Maybe you will," she said, putting her flirty voice into action. "Or at The Drunken Sailor. I bet I could teach you a thing or two also."

His smile got bigger. He nodded, then followed the others back to the truck.

"He is hot," Moira said.

"So am I," said Courtney.

They went back into the kitchen to check out the damage and Harry went back upstairs to bed.

"Well, it could be worse," Courtney said as they stood side by side. "I'll have to call the landlord. God knows what he'll charge me for this mess."

The stove was covered in fire extinguisher goop and some of that had spilled over onto the chicken. The microwave was dead, and the wall was blackened. The cupboard above it was black, as well. The ones on either side were singed also. Cans lay scattered all over the counter and floor. The half-empty baking soda box had landed on the floor clear over by the kitchen table. The room smelled of burnt wood and chemicals.

"Maybe you don't have to call him," Moira said, opening the back door to let in fresh air. "I think this is fixable. I bet you could get Seth to help pull out those cabinets and put in new ones. We could wash and repaint."

"Good suggestion. I should still tell him, anyway." Courtney frowned at the ruined chicken. "I guess I won't be bringing fried chicken to the party tomorrow."

"Just be glad you can still bring yourself," Moira said. "I think we'd better buy a fire extinguisher."

"I think you're right. Meanwhile, I guess I'd better clean up this mess."

Moira started picking up cans from the floor and Courtney got herself a piece of gum, then did some research online to find out how to clean up fire extinguisher residue.
"Oh, boy, this is going to be fun," she muttered.

They were still cleaning when Annie came back home,
Emma behind her, carrying a plastic grocery bag. "What
on earth happened?" she asked, setting her bags on the
table.

"I wanted to roast hot dogs," Courtney said.

"A little kitchen fire," Moira explained.

"It smells yucky," said Emma, wrinkling her nose.

"It is yucky. You should probably hang on the front
porch so you don't have to breathe this," Courtney said
to her.

"Good idea," Annie said. "Why don't you go over to
Addie's house and see if she can play?"

Emma was more than happy to scram.

"What were you doing?" Annie asked, and her tone
made Moira think of her mom.

"I was trying to be you, okay?" Courtney snapped and
wrung out a rag in the kitchen sink.

"Let me just put away my perishables and I'll help you,"
Annie said.

"No, we've got it," Courtney said, a little less cranky.
"Just don't ever say the word *chicken* in my presence."

"It could have been worse," said Seth, who came over
right after they called him. "I can fix it, no problem."

"Thank God," said Courtney. "Does this mean I don't
have to call Mr. Melville and tell him I tried to burn down
his house?"

"I can keep a secret," Seth told her, and she smiled.

Okay, crisis averted. Now they could enjoy the holiday.
And enjoy it Moira did. Her mother didn't come down—

a second date with a potential Mr. Perfect (Moira wasn't holding her breath)—but Victor's family came and she enjoyed visiting the various food and crafts booths on the pier with his mother and father and brother and sister-in-law. A normal family, wow.

Victor was even able to join them as part of his normal duties involved keeping an eye on things, and she enjoyed strolling among the arts and crafts booths with him. She was impressed by how many people stopped him to say hi or had a word of thanks for him.

An older woman called to him with a cheerful hello, and he took Moira over to where she sat in a booth, selling hand-crocheted items.

"Hi, Mrs. Burton. How's Dougal?" he asked.

"Now that I took your advice, fine. No more problem with him escaping."

"I guess that means I don't get any more cookies," he joked.

"It looks like you've found someone to make you cookies," she said with a sly smile.

Victor didn't blush. Instead he grinned broadly and introduced Moira, as well as the rest of his family.

"You've got a good man there," the woman said to Moira, and then he did blush.

"That's our boy," his mother said proudly.

To cover his embarrassment, he bought dish towels for both Moira and his mom.

"She's sweet," Moira said to him as they all walked away.

"Nice lady."

"Who's Dougal?"

"Her dog. He used to be a real escape artist." Victor grinned. "Sometimes I miss giving old Dougal rides home. I'd sure like to get a dog someday."

"Harry's not enough?" Moira teased. A cat was enough for her. But maybe Victor could turn her into a dog lover.

"Harry's pretty cool," Victor admitted.

Their conversation didn't get any further as another person wanted to stop and say hi to Victor, a big hairy man who had a skinny woman in ancient jeans and a faded T-shirt with him. Moira noticed a baby bump under that T-shirt.

"Officer King, my man," the big guy said, and he and Victor bumped knuckles.

"How's it going, Tommy?" Victor asked.

"I'm clean, man. I'm good. Had to clean up my act. We're gonna have a kid." He put a big arm around the woman and she beamed up at him. "Can't be doin' that shit when you're a dad."

"Good job, man," Victor said. Then to the woman, "Be sure to bring the kid by the station so we can see...her? Him?"

"Him," said the woman.

"My son's gonna grow up to be better than me, that's for damn sure," Tommy said. "Maybe he'll grow up to be a cop."

"There you go," Victor said diplomatically.

"What's his story?" Moira asked as Tommy and his lady went on their way.

"Let's just say he had some problems that involved a few visits from some of us."

"You'd think he wouldn't like you," she ventured. "If he had problems."

Victor shrugged. "We've always been fair with him and he knows it. We have to live in this community, so we try to treat everyone fairly. Some people pull out of their tailspins and when they do that's a win-win—good for them and good for the town. I like seeing success stories like that. Wish everybody who messes up could figure out how to become one."

Several more people called an enthusiastic hello as they strolled by. Victor nodded politely to all of them.

"You were right about my car needing a ring job," one woman told him. "I'm so glad you noticed it burning oil and stopped me."

"Is there anyone in this town who doesn't love you?" Moira asked as they followed his parents to a booth selling wood carvings.

Victor shrugged. "I'm sure there is. I really only care about one person loving me," he added, smiling down at her, setting off sparklers in her tummy.

The kiss he gave her before leaving for his patrol car, to check on someone setting off fireworks in a no-fireworks zone, promised even more sparklers later that night. The only thing to mar the day was a feeling that crept over her after he'd left, some odd sense of unease that she couldn't explain. Once she even thought she saw someone who looked like Lang, but he vanished in the crowd.

She eventually shook it off and was able to enjoy the bonfire on the beach behind Edie Patterson's house. "By all means, bring Victor's family," Edie had said when Moira had asked, and by the time they got to the party she and Mrs. King, who was already insisting Moira call her Janine, were becoming good friends.

"I'm so glad Victor's found a nice girl," Janine said, as they sat side by side, toasting marshmallows. "We were beginning to wonder if he ever would."

A nice girl. Moira liked the sound of that. "He's amazing," she said.

"We think he's pretty special. And I know he thinks you are," Janine added.

"Okay, announcements," declared Jenna's sister, Celeste, standing up and pulling her husband to his feet. "Henry and I..." she gave a dramatic pause, then finished "...are pregnant."

"Yes!" whooped Jenna, and she jumped up to hug her sister.

"I'm going to have a cousin," Sabrina said happily.

"Do you know yet if it's a boy or a girl?" Nora asked.

"No, and we want to be surprised," said Celeste. "Don't we, Henry?"

"We want whatever Celeste wants," Henry said, making their friends laugh.

Lucky Celeste. She not only had a good man, she was going to have a kid.

Lang hadn't wanted kids. Or marriage. Ever. And Moira had had her doubts about being a good mother. But maybe she wouldn't be so bad. Maybe someday, if things worked out with Victor.

"I think it's time for some campfire songs," Edie said a few minutes later.

Seth Waters had brought a guitar. He'd been sitting next to Jenna on a log and moved to where he'd propped the guitar case. Brody Green arrived just as Seth was taking it out and claimed the vacant spot next to her.

She smiled at him but it was hard to read that smile. Was it a simple welcome for a friend or something more?

It wasn't hard to tell how Seth felt. His lips were clamped together and a muscle in his jaw twitched.

By the time he'd found another place to sit and had tuned his guitar, he'd slipped on an easy expression, though. "Requests?" he asked.

Yeah. Tell me what the deal is between you and Jenna and Brody?

"'Girls Just Want to Have Fun,'" said Henry and winked at his wife.

She stood up and attempted to lead the others and everyone stumbled through the verses. All were able to sing the main line with gusto.

After that, it was on to "The Banana Boat Song," "Stand by Me" and "Africa."

"'Ninety-Nine Bottles of Beer on the Wall,'" Pete requested and everyone groaned. Without waiting for anyone, he began to sing and Edie joined him, Seth finding the key they were in and strumming along.

They finally gave up on fifty-nine bottles when the first fireworks began to sail up into a darkening sky. "Happy Independence Day, everyone," Edie said.

Independence Day. Moira smiled and celebrated her own independence.

She was feeling content and happy when she returned to the house around ten thirty. She found Annie already in her sleep T-shirt and getting ready to head upstairs to bed.

"I'm pooped," Annie said.

Not surprising. There'd been a pack of people milling around in front of Annie's food truck when Moira had stopped by with Victor's family to get treats.

"A successful day?" Moira asked.

"Sold out," Annie said with a smile. "Emma's staying with Grandma and Grandpa at the Oyster Inn, which means I can sleep in. Thank God. I could sleep for a week."

"Between the food truck and your catering business, I think your sleeping days are over," Moira said.

Annie nodded. "Yes, it's a good thing my parents are taking Emma for a while. I'm sure going to miss her, though." She yawned. "Guess you're in charge until Courtney gets home."

Who knew when that would be? Courtney had put in an appearance at the beach party, bringing a bucket of chicken she'd picked up at Beachside Grocery and then wandered off down the beach to where the Moonlight Harbor Fire Department had a truck parked. A certain firefighter was on duty down there.

Moira was fine with having some alone time. She had one last chapter in her Muriel Sterling book to finish. She curled up on the couch with it and began reading, digesting Muriel's final pearls of wisdom.

"Keep making your dreams come true," Muriel concluded. *"And celebrate every victory, every goal you reach along the way. I finally built the life I wanted. You can, too."*

Yes, she could. Moira had just shut the book and was on her way to the kitchen in search of chocolate when she heard a knock on the door. It wasn't the usual drunken pounding that signaled a visit from Greg. This was a polite knock. Victor must have gotten off work early and decided to surprise her.

She hurried to the door and swung it wide, a welcoming smile on her face. The smile died when she saw who was standing on the front porch.

Twenty-Two

"Long time, no see," said Lang. "Mind if I come in?" Without waiting for an answer, he stepped in, shutting the door behind him, and pushed past Moira into the living room. He wore expensive jeans and a slim white linen shirt. Casual brown shoes. No flip-flops or sandals. You could do so much more damage wearing shoes.

He stood there, looking around, nodding in mock approval. "Nice place you got here."

Any minute he was going to lose that smile, get nasty, probably hit her. Moira could feel her heart racing faster than a high wind in a winter storm.

"Why are you here, Lang?" She managed to keep her voice steady.

"Why am I here? Maybe I'm here to find out why my girlfriend left me. For God's sake, Moira, I thought you'd been kidnapped or something."

By aliens? She kept the smart remark caged firmly behind her lips. That would only be gasoline on the fire, and they'd already had one fire in the house.

He strolled around, looking up the stairs, checking

out the kitchen. "What happened in there? Did you try to cook?"

"What do you want?" She was trying hard to keep her voice calm, to stay nonadversarial. In the end, it wouldn't matter. He was there for only one reason. To punish her.

She took a step back, keeping some distance between them, edging toward the door. If only she had a gun. She'd shoot him. Not to kill, but certainly to maim.

She knew someone with a gun. She knew plenty of someones. Her cell phone was on the coffee table. If she could reach it...

"I told you," he growled. "I want to know why you left me."

"Because I was tired of what we had. We could have been good, Lang." It was true. Things had been good when they first got together. If only he hadn't turned ugly.

Not turned. He'd been ugly all along. He'd simply hidden it.

"We *were* good. Or so I thought. And then you just up and waltzed right out of my life, like I don't matter."

You don't. Not anymore. Moira raised her chin.

He closed the gap between them in two quick strides and grabbed her chin, his fingers squeezing like a vise. "Don't you look at me like that."

She tried to pull away. "Stop it, Lang. You're hurting me." As if he cared.

He tightened his grip and yanked her toward him, sending pain riding down the tendons in her neck, putting his face inches from hers. "Nothing like you hurt me. No one has ever walked out on me. Ever! Do you know how long I looked for you? I finally gave up. Then, a few weeks ago, I was surfing the internet, thought, 'What the hell, I kind of miss her. I'll try one more time.' And what did I find but an old article from a newspaper in some Podunk town about a new colorist. 'She's making everyone beautiful... I think I've found my forever home,'" he quoted, his tone mocking. "And there, babe, was a picture of you. So I come down here, stay in some fleabag motel and check things out. Yep, there you are, happy as a clam with your new job and this house, whoring around with another man." He let go of her, giving her a violent shove and sending her stumbling back against the couch. "A cop? Haven't you ever read the statistics? Cops are all violent sons of bitches."

No, they weren't. Most of them were noble and conscientious, and they cared about their community. Especially her cop.

He shook his head, frowned. "You should have stayed with me, Moira. What you did to me, the way you left me... I can't let you get away with that. You know I can't."

His hands were at his sides, clenching and unclenching, like a boxer getting ready to throw a punch. This was the windup. Could she get to the door and get out before he reached her? Probably not.

Agree. Say yes. Anything to calm him down, make him stop.

But there'd be no stopping him. Not this time. He'd beat her to death for sure. She could see it in his eyes.

So what was the point of cowering or groveling? And why should she?

Something began to bubble up inside Moira. It wasn't right, what he was saying, what he was trying to do to her all over again. She didn't deserve to be punished for anything by anyone, especially this horrible loser of a man who'd done his best to murder her self-esteem.

The bubbling turned to a full rolling boil. "No, I don't," she said. "It's you who should be punished, Lang."

"What did you say?" He stared at her, disbelieving.

Something she never would have said in the past. But enough was enough. She couldn't be afraid anymore. She wouldn't be. She was done finessing him, placating him, acting like a whipped puppy. She was better than that. She was better than him. If he did end up killing her, at least she'd die bravely.

"You heard me. You should be punished for the way you abused me, both mentally and physically. You're a bully, a worthless, insecure—"

He was on her quicker than a heartbeat. The slap to her face was so hard she saw stars. It cut off her sentence and sent her reeling onto the couch, knocking over the floor lamp in the process, breaking the glass shade. A favor, actually. Her cell phone was now in reach.

She forced herself to ignore the pain and snatched it. "Get out of here, Lang, right now, or I'm calling the cops." If only Victor were there.

Victor. She didn't want to die, bravely or otherwise. Not now, not when she was living her best life ever, not when she was with a good man. She did a quick swipe of the screen to bring up the numbers. 911. It only took a second to dial.

"I don't think so," he snarled and lunged for her, grabbing her hand.

All she needed was a second. She hung on for all she was worth, trying to free herself from him. He yanked the phone out of her hand and threw it across the room.

With a cry of desperation, she scrambled out from under him and dived over the coffee table. No use going for the phone now. It was in pieces.

"Just remember, you had this coming to you," he snarled.

* * *

Annie had heard the escalating voices. She'd left her bedroom and slipped down the hall, stood at the top of the stairs long enough to know Moira was in trouble. The man she'd run from had found her. Annie raced back to her room, grabbed her phone from the bedside table and dialed 911.

As soon as someone answered, she gave the address. "A woman is being assaulted here. Come quick!"

Even as efficient as the police were, it could be minutes before they arrived. It was, after all, the Fourth of July, and both the police and fire departments were busy. What to do?

She heard a crash as something fell to the floor and broke. She heard a half scream come from Moira. She couldn't wait for the cops.

Heart hammering, she left her bedroom and hurried back down the hall. From her vantage point, she could see Moira trying to protect her head as the man rained blows on her. He shoved her violently and she fell back over the coffee table and onto the floor. The lamp by the couch was on the floor, the glass shade broken. Moira grabbed a piece of the shade and hurled it at him, but it missed. Her attempt to fight back enraged him even more.

"Bitch!" he roared and dived for her as she tried to scrabble away.

Neither one saw Annie as she raced down the stairs toward the kitchen. She grabbed what was nearest at hand and moved to the living room that had turned into a boxing ring, opening the front door wide on her way, an invitation to Moonlight Harbor's finest. If they ever arrived.

Moira had managed to get to her feet but the man was

on her and had her by the arm. "You'll pay for this!" she threatened between sobs and he slapped her.

"Who's gonna make me, you?"

No, me, thought Annie. Annie, who had never been athletic—who was always the last chosen for neighborhood softball games when she was a kid, who couldn't hit a tennis ball if her life depended on it. She swung the broom she'd grabbed with all her might and caught the man alongside the head, sending him stumbling off to the side. She swung again and caught him on the back, making him pitch forward and Moira kicked out, catching him in the knee.

He howled in pain and fell to the ground.

They had the advantage now. Annie brought the broom down on him like a giant fly swatter and Moira kicked him in the gut.

Victor and Frank both pulled up to the house at the same time. A woman being assaulted at Courtney's house. Not Greg's style. A black Mazda sat parked out front. The perp. It was easy to figure out whom it belonged to. Victor was out of his vehicle in a heartbeat and running up the front walk, Frank right behind him.

The front door was open, like a welcome. "Police," Victor announced as they came in.

Then he stopped in his tracks at the sight in front of him. The perp was curled in a ball on the floor, trying to hold on to a knee with one hand and protect his head with the other, alternately crying out in pain and yelling threats. Moira had just kicked him in the gut and Annie was in midswing with a broom. She brought it down on the guy's head, then stepped back. Still holding it.

"We'll take it from here," Frank said, removing the broom from her hand.

She nodded and released it but still looked ready to go a few more rounds.

"They're assaulting me," the man accused.

Victor ignored him. "Did this man hit you, Moira?" Her nose was bloodied and her lip was swollen and bleeding and she was going to have one doozy of a black eye.

She nodded.

"He came in here and was attacking her," Annie said. "I saw it."

And Moira had felt it. Poor kid.

The perp was still on the floor, holding his knee with both hands now and groaning. He freed one hand long enough to point at Moira. "She broke my kneecap."

"Was that before or after you tried to break her jaw, sir?" Victor asked.

"He was yelling at her and beating her," Annie said, her voice now near hysterical.

"You're under arrest. Please stand," Victor said. And then, since the guy was having trouble doing so, Victor helped him, giving him a good yank, just to make sure he made it up all right, of course. "Put your hands behind your back."

"This is my girlfriend," the perp protested.

No, she'd been his punching bag. Obviously, not anymore. "I assume you're going to want to press charges?" he asked Moira.

"You bet," she said, glaring at the guy, tears running down her cheeks.

"You'll be sorry," he spit.

Right in front of two officers of the law. That was rich. They marched him out of the house, the guy making all kinds of threats of lawsuits and recriminations as he went. *Yeah, good luck with that.*

"You saw them. They were beating me!" he roared as they settled him in the back of Victor's car for a nice little ride to jail.

It would have been great to tell him he had the right to remain silent and suggest he exercise that right but they didn't bother. Contrary to what people saw on TV, he wouldn't get Mirandized until later.

Frank did speak to him, though. "A real shame," he said. "A big strong man like you being beat up by two little women. Boy, it'd be pretty embarrassing if that got in the news."

The perp shut up.

Once the adrenaline stopped coursing through Moira's veins she felt weak, and she fell onto the nearest chair.

"I'm getting some ice for your eye," Annie said and hurried into the kitchen.

Moira tried to breathe and waited for her heart rate to return to normal. He'd punched her and now it hurt to breathe. She was sure he'd cracked a rib. She was alive, thank God, but she felt like a soldier who'd barely survived hand-to-hand combat.

Annie returned, balancing a bottle of ibuprofen and a glass of water on a freezer bag filled with ice, wrapped in a kitchen towel. "Thanks," Moira said to her. "You probably saved my life. I think he was going to beat me to death."

Annie perched on the arm of the couch. "I was so scared for you."

"I was scared, too," Moira confessed. "But I did it. I finally told him what I really thought of him. I stood up to him. Well, sort of."

"You did great," Annie assured her.

"I feel like I've somehow broken an evil spell. I'm going to take him down, Annie. He can't be allowed to do this to another woman."

He probably would, somewhere, someday. Men like that never changed.

But the women they abused could. They could get away and get stronger. Moira had proved it.

"You're my hero," Annie said quietly.

Moira could only manage a tiny smile. She winced as she touched the ice to her eye. "Ouch."

"You took such a beating."

"But it was my last. I'm not taking crap from anyone ever again."

She said as much to Victor when he came back to insist she go to the emergency room. "I told him what a rotten bully he is," she said as he helped her into his patrol car.

"You were one brave woman," Victor said.

Well, sort of. "The one who was really brave was Annie."

"You both were." Victor shook his head. "Coming after the guy with a broom. Now I've seen everything."

"It was enough to knock him off balance and give us the upper hand."

"You probably didn't even need us," Victor said with a smile.

"Oh, we did. I still need you."

"We're here to serve and protect," he said, reaching a hand out to gently rub her neck. "Honestly, it was all I could do not to beat the crap out of that loser. But you were already doing a pretty good job of it."

"Girls rule," she joked.

"Yeah, you do," he said softly.

* * *

"I missed it all," Courtney lamented the next day as Moira and Annie filled her in on what had happened. "I wish I could have been there to help beat the crap out of him."

"We had it under control," Moira said, looking at Annie. She wasn't able to manage much of a smile with her split lip and she'd already commanded Courtney not to make her laugh. That old joke about it only hurting when you laughed was true. Broken ribs hurt.

"Yes, we did," Annie said, sounding proud of herself. "There comes a point when you can't let people push you around. And no one deserves to be hit, especially not Moira."

"I like to think I'd have been able to fight him off on my own," Moira said, "but honestly, I don't know what would have happened if you hadn't jumped in. Thank you for being so brave. And such a good friend."

Annie had no problem smiling. "I love it when things turn out the way they should."

It looked like Moira was going to finally get the kind of happy ending Annie loved in movies. She was even a little bit jealous. Yes, she finally had her food truck, but she was living her dream alone.

It was a sad day when, come September, she and Greg stood in the courthouse hallway, their divorce final. "I can't believe you did this to us," he said miserably.

It was still always someone else's fault when he screwed up. "No, Greg, I didn't do this to us. You did. Life's all about choices and you've made yours." He shoved his hands in his jeans' front pockets and scowled at her, and she sighed. "You know, I think I'll always love you a little bit. Maybe, if you ever pull your life together and become the kind of man your daughter and I can look up to, I'll be able to like you again."

He didn't look at her, just nodded, then he turned and walked away. She had full custody of Emma but he had visitation rights so they'd still be seeing each other. Maybe she'd even see him sober. Who knew?

The one thing she knew for sure was that she'd done the right thing, painful as it had been. Maybe, like Moira, someday she, too, would get that happy ending—true love wrapped in a glowing sunset moment. Anything was possible. She was sure going to do what she could to make the rest of her life better than it had been for the last ten years. Like she'd told Greg, it was all about choices.

Twenty-Three

Fall came on with sunshine, smiles and accomplishments. Moira's wounds, both physical and emotional, healed.

She hadn't felt even remotely sorry for Lang when he was sentenced to a year in jail and given a five-thousand-dollar fine. He had, indeed, broken a rib, and because of that he was charged with assault in the third degree, a class-C felony. She hoped he'd wake up and learn how to treat people better but she doubted he would. All she knew was he'd never treat her badly again. She'd signed up for karate lessons.

She and Lang did have one more dream encounter. This time he was in prison and she was visiting. It wasn't a normal prison. This was like the Château d'If, where Edmond Dantès was imprisoned before he escaped and became the Count of Monte Cristo, and Lang's cell was in a horrible, dank dungeon. He wore filthy rags, a long scraggly beard and looked gaunt and miserable.

"I'm sorry," he sobbed. "Get me out of here, Moira, please."

"I can't," she told him. "I don't have the key. You'll have to find it and save yourself."

The words were barely out of her mouth when she awoke. No racing heart, no trying to catch her breath. Only the realization that, in the end, everyone had to find their own key to escape the messes they made.

Annie had found her key. She was able to quit waitressing thanks to her food truck continuing to do hot business, right along with her catering. She was the town's new poster girl for success. Greg no longer banged on the door and made a ruckus on the front porch and the house was constantly filled with both laughter and good aromas as she concocted new recipes. Moira, Courtney and Emma devoured her spiced apple bread in one day.

Greg did manage some sporadic visits with his daughter, which left her happy with him and angry with her mom. After those visits it always took a couple of days and a visit to Nora's ice-cream parlor to restore mother-daughter relations to normal.

"The dust will settle eventually," Courtney kept assuring her and Annie hoped she was right.

Courtney ushered in the cold fall weather creating plenty of heat with Jonas, and Moira suspected it wouldn't be long before Courtney moved out and she and Annie had the house to themselves.

Fall brought Moira cooking lessons with Edie, word games with Pearl (when she wasn't busy with the new man in her life) and plenty of cozy nights enjoying a fire in the woodstove at Victor's house. Moira did spider patrol for him.

A new stylist arrived at Waves, a girl fresh out of beauty school who was in awe of Moira and more than willing to sit at her feet and learn. She'd also been pretty taken with Victor the first time she saw him walk into the salon. Until she saw him kiss Moira.

"He's probably the only decent guy around here," she'd grumbled.

"Not necessarily," Moira said. There was always Frank.

Halloween came with pumpkin carving and costume parties. Courtney sewed an elaborate fairy costume for Emma to wear trick-or-treating. She turned herself into Maleficent for the big bash she and Jonas went to at The Drunken Sailor ("'Cause I like bad girls," she said with a grin.) and Moira wore a Wonder Woman costume. Courtney took first place and scored a fifty-dollar gift card.

Then they rounded the corner into Thanksgiving, with Moira's roommates going home to their families. She spent the day with Victor's family, eating turkey and stuffing made from scratch. Under Edie's supervision, she made her first-ever pumpkin bread, which she took to the feast and Janine raved over. The Kings included her mother in the celebration and Mom brought pie. Store-bought. Come Christmas everyone gathered again, and Mom brought cookies. Chocolate mint. Store-bought.

"I love these," Victor said, choosing one from the plate instead of his mother's home-baked sugar cookies, and Moira loved him for it. She loved him, period.

By Valentine's Day she was so over being cautious and ready for major commitment.

"Maybe I should propose to him," she said to Hyacinth as she worked on turning her hair lavender with gold tints.

"I don't know if that's such a good idea," Hyacinth said. "He could already be planning to ask you on Valentine's Day. I'm sure he's planned something special."

"We're going to The Porthole for dinner. That's special."

"Maybe he's going to propose there," Hyacinth said. "I'm sure he will soon. You just have to be patient."

Hyacinth was proof that patience paid off. Pastor Paul

had popped the question to her at their church's New Year's Eve party and she was now sporting a diamond ring and planning a June wedding.

"Yeah, you're probably right," Moira agreed. "And I did tell him way back that I didn't want to rush into anything. But he should have figured out that I'm over that."

"I bet he has. Who knows what will happen when you two are out to dinner tonight. He hasn't taken the day off for nothing," said Pearl, who had her friend Arlene in the chair next to them.

Pearl's romance had hit high gear. Her someone special was coming down to take her out to dinner and finalize plans for a cruise to the Mexican Riviera. Moira would be managing the salon in her absence. Moira was doing a lot of that lately.

"Girlie girl, if there isn't a ring on your finger by tomorrow, I'll be very much surprised," said Arlene.

"You know it's coming, that's for sure," Courtney said when she came in for a hair color touch-up before her date with Jonas. "And when it does, nobody will be happier for you than me. You guys are perfect for each other. And wasn't it big of me to admit it?" she cracked. "By the way, I expect to be a bridesmaid."

"How about maid of honor?"

"I'll take it. And you can be mine. God knows Annie won't have time as busy as she is these days."

Annie was busy, and she and Emma had found a small beach cottage not far from Courtney and moved in at the beginning of the month. Which freed up a bedroom for Moira.

Not that she was there much.

"By the way," Courtney said, "I'm proposing to Jonas tonight. He'd better say yes."

That was Courtney, always one to go after what she wanted. Moira was just glad she'd decided not to want Victor anymore.

He came into the salon later that afternoon, casual in jeans and a jacket, an announcement to any and all that he was off duty and if they had problems he wouldn't be around to help solve them. He carried a huge bouquet of red roses.

"Oh, my gosh," said Chastity, who was doing Tyrella Lamb's nails. "Look at those flowers."

"Are you wanting a haircut, Victor?" teased Pearl. She was now getting Edie Patterson ready for a dinner date with her crusty old handyman.

"Nope. Something else," he replied. He moved to where Moira stood, working on Jenna Jones, who was getting ready for a drive up the coast with Brody.

"Are those for me?" Moira asked. Of course they were, but…wow.

"They are," he said. He set them on the work space. "I have something else, too. I hope you'll want it. It's been a year since we met."

"I remember when you gave her a police escort here," said Chastity, who was shamelessly listening to their conversation. Like everyone else in the salon.

Victor reached into his pants pocket and pulled out a small black jewelry box, producing a collective gasp. Then, with the Victor King blush Moira so loved, he got down on one knee and opened it, presenting an emerald-cut diamond ring.

She let out a squeak and put a hand to her dancing heart.

"Have we taken it slow enough?" he asked.

"Oh, yeah. I'm done with slow," she said.

Then to make it official, he asked, "Will you marry me?"

"Yes!" she cried, and her friends applauded as he slipped the ring on her finger.

So there in the little salon in the town at the end of the world, which now meant the world to her, Moira Wellman committed herself to the perfect man, and now her life was truly perfect.

No, *perfect* wasn't a good enough word. *Sublime.* Yes, that was it. Sublime.

* * * * *

*Recipes from Your Friends
in Moonlight Harbor*

Edie's Dumplings

Serves 6

Ingredients:
2 cups flour
5 tsps baking powder
½ tsp salt
3 eggs, beaten
⅔ cup milk
3 tbsp oil

Directions:

Sift dry ingredients into a bowl, then add eggs and mix. Slowly add milk and gently mix until the ingredients are well combined. Drop by spoonfuls into a large pan of gravy. (You can use a gravy mix, if you like.) Put on the lid and simmer for 15 to 20 minutes.

Penne with Artichoke, Olives and Bacon

*Courtesy of Theresia Brannan, owner of
East West Catering*

Serves 8

Ingredients:
1 lb penne pasta
1 can diced tomatoes (preferably Italian)
2 cups cherry tomatoes
Freshly ground pepper, to taste
1 tsp pasta seasoning, such as McCormick
¼ cup olive oil (light, not virgin)
Salt
¼ lb bacon (precooked)
2 cups marinated artichoke hearts
1 cup large Kalamata olives
1 cup basil leaves, loose
¼ cup dry fancy Parmesan cheese, grated
10 cloves of fresh garlic

Directions:

Boil a large pot of water with some salt. While bringing to a boil, slice the cherry tomatoes in half and the olives lengthwise. Drain and quarter the artichokes. (Retain some marinade juice.) Cut bacon into ½ inch long pieces. Peel and slice the garlic. Fry garlic in heated olive oil, let it sizzle and stir frequently until it browns. Remove from heat and put garlic and oil in a bowl.

Put the precooked bacon in a pan to heat and stir for about 3 minutes, then set aside.

Once water has come to a roiling boil, add pasta. Cook according to instructions on package to al dente consistency, stirring frequently with a wooden spoon so the pasta won't stick on the bottom of the pan. Drain well and let pasta continue to cook in steam in a bowl.

Drain the olive oil from the garlic into the pasta along with a small amount of the artichoke marinade and mix well. Add pasta seasoning and pepper. Mix in the canned tomatoes (with juice if served hot or drained if served cold), olives, cherry tomatoes and bacon. Finally, cut the basil thinly and add, along with garlic and Parmesan cheese, just before serving.

Spiced Apple Bread

*Courtesy of Theresia Brannan, owner of
East West Catering*

Makes 2 9x5 inch loaves

Ingredients:
3 cups flour
1½ tsps baking soda
1 tsp salt
2 tsps cinnamon
½ tsp ground nutmeg
½ tsp ground cloves
½ tsp ground cardamom
1½ cups granulated sugar
1 cup vegetable oil
4 eggs, beaten
2 tsps vanilla
4 cups coarsely chopped apples
1 cup raisins
1 cup chopped pecans
2 tsps sugar mixed with ¼ tsp cinnamon

Directions:

In a large bowl combine sugar and oil. Beat in eggs and vanilla, then stir in chopped apples, raisins and pecans. Sift in the dry ingredients and mix until well blended. Grease two 9x5 inch loaf pans and sprinkle the cinnamon sugar into the bottoms. Divide the batter between the two pans, smoothing the tops with a spatula or spoon. Bake for 50 to 60 minutes at 325 degrees F or until a wooden pick or cake tester inserted in the centers comes out clean. Cool for 10 minutes, then turn onto a rack to finish cooling. Freezes well.

Acknowledgments

I would like to thank some very special people who shared their time and expertise with me so I could write this book. First of all, a huge thank-you to Sergeant David McManus of the Ocean Shores Police Department for letting me ride along with him and see what life at the beach is like when you've sworn to serve and protect. And for responding to all those emails I barraged you with, you truly went beyond the call of duty!

Also, huge thanks to my good friend Theresia Brannan of East West Catering, who so kindly provided me with her own culinary creations to share in this book.

Thank you, Michael Lowenstein, hair artist extraordinaire and owner of Ross Michaels Salon in Bremerton, Washington, for sharing your vast wealth of beauty and business knowledge with me. And for lots of good visits every time I come in for a haircut!

Finally, thank you so much to my fabulous agent and friend, Paige Wheeler, for always being there and to my brilliant editor, April Osborn, for your insight and guidance. And a huge thanks to the whole Mira team for working so hard to turn this story into a book I can be proud of. You are all the best!

IF YOU ENJOYED THIS BOOK
WE THINK YOU WILL ALSO LOVE

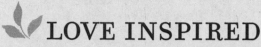

LOVE INSPIRED

INSPIRATIONAL ROMANCE

Uplifting stories of faith, forgiveness and hope.

Fall in love with stories where faith helps
guide you through life's challenges, and discover
the promise of a new beginning.

6 NEW BOOKS AVAILABLE EVERY MONTH!

Holly saw him enter but she didn't believe it, not at first. It couldn't be Colt, looking rugged but handsome, a few days' growth of whiskers on his too-attractive face as he leaned heavily on a cane and announced his arrival like she might have been waiting for his return.

He removed his hat and pushed a hand through dark hair. For a moment she was eighteen again, meeting up with a guy and not realizing the combined power of attraction and loneliness.

Just like that day twelve years ago she felt it again, hitting her hard, taking her breath for just an instant before she reminded herself that he was a two-timing, no-good piece of work that she wanted nothing to do with.

She couldn't let herself get pulled in by his looks and charm. Not again.

"Holly," he started.

She shook her head and took a step back.

"What are you doing here?" she asked. It wasn't the first time he'd come home. Nor the first time she'd seen him in the past eleven years.

It's just that he never came here, not to the café.

"I just need a few minutes of your time."

"Why?"

He had moved closer and was suddenly in front of her, smelling too good. She nearly groaned at her own weakness for this man.

"Spit it out, Colt."

He motioned her toward a table, even pulled out a chair for her.

She took the seat and he sat across from her. "Get it over with, please. I can't take much more of this. Are you sick? Did that bull hurt you worse than everyone said?"

He grimaced as he leaned back. "I'm not sick. I would tell you not to worry but I doubt worry is the first thing you feel for me."

"I would be upset if something happened to you," she admitted, her voice faltering.

"This isn't about the accident. I'm healing up fine." He leaned back in his chair and studied her face. "You're still beautiful."

"Don't. I don't want your compliments. You're obviously here on business. So why don't we cut to the chase?"

He didn't smile. "Of course, right to the point. Holly, it's about Dixie. That's why I'm here."

Dixie.

He wasn't here about the café or about them. He was here to tell her something concerning Dixie.

Their daughter.

away from taking a handful of those pain pills the doctors prescribed for me, wanting just…peace."

She'd contemplated suicide? Cash recoiled from the thought. He'd never loved Lisa the way he should have, but she'd been his wife for six years. The mother of his children. "Our life together was so terrible?" he asked.

"Yes. It was. I hated it here. You knew that. I didn't have anything for myself. A career. A purpose."

"You think I would have stood in your way? You could have done anything you wanted. I would have supported you."

"Yes. You would have. But there's one thing I needed you couldn't give. You couldn't love me, Cash. You never did."

What could he say to that? It was true. He compared what he'd felt for Lisa with the way his heart raced every time Rowena came into a room. The way he'd had sex with Lisa, as if there was still a wall between them, and no matter what, they couldn't seem to reach each other.

With Rowena, every nerve in his body seemed attuned to her, every wall crashed down, every sensation sharper, sweeter.

He didn't want to feel sorry for Lisa, or regret the pieces of himself he'd withheld from her. In the end, she hadn't loved him either. But in spite of all that, he couldn't help regretting all those barren years.

"We could spend all night talking about how we failed each other," Cash said. "But in the end, this is ancient history. What matters is now." More of Rowena's wisdom.

"That's what I want to negotiate with you. The future."

Negotiate? That sounded bad. Real bad.

"And so you appear out of the blue?" Cash challenged, the tension cinching tight again. "Take Mac to some doctor? Feed her some line about how he'd make her walk in no time?"

"John says…"

"John?" Cash sneered. "Well, if *John* says it."

"From the looks of things your social life is not exactly on hold either," she snapped. "I might as well just blurt out the whole thing. You're going to take it wrong any way I say it."

"Then get it over with."

"John is an orthopedic surgeon. I hired him to help me make sense of Mac's medical reports."

"So you didn't completely ignore Mac's condition," Cash said. "That doesn't give you the right to make medical decisions without my consent."

"And just because John is my fiancé doesn't change the fact that he's one of the top men in his field."

"You're getting married?" This interfering stranger—a goddamned doctor—was going to play stepfather to his girls? Panic jolted Cash, as if a steering wheel had just gotten yanked out of his hands and his life was careening out of control.

"The wedding is in June. He's worked on cutting edge treatments at the university hospital at Northwestern. He's been studying MacKenzie's case."

Resentment crushed Cash in his grip. "Dr. Malley is Mac's doctor. He's been with her through every surgery, every step of the way."

"Exactly which *steps* would those be, Cash? As far as I can see, MacKenzie hasn't taken any steps at all."

Cash slammed his fist into the wall. "Damn it, Lisa, Mac's starting to stand on her own now, and—"

"Losing your temper isn't going to change the truth. I know you've been doing the best you can, but this town is so far off the medical map that it might as well not exist."

"We're hardly using leeches and witch doctors around here."

"John measured MacKenzie this weekend and he's putting up handrails on every wall in our condo. So as soon as she's on her feet she'll be able to hold onto them, make her way around without that horrible wheelchair."

Cash didn't want to feel this sudden sense of inadequacy. Wanted to cling to hate, anger. "And who's going to go through Mac's exercises with her? Hold her hand while the doctors are pulling out stitches or poking where it hurts and she's scared and crying? You couldn't stomach it before. Why do you think you can do it now?"

Lisa couldn't meet his eyes. "John is going to hire someone to come to our home to help with the things that were too hard for me before."

"A stranger can do it better than her own father can?"

"A trained professional—"

"She has sessions with her physical therapist all the time right here. But nobody, Lisa, *nobody* else knows Mac the way I do."

Lisa sighed. "You always *have* felt like no one can possibly do things as well as you."

"And all of a sudden you can?"

"The whole city is handicapped accessible. She would have the best of everything. Every advantage money can buy. Museums. Culture. The finest schools in addition to superior medical care."

"So we're back to money again, are we? I can damned well support my own daughters! They've got a roof over their head. Plenty to eat. Clothes on their backs. But most of all they know when they need me I'll be right here."

Lisa fidgeted with the diamond ring on her finger. It was the size of a goddamned gumball. How had he missed seeing it?

"Cash, I've grown up a lot the last two years. When I left, those first few months it was a relief not to have to face the mess our marriage had become. A relief not to hear Mac screaming and not be able to stop her pain. I know you think I was weak, a coward, a terrible mother. I thought so, too. Then I started to miss the girls terribly."

"All you had to do was pick up the phone," Cash said, bitter. "You didn't."

"I was ashamed. Have you ever made a mistake that horrified you so much you could never forgive yourself?"

What the hell could he say? "You know I have."

"I started therapy with a really gifted psychologist. Wanted to sort through all the wrong turns I had taken, figure out how my life got so tangled up. She's the one who suggested I talk to John about Mac. It was hard, Cash, to be honest with myself, get all the ugliness out in the open. But in time I came to realize how much I love my children."

Cash gave a snort of dismissal.

"I know you think I don't deserve MacKenzie," Lisa said. "And maybe you're right. But maybe what we should both consider is what *she* deserves. And which one of us can best give it to her."

Cash reeled inwardly, trying to imagine Mac gone. Not waking her up every morning, seeing that grumpy face she always made. Not dressing her and buckling her into her wheelchair. No more battles, trying to get her to fight her way up to her feet. His life would be so much easier, a dark voice whispered. Not to have all that responsibility on his shoulders.

No. What his life would be was *unbearable*.

"We can fight this all out in court if we have to," Lisa said, "but I hope we don't have to put the girls through it."

Lisa? The voice of reason? Cash wanted to puke.

"All I'm asking you is this, Cash. Just think about it. I'm going to stay at March Winds tonight. Maybe we can meet for coffee tomorrow and discuss this further."

She was staying at the local B&B Deirdre Stone and her sister-in-law ran? Terrific. Cash wanted Lisa as far away from town as possible.

"If tomorrow is too soon, we can talk when I pick them up a week from Friday."

"What do you mean a week from Friday?"

"I'll be taking them on every one of my visitation days from now on. And their next summer vacation. John's lawyer says the court should award me at least two months."

Two months? Just these few days without his kids had left Cash ragged.

"Lisa…don't do this. Those girls are my life."

"I know," she said quietly. "That's why I plan to leave Charlotte with you when MacKenzie moves to Chicago."

"Separate the girls?" He tried to imagine the damage that would do. Cash flashed back to the years before the split. How Lisa had doted on MacKenzie. The baby she'd actually wanted, maybe hoped would fix their floundering marriage. He couldn't help but feel Lisa's rejection of their oldest child like a boot in the stomach.

"That's the arrangement I'd like to propose," Lisa said. "Believe it or not, Cash, I'm not trying to ruin your life. I want custody of MacKenzie so I can focus all my energy on her while she's learning to walk. The advantages I can give her…"

"And you're going to explain all this to Charlie how?"

"She spent most of the visit up in the loft bedroom because her sister couldn't follow her up the ladder."

"That's what kids do. Try to ditch younger siblings. I tried to ditch my little brothers all the time." Not that his mom had let him get away with it very often.

"Well, then think how happy she'll be when we sort this out. Her sister in Chicago, and her, here with you. Unless you don't want custody of Charlie."

Cash's rage broke free. "You're right, Lisa," he shouted in cutting sarcasm. "I don't want either of my kids. It's too much trouble. I want to do what you did and take two goddamn years off to do whatever the fuck I want to."

He spun around and kicked the kitchen chair. It careened across the floor, smashing into the stove with a hellacious clatter.

He didn't hear the tiny cry a dozen yards from the window Rowena had opened earlier to clear that new paint smell from the house. Didn't see Charlie drop the football she'd been tossing to Destroyer as her whole wide world fell apart.

CHAPTER NINETEEN

LISA WAS LONG GONE and the girls were finally sleeping when Cash loaded the dog crate in the back of Rowena's van, the pug puppies completely exhausted after their day in his backyard. Cash shut the hatchback, then noticed Destroyer's mangled football lying forgotten beside the fence. He picked up the dog's favorite toy and turned it in his hands, feeling chewed up and spit out himself after Lisa's little announcement.

"She wants custody of Mac," he told Rowena flatly.

"What?" Rowena paled, her eyes stark with disbelief, pain. Hell, she looked almost as rotten as he felt.

"She's got some specialist in the city who says he can get Mac on her feet faster than we can here. I can keep Charlie, as far as Lisa's concerned, but she's going to fight me for Mac. In court if necessary."

"Well, she can't have Mac!" Rowena protested, every bit as stricken as he was. "You're the one that child depends on, Cash. Every moment of every day. You're her rock."

"Am I?" Cash leaned his back against the car and stared up at the stars. Dawn was just starting to scrub them out. "Right now I feel like I'm anything but. What if this doctor of Lisa's is right? What if moving to Chicago would mean…" He hesitated, faced a possibility too painful. "You come from a family of doctors, Rowena. What if I'm just being a selfish bastard keeping her here and I'm denying my little girl her best chance?"

"Has she been to any of the university hospitals? Seen any specialists in the past?"

"Right after the accident they life-flighted her to Iowa City. She had two of her surgeries there. That's when we hooked up with Dr. Malley. Everyone said he was the best."

"What did he say?"

"He said people heal in their own time."

"I've seen that with animals, too." Rowena nodded, so earnest. "You try to rush them and it sets them back instead of pushing them forward."

"I push, Rowena."

"Sometimes. But mostly, you love her, encourage her. Believe in her."

Cash looked away. "I can't just dismiss this new prognosis as crap. No matter how much I want to."

"If you want to have this new doctor of Lisa's checked out, fine. I can call Bryony. She's tough to impress. But even if there *is* merit to what this doctor is suggesting, Mac moving in with Lisa isn't the only way to make that work. I can help you get her to the city for treatment. My mom would be thrilled if I were driving to Chicago more often."

"No, she wouldn't, if you were ferrying my kid there. And she'd have every reason not to be. You've already done too much for my family." He must have looked like hell. Rowena slid her hand down his arm, the shirt he'd grabbed after Lisa left rippling under her touch.

"That's my decision to make. I know all this upheaval is hard, Cash, but you're going to have to pull it together. Charlie suspects that something is going on. She barely even looked at the puppies. Or me."

Cash heard the hurt in Rowena's voice. Charlie *had* been wary of Rowena, that old, haunted look in his little girl's eyes. No—not the old expression at all. Something new pinched Charlie's pale face: shock, pain, as if Destroyer had suddenly wheeled around to bite her. She'd shut Rowena out completely and she didn't trust Cash at the moment either. He'd felt plenty rotten himself when Charlie had posted a KEEP OUT sign on her bedroom door an hour before. Even when he'd knocked, asking her to let him in, she'd stubbornly refused.

I got to think and I think better when I'm alone. Her muffled reply made him wince. The words could just as easily have come out of his mouth. He'd always been one to withdraw, sort things out. Maybe that's why the last two years were so hard. There had been no time, no safe place to do either.

He'd give Charlie some space, and they could talk more in the morning. By then, maybe he would have figured out what to say.

"I know Charlie's acting strange," he reasoned, "but she was just surprised to find you in my bathrobe. That's a lot for a nine-year-old to handle."

"Too much right now, with everything else going on." Rowena looked so wistful he reached for her. She slid into his arms, fitting against him as if she belonged there forever. "I think I should stay away for a while, Cash," she said, leaning her cheek against his chest. "Give the three of you time to sort this out."

"No." Cash held on tight. "Charlie will get used to us being together in time. Everyone in Whitewater is going to have to."

"What?"

"I realized one thing for certain tonight." He hesitated, the words feeling so important it was hard for him to say them aloud. He took her chin between his fingers and forced it up so she was looking right at him. "Rowena, I'm in love with you."

God, it felt good to say it out loud. Scary as hell, but good.

Cash held his breath, waiting. He knew she loved him, but he needed to hear her say it. Needed to know she was as far past the point of no return as he was. What would it feel like? To love a woman and know she loved you back?

Rowena looked so shaken it terrified him. "What's that thing lying on the grass?"

"What?" Cash drew back, confused, a little irritated. He'd just told her he loved her, and it was as if she hadn't even heard him. She was pulling out of his arms, opening the gate and hurrying toward some object that caught the light's beam with a metallic glimmer.

Cash followed her and scooped up the thing before she could reach it, in case it was something sharp—the lid of a tin can, a dangerous piece of metal. When he turned the object over in his hand, he frowned. "It's a weird thing for somebody to drop," he said, glancing up at her alarmingly pale face. "It's a can opener."

"It's Charlie's," Rowena whispered. "I gave it to her. I saw her climb up to the tree house and put it in her survival kit with my own eyes."

"She must be plenty mad," Cash said, "throwing it out like she did."

"Throwing it out when? She didn't go near the tree house tonight. And the can opener wasn't there when I came over to paint. Something's not right, Cash."

Foreboding closed in. Cash loped into the house, Rowena right behind him. His boot caught a bucket of paint as he rushed to Charlie's room. He didn't even bother to see if the can was sealed. He opened her bedroom door, the tape holding the Keep Out sign pulling loose in the draft from the wide open window, the piece of notebook paper drifting to the floor. Cash flicked on the overhead light.

What the hell? Adrenaline shot through his system. The covers were lumpy, but there wasn't a single wisp of Charlie's brown hair visible on the pillow. And the dog—he'd been glued to the kid since she got home. Now Destroyer was nowhere to be seen. Cash flung back the covers, revealing the stuffed animals Charlie had used to make it look as if she was still there.

But she wasn't. The bed was empty.

"There's a note," Rowena said, hurrying over to Charlie's desk. She handed him a piece of loose-leaf paper with "Daddy" printed on it in purple crayon.

Cash grabbed the letter, unfolded it and read aloud.

Dear Daddy,
I know it is real hard for you to take care of Mac and me all by yourself. Now Mommy wants Mac but she doesn't want me. It's O.K. It's better if I take care of myself. Don't worry. I got everything I need. Even my flashlight.
Yours Truly,
Charlotte Rose Lawless

His little girl was out there, somewhere in the night, alone? Cash's blood ran cold as possibilities flashed through his mind. He'd seen the worst of them happen before. She could run in front of a car that couldn't see her in the dark. She could fall and get hurt. Some sick sonofabitch could get his hands on her.

And what had made her run?

Cash staggered back a step under the weight of Charlie's words, his eyes finding Rowena's heartbroken gaze. "How the hell did she know all this?" Cash asked. "The door was shut when Lisa and I were fighting. I know it was. But the things we said…this is too damned close to be a coincidence."

A breeze lifted the curtains. Rowena stared at it, her face ashen. "The windows," she said. "They were all open because of the paint. Charlie must have been close enough to overhear…"

How could she have avoided it? He'd been yelling his head

off, so angry, so scared, feeling gut shot over the possibility he might lose his children. Cash flinched, remembering how ugly things had gotten when he'd stormed into the kitchen, kicked the chair. "I said I didn't want the girls. I said it was too much trouble," he choked out.

"No, you would never—"

"I was being sarcastic, but Charlie didn't know that. She just heard that her mother didn't want her. And now she thinks I don't want her either. You warned me about letting all that hate for Lisa come out. Christ, Rowena. How long ago do you think she left? Where would she go?"

"Someplace she feels safe. I'll check the tree house. The play house. You search the inside. She couldn't have gotten far."

Cash clung to that as he whistled sharply for the dog. "Charlie!" he yelled as he ran through the house, flipping on lights, flinging open closet doors. Nothing.

Mac came awake grumbling, startled from her sleep. Cash rushed into her room, the blinding glare of lights leaving Mac blinking. "Mac," Cash said, scooping her up in his arms, "your sister's gone. Did she say anything to you? Where she was going?"

"Going?" Mac scrubbed at her eyes with one fist.

"Did Charlie tell you she was running away?" Cash demanded.

"Charlie runned away?" Big tears welled up in Mac's eyes. "Bad stuff happens when you run away. Monsters eat you an' witches steal you an' you never come back." She started to sob, kicking her legs. Any other time, Cash would have rejoiced at it—Mac's movements stronger than they'd ever been before. But now, with Charlie missing, the kicks only seemed to worsen the foreboding in his gut.

"I want my sister!" Mac wailed. "I want my sister!"

Rowena bolted into the room. "Charlie's backpack is gone, and a bunch of stuff from that box up in the tree house is missing."

"She's not in the house," Cash said.

"Then she's out there, somewhere." Rowena waved at the darkened window.

Cash beat back the rush of pure terror shooting through him. *Panic is deadly.* A distraction he couldn't afford. He grappled for the focus and calm that had gotten him through combat. But this was different. It wasn't his life that could be in danger. It was his little girl's.

Think! He told himself fiercely. *Damn it think how to find her!*

"Destroyer is with her," Rowena said.

Cash latched on to that. "Charlie might be able to hide, but that dog of hers is impossible to miss."

"That dog will guard her with his life, Cash."

And yet—there were dangers even a Newfoundland couldn't protect a child from. The fact that Destroyer was with Charlie didn't guarantee that either one of them were safe.

"We're going to find her," Rowena said. "Call Lisa. She can watch Mac while we search."

Cash recoiled from the idea of asking his ex-wife for anything. *Admit I lost my own kid?* For a heartbeat Cash resisted. Wouldn't that give Lisa plenty of ammo for a custody suit? But before he could weigh out the danger, he handed Mac to Rowena and grabbed up the phone.

What mattered was finding Charlie as fast as possible. And if Lisa were here, he and Rowena could split up, cover twice the ground. He hung up bare minutes later, having started the chain that would notify whoever necessary. Vinny, Lisa, the Stones. Whoever Charlie might seek out in her pain.

Lisa, sounding as panicked as Cash felt, wanted to join the search. He'd convinced her she could help most by coming to the house to calm Mac. Vinny was calling the Sheriff's department for good measure, the dispatcher asking whoever was on patrol to keep their eyes peeled.

"Daddy's real good at finding people," Mac said. "He finded me when the big truck hit me. Didn't you, Daddy?"

Cash's stomach sank, remembering. All the guilt, all the dread, the gnawing fear that he'd damaged his child instead of saving her.

"Your daddy is going to find Charlie, too," Rowena insisted, with so much faith in him it tamed the old memories, shoved them back where they belonged.

"I'm going to check out the way to Hope's house. And the park," Cash told her.

"Go!" Rowena urged. "I'll head out in the other direction as soon as Lisa gets here. If you find them, Cash, call right away."

"I will." He opened the door and set out at a dead run, self-blame heavy on his shoulders. If anything happened to Charlie it would be his fault. For losing his goddamned temper, letting all that hate for Lisa out. His little girl had heard it. His stomach churned at the knowledge. She'd never forget the things he'd said. The things her mommy and daddy had said to each other.

Let me tell her I'm sorry. Let me try to explain...

He prayed harder than he had since the accident two years ago. But he felt no more absolution now than he had then.

This time he hadn't twisted up his child's legs. This time he'd scarred something even harder to heal.

His little girl's heart.

ROWENA'S SWEATY FINGERS clamped around the handle of the flashlight she'd gotten from the mudroom, her lungs burning, her heart pounding. For almost an hour, she'd been searching, anyplace she could think of where a little girl might hide. She'd checked in with Cash on the cell phone, but neither he, Jake Stone nor anyone else who was searching had caught a glimpse of the lost little girl or the big dog. A fact that was beginning to tighten the grip of fears pooling all around them with the night's darkest shadows.

I've looked everywhere I can think of, Rowena thought miserably. *Where else could she be? Her favorite places. Her safe places. Somewhere all those books of hers would say could shield her from disaster...*

If only Charlie knew the one place she'd be safer than any other was her own daddy's arms.

But how could you find a child as good at disappearing as Charlie was? Fading into the background? It was as if the little girl finally *had* learned how to make herself invisible.

Rowena felt queasy with remorse. She was the one who had made such a disaster out of things. If she hadn't been fresh out of Cash's bed when the girls got home none of this would have happened. With the girls still in the house Cash would never have allowed himself to lose his temper. But with Rowena watching the kids at what he'd thought was a safe distance away, he'd let his anger get the better of him.

She hadn't kept Charlie safe.

Now the little girl was out there somewhere, scared, alone, believing that even Cash didn't want her.

The very thought was absurd. And yet, Charlie had seen far too many terrible things happen before. The accident that had destroyed the only life she'd ever known. Her sister walking one day, in a wheelchair the next. Her mother disappearing, then coming back just to reject her all over again. In Charlie's world days were spent waiting for the sky to fall on her head. No calamity was out of the realm of possibility.

But the whimsy other children took for granted was. The word *impossible* was reserved for make-believe or dreams come true or magic whistles Cuchullain once played.

From the moment Charlie had gone missing Rowena had sensed the little girl's desperate need for someone to prove that she was wrong. That she wasn't invisible, that it would matter if she disappeared, that her daddy loved her enough to come after her. That maybe, just maybe there was some bit of magic left in the world that seemed so big and scary and uncertain.

Rowena remembered Charlie's reaction to the whistle and her heart squeezed, the little girl dismissing the story with a wistfulness that showed just how much she wished it was true, that Cuchullain's fairy pipe could heal even the most wounded spirits. Even Destroyer's reaction to the haunting melody Rowena had played hadn't convinced the little girl. The dog suddenly enchanted, blissful, drawing nearer to Rowena as if by a spell that lit the way to someone who would love him.

The whistle... Rowena stopped. If Charlie wasn't willing to answer when called, maybe there was someone else who would.

She ran back to Cash's, got in the van and drove to her shop. She rushed in, flicking on the overhead light. Hurrying to her desk, she drew out the antique whistle on its silver chain. She slipped it around her neck then started for the door. Suddenly she froze, staring. A handful of kibbles scattered the counter she'd wiped clean before she locked up Saturday night. Right beside it sat a little pile of money.

Rowena heard a scuffle somewhere deeper in the pet shop. One of the other animals settling in for the night? No. It had to be...

Rowena lifted the whistle to her lips, praying that Auntie Maeve was right and the pipe held mystical powers. For no one in a thousand years had ever needed the power of healing promised by the old Irishwoman more than the little girl who had gone missing tonight.

Soft, sweet, Rowena piped the haunting tune Auntie Maeve had taught her, the one that Charlie hadn't believed could be magic.

Rowena walked through the shop, searching, wooing, calling out to Charlie with all the love in her heart. Until suddenly, a pile of boxes in a corner erupted, an earthquake in the guise of a giant black dog bursting from its midst. Destroyer trotted toward her, looking almost as glad to see Rowena as she was to see the dog.

Relief shot through Rowena as she saw the small figure behind him, huddled as deep into the shadowy corner as possible.

Charlie, so woebegone that tears stung Rowena's eyes. Destroyer sank to his stomach, his big head low, and inched toward Rowena as if to say he was sorry. He should have been able to stop Charlie from running away.

Rowena dropped the whistle, wanting to scoop Charlie up in her arms, but something in the child's face stopped her. An invisible wall, as palpable as the one Charlie's father had once built around him. The kind not even the most determined person could batter through. The prisoner had to give you the key.

Like Cash had tonight, before the world fell apart, Rowena thought, his emotion-roughened voice echoing through her. *I'm in love with you...*

Rowena shook the memory from her mind, guilt raking her again as she hunkered down in front of the little girl still reeling because the adults in her life had failed to protect her.

"Are you hurt, honey?" Rowena asked quietly. She wasn't about to ask if the child was okay. The answer to that was a Destroyer-sized *no*. If Charlie had been fine, she never would have fled the house.

"Where's my daddy?" Charlie asked, and Rowena could see the salty tracks of dried tears on her cheeks.

"He's been looking everywhere for you. How about if I call him right now?"

Charlie looked down at the toes of her shoes.

"He's so worried about you, honey. Please let me?"

Charlie shrugged. "I guess."

Rowena dug her phone out of her jeans pocket and dialed

Cash's cell, the emotion in the man's voice shattering as she told him Charlie was safe at the shop. He promised to rush right over. And what would he find when he got here? Rowena winced, taking in every detail of the bedraggled little girl before her.

Charlie's jacket sleeve was torn. The zipper on the backpack Rowena had once teased could make the trek up Mount Everest lay split wide open, empty of "all the stuff" Charlie needed to feel safe. Only one can of corn and a rawhide bone were left of all her tools and provisions.

Rowena tucked her phone away and hunkered down. "Where have you been all this time? People are looking for you everywhere. Your daddy and me. Mr. Stone and Mr. Google and all the deputies your daddy works with. We didn't see you anywhere."

"First I went to the old boathouse. Me and Hope went down there once with her uncle. My backpack ripped and stuff fell in the river. I tried to get it back, but Destroyer wouldn't let me."

"Thank God!" Rowena shuddered, thinking of the Mississippi, so unpredictable, with its treacherous currents.

"He grabbed my arm and pulled and pulled until all my stuff disappeared. But then I didn't have anything for him to eat. So I came here and got the key out of that little rock you keep it in. I left money on the counter for the food I took. I wasn't stealing."

"I know you weren't, honey."

"And then, I couldn't go back outside because I figured something out that's really bad."

That your father is sleeping with someone? That your mother doesn't want custody of you? That she wants to take your little sister away?

Rowena couldn't resist smoothing a tendril of hair back from where tears had glued it to Charlie's cheek. "What did you find out?"

Hollow-eyed, the little girl peered up at her, so empty of

hope Rowena couldn't bear it. "It doesn't matter how hard you work to get ready," Charlie said. "Even disaster kits don't matter. Bad stuff happens anyway."

Rowena searched for wisdom, wanting so badly to find the words to reach past the fears gripping this child she'd come to love. "It may seem that way sometimes," she reasoned. "But maybe the problem is counting on things like bottled water and extra flashlight batteries to keep you safe. Maybe it's magic you should be depending on instead."

"Magic's not real."

"Isn't it? The magic whistle called to me all the way across town tonight. It made me come here. It helped me find you, safe and sound." Instinct made Rowena draw the chain over her head, the whistle cupped in the palm of her hand. "You want to know what its secret is?" she asked as she tilted the silver tube to catch the light. It glimmered, drawing Charlie's gaze. "It's love, Charlie. That's the magic. And I want to give it to you."

Rowena slipped the necklace over Charlie's head. The little girl touched the tin whistle with her finger as if she wanted so badly to believe.

"I know the world looks scary sometimes," Rowena said, "and it's true you can't count on some things. But there are others you can depend on."

"Like what?"

"Someone who won't ever let you disappear, even if you try to run away or fall in the river. Someone who loves you with all their heart."

"Remember I told you people only love the cute ones. Like the puppies Mommy got rid of when they got too big. Like the kitty Hope's going to get. Like Mommy loves Mac because she's little and looks like a Christmas tree angel."

"Destroyer wouldn't ever leave you alone, would he? I knew it the instant I saw the two of you together. You were a perfect match."

As if in answer, the dog scooted over and laid his head in Charlie's lap.

"Your daddy would never leave you alone either," Rowena assured her.

Charlie picked at a tuft of Destroyer's fur. "But I'm alone lots of time after school when Daddy's busy with Mac. He's like—like a birthday cake cut up in so many pieces there almost isn't any left. That's why…"

Charlie chafed her bottom lip with her teeth, and Rowena could see the child teetering on the knife's edge of confessing her true feelings, terrified about the calamity such honesty could bring.

"Why what, sweetheart?" Rowena asked. "You can tell me."

Charlie's little voice got gruff, her eyes pleading for understanding. "I can't like you anymore, Rowena," she confided. "If my daddy gets in love with you, I'm scared there won't be any room left for me."

Rowena felt pain pierce her heart, the memory of Cash declaring he loved her still fresh, a little raw, a little too precious to touch. Something she'd longed for. Something this child would view with dismay.

"I try not to care he's so busy," Charlie went on, "but I want my daddy back the way he was before. I want my tree house to get done with a roof and a slide. And I want my mommy to love me as much as Mac. But nobody ever loves me best."

"Your puppy loves you best in the whole world."

"No. He and Mac get locked up in her room and I've got to share because she can't go play with other kids and…I want Daddy even more than I want my doggy. Does that make me bad?"

"Of course not!"

"I've already lost Mommy. And now Mac's going to go away. When I heard Daddy say he didn't want me either I just wanted to really get invisible. 'Cause maybe then it wouldn't hurt so bad. But it didn't matter. It still made my tummy feel all icky inside."

"Well, you don't have to get invisible, not ever again," Rowena promised.

"But I don't know what else to do."

"How about if we try something different?" Rowena suggested, fighting to keep her voice from breaking just like her heart. "This time I'll disappear instead."

"You would do that? For me?" Charlie's eyes clouded, so old, so sad.

Rowena nodded, her own chest aching. "Cross my heart."

Destroyer woofed as a car screeched to a halt at the curb, lights flashing, and Rowena knew Cash had caught a ride in the patrol car nearest wherever he'd been. He rushed into the shop, haggard, his face seeming to have aged ten years.

"Jesus Christ, Charlie!" he swore, scooping his little girl up in his arms. "I was so scared I lost you!"

He kissed her cheek fiercely as she buried her face in his neck.

"I'm sorry, baby," he soothed, hugging her tight. "I'm so damned sorry for everything you overheard between me and your mom. I was just angry, saying things I didn't mean. If I ever lost you..."

His voice cracked, and Rowena knew the images flashing through his mind, how close he'd come to losing Mac to the accident, how many ways Charlie could have disappeared into the night. "You're my whole life, Charlie."

Rowena loved him all the more, knowing that was true.

Charlie leaned back, cradled Cash's face between her hands. "You're *my* whole life, too, Daddy. I know you found Mac after the crash. But...tonight...want to know a secret? I was scared you'd give up because it was only me."

"Only you?"

Rowena saw his face contort with disbelief.

"Charlotte Rose Lawless, don't you know how special you are? You were my very first baby. The first baby whose smile made me...feel love so big my heart couldn't even hold it. From the minute you opened your eyes, I knew the most important thing in my world was being your daddy. And I knew I'd hold on to you with everything inside me and never, ever let you go. You were the most beautiful baby I'd ever seen."

Rowena saw Charlie frown, doubtful.

"But in the picture the hospital took my head was all pointy on top and I had a big red scratch on my face," Charlie said. "I think you got me confused with Mac."

"I do not, Charlie. I remember exactly how you looked the first time the nurse put you in my arms. You didn't even cry when you were born. You were so patient, Charlie. You looked up at me. And...I fell in love. I'm sorry I let you down. I'm sorry for everything. For not paying enough attention to you. For not noticing that you needed me. That you were feeling invisible. I'll do better from now on. I promise."

Charlie looked into his eyes, so earnest, so much like her father, Rowena felt her heart break, felt their hearts heal as Charlie promised.

"I'll do better, too. See, I've got magic now." She pulled the whistle up on its chain and showed it to him. "It came from a fairy godmother and it makes hurting stuff all better 'cause it's got love inside. Rowena said so."

Cash's gaze found Rowena's, and in that instant Rowena knew just how much she'd lost.

"Rowena can teach you everything there is to know about magic," Cash said, his heart in his eyes. "And love."

No, Rowena thought. Not everything.

Cash held on tight to those he loved.

She let go.

CHAPTER TWENTY

CASH SAT ACROSS the kitchen table from his ex-wife and tried to squeeze his heart back into his chest. He felt slashed wide open by the night's events, every nerve bare, every mistake he'd ever made lying right out in the open. He wished he'd been able to convince Rowena to stay, needing her near him. But she'd insisted they could talk later. His family needed time alone.

He'd let her go for the time being, secure in the knowledge she loved him, grateful, so grateful he'd been given this second chance. To build a life. To be a parent. To make a new family with a woman he loved, and show his little girls by example just how beautiful life could be.

And life would be beautiful here in this house now that Rowena had transformed it: turned its gray walls bright with color, banished the gray of dreams lost and brought hope back into the lives of Cash and his children. Made Charlie believe in magic again. Feel safe.

And Charlie did. He's seen it in his little girl's eyes when he'd held her on his lap in Rowena's van, as she'd dropped them off and he'd carried Charlie in to bed. His bed, not hers.

It was the only one big enough to fit the dual guardians who not only stubbornly insisted on keeping the runaway in sight, but had to be touching her at all times just to make sure she couldn't escape. It had moved Cash to the core, seeing De-stroyer plastered against one side of his daughter, keeping watch, while Mac snuggled in on the other side of her sister, her little hand holding tight to Charlie's pajama top just to make sure her slippery older sister didn't disappear again.

Even Lisa seemed subdued by what had happened. Cash was thankful his ex-wife had greeted their oldest daughter with tears and hugs, as relieved as Cash was to see Charlie safe. And yet, even that couldn't bridge the gap between two warring parents. Cash knew he had to do that himself.

"I lost my temper tonight," he admitted. "Let all that poison between us spill out. And Charlie paid the price."

"She always paid the price, didn't she, Cashel?" Lisa gripped her hands together, her voice shaking. "Somewhere deep inside I blamed her for the fact that we had to get married. And I was jealous when I saw the way you looked at her. But when Mac came along—it was so much easier for me to love her. God, what an ugly thing for a mother to admit. But tonight, while Charlie was missing I had to face the truth about myself. The reason I ran."

"Because it was too hard for you to see Mac in pain." He'd always known the reason. Lisa had told him long ago.

"No. That's what I told you. Told myself. Because it was easier than admitting the truth." Tears welled up in Lisa's eyes. "I left because I was terrified someday Charlie would look in my eyes and guess the truth. That if one of my girls had to be hurt so badly in that accident, I wished it had been her."

Lisa looked at him, and he could sense what she expected to see. Revulsion. Disgust. Hate. But in that moment what he felt was grateful. Cash realized he'd known how she felt the whole time. She'd been trying to protect Charlie, in her own way. One he never would have chosen. And yet, trying to protect a child, even in the most misguided way, was something he could understand.

"You didn't want Charlie hurt, Lisa," he said at last. "You wanted Mac well. We both wanted that."

"I kept thinking God was punishing me," Lisa confessed, twisting her engagement ring around her finger. "Because I loved MacKenzie too much and Charlie too little. I can't tell you how many hours I spent with my therapist, trying to believe I could make things better. But I didn't know until tonight how cruel I'd been. When I thought of Charlie alone out there in the dark, thinking I didn't want her...it hurt me so badly, Cash. Then I knew for the first time how much I loved her, too. If I could go back and change the way I held my heart back from her, I would. But all I can do is try for the rest of my life to show her just how much she means to me."

"There are plenty of things we'd both change, Lisa," Cash said. "Tonight Charlie could have been killed because you and I were too busy hurting each other to do what parents are supposed to do—love their children together even if they can't stay married to each other."

"We've never been good at working together. Everything in our marriage was a contest. Either you won or I did. Never both. What are we going to do now? About treatment in Chicago? About custody?" Lisa asked. "And how am I ever going to make it up to Charlie now that I've hurt her so badly?"

Cash lowered his face into his hands. He had plenty of his own fences to mend when it came to his little girl. But Rowena would help him figure out how to heal things in time. "We'll have to put our own needs aside. Think of what's best for the girls. Both of them."

"Even if that means moving them to Chicago?"

"I want Mac to walk as much as you do, Lisa. And I feel like she really is starting to make progress. She's pulling herself up, and—"

Cash stilled, hearing the creak of the bedroom door. A metallic thump he recognized as Mac's wheelchair whacking into the wall.

"It's the girls," he warned, getting to his feet. As if she didn't know. He saw Lisa fight to hide the misery in her face.

"Let me do it!" he heard Mac grouse as the wheelchair banged against something again.

"You're gonna scratch the wall," Charlie warned. "Daddy worked real hard to paint it."

"I don't care about any old paint! Even pink!" Mac insisted.

Cash headed through the living room, then down the hall to see what all the commotion was about. Not only had Mac wrestled her way into the wheelchair, she'd gotten Charlie to put on her leg braces and her sturdy-soled shoes. The kid was definitely dressed for battle and not planning to go back to bed anytime soon.

"You're supposed to be asleep," he said. But the only one who seemed to care about his opinion was the dog. Destroyer dropped down onto his belly and laid his head on his paws.

"Well, I'm not sleeping," Mac insisted with her best "off with their heads" regal glare. "I got important stuff to say and you an' Mommy got to listen."

Cash sighed. He knew he'd have to deal with whatever was on Mac's mind, but he'd be better prepared to face the kid's inevitable questions once he and Lisa finished sorting things out themselves.

"It's been a pretty tough night, kiddo," he said. "Can't it wait until tomorrow?"

"No way." Mac gripped the metal rail that spun her wheels and gave the chair a shove so hard one of the footplates banged into Cash's shin.

"Ouch! Hey, you! Watch it!"

"I'm going to run you right over if I got to!"

"It's that important, huh?"

It must've been. He dodged as she propelled the chair forward with another shove.

"I'm sorry, Daddy," Charlie said, looking miserable again. "I just didn't want her to get a bad surprise like I did. I was just trying to explain—"

"—why Charlie runned away," Mac blustered, hijacking the spotlight again with one of the direst expressions Cash had ever seen. *"Mommy maked her."*

Oh, God. Cash closed his eyes for a moment, surrendering to his youngest daughter's iron will. There was no way Mac would let this subject wait until tomorrow.

Mac all but ran over Cash's feet as she wheeled her chair into the kitchen. He hadn't realized avenging angels came in the guise of five-year-olds wearing Hello Kitty nightgowns, but Mac fit the bill perfectly. Cash, Charlie and the dog followed in her wake.

"Remember, I told you that Mommy and Daddy made a mistake," Cash began, but Mac wasn't hearing any of it.

"Mommy sure made a great big giant-gantic one." Mac leveled a baleful glare on Lisa. "Charlie says you're making me move to your house. But she's got to stay here."

Lisa flushed, struck speechless. Cash knew Mac's translation of the situation was making his ex-wife even more uncomfortable than she already was.

"Well, you're not the boss of me!" Mac crossed her arms over her chest. "Me an' Charlie got important stuff to do right here. We got to take care of our dog and go to school and Charlie's got to come get me at the playground door every day and tell me all the bad things Tyler James did in fourth grade. And me and Daddy got stuff to do, too."

"Your therapy? Maybe I could learn to do it," Lisa said, and Cash knew she meant it. She was willing to try. It surprised him. Warmed him toward her, just a little.

"Therapy stinks! It's *dancing* I got to do."

Cash felt the old knife twist in his chest. How many times

had he and Mac watched that old recital tape, her little body swaying to the music, her arms going through the ballet moves even though her legs couldn't hold her up.

Lisa was trying hard not to cry. "Dancing's not the only thing in the world. There are lots of other things you can do. I could buy you a piano. You could play the pretty music sitting down."

"What are you? Crazy?" Mac gaped at her in horror, as if she were Baryshnikov himself and someone had just suggested he turn in his tights to play Chopsticks. "I'm a dancer. And my daddy dances me whenever I want to. Round and round with my recital dress on."

"In Chicago you could see real dancers do ballet on a great big stage." Lisa tried to tempt her.

"I *am* a real dancer," Mac insisted, in high outrage. "I don't want to sit around and watch. And know what else?"

"I'm listening, MacKenzie," Lisa said, and for once Cash could see that Lisa was.

"I'm *keeping* my sister. 'Cause right now I like her lots better than either one of you!"

Cash saw Charlie's jaw drop. She stared at Mac, and he could see the conflict going on inside, that Charlie was still almost afraid to hope.

"And if you or Daddy even *try* to take us apart, you'll be sorry! Me an' Charlie won't live with either one of you."

Cash glanced at Charlie, saw something wonderful dawn in his little girl's face. Her eyes started to shine.

"Mac, kids have got to live with a mom or dad or I think we'd get arrested," Charlie said. "Besides. We don't have anyplace else to go."

"Oh, yes we do. The tree house! And we'd eat corn every single day and have a flashlight and everything."

Charlie scooted over to her sister, leaned against Mac's chair, looking as if she'd just won something precious.

"Kids, your mom isn't trying to be mean, talking about taking Mac to Chicago," Cash tried to explain. "She was trying to figure out what's best for you, just like I am. We both want the same thing, Mac. You back on your feet."

"I'm *already* on my feet," Mac asserted, thrusting out her chin. "My doggy helped me."

"He did," Charlie affirmed. "Daddy and I saw it, right, Daddy?"

"We did," Cash said, remembering the day she'd gotten her bear from the shelf and the sweet burst of hope he'd felt. She'd been standing now at therapy, too. A little longer every time. "You're so brave, Mac. So strong. I know you'll walk—"

"Walk, walk, walk. I'm sick of hearing 'bout it. If I do it right this minute will you promise to leave me alone? Will you, Mommy?"

"Sweetheart, you can't—"

"You better promise."

"I'd give anything if you'd walk," Lisa said. Cash knew that he would, too. Because walking was the first step toward dancing. And he wanted that for Mac now, more than ever before.

"C'mere, doggy," Mac ordered, regal as a queen. "Charlie, pull me. I'm stuck."

Charlie eyed her parents nervously, then did as she was bid.

Lisa started to protest, but Cash laid a hand on her arm, stopping her.

Mac clenched her little fist in Destroyer's plush fur and grabbed tight to her sister's arm. She scooted her bottom forward to the edge of the wheelchair's seat. "Fold up my feet thingies so I can reach the floor."

Charlie bent down to flip the footrests up at her command. "Like that?"

"Egg-zacly. That's what I like 'bout you, Charlie. You do everything just right. When I grow up, I'm going to be just like you."

Charlie's chest seemed to puff out just a little, her chin a little higher at Mac's praise. "You ready to try standing up?" she asked.

"I'm sick of trying. I'm just going to do it so everybody stops bugging me crazy."

Cash held his breath as Mac set her jaw and pulled, pulled herself hard, pulled herself up, her face turning red with exertion as she got her feet underneath her. She was balancing there on the stiff soles of her shoes, braced between the dog and her sister. Standing, stronger than she'd been since the day her legs had been crushed.

"MacKenzie!" Cash breathed in amazement. "Look at you!"

"You ain't...seen nothing yet." Mac's brow furrowed and she glared down at the floor as if it were an enemy soldier. Slowly, painfully she shifted all her weight to her left foot then slid her right forward three inches. Four. Readjusting her grip on the dog and her sister, she concentrated on shifting her weight again, this time sliding her left foot up to her right.

One step.

Cash held his breath as she fought for every inch.

Two steps.

Three.

Charlie nearly dropped the kid, she looked so stunned. "Mac, you—you're walking."

Mac held her ground, panting, her face glowing with triumph. "Yeah. So there. Me an' Destroyer been practicing. An' I'm not going to Chicago and I'm keeping my sister 'cause Charlie and our doggy are lots better at making me walk than any old doctor ever is. Right, Daddy?"

"I guess so!" Cash fell to his knees. He opened his arms.

Mac let go of her hand holds and reached for him, taking one last step on her own. Into a future far brighter. Into arms she knew would always be there to catch her if she fell. Charlie piled on, too, hugging them both. He wished Rowena was here to see this. His children together, his anger at Lisa tempered, on its way to being healed. Maybe Rowena was right in the end: love could fix what was broken now that he finally believed.

Lisa stood a little way off, crying, suddenly looking so alone. The woman who'd given him these two children. That alone was a gift beyond measure.

He promised himself that he'd try harder to work with her, reason with her, make her a part of their daughters' lives. Mac and Charlie would have Rowena—all her warmth, all her joy. But even then, they deserved the chance to know their real mother, too.

Cash held out his hand to Lisa, inviting her into the circle he and the girls made, a ring of healing. Hope. And she came, hugging Mac, hugging Charlie, her eyes thanking him.

"You did this, Cash," Lisa whispered to him. "Thank you."

Mac's mouth popped open. "What'd you mean, *he* did it?" she complained, pulled back in Cash's grasp. "*I* did it. An' Charlie an' Destroyer. And I'll tell you something else right now, Mister Daddy."

Cash laughed, standing up with his youngest daughter in his arms. "What's that, kitten?" He perched her on the edge of the kitchen table.

"You better get busy makin' our tree house. 'Cause maybe Charlie doesn't like either one of you anymore. An' maybe me an' her'll go out an' live there even when it rains!"

"I like Daddy," Charlie said, a little shyly, leaning against him. "I *love* Daddy." She hesitated, and Cash could feel how big a chance his daughter was about to take. "And I love Mommy, too. But its okay you don't want me, Mommy. I know it's 'cause it's my fault Mac's legs got all smashed."

"Your fault?" Cash asked, dumbstruck. "That's ridiculous, honey. It wasn't—"

"It was so. Remember how me an' Mac always used to fight over the good seat? The side where you could see people's yards?"

Cash remembered. "My brothers and I used to have the same fight. All kids do."

"On the day that truck hit us it was Mac's turn to sit in the good seat. But I wanted to see Jimmy Wong playing Frisbee with his dog. He took it to all kinds of contests and it'd jump way up in the air and catch everything Jimmy threw. I promised Mac could sit in the good seat the next two times if she'd trade that day."

"Charlie, you couldn't know Mac would get hurt," Cash insisted.

But Lisa cut in. "Charlie, I know it's easy to blame yourself when bad things happen to someone you love. I—I've blamed myself for not being quicker to hit the brakes. Not seeing the truck sooner."

"I blamed myself, too," Cash confessed to both of them. "Maybe if I hadn't been so desperate to get Mac out of the truck, the EMTs could have done a better job. I was so scared. All that gasoline spilled."

"You guys are crazy!" Mac said. "The truck man was the one that was bad. He didn't stop at the stoplight. 'Member, Charlie? Daddy said Mr. Google 'rested him."

It had been an arrest Vinny had been thrilled to make. Cash couldn't count the times his ex-partner had said that collar was the one that drove him to retire. He came far too close to putting the trucker's head through a wall.

Lisa gathered Charlie up into her arms. "Maybe it's time we all let the past go and focus on the future. I love you, Charlie. Maybe I didn't know how much until I thought I'd lost you. We'll start all over. Can we? Will you give me another chance?"

"I want to," Charlie confided. "But I'm scared."

"I'm scared, too," Lisa said. "I don't want to make any more mistakes with you. I've made so many."

"Destroyer made lots of mistakes, too, before he got to be our dog," Charlie said. "He even gave Daddy a black eye. But I still love him anyway."

"That's good news," Lisa said, trying to smile. "Maybe there's still hope for me."

"There's hope for all of us," Cash promised. Rowena had taught him that.

He knew it would take time for Charlie's wounds to mend, but at least they were all uncovered. Out in the light and air Rowena promised could heal them.

"Can Mac and I stay with Daddy?" Charlie asked.

"Will you visit me sometimes?" Lisa pleaded. "And let me visit you here? I've missed you. Both."

Charlie looked to her sister and Cash had to smile as Mac balanced her small legs on the Newfoundland's back, using Destroyer as a footstool. "Is that okay with you, Mac?" Charlie queried.

Mac paused to consider. "I guess so. On one condition." The kid might as well have been threatening to turn Little Rabbit FuFu into a Goon. "That you *never* make my sister sad again, Mommy. And Daddy finishes that tree house right away."

The tree house. A symbol of everything Cash had lost. And yet, now it seemed full of possibilities. For the first time since the accident he could imagine Mac climbing up the ladder. He could picture his children storing not disaster kits in the oak's broad branches, but rather, dreams. He could weave fantasies of taking Rowena up there when she was his wife, making love with her under the stars, maybe creating a new life, a baby of their own.

"You said you only had one condition, Mac," Charlie's earnest correction jarred him from picturing joys tomorrow might bring. "You gave two."

Mac plumped out her bottom lip. "I don't care. You ran

away too far this time an' we couldn't find you forever an' ever. You got to have a better place to hide next time so you don't scare me so bad."

"I'm not going to run away," Charlie promised solemnly. "Never again."

"Well, I s'pose that's good." Mac scratched her nose, obviously weighing her sister's promise. "But Daddy's got to finish the tree house anyway. I got to teach you how to play good again before it's too late."

AFTERNOON SUN MADE the shop window glisten like gold as Cash pulled his SUV up to the curb and parked. He fingered the small velvet box in his jacket pocket, nervous as hell, and maybe happier than he'd ever been.

He had so much to tell Rowena. So much to share. MacKenzie's first steps. The way she'd clung to Charlie and the dog. The way Charlie's face had lit up when Mac insisted that she was keeping her sister.

Even the tree house clause in Mac's negotiations would make Rowena laugh. But as much as any of these miracles, he hoped the last one he offered would bring joy to Rowena's heart.

Asking her to be his wife.

And yet, Cash couldn't help but sense Rowena was avoiding him. Not picking up the phone the past week. Not returning his calls. He knew she was trying to give him and the girls the space she thought they needed after the hell they'd gone through the night Charlie had gone missing. But what Rowena had to understand was this: the enchantment the Lawless family really needed most at the moment was *her.* The colorful paint didn't brighten the house nearly as much as Rowena's smiles. The dog didn't shower his girls with even half of Rowena's unconditional love. And not even Cuchullain's magic whistle could awaken in Cash an ounce of the enchantment he felt holding Rowena in his arms.

And she loved him right back.

What could possibly go wrong?

He drew in a deep breath and opened the door. Saw Rowena at the register ringing up what looked like a sack of parrot food as Miss Marigold counted money out of her old-fashioned beaded bag.

As Cash approached, the older woman turned and flashed him a smile beneath the brim of what looked like an old-fashioned Easter bonnet. "Bless my soul! If it isn't that handsome Deputy Lawless!"

Rowena started at the sound of his name. He'd hoped she'd look happy to see him. Instead she looked...ragged around the edges, the light in her eyes so different it sent a shiver of unease down his spine.

"Ma'am," he greeted Miss Marigold, trying to figure out what the devil was wrong. Who had put the sadness in Rowena's glen-green eyes.

"So you're back at the pet shop again," Miss Marigold said. "I'd never have guessed you were an animal lover after the words you said when you chased that awful monster of a dog out of my tea room! I declare, you near burned my ears raw, but I expect I'd be a lot less shockable these days than I once was, considering the company I've started to keep."

"Ms. Brown here has a gift for changing people's minds. Actually, my girls adopted Destroyer. Although I do confess I get tempted to swear at him when he misbehaves now and then."

Miss Marigold tittered and pressed her fingertips to her rather buck teeth. But Cash looked right past her to the golden-haired gypsy who'd snagged his heart. Why was it that even her bracelets didn't seem to jingle quite so merrily today?

"Rowena," he said, low, husky. Her name. It was just her name. And yet he infused it with all the love he felt for her. Why wouldn't she meet his gaze?

"Have you heard the news?" Miss Marigold asked him. "I've finally found a gentleman who appreciates my finer qualities. I always told my folks I was waiting for Cary Grant to sweep me off my feet, but I've decided to settle for Elvis."

"So Vinny sweet-talked you into the parrot at last?" Cash reached for his cop mask, hiding the mounting tension he felt.

"It's true, Vincent did introduce me to my feathery soul mate. But it was that rogue bird himself who won my heart. And in the end, I fell head over heels for Vincent, as well. I just couldn't help myself. Vincent claims that someday he's going to sweep me off to Vegas to get married in an Elvis chapel—in honor of the King who introduced us."

Cash grinned, happy for both of them. One more miracle Rowena had made happen. "You in an Elvis chapel?" he teased. "It's hard to picture."

"Well, young man, there's a lot about me you don't know. I haven't a drop of willpower at all when it comes to love."

"I understand completely." Cash tucked his hand in his pocket, his fingers skimming the velvet on the box. "Love—" he grimaced with a shake of his head "—sneaks right up and bites you in the—"

"Cash!" Rowena protested, and he hated how pale she seemed. "As you can see, I'm sort of busy."

"I can wait. Forever if I have to." As long as she'd let him drive the shadows from her eyes.

Miss Marigold's gaze sharpened. "Well, I declare! Elvis isn't the only one who's looking to 'love me tender.'"

"Miss Marigold," Rowena protested. "This isn't what—what it looks like."

"I may be an old maid, dearie, but my glasses work just fine.

I'll be getting back home. I've a tea party for six in two hours. And I'll wager it'll be an adventure. Elvis has a spicy vocabulary, Deputy, but I confess, I can't wait to hear what he'll say next."

She scooped up her purchases and started toward the door. "Hmm." Miss Marigold turned at the door, surveying Rowena. "You make a very striking couple, the two of you. You might want to consider taking on a man of your own, Ms. Brown. One without feathers or four paws."

Rowena flushed. "I don't think…"

"Just consider the possibility," Miss Marigold suggested. "I must warn you, dear, that being the town's maiden lady isn't all it's cracked up to be. It gets tiresome, being alone. I thank God for my two men every day. Well, my man and my parrot."

Cash went to the door and opened it for the older woman. The bell jangled as it shut.

He turned back to Rowena, a nagging weight in his chest. Something was very wrong. "You haven't been answering my calls."

"No. I've been busy. How—how are the girls?"

"Pretty damned amazing, actually. Charlie's smiling. Mac's taken four steps."

Finally a spark lit her eyes. "Really? Oh, Cash! Thank God!"

"*And* you. She held on to Charlie and that damned dog you foisted off on me. I wish you could have seen her, Rowena."

"You did. That's what matters."

He touched one of the brass dogtags decorating a miniature tree near the register. He could make out the familiar figure etched into the medal. St. Francis of Assisi. The patron saint of animals came complete with a hook ready to be attached to a beloved pet's collar. Cash would have to pick one up for Destroyer. Even Rose Lawless would have to approve of the dog now, looking down from her seat in heaven. Especially since before Rowena and that Newfoundland had come into Cash's life, his family would have fit far better under the jurisdiction of St. Jude, patron of hopeless causes.

"I took your advice about Lisa," he said. "We're working things out. We're not exactly sure what we *are* going to do yet, but we know what we're *not* going to do. Fight with each other, tear our girls apart."

"I'm glad."

"I still don't agree with the way Lisa handled things. But at least I understand what she was trying to do. She's worked hard on herself these past two years. And in her own way she loves the girls."

"I'm…happy for all of you."

She sounded so strange, so withdrawn, her eyes red, their lids heavy as if she hadn't slept. He'd had insomnia long enough himself to know what it meant: a troubled heart.

"If you're happy, why do you look like you want to cry?"

She said nothing. He saw her throat work.

"Rowena, I know everything has been changing, happening so fast. But there's one thing I'm absolutely sure of. You're the reason my daughter is walking. You're the reason Charlie has the dog who kept her safe when I couldn't be there. You gave her your magic whistle. I guess I want to give you something to take its place." He pulled the box out of his pocket. "This didn't come from a fairy godmother, but it's got all my love inside it. Maybe that will be enough."

He opened the box, the engagement ring he'd bought just that morning sparkling. He slipped it out, holding it in the palm of his hand. "I was so sure I'd blown my chance at this kind of loving. But I want to spend the rest of my life with you, making up for lost time. I've even imagined the two of us in the tree house when it's finished. Making love. Making more babies. Making…all the good things you promised life could be."

Anguish welled up in Rowena's eyes. "I can't. We can't."

Cash's chest felt too small. He struggled to quell the dread that gripped him. "What do you mean we can't? You love me. I love you."

"The two of us together would have been complicated before Charlie ran away. But now—it's impossible."

"You don't believe in impossible. That's what you told me."

"I believe in it now. Your girls have been through so much, Cash. And Charlie is so afraid of losing you. Marrying me and forcing them to accept a mother they don't want would be a mistake. I won't be the cause of more hurt in their lives."

Cash reeled in disbelief. "But you're the best thing that ever happened to them."

"Charlie doesn't think so."

"Give her a little time. Remember what it was like between the two of you before she ran away? If it wasn't for you she wouldn't have that dog she loves. I still wouldn't know she felt invisible. You helped my little girl see magic in the world again, Rowena. Don't take it away from her now."

"You're the magic in her world, Cash. You always were. She lost you after the accident and she just got you back. She's scared I'll take you away from her."

Charlie's small, lonely face rose in his memory, how lost she'd been, how brave. Giving her mother a second chance. Forgiving him for the things he'd said, the things he didn't mean. God, he didn't want to put any more fear in her eyes. And yet, he felt as if in losing Rowena he was surrendering a part of his soul.

Cash skimmed his thumb over the ring he'd bought with so much hope, never dreaming she'd turn it down. "But I need you, Rowena," he said, low. "Doesn't that matter at all?"

"It matters. But not enough to change anything. I know you, Cash. You don't know how to do anything but your best. Especially when it comes to your girls. If there were problems later because you married me, you'd never forgive yourself. And I couldn't bear that. I won't have you feel guilty for marrying me. I won't have you look back and resent me."

"I wouldn't. I couldn't," Cash rasped. "Good God, Rowena, I love you."

"I know. But you loved them first." She took his hand, closed his fingers gently over the ring, blocking out its shine. "I won't be changing my mind, Cash. I promised—"

She cut herself off, and he wondered what it was she was about to say. "You promised what?" he asked.

"I promised myself I'd disappear now that you and the girls are—are all healed." She smiled, a wobbly smile. "Giving up something you want with all your heart is the part in fairy tales that makes the magic stick. The miller's daughter giving up her baby so she could spin straw into gold. The Little Mermaid giving up her beautiful voice for a chance to love the prince. I have to give up you."

"What about happily ever after? That's the way the stories I read to Mac always end."

"The watered-down versions, maybe. But if you read the real ones, the old stories, you'd see that sometimes the prince has to love somebody else and the mermaid turns to foam."

"Damn it, Rowena, this isn't some fairy tale. This is real life. *Our* lives."

"I know. But it's not like the ending is any big surprise to me. It's what I always do, you know. Disappear once things are fixed."

She meant it. And the knowledge was killing him. He'd ended up hurting her the way Bryony had feared he would. Rowena had given too much and he'd taken it. All her hope.

All her heart. After everything she'd sacrificed to make his family whole it seemed so damned unfair to leave her all alone.

And yet, her resolve seemed so steely. Her fears all too real.

"You did fix us, Rowena," Cash said softly. "In so many ways." He cradled her cheek, wanting with all his soul to kiss her one last time. But she caught his wrists to stop him. Pain flared, hot in her eyes.

"God, Rowena," he pleaded. "I just wish you'd let me…let me try…"

"It's not worth the risk. You know that even better than I do. Go home, Cash. To your daughters. And if you love me, even a little, respect my decision."

It tore him apart to step away from her, walk out the door. He went back to his house. To the colors she'd chosen, the walls she'd painted, the children she'd healed.

To the lives that she'd changed forever.

The life she was so damned sure that Cash had to live without her.

I TOLD YOU SO was an ugly bunch of words, but tonight Rowena was just miserable enough to risk hearing them. She pulled off Michigan Avenue into her sister's parking garage. Even at four in the morning with her eyes nearly swollen shut, the spacious building Bryony lived in looked gorgeous, elegant, soaring with confidence and all the other things Rowena knew she could never be.

She rushed up to the doorman who'd known two generations of Browns. He took one look at her and buzzed her in, his leathery face worried as he let Bryony know she was on her way to the apartment on the twenty-seventh floor.

"Dr. Brown just got in," Michael said, rushing to push the elevator button for her as if he was afraid she'd miss it. "An emergency at the hospital last night…I hope everything is all right…"

But for the first time in her life, Rowena doubted anything would ever be right again. She leaned against the elevator wall, watching the numbers flash by. The trip seemed to take forever. But when the doors slid silently open, Bryony was waiting on the other side.

"Oh, sweetheart," Bryony said, rushing toward her in a cream silk robe. "What happened?"

"I love him, Bry. And I can't…we can't…be together." Rowena's voice cracked, sobs that had built up during the drive finally breaking free. "It hurts, Bry. It hurts so bad."

For the first time Rowena could remember, no "I told you so" left her sister's lips. Bryony's mouth didn't thin. She didn't even give a long-suffering shake of her head. Instead, Bryony's eyes filled with grief, with love, with understanding.

She opened her arms and pulled Rowena in.

CHAPTER TWENTY-ONE

ROWENA STOOD at the pet-shop window, peering at the playground beyond the chainlink fence. Snowflakes drifted in puffs of white. Bright red ribbons trailed from the lightposts marching down Main Street. Across the way, school windows were trimmed for the holidays, one boasting a snowman tall as any kindergartener. Every morning, some lucky kid got to change the number on its cotton batting tummy, counting down the days until vacation started.

But even Christmas had lost its luster. What was the sense in putting up decorations in her apartment when no one but her would see them? Besides, it only made her wonder what kind of tree the house on Briarwood Lane would have. Not an artificial one like her mother's interior designer had created for the sprawling house in Forest Park, decked with white flocking and cut crystal balls and no colors at all. A real pine would fill Cash's house with the scent of winter and the girls' memory with wanderings through a Christmas tree farm all blanketed in white.

She could imagine Cash carrying Mac up on his shoulders as Charlie earnestly inspected each prospect. Could see him seating Mac on a stump, then kneeling in the snow to cut down whichever tree his girls had chosen.

It was so easy to imagine him selecting the gifts Santa would leave. His beautifully shaped hands putting together a doll's house or a scooter or a new bike. She wondered what it might have been like to creep out to the new green living room with him long after midnight and fill stockings together. Curl up with him and share kisses flavored with peppermint and hot chocolate and the passion she knew would never cool between them.

But the chance for that kind of magic had passed Rowena by. No, not passed. She'd given it up herself. Hadn't done as Cash had asked her, giving Charlie a chance to adapt, get used to…what? Her daddy's love being divided up one more time? His precious time with Charlie subtracted away? Charlie spending her days afraid she'd become invisible again? No.

Charlie had been through so much. The little girl deserved this chance to make up for everything she'd missed. Rowena wouldn't be the one to take it from her.

But knowing that she'd done the right thing didn't stop the ache that kept Rowena awake at night, and none of the projects she'd tried to distract herself with could fill the hole in her heart left by Cash Lawless and his children.

Christmas just seemed to make the loss worse. Rowena couldn't muster the least bit of enthusiasm for the shopping that had once delighted her, finding whimsical presents that would make her too-serious sisters laugh in spite of themselves. And the prospect of one of her mother's elegant formal dinners where everyone would scrupulously avoid the subject of Rowena's latest disaster seemed about as appetizing as turkey-flavored cheesecake.

It wasn't that they were bombarding her with the usual round of "I told you so" phone calls. Or saying "I know this hurts now, but someday you'll see it's better this way." Rowena knew her reprieve was Bryony's doing. Her older sister must have threatened her mom and Ariel with something dire indeed.

Or maybe they'd just realized the truth, as well. That this time Rowena had finally really done what they'd all feared for so long. She'd gotten her heart so chewed up she wasn't sure she'd ever have the courage to risk being bitten again.

So why was she staying here in Whitewater? Because the

shop was finally starting to blossom, now that it had her full attention? The people in the town not only accepting her gift, but delighting in it? That she'd begun to make friends—Miss Marigold and her new fiancé, Vinny, Deirdre Stone and Ms. Daily? Those were logical enough reasons to give her family.

But Rowena had never been good at lying. Even to herself. She stayed because she could peer out of her pet-shop window and catch glimpses of the children she might have called her own and the man she would love forever.

She knew the girls were healing. She could see it for herself. The whole world was moving on. Even Cinder the cat and her litter of kittens had been swooped away from her. When she'd called the vet to ask about bringing them to the pet shop after they'd finished recuperating, Dr. Wilcox had laughed out loud.

Don't you read the newspaper? Every one of those animals is spoken for. At least, they are as of this Friday. That's when their new owners can pick them up. Big doings at the Holiday Program at school.

That little Lawless girl is a kid after your own heart. She found homes for every one of those kittens. Her best friend is taking Cinder on. Cat looks like something from a horror movie after the burns it suffered, but Hope is downright crazy about that animal.

So the little girl who had wanted the "prettiest kitty in the whole world" had come to love the bravest one instead. She wished she could hear Charlie's version of how that transformation had come about.

But when Cash and the girls had stopped by the shop for their monthly supply of dog food Rowena hadn't been able to bring herself to ask the silent, painfully stoic little girl. If you kept picking at a wound it would never heal. Even then, this was one she wasn't sure ever would.

Still, Mac had jabbered like a little jaybird the whole time. *I get to pick a pet of my very own. See, Destroyer can lick me and play dolls with me but he's Charlie's dog, not mine. Daddy e'splained it to me.*

That's wonderful, Rowena had told her. *Your daddy is a very wise man.*

Yeah, Mac had agreed, jumping right into the holiday season. *But he doesn't ride on a camel or anything like the Christmas ones. Maybe Santa Claus will bring me one of those dogs with a pushed-in face like Lucy. Or maybe a kitty. Which one do you think would look pretty in a tutu?*

The postman blotted out Rowena's view of the playground for a moment, scattering the poignant memory. She opened the shop door to take the mail. She sifted through the bills, the advertisements and Christmas cards, then suddenly glimpsed an envelope that made her heart stop.

Charlie's neat printing marched across the envelope. Rowena's fingers shook a little as she opened it.

The students and staff of John Glenn Elementary School invite you to Winter Magic, December 15 at 7:00 p.m.

Beneath it was a personal note. "Be there or else." In parentheses Charlie had noted "Mac made me write that. I just wanted to say please instead."

So Mac was behind the invitation being sent. Rowena could see Mac giving one of her comical regal commands. Charlie reluctantly doing her sister's bidding, trying to soften Mac's orders with "please" even though Charlie would doubtless have anybody come to the performance besides the threat she'd managed to get rid of six weeks before.

Why would Mac want Rowena there? Was the little girl performing somehow? One thing Rowena knew for certain was that Charlie had only sent this under duress.

Rowena didn't want to go. Didn't want to see everything she'd never have.

But when the night of the program came, she watched the cars turn the playground into a parking lot, families spilling out in their holiday finery. Little girls in poufy dresses, boys with their hair neatly combed. Fairy lights twinkling, the winter wind piping a haunting tune.

What if Mac *was* going to be performing again somehow, not dancing yet, but still on her feet? What if Rowena missed this chance to hang back in the shadows and see…see how much stronger Mac had grown, see how much happier Charlie might be. See Cash. Drink in the sight of him, remember the feel of him, his mouth, so hard, so tender, his eyes that hadn't dared look up from duty for so many years. She hoped he was seeing rainbows again and tree houses high overhead.

The clock over the counter read quarter to eight when her resistance finally snapped. Rowena grabbed her keys and locked the door, not even stopping to put on her coat because she was afraid she might change her mind. She dashed across to the school door, snowflakes in her hair.

The school gym was dark, quiet, and for a moment she feared she'd missed the whole program. But then, a teacher announced "We'll close tonight's program with a reading by the winner of our holiday essay contest. Miss Charlotte Lawless."

Charlie. Her hair in French braids, her dark green dress decorated with a puppy in a Santa hat. Rowena glimpsed something silver sparkling in the stage light. Cuchullain's pipe making magic real for another little girl. Charlie crossed the stage, the heels of her patent leather Mary Janes clicking, a look of intense concentration on her face. She adjusted the microphone, then unfolded a piece of paper, its edges crumpled by her hands.

"*Winter Magic* by Charlotte Rose Lawless," she announced. Rowena saw the child look up, knew Charlie had seen Cash when some of the tension melted out of her little shoulders.

"People talk about magic like reindeers that fly," Charlie read. "I never met a single person who saw one. But magic is tricky that way. It doesn't come from big bangs out of magic wands. It would be lots easier to know it was magic if it did.

"Sometimes magic sneaks up on you. Magic is when your sister can't walk but your daddy makes her dance. Magic is getting to keep a dog even after it gave your daddy a black eye. Sometimes magic is somebody seeing you, even when you feel like nobody can.

"Magic can make an ugly cat look pretty. My friend Rowena told me that. I didn't believe her, but the cat my daddy saved from the fire is going to live at Hope's house. Hope thinks Cinder is the most pretty cat in the world.

"That kind of magic is better than being able to turn some-one into a frog.

"Turning people into frogs is a very bad idea. Later you get sorry and wish you could change things back. You would even trade your magic whistle if you could. Maybe Christmas is a good time to try."

Rowena's eyes burned, a tiny cry rising in her throat. She saw parents glance up at her. She turned and fled out of the hall. Cold air hit her face and she stumbled, a hand catching her elbow, keeping her from tumbling to the snow-spattered asphalt.

She felt herself being hauled up into strong arms. Cash. She could smell the woodsy scent of his aftershave, feel the familiar hardness of his body. She turned and found herself staring up into dark eyes full of yearning. Why on God's earth had she put herself through this? Seeing him hurt too much. Charlie's words haunted her, making Rowena want to hope. But she didn't have the courage anymore.

"I kept watching for you," Cash murmured. "I was afraid you weren't coming. Mac was sure you would."

"She threatened me." Rowena tried to keep it light, put space between them. "I found out in the grocery store just how harrow-ing one of her 'or elses' can be. Tell her I'm sorry I missed... whatever it was that she did."

"She got to be a snowflake. It involved wearing a tiara. Jake and Deirdre are taking bets as to how long it'll be before I get that thing off her. Jake's got Halloween. Deirdre's going for a year from this Easter."

"Then maybe I'll get to see it sometime after all. When she's on the playground or…or you're picking up dog food."

"Actually, it was Charlie who wanted you to come to the program so much. Her teacher made her shorten her essay a little for the performance. I thought you might want to read the rest."

Cash reached in his jacket pocket. Rowena took the note, but couldn't read it in the dim light.

"I can't see…"

"I know it by heart," Cash said. "If I really could make magic, there are things that I would do. My sister would dance even without Daddy holding her up. Dr. Malley says she will. I would change Rowena, too. I would turn her into my mom."

Cash cleared his throat. "I didn't put her up to this, Rowena. I swear. One night she just asked me to check her spelling. We talked about it. She told me about your fairy godmother and the magic whistle and we thought maybe all our love and all your magic together could be so strong it could make this appear on your finger."

Rowena stared as she saw him uncurl his hand. The engagement ring lay there against the callused palm she'd felt search every inch of her body during nights filled with his love.

"I thought you'd take the ring back to the jewelers."

"I might have given up before I knew you. But someone very wise told me that nothing is impossible. That a little girl can disappear even though she's still sitting right at the kitchen table. That demon dogs have destinies and love happens even if you don't have time to find it. It barrels into you and leaves you with a black eye to go with your—your broken pieces inside. Pieces the right woman can put together and make whole. It's a gift, you know. Seeing all of that in a world that seems so—so shattered sometimes. Your gift, Rowena."

"Oh, Cash."

"You gave that gift to me. To my children. Do you have any idea how amazing that is? You showed me that if that monster of a dog can find someone who loves him even after all the mistakes he made…maybe it's not impossible to believe that I can, too."

Rowena caught her bottom lip with her teeth, hearing the awe in Cash's voice, sensing the wonder in him. Redemption, pure and sweet.

"You might want to know that we finally settled the great doggy-name war. We decided to call him Destroyer. It's ironic, I know, since he put a broken family back together and healed us in so many ways. Charlie says it's like a secret joke every time she calls him that." Cash swallowed hard. "Who would have believed it six months ago? My Charlie making a joke?"

Rowena's eyes burned. "That's wonderful, Cash."

His hand closed warmly over Rowena's. She felt the smooth kiss of his ring against her finger. "Marry me, Rowena. I want you in my bed. In my life. In my kitchen making me coffee."

"We're back to coffee again, are we?"

"No," Cash said, sliding the ring home. "We're back to *this*." He gathered her up onto her tiptoes, then against his chest, his mouth coming down on hers with so much joy, so much love she drowned in it. Hungry, hot, he kissed her as if he never wanted her to forget this moment. And in spite of the wintry wind and the coat she'd forgotten, Rowena doubted she'd ever feel cold again. She didn't even notice the crowd from the program spilling out the school doors, never felt eyes watching them until she heard a warning whistle.

Cash and Rowena sprang apart, flustered, to see Jake Stone approaching, Mac up on his broad shoulders and Charlie and Hope beside him.

"Woo-ee, baby!" Mac's high-pitched voice split the air. "Daddy's kissing Rowena in front of the whole school! Can you get arrested for that?"

Laughter rose from the crowd.

"How about you let us off the hook this one time?" Cash took Rowena's hand and held it into the light. The diamond shimmered, chasing rainbows into the dark. "Look, girls. Rowena's going to marry us."

Applause broke out and Rowena could feel the affection these people felt for Cash, felt for the first time that she belonged here, too. She'd found her destiny right here, just as her fairy godmother had promised. Whitewater was home.

"What do you think of a wedding as a Christmas present?" Cash teased, tugging one of Mac's shiny pink shoes.

Mac wrinkled her nose. "Well, I guess it's okay as long as I get to wear my tiara. But don't be trying to give me a baby for Christmas like Tyler James got last year. I'd like a kitty better."

"Some kids are lucky and get both," Charlie said softly, slipping her hand into Cash's. Her optimism made Rowena's heart soar.

"But you said you only got *bad* luck, Charlie," Mac complained.

"Now I've got magic instead." Charlie tugged the silver chain, and Cuchullain's pipe sparkled in the twinkling fairy lights. Suddenly her brow wrinkled, and Rowena could tell she was deep in thought. "I don't 'spose you've got any *more* magic stuff lying around somewhere, do you, Rowena?"

Rowena thought of her sisters, Bryony with her earrings and Ariel with the dagger centuries old. Magic, as yet not spun. It was hard to think they might not ever dare to give Maeve MacKinnon's gifts a chance. Rowena could only hope her happiness would give her sisters the courage to try.

Cash drew Rowena into the crook of his arm, into a future twinkling bright with love. "You think you'll need more magic than this, Charlie?" he asked, kissing Rowena's cheek.

"The magic's not for me, Daddy," she explained earnestly. "It's for Mac and Hope and a baby if we have one. It never hurts to be ready just in case."

REQUEST YOUR FREE BOOKS!

2 FREE NOVELS FROM THE ROMANCE/SUSPENSE COLLECTION PLUS 2 FREE GIFTS!

YES! Please send me 2 FREE novels from the Romance/Suspense Collection and my 2 FREE gifts. After receiving them, if I don't wish to receive any more books, I can return the shipping statement marked "cancel." If I don't cancel, I will receive 4 brand-new novels every month and be billed just $5.49 per book in the U.S., or $5.99 per book in Canada, plus 25¢ shipping and handling per book plus applicable taxes, if any*. That's a savings of at least 20% off the cover price! I understand that accepting the 2 free books and gifts places me under no obligation to buy anything. I can always return a shipment and cancel at any time. Even if I never buy another book from the Reader Service, the two free books and gifts are mine to keep forever.

185 MDN EF5Y   385 MDN EF6C

Name _____ (PLEASE PRINT) _____

Address _____ Apt. # _____

City _____ State/Prov. _____ Zip/Postal Code _____

Signature (if under 18, a parent or guardian must sign)

Mail to **The Reader Service:**
IN U.S.A.: P.O. Box 1867, Buffalo, NY 14240-1867
IN CANADA: P.O. Box 609, Fort Erie, Ontario L2A 5X3

Not valid to current subscribers to the Romance Collection,
the Suspense Collection or the Romance/Suspense Collection.

Want to try two free books from another line?
Call 1-800-873-8635 or visit www.morefreebooks.com.

* Terms and prices subject to change without notice. NY residents add applicable sales tax. Canadian residents will be charged applicable provincial taxes and GST. This offer is limited to one order per household. All orders subject to approval. Credit or debit balances in a customer's account(s) may be offset by any other outstanding balance owed by or to the customer. Please allow 4 to 6 weeks for delivery.

Your Privacy: Harlequin is committed to protecting your privacy. Our Privacy Policy is available online at www.eHarlequin.com or upon request from the Reader Service. From time to time we make our lists of customers available to reputable firms who may have a product or service of interest to you. If you would prefer we not share your name and address, please check here. ☐

BOB07

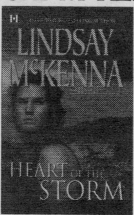

Kimberly Cates

| 77189 | THE WEDDING DRESS | ___ | $6.99 U.S. | ___ | $8.50 CAN. |
| 77178 | THE GAZEBO | ___ | $6.99 U.S. | ___ | $8.50 CAN. |

(limited quantities available)

TOTAL AMOUNT	$ _____
POSTAGE & HANDLING	$ _____
($1.00 FOR 1 BOOK, 50¢ for each additional)	
APPLICABLE TAXES*	$ _____
TOTAL PAYABLE	$ _____

(check or money order—please do not send cash)

To order, complete this form and send it, along with a check or money order for the total above, payable to HQN Books, to: **In the U.S.:** 3010 Walden Avenue, P.O. Box 9077, Buffalo, NY 14269-9077; **In Canada:** P.O. Box 636, Fort Erie, Ontario, L2A 5X3.

Name: _____
Address: _____ City: _____
State/Prov.: _____ Zip/Postal Code: _____
Account Number (if applicable): _____

075 CSAS

*New York residents remit applicable sales taxes.
*Canadian residents remit applicable GST and provincial taxes.

HQN™

We *are* romance™

www.HQNBooks.com

PHKC1207BL